"You said the babe is not yours?"

Raesha Bawell's pretty face paled to a porcelain white. "We found her on our porch night before last," she said, her gray eyes stormy with emotion.

Josiah's heart beat too fast. He took in a breath. "Found her?"

"*Ja*. Someone left her in a basket with a few supplies and a note."

"Her bonnet," he said. "Could I take a look at it?"

Raesha lifted the dainty little knit cap from the baby's head and handed it over to Josiah. He clutched the soft, warm fabric, his eyes misting when he saw what he'd been looking for. "There," he said. "My *mamm* stitched my sister's initials in the tiny cap. DJF. Deidre Josephine Fisher. Josie loved that little hat. She took it with her when she left."

Josie's sudden departure from Kentucky had rattled Josiah to the core. Now he felt hopeful for the first time in the last year of searching for his sister. Josie could still be nearby.

He hated to hurt Raesha any further, but he had to believe what his eyes were telling him. "*Ja*, I do think this *bobbeli* could be my sister's baby."

D0012205

With over seventy books published and millions in print, **Lenora Worth** writes award-winning romance and romantic suspense. Three of her books were finalists in the ACFW Carol Awards, and her Love Inspired Suspense novel *Body of Evidence* became a *New York Times* bestseller. Her novella in *Mistletoe Kisses* made her a *USA TODAY* bestselling author. Lenora goes on adventures with her retired husband, Don, and enjoys reading, baking and shopping...especially shoe shopping.

Maggie K. Black is an award-winning journalist and romantic suspense author with an insatiable love of traveling the world. She has lived in the American South, Europe and the Middle East. She now makes her home in Canada with her history-teacher husband, their two beautiful girls and a small but mighty dog. Maggie enjoys connecting with her readers at maggiekblack.com.

New York Times Bestselling Author

LENORA WORTH

Her Amish Child

&

MAGGIE K. BLACK

Amish Hideout

LOVE INSPIRED
INSPIRATIONAL ROMANCE

LOVE INSPIRED®

INSPIRATIONAL ROMANCE

Recycling programs for this product may not exist in your area.

ISBN-13: 978-1-335-22982-3

Her Amish Child and Amish Hideout

Copyright © 2020 by Harlequin Books S.A.

Her Amish Child
First published in 2019. This edition published in 2020.
Copyright © 2019 by Lenora H. Nazworth

Amish Hideout
First published in 2018. This edition published in 2020.
Copyright © 2018 by Harlequin Books S.A.

Special thanks and acknowledgment are given to Maggie K. Black for her contribution to the Amish Witness Protection series.

This edition published by arrangement with Harlequin Books S.A.

For questions and comments about the quality of this book, please contact us at CustomerService@Harlequin.com.

Harlequin Enterprises ULC
22 Adelaide St. West, 40th Floor
Toronto, Ontario M5H 4E3, Canada
www.Harlequin.com

Printed in U.S.A.

CONTENTS

HER AMISH CHILD

Lenora Worth

To one of my favorite readers, Patsy Thompson.
Thank you, Miss Patsy, for your encouraging letters
and for your continued prayers!

Whosoever shall receive one of such children
in my name, receiveth me: and whosoever
shall receive me, receiveth not me,
but him that sent me.
—*Mark* 9:37

Chapter One

The gloaming sparkled in a brilliant gold-washed shimmer that covered the sloping valley and glistened through the trees.

Raesha Bawell took a moment to stare out at the end of the day, a sweet Friday in late summer, and sighed with contentment.

It had taken her a long time to reach such contentment.

Even now, with the soft breath of fall hinting in the wind, she still missed her husband, Aaron. Her heart twitched as if it had been pierced but the piercing was now dull and swift.

She'd had to watch him die. How could a woman ever get over that kind of torment? Cancer, the doctors at the big clinic had told them. Too late for surgery or treatments.

Too late for children and laughter, for growing old together, for taking long walks on nights such as this.

Too late.

But never too late to remember joy. She sometimes felt guilty when joy came to her, but tonight she studied the trees and the big creek that moved through the heart of this community. Tonight, she thanked the Lord that she had her mother-in-law, Naomi, to guide her and keep her grounded.

Naomi had been a widow for several years so she knew the pain of losing a dear loved one. Knew it well since she'd also lost two infants at birth. Aaron had been her pride and joy.

But now, Naomi and Raesha had each other.

They worked side by side each day, but Raesha spent a lot of time in the long rectangular building around back of the main house. The Bawell Hat Shop had become more than just hats. They quilted and sewed, canned and cooked, laughed and giggled, and held frolics for their friends almost every month. They had loyal customers, both Amish and Englisch. They'd taken to making not only men's hats, both felt and straw, and bonnets for Amish women and girls, but Easter hats and frilly scarves and caps for tourists, too.

"You don't need to stay here with me," Naomi always said. "You are young and full of life. You should get married again."

"I am content," Raesha would always reply.

"You could go back and be with your family. I'm sure they miss you."

"My family is two hours away and they have other children and grandchildren," she always replied. "They know my place is here with you."

Her siblings often came for visits and to see if she wanted to return two counties away and start over there. She did not.

Now as she watched the sunset and thought about the beautiful wedding bonnet she'd made for a young neighbor who was about to become a bride, she knew she *was* content.

And yet, she still longed for a husband and a family.

Raesha turned to go inside and start supper, prayers for comfort foremost in her mind. She had nothing to complain about. The Bawells had built a fine house that kept growing since her in-laws always welcomed nieces and nephews and friends. People had moved in and out of their lives, filling the void after they'd lost two children. The house and outbuildings were neat and symmetrical, steady and solid. From the red big barn that held livestock and equipment to the *gross-daddi haus* beyond the main structure to the big shop that covered the length of the western side of the house to allow for parking, the Bawell place was a showpiece but in a plain, simple way. She and Naomi had a lot of help keeping up this place. Raesha never wanted to live anywhere else.

Turning to go and assist Naomi with lighting the lamps and warming dinner, she heard something round on the other end of the long porch, near the front door. A sound like a kitten meowing.

Listening, Raesha moved across the wraparound porch and turned the corner toward the front of the huge house. Had a stray come looking for milk?

The cry came again. And again. Soon soft wails echoed out over the fields and trees.

Then she saw the basket.

And a little pink foot kicking out in frustration.

Raesha gasped and put a hand to her mouth.

A *bobbeli*?

Raesha fell down beside the big, worn basket and saw the pink blankets inside. Covered in those blankets and wearing a tiny pink hat stitched with darker pink roses lay a baby.

"Sis en Maedel." A girl.

A very upset and wailing baby girl.

Grabbing up the basket, Raesha spoke softly to the baby. "Shh, now. Let's get you inside and see what we have to feed you."

What did they have? Goat's milk. Cow's milk, but no mother's milk. What was she to do? Naomi would know.

Telling herself to stay calm, Raesha lifted up a prayer for help. Then she glanced around, searching for whoever might have left the babe at her door.

But the sunset had changed to dusk and all she saw was the last shifting shadows of the day as darkness settled over the field and valleys of Campton Creek.

Who had abandoned this child?

Please take care of my little girl. I'm sorry but I am not able to do so at this time. Her name is Dinah and I was once Amish.

Naomi squinted down at the kicking baby and then laid the note they'd found inside the basket on the kitchen counter. "I'm *verhuddelt.*"

"I'm confused, too," Raesha replied as she changed the little girl's soiled clothing, glad they had a few baby gowns and such stocked in the shop and some leftover clothing from the comings and goings of relatives. Thankfully, she had found a supply of commercial formula inside the basket, along with a few disposable diapers and some clothing.

They'd warmed a few ounces of the formula and fed it to her after sterilizing a glass baby bottle Naomi had found in the pantry, hoping that would quiet her until they could figure a proper diet.

"Who would abandon a baby?" Raesha asked in between cooing and talking to the tiny infant. "Such a poignant plea in that note."

"And who would leave the babe with us?" Naomi replied, her once-blue eyes now blighted with old age, her face wrinkled but beautiful still. "Do you think she could belong to a relative? We have sheltered so many here."

"I do not know," Raesha replied, her heart already in love with the darling little girl. "She did say she was once Amish. Does that mean she is never coming back?"

Naomi did a thorough once-over of the kicking baby. "The note gave that indication. But this child doesn't look like any of our relatives."

The child had bright hazel eyes and chestnut curls. Raesha checked her over, too. "She looks to be around three or four months, *ja*?"

"'Spect so," Naomi said, a soft smile on her face. "She is pretty. Seems healthy and she did come with a few supplies, but I still cannot understand."

"God's will," Raesha said, thinking they could easily take care of this *bobbeli*.

"Or someone's free will," Naomi replied, her eyes full of concern. "We need to report this to the bishop."

"First thing tomorrow," Raesha said, her heart already breaking.

Of course, they'd keep the baby within the community if she'd truly come from an Amish mother. The Amish did not always bring in Englisch authorities for such things. Someone had left her here for a reason, though. It would be a shame to let this precious child go back out there to someone who didn't want her or to strangers who might not treat her kindly.

"I think her *mamm* left her with us because she wants her to be raised Amish."

"We will pray on this and do what we must in the morning," Naomi said, her tone calm and firm. "For now, little Dinah, you are safe."

Raesha nodded. "*Ja*, you are right. I worry about the mother but we will pray for her, too." She smiled down at the pretty little girl. "Your *mamm* might come back one day."

Naomi patted her hand and then Raesha finished bathing and dressing the baby. Soon after she gave little Dinah the rest of the bottle of formula, the child calmed, her eyes drooping in a drowsy dance, the long lashes fluttering like tiny butterfly wings.

"I'll sit with her," Raesha said. "Once she's asleep, I'll take the basket into my room in case she wakes."

"I'll heat up the stew we had left from yesterday," Naomi replied. "You'll need nourishment."

"What will we do if someone comes for her?" Raesha asked, her heart clenching, her mind whirling with images she couldn't hold.

Naomi laughed. "We've had a lot of experience in dealing with children, 'member? Some would say we are akin to the foster parents who do the same in the Englisch world. Maybe that will work in our favor, *ja*?"

Raesha's heart filled with a new hope. They did have experience and the Amish way was different from the Englisch way. Maybe they could keep this little one a few days longer. Or weeks even. But if the mother gained remorse and returned, they'd have no choice but to let her take the baby. If she would be capable, of course.

"We could have helped the woman if she'd only asked," she said.

"We will do what we can for this one," Naomi said, always relying on the Lord for her strength.

It would be hard to let this precious one go but Raesha knew it was out of her hands. God would give them the answers they needed.

And she'd have to accept that and stay content.

Two days later, Josiah Fisher stared into the early morning sun and wished he could turn back time. But time wasn't his to hold or change. All things in God's time.

He had work to do. He'd arrived in Campton Creek late last night and found a room at a nearby inn but he had checked out early to come here. Now he stood surveying the homestead his family still owned. It was his land now and he planned to fix it up to either stay here and work the land or sell it and go back to Ohio. Most likely the last choice.

Unless…he could find his missing sister. He hoped he'd hear soon from the private investigator he'd hired. He had told the man he was returning to Campton Creek.

Now he wondered if that decision had been wise, but Josie had been seen in this area. And it was time to face his past.

The neglected property looked sad and forlorn next to the big Bawell acreage just across the small shallow stream that trickled down from the big creek. He'd have to survey the burned-out barn and decide how to renovate it and the part of the main house that had also caught fire, but first he needed to alert the neighbors and introduce himself. Two women living alone would wonder who he was and what was going on.

Besides, he hoped to bargain with them about possibly renting some of their equipment. The Amish innkeepers had told him two widows lived on the big place and rented out equipment and such to bring in funding. Josiah counted that tidbit as a blessing.

Turning away from the memories of how his parents had perished in the barn fire that had jumped to the main house, he was glad the local volunteer fire department had managed to save most of the house.

But not the barn. His father had run in to save the animals and his mother had run inside to save her husband.

Or so that was the story he'd heard.

He walked the perimeters of the gutted, jagged building, amazed to see the pink running roses his mother had loved still growing against what was left of the barn.

Placing his hat firmly back on his shaggy hair, Josiah hurried toward the small wooden bridge someone had built over the meandering stream and crossed the pasture toward the Bawell house. Taking in deep breaths of the crisp early autumn air, he hoped coming back to Campton Creek had been the right thing to do. He wanted to start fresh, but he couldn't do that in the place where he and his sister had been born and raised. Better to fix the place up and sell it so he could finally be free.

Soon he was on the big wraparound porch, the carpenter in him admiring this fine house. He knocked firmly on the solid oak door and waited.

And then he heard the sound of a baby crying.

Was one of the widows a mother?

The door opened and an older woman dressed in

brown and wearing a white apron, her *kapp* pinned precisely over her gray hair, nodded to him. "*Gut* day. The shop isn't open yet. If you'd like to wait around by the door—"

"Hello, ma'am," he said, nodding back. "I'm your new neighbor over at the Fisher place. Josiah Fisher. I'm just letting you know I'll be around doing some work and I also…"

He stopped when another woman appeared at the door, holding a baby.

Josiah took in the woman. Pretty and fresh-faced, she had gray eyes full of questions and hair that shined a rich golden brown. She wore a light blue dress with a crisp white apron. His gaze moved from her to the baby. The child's eyes were open and she seemed to be smiling.

Josiah stepped back, shock and joy piercing his soul. "Is that your child?"

The young woman looked confused and frightened. Giving the older woman a long stare, she finally came back to him. "*Neh*, she is not my child."

"Why do you ask?" the older woman said, her shrewd gaze moving over Josiah.

He didn't want to scare the women but he had to know.

"Her bonnet," he said, emotion welling in his throat. "My younger sister, Josie, had a bonnet like that one. Our *mamm* knitted it special for her but never let her wear it much—not plain enough for our *daed*."

He gave the baby another glance that brought on an uncomfortable silence. "I don't mean to stare, but she looks like my sister, same hair color and same eyes."

The woman holding the baby took a step back, something akin to fear and dread in her eyes.

"I didn't mean to frighten you," Josiah said. "It's just that my sister...has been missing for a while now and I'd gotten information that she could be in this area. Seeing the *bobbeli* wearing that little bonnet brought back memories."

The old woman opened the door wide, her eyes filling with recognition. "You're that Josiah. *Joe* they called you sometimes. Your parents were Abram and Sarah Fisher? Used to live across the stream?"

"Yes, ma'am." Josiah lowered his head. "They died in the barn fire ten years ago. Josie was nine and I had just turned eighteen."

Glancing toward the old place, he went on. "I had left to help some relatives in Ohio when I got word of what had happened. I came home and took care of Josie. We moved to Ohio to be near kin but Josie left Ohio a couple years ago during her *rumspringa*."

The women looked at each other and then back to him, sympathy in their eyes.

"*Kumm*," the woman holding the door said. "We will talk about this."

Josiah removed his hat and entered the sunny, warm house and inhaled the homey smells of coffee, bacon and biscuits, his heart bursting with an emotion he'd long ago buried and forgotten.

This house held hope.

Maybe God hadn't sent him here to rebuild the homestead.

Maybe God had nudged him back to Lancaster County to find his missing sister.

Chapter Two

"I'm Naomi Bawell and this is my daughter-in-law, Raesha," Naomi said, guiding Josiah Fisher into the kitchen. "We have fresh coffee and some bacon and biscuits. Are you hungry?"

Josiah noted how she pronounced her name as *Nah-oh-may*. It rang lyrical inside his head. Naomi's hair shined a grayish white but she had eyes of steel.

Josiah's nostrils flared and his stomach growled. "I don't want to be a bother."

"No bother," Naomi said. "Have a seat at the table and we will bring you food."

Josiah nodded. *"Denke."*

He kept glancing at the young woman who held the *bobbeli* so close. She averted her eyes and pressed the baby tight with one arm while she served him coffee with her free hand.

Soon Josiah had a plate loaded with two fluffy biscuits and three crisp strips of bacon in front of him. But he couldn't take a bite until he knew the truth.

"You said the babe is not yours?"

The room went still. Raesha Bawell's pretty face

paled to a porcelain white. She sat down across the table from him, her eyes on the now-sleeping baby in her arms.

"We found her on our porch night before last," she said, her tone low and calm, her gray eyes stormy with emotion. And resolve.

Josiah's heart beat too fast. He took in a breath. "Found her?"

Naomi nodded. "*Ja.* Someone left her in a basket with a few supplies and a note. We got her all fed and cleaned up and we called in the bishop this morning. He agreed she could stay here for a few days to see if her mother returns. If that doesn't happen, we might need to bring in the authorities. We can't harbor a baby that might not be Amish."

"Josie—my sister—is still Amish. She has just lost her way."

Raesha's head came up, her gaze full of determination. "Eat your food, Mr. Fisher. It's growing cold."

Josiah bit into a biscuit, his stomach roiling but hunger overtaking him. Then he took a sip of the strong coffee. He knew they were waiting for him to say what was on all of their minds.

"The bonnet," he finally said. "Could I take a look at it?"

Raesha glanced at her mother-in-law. Naomi nodded. Carefully, she lifted the dainty little knit cap from the baby's head and handed it over to Josiah. Then she rubbed her fingers through the baby's dark curls, her eyes full of sweet joy.

Josiah's heart did something odd. It slipped and stopped, then took off beating again. This woman holding that baby—it was a picture he would always remember. Raesha looked up and into his eyes. The warmth from the baby's head was still on the soft threads of the little bonnet. He clutched the soft, warm fabric while the woman holding the baby watched him in a calm, accepting way.

Then he glanced down at the pink bonnet, his eyes misting when he saw what he'd been looking for. "There," he said, a catch of emotion clogging his throat. "My *mamm* stitched my sister's initials in the tiny cap. DJF. Deidre Josephine Fisher. She did the same with all of our clothes but never made a big deal out of it in front of others since our father did not approve of showing off. Said it made them even more special because they were made with a mother's love."

Rubbing his fingers over the tiny worn cap, he added, "Josie loved that little hat and kept it hidden in her dresser drawer. After the fire, she found it and made sure we took it with our other things to Ohio." Holding tight to the worn knitted wool, he said, "She took it with her when she left."

Raesha let out a sigh that sounded like a sob. "Are you saying you think little Dinah could be your niece?"

Josiah's eyes held hers. "Her name is Dinah?"

"We found the note," Naomi explained. She stood and walked to where a basket sat on a counter. Then she brought him a white piece of paper.

Josiah read the note, blinking back tears of both relief and grief. "My grandmother's name was Dinah," he said. "My sister, Josie, left Ohio two years ago and wound up in Kentucky. She was engaged to an Amish boy there. A *gut* man from what she told me. But I got word she'd broken the engagement and left. That was over a year ago."

Josie's sudden departure from Kentucky had rattled Josiah to the core. She had written that she loved it there and she was very happy. He should have gone to Kentucky with her but he had work to do. They lived off their relatives' kindness and Josiah felt obligated to stay and pay his *onkel* back. But then Josie had gone missing and one of his cousins had accused Josiah of not doing his share of the work. His family had become tired of his leaving to search for Josie.

Now he felt hopeful for the first time in the last year of searching for his sister. Josie could still be nearby.

"I hired a man to help me search," he explained.

"And did this man find anything?"

"He is supposed to get in touch with me when he does. He knows I'm here. He is from this area and came highly recommended."

He hated to hurt Raesha any further but he had to believe what his eyes were telling him. "*Ja*, I do think this *bobbeli* could be my sister's baby. I heard Josie might be headed this way and one reason I came back to Lancaster County was so I could search for her here."

Holding the bonnet tight in his hands, he looked at Raesha. "I might not find my sister but if this is her child, I've found something very precious." Then he handed the bonnet back to Raesha, their eyes meeting. "But I have to believe my sister hoped I would find her baby and that's why she left the child with you."

Raesha stood and took the cap back from Josiah Fisher, a great tear rending her heart. While she felt for him, she couldn't let him take this babe. He seemed to be a reasonable man. She prayed he'd listen to reason and not demand to take Dinah with him. "We will have to decide how to handle this."

"We should consult someone at the Campton Center," Naomi said, her hands holding tight to her coffee cup. Then she looked at Josiah. "A few months ago, Judy Campton, an Englischer whose husband descended from the founders of Campton Creek, became a widow. She still lives in the Campton house in an apartment over the garage with her friend and assistant, Bettye, but she has opened her big home to the Amish as a community center where qualified Englisch can help us with certain issues. We now have doctors and lawyers and other experts available for no charge there. Even counselors. All volunteers."

Raesha watched Josiah's face and saw his eyes widen. The man was handsome but the intensity in his brown eyes scared her. "Are you saying someone there can counsel us on this situation?"

"Ja," Naomi replied. "Now that we know you might be related to Dinah, we will also seek advice again from the bishop. We already love little Dinah and we will protect her until we know the truth."

Raesha tugged the baby close, the sweet bundle already embedded in her soul. "We will do the right thing but until we can talk to someone, Dinah remains here with us. She will be well taken care of, I can tell you that."

Josiah came out of his chair and put his hand in the pocket of his lightweight work coat and then shoved his hat back on, his eyes full of a troubled regard as he studied her and the baby. "I will call my investigator. I'll have him search for proof."

"If she had the baby in a hospital, there would be a record," Raesha said. "Maybe even a birth certificate."

"That would certainly show proof," Naomi said. "But most Amish don't have official birth certificates. You might check with midwives in the surrounding counties and communities."

Josiah scrubbed a hand down his face. "I do not mean to snatch the child away. I am thankful that she is safe and warm, whoever she belongs to. But that little cap has my sister's initials stitched in the lining."

"It could be someone else's initials," Raesha said, sounding defensive in her own mind.

"I don't think so," he replied. "My *mamm* went against our father's wishes to make pretty things so she could sell them to help our family. But some she kept. It's clear to me the baby hat belongs to my sister and this child looks like my sister. The note said she was Amish. How can it not be so?"

"It very well could *be so*," Raesha echoed, torn between her own heart's desire and doing the right thing for the baby. "We will have to find out what needs to be done to prove your claims."

Then she softened her stance, hoping to make him understand. "We have taken in lots of young relatives through the years. We are both widows and I am…childless. We will keep Dinah fed and warm and you can visit her anytime you want, ain't so, Mammi Naomi?"

Naomi bobbed her head. "She could not be in a better place for now. What do you know of children, Josiah?"

His dark eyes flared with regret. Shaking his head, he looked at Raesha again. "I know nothing much about children except my sister, but I have no kin left around here. I need to find Josie and hope she'll change her mind about giving up her child. Little Dinah could be my only close relative and she'll need to know that one day."

"Then we will work together to figure this out," Raesha said, standing her ground. They all knew he couldn't take care of a *bobbeli* right now. "As I said, you are *wilkum* to visit Dinah."

He studied the baby again. "May I hold her? And then, I'll leave. But I'll be glad to go with you to the Campton Center, both of you. We should all be there to talk with someone."

Raesha indicated she agreed. "Then it's settled. We could go later this afternoon. We have a girl who comes to watch the shop when we have to be away."

"I have much to do today," he said. "But I will make time for this. I plan to stay in the house if I can get it fixed up before winter sets in. I need to find lumber and supplies and get the back bedroom fixed, at least."

"Maybe we should wait," Raesha suggested. "Maybe the mother will come back."

"I still need to call the man I hired," he said. "I'll give him this new information and ask him to talk to hospitals and to check as many Amish communities as he can."

"We have a phone in the shop," Raesha said. "Meantime, we have supplies enough for this little ball of energy. I have learned how to make homemade baby formula since she can't be nursed."

"I will consult with the bishop regarding your information," Naomi said to Josiah. "I hope he will agree we need to protect the child first and worry about the rest later."

"I'd feel better if we brought in a midwife," he added

as Raesha carefully handed him the baby. "To make sure she is well."

Raesha looked to Naomi. The older woman nodded. "I'll go and get word to Edna Weiller. She lives around the bend. I'll send one of our shop workers over for her."

"Denke." His big hand touched Raesha's when he took Dinah into his arms. Their eyes met and held, causing a keen awareness to envelop her in a warm glow.

"There you go," she said to hide the swirl of disturbing feelings pooling inside her stomach. "Dinah needs to know we will provide for her. She'll need to know her uncle, too."

"If I am truly her uncle," he said, a soft smile on his face as he stared down at the sleeping baby, "I will take good care of her and raise her as my own." Then he handed her back to Raesha. "But maybe I will find my sister and then she can explain all of this—especially how she came about having a baby in the first place."

"I expect she did it the natural way," Naomi said later that day, shaking her head while she rocked Dinah. "If she no longer considers herself Amish, she might not be able to return to the old ways. But if she wants to return, she will have to confess all. Josiah seems to want to find her, regardless."

She paused, her brow furrowing. "His mention of his father brings back some memories. Abram Fisher was very strict and a stickler for following the *Ordnung*."

"There is a reason we have a rulebook," Raesha replied. And yet her heart went out to Josiah and his lost sister. The lost sometimes did return. She prayed he'd find the girl, but that meant Dinah would have to go back to them.

Your will, Lord. Not mine.

Naomi gave Raesha one of her serene stares. "Abram went beyond the rulebook."

"What do you mean?"

Naomi lowered her voice. "He was not above using his physical strength to make his point."

"You mean, he abused his family?"

Naomi nodded. "Sarah never spoke of it, but the proof was in the many bruises we saw. She had a black eye once and said she'd fallen and hit the floor too hard." Gazing down at Dinah, she added, "We mustn't speak of this, of course."

"No. We mustn't," Raesha agreed, her heart hurting for Josiah and Josie. No wonder neither of them had stayed here.

Earlier, Edna Weiller had come by and looked over little Dinah, examining her from top to bottom. "This child seems fit as a fiddle," the stout woman announced, her blue eyes twinkling while she danced Dinah around. "And probably much better off now that she is with you two."

"We are going to try to find her mother," Raesha had explained. Then she told Edna about Josiah.

Naomi had talked to Bishop King earlier. "The bishop thinks we're doing everything in the right way. But he expects us to alert the authorities if the woman doesn't return in a week or so, to find out what we should do."

"You'll need proof on this Josiah being related," Edna said. "If no proof is found, the Department of Child and Family Services will want to place her with a foster family until they find proof that the mother can't be located or that Josiah Fisher is truly her *onkel*. The sooner you turn her over, the sooner you could have her back. Or he will, at least. But it'll be a long shot and he might be required to go through foster training. Just warning you, but I don't think it will come to that." Her gaze softened. *"Gott segen eich."*

God bless you.

"Denke."

Edna handed the baby back to Raesha. "I can ask around amid the midwives. See if any of them know of this child being born."

"That would be helpful," Naomi said.

Troubled after Edna left, Raesha scrubbed down the house, made a chicken casserole for supper, and washed a load of clothes and brought them in to finish drying since the sky had darkened and a cold rain seemed to be on the horizon.

But she still couldn't get Josiah Fisher out of her head.

She wanted to *not* like him. But something had happened to her when he'd held that baby. Raesha's heart had felt as if she'd just fallen off a cliff. On the one hand, she prayed the baby wasn't his niece. But there was no denying the strong possibility. Even so, *she* might not be able to keep the child.

She didn't know which would be worse. Watching a stranger remove Dinah from their home or watching Josiah take the baby away but knowing Dinah was right next door. *If* he stayed on the old farm. What if he took the child back to Ohio?

Well, if he did stay here, Raesha could catch glimpses of the child and watch her grow up. Maybe with a new *mamm* if Josiah found a suitable wife. He obviously wasn't married since he had no beard and she didn't see a wife lurking about.

That thought made Raesha rescrub the counter.

"*Ach*, you've done enough. Stop and rest here with Dinah and me," Naomi said, her words low while she smiled down at the sleeping baby.

Dinah had been fussy earlier. Raesha would make the short drive to the general store tomorrow since a baby's needs never ended. For now, they had enough formula to get through the next couple of days. Raesha would have preferred mother's milk, but that wasn't an option. She would buy more supplies to make a more natural formula for little Dinah.

"Stop spluttering and talk to me," Naomi called again.

She and Dinah sat by the heating stove since the day had turned chilly. The afternoon skies looked stormy and the wind blustered around the house. They'd opened the shop for a few hours but had not had a lot of visitors. So they closed the front early and left the workers in the back to their tasks.

People knew to knock on the front door if they needed to pick up an order. They also took orders to the Hartford General Store in town, the closest thing they had to a Pennsylvania Dutch market. Mr. Hartford, an Englischer, sold a lot of Amish wares on consignment and paid them as needed.

When she heard a knock, Raesha jumped. Her nerves were sorely rattled today.

"I'll see who it is," she said, nervous energy bouncing off her.

Raesha opened the door to find Josiah Fisher standing there, wet and shivering in the wind, his hat dripping a pool of water on the porch rug.

"Josiah," she said on a surprised gasp. "*Kumm* inside."

Why was he back so soon? Why did he look so wonderfully good, his dark eyes moving over her in shades of doubt? He had broad shoulders and a sturdy build. Why was she even thinking such things while he stood there in the damp air?

He stepped inside and she shut the door, her arms gathered against her stomach. "Did you need something?"

"I'm sorry to bother you again but it's going to take longer than a day to fix up the house. I was headed back to the inn after I went into town to load some wood, but Mr. Hartford at the general store said you sometimes rent out rooms. I was wondering if I could possibly rent the *grossdaddi haus* out back. It would help me so much to be near my place and I can visit with Dinah some, too." He paused, his head dipping down. "If that would be all right."

His expression held a longing and a need that Raesha couldn't deny.

But could she tolerate his being so close to Dinah? And so near to her?

Chapter Three

Josiah took off his hat and hung it on a peg Naomi indicated by the door. Then he sat at the kitchen table while the woman took Dinah with her and Raesha into another room to discuss whether or not they could rent the *grossdaddi haus* to him. He hadn't thought this through and now he regretted blurting out his proposal to Raesha.

She obviously didn't want him around. Did she find him revolting and unappealing or was she afraid he'd take the babe away in the middle of the night?

He'd been so frantic earlier while loading boards at the general store. With the weather turning bad and the idea of either sleeping in a cold house with a burned-out roof on one side or taking his buggy back the fifteen miles to get another room at the inn since he'd given up the one he had, Josiah had voiced his worries to Mr. Hartford.

That's when the kindly storekeeper had suggested this solution. "The Bawell ladies are kind and they have often opened their home to those in need. They make money off their millinery shop and sell other items there—mostly for the tourists who come through. But they need all the income they can find. That's a mighty big place."

Josiah stood and stared out the wide window over the sink. Such a pretty spot, too. He barely remembered the Bawells but then, he'd tried to put his memories of Campton Creek behind him. He did remember that their son, Aaron, maybe a year or so older than Josiah, had spoken to him often at church gatherings and such. Raesha must have come along after Josiah and Josie had moved away.

A big mistake, that. His feisty younger sister had started acting out when she reached her teen years. He'd hoped she'd sown all of her wild oats during her *rum-springa* but Josephine Fisher was determined to see the world outside their small settlement. He still didn't know if she'd ever been baptized.

But he did believe his troubled sister had been running from something.

Well, she'd seen the world all right. His heart bumped at the weight of seeing that *bobbeli* that only reminded him of his failure as a brother. Was the man she'd been engaged to the father of that baby? Or had she strayed?

If Dinah was even her child, of course.

He'd come back here to salvage the farm and maybe sell it to help pay back his cousin's kindness. But he'd done that only in hopes of finding Josie. But if she'd been here and left this child with these kind women, she'd also done her homework.

What better place to abandon a baby?

He wondered if she'd come home, thinking to open up the house and instead, alone and afraid, had found it wasn't livable. Had she dropped off her child in a fit of despair?

Could she still be in the area?

He'd reached Nathan Craig, a man known for tracking down missing Amish. Nathan had already talked to several people who'd seen a young woman fitting her description and carrying a baby. But she could easily blend in here among the other younger women. Someone could be hiding her. He didn't know and now he had other things to consider. The house repairs and, possibly, an infant niece.

Thinking he'd leave and not bother these women again until they all went to the community center tomorrow, Josiah turned to leave.

"Josiah?"

He pivoted at the door to find Raesha standing at the edge of the big long living room. "I'm sorry," he said. "I was aggravated and cold and hungry earlier. Never mind me asking about staying here. I do not think that's wise."

"We don't mind," she said, but she didn't sound sure. "I will have to clear it with the bishop and we'd lock the door to the long porch that connects the *grossdaddi haus* to this house. We don't use that way much now so it's usually locked anyway. We tend to go out the side door by the shop."

"I would not harm you or bother you," he said, hope gaining speed again. "I won't show up on your doorstep again. I just need a place close by while I rebuild my house."

"I understand," Raesha said. "It makes sense and we do often rent out equipment and the occasional room. We often have relatives visiting for long periods and they find the *grossdaddi haus* comfortable."

"I don't want to impose."

"It's no bother," she said. "But we will have to consider what to do if Dinah is truly your niece."

"I had planned to sell the place, but I wouldn't want to take her away." He paused. "I told my *onkel* and cousins I'd be back. I borrowed traveling money from my *onkel* and one of my cousins is angry with me."

Raesha's expression softened at that. "I'm sorry to hear of your hardship. Maybe you can send them the money even if you decide to stay. It might take longer to pay off but at least they'd know you mean to do so. Once you have your house in order she—Dinah—would be right next door."

He grabbed at hope. And he'd be right next to Raesha. "You could visit her often."

"And watch her if you need us."

They seemed to be reaching a truce of sorts.

Josiah gazed at the woman across the room, their eyes holding with a push and pull that reminded him of a rope tug.

"I did call Mr. Craig. People have seen someone matching her description in town and the woman was carrying a baby. But no one can be sure."

"Then there is hope that she will return," Raesha said. "I pray God will give us insight.

"If your sister comes back, we will do what we can for her," Raesha said, her tone soft and quiet. "You can still do what you set out to do and Naomi and I will continue on."

Josiah nodded and rubbed his face. "This is a *gut* plan, *ja*?"

"That remains to be seen," Raesha replied. "Meantime, you are here and it's storming out there. You will stay for supper."

"I will?"

She smiled at the surprise in his question. "If you are so inclined."

"I'm inclined," he said. "Whatever's simmering on that stove smells mighty *gut.*"

"Then sit by the fire and I'll go and tell Naomi we have reached an agreement. We will discuss the details after supper."

"You are a very forceful woman," he said, moving across to the welcoming heat coming from the woodstove.

"I am a woman on my own with a mother-in-law I hold dear and with way more property than I can handle. I've learned to be forceful. Some frown on that, however."

He smiled. "I'm not one of them."

She inclined her head, her eyes going dark gray in the glow from the gas lamps. Then she turned and went into the other room to get Naomi.

Raesha let out a deep breath. "It's settled."

Naomi watched over Dinah. They'd found a huge straw basket that would make do for a bassinet for now and covered it with blankets so Dinah would be comfortable and safe. It sat by Raesha's bed. She had a comfortable room that held the bed, two side chairs and a large but simply made armoire that had stored her clothes along with Aaron's. His were gone now, donated to someone in need.

The room seemed cheerier with the big basket on the floor, a baby sleeping inside.

Naomi rose from the chair she'd taken near the baby's bed. "*Gut.* Our neighbor is in need. We will help him as we can."

"At what cost?" Raesha asked in a whisper.

"It costs us nothing to be kind," her mother-in-law reminded her.

"But the baby—"

"Is not ours either way."

"You're right," she said, feeling as if she were sitting on a fence and couldn't decide which way to jump. "You're right."

"Let's go and have our supper," Naomi replied, taking Raesha by the hand. "A good meal will ease our concerns and maybe we can get to know Josiah a bit more, ain't so?"

Raesha nodded. "*Ja*. I need to know all kinds of things."

Naomi gave her a knowing look, her shrewd eyes still strong enough to see more than she let on.

"For the *bobbeli*'s sake."

Raesha echoed that. "For Dinah's sake. Nothing more."

But there was a lot more going on here than an abandoned baby sleeping away and a stranger eating supper with them.

Her life had changed dramatically overnight.

But she wasn't so sure she would like this change.

"The meal is wonderful," Josiah said, glancing across the table at Raesha. "Do you share cooking duties?"

Naomi held up a wrinkled hand. "I used to run this kitchen but old age has slowed me down. But Raesha is a fast learner and her mother taught her well before she came to live with us."

"We cook for special occasions and frolics, church gatherings and market days," Raesha said, the coziness of the night making her mellow. "But for the two of us, we measure out and don't waste anything."

"A good rule," Josiah replied. "Josie and I were not the best of cooks but we managed. When we first moved to Ohio, we were both so distraught. We'd lost our parents and our relatives didn't much know what to do with us."

"Did you live with some of them?" Raesha asked, her mind wound tight with so many questions.

"For a while we lived with our uncle but he had a large family to begin with. I made a little money doing odd jobs and we moved into a small house that my cousin owned near them. That worked for a while but Josie was not happy. It's hard to explain death to a child who is old enough to grasp it but still young enough to want her parents." He took a bite of the chicken casserole and broke off a piece of freshly baked bread. "She only got worse as she grew. I think she'd held a lot inside for a long time. We both had."

"I'm sure you did your best," Naomi said, her tone gentle.

"I tried."

He looked so dejected Raesha again felt an overwhelming sympathy for him. "You were young, too. Did you seek help from the ministers or the bishop?"

"I tried to get Josie more involved in the youth singings and frolics. She always was shy and quiet. She wouldn't speak up and she didn't know how to fight for herself." He looked down at the bread on his plate. "Our *daddi* didn't like women to speak up much."

Naomi shot Raesha a measured glance.

They both knew that the man was the head of the household but what most didn't know or understand was that the woman was the heart of the household and kept things running smoothly, all the while holding things close to her heart and praying to God to show her the strength she needed each day.

"We all have our roles to play," Naomi said.

"*Ja*, and some take their positions very seriously," Raesha replied. "My husband, Aaron, was a *gut* man who followed the tenets of our faith but he was never harsh or cruel."

"Nor was his father, my husband, Hyam Bawell," Naomi said, nodding. "Different people have different ways of doing things."

"I didn't mean to imply I went against my father," Josiah said, clearly shaken. "He took care of us and provided for us. But he never seemed content."

Content.

That word echoed inside Raesha's head. She'd been content a few days ago. Today, her life seemed confusing and unpredictable.

The man sitting across from her wasn't helping matters.

She wondered what would have happened if he hadn't shown up at their door. Or if they'd hidden the baby away until he was gone.

But no, that kind of attitude went against her nature and she was very sure Naomi felt the same way.

"May he rest in peace," she said. Then she looked over at Josiah. "And may you live in peace."

Josiah's eyes widened. "*Denke.* You have both been very kind to me."

After they'd each had a slice of spice cake, Naomi stood. "My bedtime has arrived. I'll help with the dishes and then I'll say good-night. Raesha, you can give Josiah the keys to the *grossdaddi haus*. I trust him to do what is right."

"And what about the bishop?" Raesha asked. "He still needs to hear what we've planned."

"I will speak again with the bishop tomorrow when we are out and about," Naomi said. She shrugged. "He probably will nod and bless us since he's used to this house being a refuge for those in need."

"Go on to bed, then, and sleep well," Raesha replied. "I'll take care of cleaning up."

"Let me help," Josiah said. He must have seen her shocked expression. "I batch myself. I know how to clean a kitchen."

"That is kind of you," she replied, acutely aware that they were alone but Naomi was in the next room. "Once we're done, I'll take you across the porch and show you where everything is."

His rich brown eyes brightened. "It will be nice to have a dry, clean place to sleep."

They went about their work in silence but Raesha had to wonder what he'd seen and done since he'd been away. Had this lonely, hurting man been sleeping out in the elements? He'd mentioned the inn on the other side of town. But where had he been before then?

Just one of the many mysteries surrounding her handsome new neighbor.

No, make that the handsome single man who would now be staying on her property.

Confusing and unpredictable.

But she couldn't turn back now. She had a child to consider. Tomorrow would the beginning of something new either way.

Chapter Four

"You two go on," Naomi said the next morning. "It's too cold out there for old people and tiny babies."

Raesha glanced from where Naomi sat by the fire holding Dinah, her gaze meeting Josiah's. He stood in the kitchen, waiting with a tight somber apprehension.

He'd knocked on the door bright and early, stating a call had come in to the shop for him. One of the workers saw him outside on the tiny back porch and gave him a message to call back immediately.

"Mr. Craig has news," he said the minute Raesha let him inside. "He will meet me at the Campton Center." Then Josiah had asked if they wanted to go with him.

But Naomi had decided she didn't want to do that.

"Your mother-in-law does bring up a good point," he said now. "It is cold out there and damp at that. You and I can talk to him. We need advice on how to handle this."

Raesha couldn't refuse. They needed to know if Dinah was his niece or not. He had to be there to explain and ply his case and she needed to be there to hear the instructions and see to it they both understood how to proceed. She'd also back him up on his claim. How could she not?

"Well, you certainly do not need to be out in this weather," she told Naomi. "Are you sure you'll be okay here with little Dinah?"

"I'll be just fine," Naomi replied, her eyes on the *bobbeli*. "Dinah and I will have a *gut* talk about life."

"We do have Susan Raber coming to run the shop today," Raesha said, glad she'd been able to send word to their reliable helper. "If you need anything, she will be right next door and she has experience with little ones."

"Ja," Naomi said on a chuckle. "The girl has eight brothers and sisters."

Raesha had long ago learned to ignore the pang of hurt in her heart each time she thought of big families. "That she does, so I shall not worry. Josiah and I will find out what needs to be done and then we'll stop at the general store and get what supplies we might need."

"Don't forget to pick up what we need to make fresh formula," Naomi reminded them, her eyes bright with expectation.

And something else that Raesha hoped Josiah didn't notice.

Naomi loved to try to match Raesha up with eligible men. She tried to be subtle about it, but Raesha had sat through too many painful suppers to miss that gleam in Naomi's kind eyes.

"We will get what we need," Raesha said as she went about gathering her heavy cloak and bonnet. She'd dressed in a dark maroon winter dress and dark sneakers and stockings. This first burst of cold weather had come on suddenly.

Just like the man who was about to escort her to town.

She shouldn't feel so nervous but her jitters were from anticipation and a bit of anxiousness to find out the truth about little Dinah. But she was also nervous about being alone with Josiah. She trusted Josiah and knew he would respect her and keep her safe, but something about going off alone with a man who wasn't her husband did give her pause.

She missed Aaron with the sharpness of a knife carving out her heart, and the guilt she felt at even thinking about Josiah as handsome and strong made her purse her lips and stick as close as she could to her side of the big black covered buggy they used during the winter. Chester, the standardbred horse, was not happy being out in the cold. The gelding snorted his disdain and tossed his dark mane. Maybe the usually docile animal sensed the tension between Raesha and Josiah?

"The Campton Center is in the middle of town," she said to ease that tension. The cold wind whipped at her bonnet and cloak, making Raesha shiver.

She loved spring and summer. Winter, which seemed determined to arrive early, made her sad. Aaron had died a few weeks before Christmas. But this year, they might have a baby in the house. Or nearby at least.

Josiah didn't say much. Was he as wound up as she felt?

"I'm sorry you don't know where you sister is," she said, wishing she could ease that burden. Wishing she knew the truth about this whole unexpected situation.

"I appreciate that but she must be close by." He watched the road for too-fast cars and clicked the reins. Chester pranced and settled into a steady, chopping gait. "I searched for her down in Kentucky but no one knew anything. The man to whom she was engaged went off on his own to search for her so I didn't even get to talk to him."

"I can't imagine how hard that must be for you," Raesha said. "Naomi and I said a prayer for you and your family last night."

And she'd been in constant prayer since little Dinah had shown up on her doorstep. The adorable girl was so sweet and had such a happy disposition Raesha didn't want to think about having to let her go.

"I came back here to check on the property but mainly to see if Josie might be here," he said, his gaze slipping over her face. "And because a friend of Josie's heard her talking about wanting to come back to Campton Creek and the home she remembered. She was never happy living in Ohio. She's had a hard time of it since our *mamm* and *daed* passed."

"I suspect you have, too," Raesha said before she could stop herself.

"I have at that," he replied, his eyes on the road, his expression stoic and set in stone. "I worked hard for my uncle and cousins but I never did fit in with them. I couldn't find a suitable wife even when they tried to marry me off. Coming back here seemed a good choice since I hoped to find Josie here, too."

So his family had tried to match him with someone, but had obviously failed. Was he that hard to deal with?

Not from what she'd seen.

"But you've possibly found your young niece."

"Hard to believe but I do hope it's so." He clicked the reins. "I know it is so."

They made it to town and the main thoroughfare, aptly called Creek Road since it followed the many streams jutting from the big meandering creek. Raesha pointed as they passed the Hartford General Store. The building, painted red and trimmed in white, covered a whole block.

"The Campton Center is just around the corner. The big brick house with a clear view of the creek and the other covered bridge that we call the West Bridge."

Josiah nodded, eyeing the massive house on one side and the creek and bridge on the other. "It's smaller than the big bridge to the east."

"*Ja*, the creek deepens there toward the east," she said, going on to explain how a young girl almost drowned there a while back. "Jeremiah Weaver, who returned to us almost two years ago, now teaches swimming lessons for all the *kinder*."

"*Gut* idea," Josiah said as he pulled the buggy in to the designated parking for the Amish across from the Campton Center. "This place is impressive."

"Yes. Mrs. Campton has been generous with our community. She has no living children and her husband, who served in the navy, died last year. They lost their only son when he was off serving the country."

Josiah stared up at the house. "We all have our battles to fight."

Raesha stared over at him and saw the anguish in his expression. She had to wonder what kind of battles he'd fought to return to a place that brought him both good and bad memories.

What if he never found his sister? What if Dinah truly was his niece? Would he take the child and leave again once he'd sold the old place?

He glanced over at her, his eyes holding hers. He

seemed to want to say something but she didn't give him time.

"We should get inside."

Josiah nodded and tied up the horse before coming around to offer her his hand.

Raesha let him help her out of the buggy, then she moved ahead of him, his touch burning a reminder throughout her system.

You can't do this. You mustn't get attached to this man. The child needs you. He doesn't.

And I don't need him either.

She'd be wise to remember that.

"Hello, I'm Alisha Braxton."

The young female lawyer smiled and reached out her hand. Josiah removed his hat, and held it against his chest and then shook her hand. Raesha nodded and gave her a smile.

Josiah introduced himself and then turned to Raesha. "This is Raesha Bawell."

The other woman took Raesha's hand. "It's nice to meet you, Mrs. Bawell. I've shopped at your place many times while doing pro bono work here."

"Denke," Raesha said, glancing at the pastoral painting on the wall that depicted an Amish farm in the mist. She recognized the work as belonging to a local Amish woman who painted.

Alisha Braxton had golden blond hair that fell around her shoulders and pretty green eyes that held a strong resolve. She wore a navy blue business suit. "Have a seat and let's see what I can do to help you two. You look like a nice couple. Why do you need legal help?"

Raesha shook her head. "We are not a couple."

Looking confused, the pretty woman with the expressive green eyes laughed. "Oh, I just assumed you might be remarrying, Mrs. Bawell. I'm sorry."

Raesha let out a gasp, a blush heating her face. "No, that is not the case."

Josiah took over. "Mrs. Bawell is my neighbor. We need to find out if the baby she found on her porch is my niece."

The woman's eyes went wide. "Oh, I see." Turning to Raesha, she said, "Let's start at the beginning. You found a baby on your porch? When did this happen? And where is the baby now?"

"Three nights ago. My mother-in-law has the child at my home." Raesha cleared her throat and tried to explain things in chronological order. "We have taken in children before but those were mostly family and friends. But we talked to the bishop and since the note indicated the mother is Amish, he allowed us to keep the child for a while."

"I see," the woman replied. "So why are you here?"

Raesha began to wonder why herself.

But she went on. "Yesterday, Mr. Fisher showed up and he believes, based on her appearance and a baby *kapp* we found in the basket with his sister's initials stitched inside, that the child is his niece."

Glancing at Josiah, she said, "I came here with him to seek advice and to see what his investigator has found. My mother-in-law has Dinah and we have a woman nearby in our shop if she needs help."

Looking impressed, the young woman nodded, her wavy hair grazing her shoulders. "Who is your investigator, Mr. Fisher?"

"Nathan Craig," Josiah said. "I first contacted him

when Josie went missing in Kentucky. But we never found her. When I got word she might be back in this area, I called him again. He is supposed to be good at tracking Amish."

The woman's face went blank but her eyes said a lot that didn't seem in Mr. Craig's favor. "Yes, he is good at that. He used to be Amish."

Raesha let that settle. It happened. People who left somehow always came back around in one way or another. But they didn't always rejoin the Amish community or confess and ask for forgiveness.

"So you know him?" Josiah asked.

"More than I care to admit," the lawyer lady said. "But he is the best at his job. Is he meeting you here?"

"*He* has arrived," a deep voice said from the open door.

"Mr. Craig." Josiah stood and shook the man's hand while Raesha took it all in.

The man looked world-weary, his expression edged with darkness while his brilliant blue eyes burned bright. His gaze moved over them and bounced back to Alisha Braxton and stayed on her for longer than necessary.

"Good to see you again, Alisha," he said.

"I wish I could say the same," Miss Braxton replied.

Raesha noticed the way the lawyer woman said that.

Seemed the pretty female lawyer might have a beef with the handsome private investigator. Raesha hoped their personal differences wouldn't interfere with Josiah's problem.

Maybe Raesha had read too many Amish mysteries.

The man leaned back against a table off to the side,

his boots scraping the hardwood floor. "Okay, so let's get to this."

"What have you found?" Josiah asked, the hope in his voice piercing Raesha's resolve.

Mr. Craig reached inside his leather jacket pocket and pulled out a notepad. "Exactly what we needed. A lead on your sister," he said. "According to several people I talked to in another Amish community not far from here, about three months ago a young girl matching Josie's sketched picture was rushed to a nearby hospital where she had a baby girl."

"That's not definitive information," Alisha said. "Amish women about to give birth are rushed to the hospital all the time. It could have been someone who resembled the missing girl."

"Yes, but several people knew of her and said she kept to herself. She was staying at a bed-and-breakfast and the owner verified that and the fact that she was pregnant. She went into labor in the middle of the night. The owner called for an ambulance. I also went to the hospital and asked around."

Standing, he turned to lean against the wall. "They couldn't tell me everything but when I explained this was an Amish girl and that her brother had hired me to find her, the hospital officials verified that a woman matching her description had been a patient there but she'd left without officially checking out."

"Did they verify that she'd had a baby?"

"No."

"What else?" Alisha asked. "Because you always manage to dig information out of people."

"I might have cornered an aide in the maternity ward."

She gave him a stern look. "And what might you have found?"

"I told her the truth. That Mr. Fisher was searching for his sister, and that he was concerned for her safety. The aide verified by nodding to my questions, that a woman named Josie had a baby there and that she'd left without being discharged."

Alisha shook her head. "One day your backdoor tactics are going to get you in serious trouble, Nathan."

"I'll take what I can get to help that girl and her child."

Turning to Raesha, Josiah nodded, tears in his eyes. "Dinah is my niece."

Mr. Craig twisted to smile at Alisha Braxton. "While we haven't verified proof yet, Josiah, I believe you're kin to the baby the Bawell women found."

"Does that mean we don't have to report this or send Dinah away?"

Mr. Craig turned to Alisha, lifting his hands up. "Well?"

She glared at him for a moment and then said, "If the mother didn't receive an official certificate at the time of birth, it's going to be hard to prove this. The HIPAA rules won't allow for much more."

"And I can't get access to the birth certificate," Nathan said. "But Josiah could file for a copy at the Department of Vital Records. You have the mother's name and the baby's name. And in the state of Pennsylvania, the father can't even be listed on the birth certificate if they're not married. He has no rights if his name is not on that document."

Crossing her arms, Alisha gave Nathan Craig a heavy

appraisal. "He's right there, but none of your tricks, Nathan. This is a serious matter."

"I told you," he explained. "I'm doing this close to the book, but with the Amish, certain English rules don't necessarily apply. The searches are difficult at best."

The lawyer lady's eyebrows went up. "In this case, we have a missing Amish mother fitting the description of Josie Fisher, who left the hospital with her baby in the middle of the night. Most Amish don't have an official birth certificate, and if this was Josie, she obviously didn't take the time to grab one."

"Should I try to get a copy of the original?" Josiah asked.

"We can do it right here, online, since we have most of the information," Mr. Craig said. "If Josie used her own name and recorded the baby's name, it's worth a shot. You can file since you are related and have the same last name."

"I can walk you through it, Mr. Fisher," Alisha Braxton said. "We have to try but it might be hard if the baby wasn't assigned a social security number and you can't provide one."

Josiah bobbed his head. "You see, Josie wanted me to find the baby. She must have come here to the old place and seen it wasn't livable. Somehow, she knew about the Bawells taking in people. Maybe she wanted to ask for their help and panicked. But she left Dinah, to keep her baby safe."

"She didn't return to the bed-and-breakfast where she'd been staying," Nathan said. "That means she must be moving around. I'll start checking homeless shelters and women's shelters next, with your permission."

Alisha lifted up in her chair. "Okay, your findings

give us a strong indication that we're on the right track. Even with access to her medical records, the hospital can't just hand over information. But a birth record would help solidify Dinah staying within the Amish community."

"So she could stay with Josiah?" Raesha asked. "Maybe if Josie knows her child is with her brother, she'll return to Campton Creek."

"I hope so," Alisha said. "Normally, Mr. Fisher, you'd have to file for guardianship, but seeing as your sister is Amish, that makes the baby Amish. And I understand the Amish tend to take care of their own."

Mr. Craig leaned down to stare at Alisha Braxton. "I'm impressed. You rarely veer from the letter of the law."

"Sometimes, the laws become a little gray in certain areas," she explained. "And the Amish are one of those areas." Then she looked at Josiah. "But I expect you to be responsible for this child. The Bawells will help you, because it's the Amish way. But ultimately, the responsibility falls on your shoulders since her mother is missing and, apparently, her father is not legally involved."

Josiah nodded. "I wonder if that's why she ran away. Maybe something happened to the man she was to marry."

"That's a question to ask her if you ever find her," the lawyer said. "I know this is hard on you but the bonnet with the initials is a strong indicator, as is the fact that she left the baby near your old home, with two women known for taking in orphans and people in need. That shows she was thinking of the baby's safety, and you came here not long after she had to have been nearby. She might be keeping tabs on you and could come back on her own."

"So we're all clear?" Josiah asked. "I won't do anything illegal but I want my niece with me."

"You've done everything right, Mr. Fisher," Alisha Braxton said. "Even hiring this irritating man."

"Thank you," the man said, his expression full of gratitude. Then he looked at Josiah. "But Josiah, your sister is still missing. She allegedly left the hospital at the end of May. Now I can focus on my continuing search, loaded with a lot more information."

"Please keep searching," Josiah said, worry clouding his features. "We will keep Dinah safe but we need to find Josie."

Mr. Craig stood. "Sometimes, people don't want to be found."

Again, a look passed between him and the lady lawyer. *What secrets do they have between them?* Raesha wondered.

Chapter Five

"I have to get back at it," Mr. Craig said while Alisha filed for the birth certificate and explained the process as she went. Glancing at Raesha, he offered his hand. "We weren't formally introduced. I'm Nathan Craig."

"Raesha Bawell," she said, briefly shaking his big hand. "Thank you. Dinah is precious and we so want to keep her safe."

"Now you can do it legally," he replied. "Nice to know Josiah's got some good people to help him."

Alisha stood and scooted around him. "So we don't need DNA and no need to call in social services. You should receive a copy of the birth certificate in a few days, Mr. Fisher. It will arrive at the shop's address. Is there anything else I can help you with?"

"I just need my sister found," Josiah said. *"Denke."*

"I'll do my best," Nathan Craig said. "I'll walk you two out."

Raesha stood and nodded to Alisha. *"Denke."*

"Of course." The other woman's smile held a trace of sadness. Her work had to be difficult.

Giving Alisha a good long glance, she felt Josiah

nudging her toward the door where Mr. Craig stood waiting.

"We don't want to get lost on the way out," Josiah said with a smile.

"It is a big place." Alisha followed them out into the long, wide entry hall. "But I'm the first door on the left. Always. Used to be the dining room."

"You've been very helpful," Raesha said.

"I hope this all works in your favor," Alisha replied.

"So do we." Josiah turned, his eyes on Raesha.

Alisha sent a knowing glance to Raesha, matching Raesha's earlier one to her.

Raesha decided Englisch and Amish women had something in common at least.

Trying to understand men.

When they arrived back home, Josiah took care of the buggy and the horses and then turned to stare at Raesha. "Are you sure you want to do this?"

"What do you mean?" she asked, fear clogging her throat.

"I'm asking so much of you already, and now, a little one to watch over and take care of. It's not fair to you."

"It would be unfair for you to have to hire someone else when I am standing right here and I'm able and willing to help for the sake of the child," she retorted, her tone firm. "Now stop your spluttering and let's get inside."

He lowered his head, a smile twitching at his lips.

"Do you find my words amusing, Josiah?"

Lifting his gaze, his eyes filled with mirth. "*Ja*, I do. You are one bossy woman."

She raised her chin. "I have learned to be firm. I employ several people, both men and women. I'm trying to be practical. There is a need and I'm filling it." Then she looked toward the house. "How could I not want to hold Dinah and take care of her? She is beautiful and she needs a woman's touch."

"So you think I can't handle a child on my own?"

"No, I think you should not have to handle this all on your own. We are friends and, for now, neighbors. You are renting rooms in my home. It makes sense to me to leave her with Mammi Naomi and me while you are doing your work." Giving him her best stubborn glare, she added, "Unless you have a plan on how you can do both."

Josiah shook his head. "My only plan was to get her back." Looking sheepish, he said, "I accept your help. I will never question you about this again."

Relief washed over Raesha. "*Gut.* It's early yet but I have not eaten since breakfast. Now let's go in and have some dinner."

"Are you inviting me, then?"

"It seems I am at that. We might as well feed you, too, ain't so?"

"I will do what I can around here to help pay you back," he said, humility coloring the words. "I owe you and Mammi Naomi a great debt."

"We do this out of love," she retorted. "Love for a helpless man." Then her lips crinkled. "And for a helpless friend, too, it seems."

Josiah's expression changed from agony to happiness again. "I am helpless in this area and many others, that is true. But I believe your good habits will rub off on me."

"We will see about that," Raesha replied before marching past him to get out of the brisk wind.

Once there, she fussed with sandwiches made with fresh bread and juicy baked ham and fresh cheese. She poured tea and heated up the coffee on the big stove. She placed fruit and cookies on the table. But her eyes wandered to the little crib in the corner over and over.

Naomi glanced from her spot cutting up fruit to Raesha and then back to Josiah. "I am so proud that Dinah can stay with us."

"I thank God," Josiah said, his gaze following Raesha. She wanted this, too, but he wondered what would happen if she got too attached to his niece. How could he take the child away if Raesha didn't want to let her go?

She is my kin, he reminded himself. *It is my choice.* He'd come here determined to fix the place up and sell it so he could pay back some of the money his uncle had loaned him to find Josie. Or maybe he'd used that as an excuse since he needed to get away from his relatives for a while. Not run away, but take some time. He'd never really taken time after his parents died to mourn them and the life they should have had here, to console himself and to do right by Josie. He'd dragged her away, unable to think straight.

Now he wondered if God hadn't nudged him here for many reasons. Raesha would make a good mother to any child.

Did he want to stay? Could he? Too many questions.

The weather cleared, warming but still with a nip in the air and the sky shining a brilliant blue in the sun. Early on Sunday morning, they all bundled up to head to church, which would take place at Bishop King's house. Here, church rotated from houses or farms to barns and basements, depending on who could accommodate the congregations.

Thinking about how they'd received stares and raised eyebrows during their quick trip through the general store yesterday, Raesha was quiet as she got in the buggy and took Dinah from Josiah. To distract herself, she made sure the baby had plenty of blankets and that her head was covered.

Josiah checked on Dinah. "She's always so happy."

The little girl smiled a lot, which made Raesha smile, too. "*Ja*, such a good girl."

Josiah's fingers briefly touching hers and his solemn eyes glancing over her face made her only too aware of the man.

Last night, they all sat around the woodstove, taking turns holding Dinah.

Naomi cooed and talked to the little one, promising that no matter what happened they had all been blessed by Dinah's presence in their home. "*Gott* will be with you."

Josiah then held the baby close, not speaking. Just staring down at her with awe. Finally, he'd kissed her little forehead, tears in his eyes. "*Gott* will return your *mamm* to me, I pray. His will and my prayers. Your mother would want it so."

He'd looked up and into Raesha's eyes, a binding connecting them with an invisible thread. When her turn to hold Dinah had come, she blinked back tears and refused to look over at Josiah.

But she voiced what they were all thinking. "You

are loved, little one. We will keep that love even if you have to move far away."

Now Raesha's heart bumped each time the buggy hit a rut in the road. How could she love someone she'd known for only a week? Was this how it felt to have a child of your own? It shouldn't hurt this much to think of letting Dinah go. But the choice would not be hers.

Josiah would have to decide what to do, even if his sister was found.

It would be an honor to help him take care of Dinah until that time. If Josie never returned, he'd need even more help.

But what if he decided he didn't want them in his niece's life? He'd indicated he might allow them to help, but what if he changed his mind once he knew he truly was Dinah's *onkel*? Too many questions.

Naomi remained calm and serene, her gaze admiring the countryside. She was good at waiting on the Lord. Raesha should learn from her but patience and waiting had never been her strong points.

Raesha missed her own mother. Ida Hostetler had died when Raesha was a teenager and her father, Robert, had passed not long after she'd married Aaron and moved away. She had three siblings. An older brother, Amos, who lived with his family in the house where they'd all grown up, and Emma and Becca, twins who lived right next to each other. They all had children and she loved helping to take care of her three nieces and two nephews when she went to visit or when they came here.

She hadn't told any of them about little Dinah yet, of course. But her sisters would come calling sooner or later and they'd be shocked to find a baby in the house.

Or worse, even though they lived in another community, word could get out to her family no matter how quiet Josiah and she wanted to keep this until they knew what would happen next. They'd certainly have questions regarding Josiah living on the Bawell property.

"Hold on," Josiah said when a vehicle came up behind them. "We will let the Englischer get by since he seems in such a hurry."

He moved the buggy to the side, careful and considerate.

He looked handsome in his clean black pants and white shirt, his dark hair curly underneath his black hat. His jacket was clean and he smelled of fresh soap. Apparently, he was enjoying living in the *grossdaddi haus.*

She shouldn't be admiring the man guiding Chester, and yet she couldn't help it. She'd been isolated and in mourning for so long, she had not realized that her heart had shriveled to almost nothing. Little Dinah had brought her back to life, and now Josiah was adding more beats to her heart, too.

She'd been content.

She needed to remember that and not jump beyond content. But being content wasn't as pleasant as the many feelings stirring inside her heart right now.

She couldn't allow those feelings to take over.

Not until they grew to know each other more and she might have some hope to add to her blossoming happiness.

They made it to the King place and after securing Chester at the hitching rail, Josiah helped her down and then assisted Naomi.

Naomi smiled and thanked him, her eyes twinkling.

How could she be so chirpy when their life had become so shaken and changed?

I need to have a stronger faith, Raesha reminded herself. If Naomi did worry, she sure hid it well enough. Raesha's emotions usually came out in her expressions, according to her bossy sisters.

She'd work on controlling her feelings this morning. For Dinah's sake, at least. People would be curious and they'd all agreed to speak the truth.

Once they were out of the buggy, they made their way to the basement of the big house, where the service would take place. Naomi took the foods they'd prepared earlier and went to a gathering of older women, all of them spluttering on about the meal they'd all share later. One of the women took the pickled beets and coconut pie into the kitchen.

Raesha held Dinah tight and waved to some approaching friends.

The men would go in first, followed by the younger boys.

Josiah stood to the side, looking lost. But some of the people he'd met in town, including Jeremiah Weaver, who'd returned to Campton Creek a couple of years ago, came up to Josiah and guided him into the service. He glanced back, his expression hard to read. Did he worry about the *bobbeli*?

A group of women came up and started admiring Dinah.

"So it's true, then?" Beth Weaver asked, smiling. "You found a baby on your porch?"

"That is true," Raesha replied, smiling at Dinah's wide-eyed expression. "But her *onkel* is renting rooms from us and we are helping him out while he rebuilds his place."

"Was that him?" someone else asked, pointing to where the men were moving slowly down into the open basement doors. "The new fellow who walked in with the others?"

"His name is Josiah Fisher," she explained. "He came here to fix up his family farm and maybe sell it but he also came back to find his younger sister. Now he will have this little one to think about, too."

"Where *is* her mother?" nosy Rebecca Lantz asked, her smile prim while her eyes glistened for details.

"She had to go away for a while."

"I heard she left the babe. Abandoned her own child. If she does come back, she might have a ban on her. She's not even from our district."

"But they used to live here," someone replied.

"Josiah has someone searching for her," Raesha explained, her tone firm and calm. "I ask that you pray for both of them, Rebecca. You are kind to worry so about someone you don't even know. Until she returns, Mammi Naomi and I are helping with the baby, with the bishop's approval. It's the right thing to do, don't you agree?"

Rebecca huffed a breath, but with the other women watching her with amused expressions, she nodded. "Of course I'll pray for them. That is a cute baby girl and yes, you always do the right thing, Raesha."

Leave it to Rebecca to wrap an insult inside a compliment.

Naomi came up and greeted everyone and then said, *"Gott verlosst die Seine nicht."*

God does not abandon His own.

Rebecca smiled and walked away with a flip of her skirt.

"I pray so, if it is God's will," Naomi said. "I pray Josie will find her way back to this child and her brother."

They made it through the long service but Raesha had to take Dinah upstairs once to feed her and change her nappy. No one seemed that concerned since the truth had come out. Just another person needing the Bawell widows. Some of the teen girls passed the baby around and helped out so Raesha could eat. They all loved Dinah.

But Raesha knew taking care of this child and standing by this man went beyond her sense of duty.

Once the meal was over and they were heading home, Naomi sat with Raesha inside the buggy. Her mother-in-law took Raesha's hand and held it tightly to hers. "You will make a good *mudder* someday."

Raesha prayed that so, too. She wanted Dinah with a heart that burned to love someone. "One day. But I have to remind myself that this child does not belong to me."

"Are you going to be able to deal with whatever might come?"

"I will," Raesha said. "You know I will."

"I think the Lord has plans for you," Naomi replied with a pleased smile.

As she watched the broad shoulders of the man who'd come so unexpectedly into their lives right on the heels of finding the babe on her doorstep, Raesha had to see God working on all of them in some way.

What are You trying to teach me, Lord?

How could her heart be so full and yet so completely empty at the same time? She could see everything just out of her reach and it seemed she'd lose out yet again.

But Josiah aimed to stay around a while to get the old farm back into shape and to wait for word on his sister. She had a little time with the baby yet. She would cherish each moment for the gift given to her.

A lot could happen before the year was out.

She'd just have to wait.

Be still, she told herself. *Just be still.*

It would be a long winter and a lonely one if Dinah and Josiah had to leave them.

Chapter Six

Josiah looked up a couple of days later to find a convoy of buggies headed up the rutted lane to the old farm. Surprised, he walked to the front of the run-down house and watched as, one by one, the men in the buggies pulled up and got out with tools and supplies.

"What is this?" he asked as one of the men introduced himself as Samuel Troyer. Josiah nodded and shook his hand. "You are one of the ministers for this district, *ja*?"

"That is correct," Samuel said. "Jeremiah Weaver is my son-in-law and he mentioned you might need some help. He'll be here later."

Josiah lowered his head. He knew this was the Amish way but he still felt inadequate. He should have come back here long ago to take care of this place and face the harsh reality of his past. But he'd tried to raise his sister and he had wanted to protect his parents' memory. Instead, this place shouted loud and clear about the unhappy times here.

"I would appreciate the help, *ja*."

"Winter will set in soon," Samuel reminded him. "You'll need the place strong if you aim to sell it."

"Word travels in this community," Josiah said. "I haven't decided what to do but the house needs repairing, no matter."

"So you'll be here a while, then?"

Josiah didn't want to blurt out his business so he just nodded again. "I'm staying at the Bawell place." He motioned toward the footbridge. "In the *grossdaddi haus*."

"So I heard. The Bawell women are good landlords, ain't so?"

"They have been kind to me," Josiah replied. "They seem to take in strays from what they've told me."

"They are good women, caring and loving. And smart, businesswise, too," Samuel replied.

Samuel Troyer had to already know all about his situation but the other man wouldn't question him outright. He did speak of his hopes of Josie returning. In his heart, he felt God had led him home.

"We will pray for you, Josiah," Mr. Troyer said. "And for your lost sister."

"*Denke* for coming," Josiah said to change the subject. "I'll take all winter if I do this alone."

Soon he was shaking hands and being introduced to a dozen or so able-bodied men who'd come to help him renovate the house.

"The barn will be next," Samuel told him when they took a break to warm themselves by a fire someone had started in an open area. "Hopefully, we can get it repaired and built before the weather takes a turn."

"I am mighty obliged," Josiah said as they went back to work on the side of the small two-storied house that the fire had gutted. Soon they had the charred remains of the old walls torn away and were working to rebuild from the floor up.

The work went quickly and got done much faster than if Josiah had tried to do it all on his own. He'd torn out a lot of rotting, scorched wood already, his body willing since it kept his mind off Dinah and his missing sister. And off the woman across the way who'd been so kind to him.

Raesha's smile shined in his mind like a beacon. He couldn't seem to get her out of his head. But then, it would be hard to avoid her if he tried.

At the end of the last few days, she'd either invited him to supper or brought him a plate. She was shy and reserved but she didn't have any qualms about speaking her mind either.

"The Bawells stay busy," Samuel said while they measured and hammered. "The hat shop has a long history here. Mrs. Bawell's husband and son ran it until… Mr. Bawell passed. Then Aaron and Mrs. Bawell did their best to keep it going. When Raesha came into the family, she dived right in and made a few suggestions to add this and that. She learned all about hat-making and suggested that Aaron hire extra help."

"Wise woman," Josiah replied, careful not to grin too much since he'd seen that feisty side of her. "They do seem to stay busy and they have given work to others."

"Busy, kind and she's single."

Josiah couldn't hide the grin now. "*Ja*, I noticed that."

"And pleasant to look at."

"Noticed that, too."

Samuel chuckled. "I will comment no further on that subject."

"Duly noted." They continued in a pleasant silence until it was time to find some dinner.

"My wife and daughter packed us a meal," Samuel

said. "And the others brought their own dinner, too. Let's sit by the fire and eat."

Josiah didn't argue with that. He'd had an egg and toast in his temporary place this morning. Soon, they were sitting on logs eating roast beef sandwiches made with freshly baked bread and fried apple pies that reminded him of his own *mamm*.

Josiah couldn't help but glance at the big place across the way. Part of Samuel's job as an elder had to be placing people together. Did he think Josiah and Raesha would make a good match?

Josiah didn't know how to go about courting a woman. He'd tried a few times back in Ohio, but he'd always been an outsider there. He didn't have a way with women. Too grumpy and shy, one had told him. Too moody, another had confessed.

Staring out at the pastures, he noticed hay bales stored near barns and plowed, fallow ground that would go dormant during the winter. Past the pastures and hills, he could see the waters of the big creek.

"It's nice here," he said. "I'd forgotten how nice."

"You don't have to sell," Samuel pointed out. "The land on this place just needs tending and clearing. Come spring, you could have it in good shape for planting."

"I know. But I owe my uncle and cousins so much. I thought I'd go back to Ohio and pay them back by helping them as much as I can."

But first, he needed to find Josie. So many questions. If he couldn't find her, and if Dinah would be his to raise, he'd have to decide if he should take her to Ohio or stay here. He'd have plenty of help back in Ohio, but would his strict uncle even allow the child to live there? Would the community accept her without question?

Thinking about Raesha next door didn't help his confusion.

"I'd think you've paid that debt," Samuel said, regarding his return to Ohio. "If you worked hard for your kin I doubt they expect more. Surely they'd understand why you want to come back to your home."

He couldn't argue with that, but Josiah had a need to pay his family back, whether with money or hard work or both. They'd tried to match him to a good woman but none of them worked out. He left on bad terms with his uncle because he refused to marry any of his hand-picked choices. Maybe a baby would make Josiah come to his senses and listen to his uncle's wishes. He'd need a mother for Dinah.

He thought of Raesha again.

"Can I tell you a story?" he asked Samuel, his heart burning with a longing to unburden himself.

"I like to hear a good story," the older man said on a quiet, knowing note.

Before long, Josiah had spilled the whole truth of his past and what little he knew of his sister's life. The other men had discreetly talked in clusters while he talked quietly to Samuel.

Finally, he finished and stared down at his brogans. "So you see, I have much to consider. The child is my niece and I have an obligation to provide for her and raise her. If I find my sister and she is all right, she can be a mother to her child. But first, we'd have to go before the bishop and see how to handle this situation. I won't be able to stay here if Josie is shunned."

"And how will you be received back in Ohio?" Samuel asked.

Josiah lifted his head. "It would not be *gut*, but I won't abandon my sister or her child."

"You do have a lot to consider," Samuel replied. "But if you find Josephine and she confesses all and asks for forgiveness, I believe you could live here with her. Quietly and she'd have to find a husband soon enough."

"But you can't be sure how anyone will react," Josiah said.

"No. It would be up to the bishop and the other ministers," Samuel replied. "And it will be *Gott*'s will."

"I felt a tugging to come home," Josiah admitted. "I think Josie is nearby."

"You might well be right on that," Samuel said. "Let's get your home ready in case she is close and waiting. I think the girl needs her home back, *ja*?"

Josiah nodded, too choked up to speak. He admired Samuel's kind nature and understanding, wise counsel. He liked Jeremiah Weaver, too. He'd heard how Jeremiah had left but returned and was now back in the Amish way.

He wanted that for Josie, if it wasn't too late.

Maybe he could have a new life here in the place he'd never wanted to see again. In a house that held horrible memories, maybe through restoration and redemption he could create new memories.

And…he might be able to do that with the woman who lived next door.

"There is much going on next door," Naomi said from her chair by the side window.

Raesha turned from finishing the last of the apple and sweet potato pies she'd been baking all morning. She had to go to the shop in a few minutes to relieve

Susan. The girl's *mamm* was sick and Susan was needed to help with the younger children.

"I saw the buggies arriving earlier." Handing Naomi her afternoon tea, Raesha glanced out the window. "They have done a lot since early this morning."

"That could be a nice house. Small but cozy. Just needs some love," Naomi said, her hand holding the cup underneath the plain white teacup.

"Tell me what you remember," Raesha said. "Josiah is such a quiet, polite man. I can't see him coming from a *daed* who would abuse his family."

"Josiah is trying to be the opposite of his father," Naomi replied with a nod. "He doesn't seem to invite confrontation. He mentions trying to please his uncle and cousins but I wonder if he ever tried to stand firm with them."

"Do you think he's weak, then?" Raesha brought her own tea over and sat for a moment, her mind on Josiah and the odd feelings he brought out in her. Little Dinah slept snugly in her crib, only reminding Raesha of him.

"No, not weak. Trying to hold it all in, trying hard to be a *gut* man and not cause trouble. But as you've seen, he will fight for his own."

Raesha believed that and she didn't consider Josiah as weak. He'd been working hard to find his sister and he was determined to raise little Dinah, if need be. He'd come home to do what needed to be done.

"What happens if he becomes weary of holding things inside?" Raesha asked.

"He will have to come to terms with that," Naomi replied. "He will need to listen to the Lord and be steady in his ways."

"Josiah has a lot on his mind," Raesha said, getting

up. "But seeing the work our community has helped him with today should ease his troubles, *ja*?"

"I believe so," Naomi replied. "Now it's time for my nap. I will pray for our Dinah before I shut my eyes."

"Pray that she stays asleep while you nap," Raesha said. "Josiah has been doing a good job with her when he comes to fetch her each night. I had to show him how to change her diapers. He made a funny face but he is a quick learner."

"He makes you laugh," Naomi noted.

"He's a funny man."

Raesha helped her mother-in-law to her bedroom and made sure she had a warm blanket. "Rest, Mammi," she said with a tenderness that made Naomi smile.

"Denke." Naomi eased into the covers and then added, "You do know you are not required to stay here with me."

"I do know that since you remind me at least once a week," Raesha replied. "Are you trying to get rid of me?"

"Not at all," Naomi said, a playful slap warming Raesha's hand. "But you are young yet. You should get out and about more."

"And for what reason would I need to be out and about?"

"I can see a couple reasons," Naomi replied. Then she shut her eyes, her smile still intact.

Raesha gathered her things to take to the shop, mindful that she'd be going back and forth to keep an eye on the baby and Naomi. In the last week, she hadn't been on task so she had a lot to catch up on. Naomi was still good with needles, so she helped with making bonnets and children's hats and she was wonderful with embroidery, too. But her mother-in-law was declining so Raesha tried to encourage her to rest after dinner each day.

Hopefully, both baby and Mammi would sleep until she unloaded her things, checked on the shop and hurried back to the house. She'd never realized how taking care of a little one changed everything.

And now, she had Naomi hinting at matchmaking.

Naomi worried about Raesha's future. Even though they both knew God had a plan for them, her beloved mother-in-law wanted to know she would be safe and taken care of once Naomi was gone.

Raesha didn't want to think that far ahead. This big house would be so empty without Naomi. She had always been the heart of this house, loving and open and kind. Raesha wanted to be the same but it would be hard, going it alone. She'd keep the shop up and running and she'd bring in people to keep her company. She had so much love to give. Maybe that was why she enjoyed being a shopkeeper and hatmaker. Her work involved being around others.

But she wouldn't make a move until she knew what would become of baby Dinah. The baby had been in her thoughts all week as she trained Josiah on how to handle a tiny child. He wanted the responsibility, took it in stride and he'd insisted on doing his part by taking Dinah to the *grossdaddi haus* with him each night.

"We are getting to know each other," he told Raesha one early morning. "I cannot thank you enough for watching her during the day."

It was easy to see the baby was related to him. Dinah's eyes looked a lot like his, golden brown at times and a richer brown at other times. Always changing.

"It is a pleasure," she'd assured him. "Dinah is a bundle of sweetness."

At least she could hold on to the child until they could find her real mother.

Raesha prayed about that, too. Josie had to be alive and safe. Josiah would be heartbroken if anything bad had happened to his sister.

He needed to know the truth. What had caused Josie to run away and have a baby all on her own?

Chapter Seven

The next day, Raesha sat at the tall stool behind the counter in the front of the hat shop, making a list of all the winter chores that had to be done before the first snowfall.

A friend had come to visit Naomi and assured Raesha she'd be happy to sit with Dinah for a couple of hours, too.

That left time for Raesha to focus on business, something she'd found soothing in the months after Aaron had died.

Earlier in the season the hay had been dried, baled and stacked by the barn. Some of it was already stored in the hayloft, ready to use. The two men who farmed the land for them would move the rest to the barn before hard winter set in. The fences had been checked and mended and the livestock—just the horses, a few cows and some goats—were in good shape.

She'd have to make sure the hay cart was in working order and the draft horses had sturdy harnesses. There was wood to gather and cut for the stoves and they'd need to make sure they had a winter supply of propane for the shop. While they had a phone in the shop, they used it only for business or emergencies. She filed the handwritten invoices on any transactions and worked with a neighbor who was an accountant to keep business in order.

The phone rang, causing her head to come up. "Bawell Hat Shop. How may I help you?"

After taking an order for two felt hats, with measurements written down by hand on the invoice pad, she said, "*Denke*. I will get these back to the sewing room today."

Then an Englischer came in looking for shawls and bonnets.

"I want something handmade and Amish," the robust woman said, waving her hand in the air. "I admire the quality of these quilts, too. Maybe I should buy one of those."

Thirty minutes later, she left happy with two shawls, three bonnets and a log cabin quilt. Raesha waved goodbye to the spry woman and took a sip of her lukewarm tea, her gaze moving over the long, wide retail building. Two doors with glass windows centered the long planked-floor room. Rows and rows of hats lined the walls on one side, while clothing and quilts covered the other side. Then a long row of open shelves moved from the heavy oak purchase counter centered in front of the doors to both sides of the room. Those shelves were full of jams, jellies, breads and pastries, most provided by local Amish women trying to make some spending money. Ava Jane Weaver had a whole shelf of her wonderful sweets, mostly cakes and pies and muffins. She sold her bakery goods here and at the Hartford General Store in town.

Then there were the handmade items that the Englischers loved. Crocheted and knitted caps and hats in all sizes, similar to the pink one little Dinah had been wearing.

Her heart pierced, thinking about how much she missed the *bobbeli* when she came here to work. Lifting her gaze over the tiny clothing and head covers, she touched her own tummy and wondered what God's plan was for her.

Will You leave Dinah to us, Father?

Shaking her head, she skimmed the walls lined with landscape paintings and colorful wooden signs that held Amish proverbs and verses of Scripture.

The hat shop had come a long way in the last ten or so years. But it felt big and lonely without her Aaron and his *daed*. Business was slow but it would pick back up with the Harvest Festival in a few weeks and the holidays after that.

Thinking she could set up a corner for Dinah and bring the baby here with her some days, Raesha made notes on her big calendar, trying to mark down all the things she needed to supervise. She and Naomi employed a dozen or so people. It took that many to keep things running smoothly here. One reason she didn't have time for courting.

Josiah came to mind and she pushed his image away and made a note to check the employee gathering room.

They had a small efficiency kitchen in the back of the shop, so employees could take breaks and eat meals, especially during the busy Christmas season and the high tourist seasons of spring through fall. Winter was for repairing things, building up inventory and making sure everything was in order for next year, and they had to prepare for the busy weeks before Christmas.

Aaron used to help her with such chores. He'd get the wood gathered and stacked and, together, they'd make sure the outbuildings and stables were secure and ready for winter. He'd let the horses out for air, their winter coats keeping them warm while they ran in the snow.

She could see him out there now, laughing at the big draft horses or trying to encourage Chester to come out and play. Aaron would have been the best father. Watching how gentle he was with the animals had always made her smile.

He'd turn and motion for her. "*Kumm* and play. *Kumm,* Raesha."

She thought about the man living on the property now. Josiah had kept his distance the last few days. Other than taking him meals when he came to get Dinah, she rarely saw him. He was up before dawn, handing her the baby with few words exchanged, then heading to work on the house next door. But she'd noticed little things he'd done here, too.

The big barn looked cleaner and better organized and the horses had fresh water and feed before she could even get out there to take care of them. Josiah worked hard and kept his rooms clean, gathered his own laundry and tried to wash his own clothes. But Naomi and Raesha had insisted it was no bother to throw his clothes in with theirs. During the winter months, they stretched a line across the basement from wall to wall and hung clothes there to dry. His were lined up on the end where he could find them when he needed them.

But it had been nice, seeing a man's clothing hanging there not far from her own. Nice, but she felt as if she was betraying her beloved Aaron.

"I want you to be happy," he'd told her many times. "Find a *gut* man to take care of you and Mamm. Promise me."

"I only want you. Stop spluttering about that. I'll never love another man."

"You will have me always. But I want you to be happy."

Wiping at her eyes, Raesha had tried to be happy. She'd been content and settled and she loved her work and she loved Naomi. Her life had become complacent and constant.

And then little Dinah had come along, followed by Josiah Fisher. Now she was restless and unsettled, that longing she'd tried so hard to temper piercing at her heart and reminding her of all she had lost.

He might be avoiding her, but Raesha couldn't stop thinking about Josiah. Which only made her miss Aaron even more.

While the tree line sheltered most of the Fisher property, she could catch glimpses of Josiah and the various neighbors who stopped by to help when they could. The stream of able-bodied men had been constant. That was the Amish way. The brethren needed help and they came and worked together. Josiah might think he didn't belong, but he was a child of God. He belonged to the Lord and that made him belong to this community.

The door to the shop opened and Susan rushed in. "I'm back. And happy to say everyone at our house is now well." Glancing around, the young girl heaved a sigh. "Ah, peace and quiet."

"*Gut* to see you and so bright and cheery on this

chilly morning, too," Raesha said, glad to have her thoughts taken away from Josiah. "Blessing on your family. I hope they all stay well."

Susan's sandy-colored hair was covered with a dark winter bonnet that had been made here in the shop. "I'm glad to be away from the *kinder* for a while," she admitted as she took off her heavy gray cloak. "Mamm says to tell you hello."

"Your mother is kind," Raesha replied, wishing with all her heart she had a big family to fuss over.

Susan fussed with her apron pins and then straightened her prayer *kapp*. "And she wants details on your new boarder."

Raesha chuckled. "I think the word is out. Mr. Hartford gossips like a chattering *grossmammi*."

"And knows all the gossips, too," Susan said, nodding. "But we are curious. I hear he's tall and fiercely handsome."

"He is tall," Raesha said. "And moderately nice looking."

"And single."

"So I'm told."

"You know more than you're letting on."

"I won't gossip about Josiah. He is a *gut* man."

"We have no need to gossip," Susan said with a jaunty grin. "But you do need to tell me everything."

Raesha listened to the steam machines in the back of the building, followed by the hum of the two Singer sewing machines. She had four workers here today. They had to stay ahead of the Christmas season, when tourists would come by and when customers would want new hats to give as gifts.

Susan glanced toward the big double doors to the

factory. "Do you not want anyone to know you have a crush on him?"

"I do not have a crush on him," Raesha denied a little too quickly. "That's ridiculous. I only just met the man."

"Right," Susan said, her cornflower blue eyes bright, her high cheeks rosy from the cold.

Raesha shot her a wry smile. "Okay, then, do you not have a crush on Daniel King?"

"Shh." Susan put a finger to her lips. "He's working today."

"I know he's working," Raesha replied on a smug note. "Since I'm his boss." Then she grinned. "And I'm thinking that is why you couldn't wait to get back to work, too."

Susan blushed, a sheepish smile broadening her heart-shaped face. "Let's call it even and I will be quiet."

"I think that is the best solution," Raesha replied.

But she had to wonder. Did everyone in Campton Creek know her heart? What kind of rumors were flying around? Maybe she should talk to Josiah about the gossip going around, so he could speak for himself. And leave her out of it.

Although, she was pretty much in the thick of it now.

Susan hurried by with a duster. "The midwife told my *mamm*. That's how I found out about him. And the baby, too, of course."

Raesha couldn't deny the truth but she wished Edna didn't prattle so. "The bishop knows of the situation but we were trying to keep it normal for the *bobbeli*'s sake. And because Josiah is concerned about his missing sister."

"There's a missing sister?"

"You already know that, I'm thinking." Raesha

slapped a hand over her mouth. "Now I have to tell you everything to set things straight."

Susan nodded, her expression serious now. "I do believe you need to tell someone since I hear mixed messages. Seems a lot has happened over this last week."

Raesha wanted to tell her friend that her whole world had been turned upside down and she needed to share how her heart had beat strongly again after holding little Dinah. But she would cherish those thoughts and keep them to herself.

"When we take dinner," she said, "I'll explain but, Susan, I do not want gossip to spread. I'll tell you the truth but I need you to not repeat it. It's getting out of hand as it is."

"I will do so, all joking aside," Susan replied. "I have never broken the confidences we share during work time."

"Nor have I," Raesha replied, the unspoken truce between them now stated. "It's *gut* to have a friend I can trust."

"*Ja*, and it's good to have an adult to talk to," Susan replied with a jaunty smile.

The girl had a strong sense of righteousness. She and Raesha shared a lot of woman talk. Raesha knew she could trust Susan.

"*Denke,*" she said. "Now I have busy work on the accounts."

"And I have to dust and polish," Susan replied. "And check on the workroom to see if anyone needs water or coffee."

"You mean Daniel King, *ja*?"

"I said everyone," Susan replied with her hands on her hips.

Two hours later, the phone rang and Raesha picked it up, expecting an order from a customer.

But her heart stopped when she heard the voice on the other end of the phone.

"Raesha, it's Edna Weiller. I asked around about Josephine Fisher and my friend Martha Pierce, who lives in the Goldfield Orchard District, remembers helping a girl who was pregnant and working at a bakery. The girl got dizzy and Martha checked her over and told her she was near term, suggested she get off her feet for a few hours. She wore Englisch attire and stayed at the Goldfield B and B."

Goldfield Orchard? Mr. Craig had mentioned he'd talked to people in a community about two hours from Campton Creek.

Raesha took a breath. "Do you think it was Josie?"

"It sounds so," Edna replied. "Martha said the girl worked in a bakery for a couple of months, but went into labor. She had her baby at the hospital."

"That verifies what we've put together so far."

"I have more," Edna said in her blunt way. "Martha said she saw the girl again just a few days ago. Said she looked frail and unwell. When Martha approached her, she turned and ran away."

"So she might be somewhere close still," Raesha said, her heart hurting for this frightened young girl.

"You should let Josiah know. He could go and search for her."

"Thank you, Edna. I appreciate the news. I'll tell Josiah."

Chapter Eight

Josiah pumped water from the old well so he could heat it over the fire and wash his hands and face. He and the other men had cleaned the well and got it pumping again. It would do for now. But he'd planned to install a pump inside the house and purchase a solar panel to help with heating water that could be pumped directly through the kitchen sink. He'd clear that with the bishop since some Old Order Amish frowned on such things.

This community seemed somewhere in between Old Order and the less conservative Amish. He only wanted a warm bath now and then and to be able to cook and wash clothes. But it would be a slow process. This morning, he was cleaning up scraps here and there since the house renovations were now finished. Soon, he could move in here with little Dinah.

That realization brought him both comfort and pain. He'd miss living at the Bawell place. But that arrangement could never be permanent.

Best to live here for a while and hope Josie would show up. If he had a stable home for the *bobbeli*, maybe his sister would be happy to join them and find some peace.

After he'd warmed the bucket of water over the fire he'd built earlier to burn wood scraps, he quickly washed up. He was about to go inside and admire the work his neighbors had done on the house and figure out if he wanted to build or buy some furniture to put inside.

"Josiah?"

He turned, surprised to see Raesha running across the tiny bridge between their property, her hands waving, her lightweight cape flying away from her shoulders.

He rushed toward her, afraid something had happened to Naomi. "What is it?"

Raesha stopped, her breath rushing out. "Edna Weiller called the shop. She's the midwife who visited Dinah. She had news regarding Josie."

His pulse quickened. "Is it bad?"

"*Neh.* At least, I think not. She has a friend who lives in Goldfield Orchard who saw a young girl, pregnant and staying at the Goldfield Bed-and-Breakfast. The girl went to a hospital to have her baby. But Martha, the friend, recently saw her again. She might still be in that area."

Josiah's heart stopped and then restarted with a rush. He whirled around and then turned back. *"Loss uns geh."* Let's go. "We must search for her."

"Do you want me to go with you?" she asked, surprise in her pretty eyes.

"I would appreciate that, *ja.*" Then he stopped. "But…you'd be better help watching out for Dinah."

Her eyes filled with understanding. "You should clean up. You can call Mr. Craig to meet you at the

Campton Center. He can go along with you and drive you to look for her."

She made good sense. He wanted to go right now but he was filthy. Looking down at his shirt and pants, he nodded. "I'll wash up and put on fresh clothing. I can clean up back at your place."

"I'll go on ahead. I need to get back to the shop. I'll check on Dinah and alert Mammi Naomi to what we've learned."

Nodding, he said, "I'll let you know when I'm leaving."

Raesha gave him a kind smile. "I pray you find her, Josiah."

"*Denke.* So do I."

After Raesha hurried away, Josiah stopped, took off his hat and looked out over the woods and fields. The sun shone brightly in a crisp midmorning glow. He closed his eyes and said a prayer.

"Your will, not mine."

But he prayed the Lord would show him favor.

Then he hurried to put away his tools and get to his buggy. He saw Raesha up ahead and caught up with her on the bridge. Her eyes met his and she offered a shaky smile.

"No matter what," she said, "you are a *gut* man, Josiah."

He wanted to be the kind of man who deserved a woman like her. He wanted to be a good uncle to Dinah and a good brother to Josie. He'd failed everyone in his family in so many ways.

Mostly, he wanted to find his sister and help her to turn her life back around.

The Lord had brought him here.

He'd wait on the Lord and then Josiah would set out to see that all of his wants became his reality. But the waiting would be so *hatt*. Hard. So very hard. Maybe that was the lesson the Lord wanted him to learn. Some things might be worth the wait.

Josiah pulled the buggy up to the Campton Center and hurried to secure the horses. Then he went inside to wait for Mr. Craig. Since he was staying nearby, he should arrive here quickly.

An assistant seated him inside Alisha Braxton's office. The attorney gave Josiah an encouraging smile. He brought her up-to-date, anxious while he fidgeted with the brim of his worn, faded hat.

"I'm still waiting on the birth certificate," he said. "I hope it will come through soon."

"It should have been there by now," Alisha said. "If you don't receive something in the next week, let me know and I'll try to track it for you."

Josiah thanked her and then waited.

"How did you meet Nathan?" she asked, her tone just below neutral.

"When I found out Josie had left Kentucky, I panicked. I had no idea where to start. A friend recommended him."

"But he lives in Pennsylvania. You were in Ohio."

"I heard he travels as needed. He was willing to go to Kentucky and ask around with me. And he's done some checking on his own now that I'm here."

That seemed to satisfy her. "I hope you find your sister, Mr. Fisher. It's tough when a loved one is out there alone and scared."

"*Ja*, she has been through so much."

Miss Braxton looked at her watch. "Just like Nathan to be late."

"Are you displeased with this man?" Josiah said, getting the feeling there was something amiss with this woman and the investigator.

Alisha tossed her thick hair back. "We don't always see eye to eye, but if I were searching for someone I loved, he'd be the only one I'd want to do the job."

"I'm reassured by that," Josiah said. "He has worked hard for me."

The front door of the big house creaked open and Nathan Craig walked in. Josiah stood and shook his hand. "Can we get going?"

Nathan's gaze moved from him to Miss Braxton. "I think we can. I know my way around Goldfield Orchard. I should have dug deeper last time I was there, but as you well know, the Amish can be tight-lipped about protecting one of their own."

Josiah bobbed his head. "I do know that. Makes it *hatt* to get anywhere sometimes."

"You two will make a good team," Miss Braxton said, her gaze touching on Nathan's. "Now go. You have all afternoon but this might take longer."

"Wish us well," Nathan said.

"Always," she replied.

When her phone rang, she waved to them and went about her business.

"We'll make good time," Nathan said after they were in his sedan. "I won't drive fast, Mr. Fisher. Don't want to rattle you."

"I appreciate that," Josiah replied, feeling odd in this fancy roaring vehicle. "And you can stop calling me Mr. Fisher. Josiah is fine."

"All right, then," Nathan said with a rare grin.

Soon they were going over the details of all the clues they'd discovered in finding Josie. Nathan Craig seemed devoted to his job and he had the details down, from having Josiah describe her to a sketch artist to gathering every little morsel of information he could even if it didn't amount to anything.

"I'll track down that birth certificate copy for you, too," Nathan said.

"Why do you do this?" Josiah asked, wondering why the man seemed so committed.

Nathan watched the road and then said, "I was born Amish but I left during my *rumspringa* and never looked back. But I regret that at times. I had two brothers and a sister. She was the baby of the family. She went missing when she was twelve. We found her a few weeks later. Dead. And we never found her killer."

Josiah held to the dash, but glanced at his friend. "I am sorry, Nathan."

Nathan stared straight ahead. "I've made peace with it but I should have been there. I could have protected her."

"So this is why you help others search for their loved one, especially Amish who don't have the resources of most."

"Yes, no resources and no help. It's challenging but I know the life, know how difficult things can be at times."

"I will forever be grateful to you, Nathan."

"Don't thank me yet. I sure hope we find Josie."

"I pray so," Josiah said.

They rode in silence until they reached the quaint village of Goldfield Orchard. Josiah couldn't help but stare at every woman he saw, thinking it might be Josie. But he did not see his sister.

She'd probably stay out of sight or she might be working somewhere. Trying to make enough money to support her baby.

"Let's start at the bed-and-breakfast," Nathan said.

Josiah nodded in agreement, his stomach roiling with apprehension.

Father, please let me find her and make this up to her.

Naomi finished her work and grabbed Raesha by her sleeve. "Sit and eat. Dinah has been fed and changed. She is sleeping again. You are too worked up."

Raesha did as her mother-in-law asked. She sat down and stared at her food. "I have much to do in the shop. I think I should set up a little nursery there, too, so I can watch Dinah there at times."

"Are you concerned that I cannot watch the child?" Naomi asked, her tone gentle, her eyes keen.

"Neh," Raesha replied, her eyes full of love for Naomi. "You are gentle and loving but your balance is not what it used to be."

Naomi nodded at that. "We could both go tumbling down and I would not want that to happen."

"It's a concern," Raesha admitted. "I hope Josiah comes home with good news."

An hour later, she heard a knock on the back door.

Rushing to open it, she found Josiah standing there with his hat in his hands, his expression full of disappointment.

"You did not find her?"

"Neh."

"Kumm," she said, wanting to comfort him.

He slipped inside and glanced around. "I came for Dinah."

"She's sleeping," Raesha said. "Sleeping and full but it's about time for her to wake. If you're tired we can keep her with us awhile longer."

He smiled at her. "I'm tired and frustrated but she brings me comfort."

Raesha's heart felt a shard of pain. He only wanted to see the babe. Did he not see that she wanted to comfort him, too?

But that would be wrong. She could offer support and friendship and nothing more.

"Can I get you a bite to eat?"

He didn't argue with that.

Naomi came into the parlor and smiled at him. "Hello, Josiah. From the looks of you, I don't think you bring us good news."

"We searched everywhere," he said. Taking a place at the supper table, he shook his head. "Many had seen a woman matching her, but that was weeks ago. No one has seen her recently. They were kind in answering our questions but I think Josie has moved on."

"Keep searching," Naomi said. "She will feel your presence and, hopefully, she will feel God's love, too."

After he'd eaten a meat loaf sandwich and some mashed potatoes, Josiah turned to Raesha. "I can't thank you enough for helping me so."

"Dinah is a joy," she admitted, now holding the smiling child. "We love her dearly." Then she cooed at Dinah. "Don't we, sure we do."

The baby gurgled and kicked her little legs.

"I can rest knowing she is in *gut* hands. I owe you a great debt."

"You have helped out around here," Raesha pointed out. "Our machines are humming away without all the creaks and groans and my workers are impressed with your talents."

"Denke." He'd been disheartened when he'd come here tonight but now, as always, these two loving women had nurtured him with food and assurances.

Now he sat and watched Raesha holding his niece while he finished his meal. It hurt to see Josie and his *mamm* in Dinah's features. But seeing the way Raesha cared for her did bring him peace. What if Josie had left Dinah at another, less loving home?

He should be thankful for God's grace and for Raesha's and Naomi's good hearts. Dinah was thriving here.

Raesha watched him and then said, "Josiah, I was thinking about setting up a place for Dinah in the shop, up front with me just behind the counter."

He stared from where she sat across from him, Dinah balanced on her lap, to where Naomi sat in her favorite rocking chair, mending clothes.

"Nowhere near the workroom," Naomi cautioned. "But Raesha is concerned with my old age and frail body and rightly so. I care about Dinah's safety so it might be best if she is with Raesha in the shop, where she will have plenty of able-bodied people to step up."

Josiah took it all in and then said, "I have a suggestion."

"What?" they both asked.

"Why don't we let Naomi be in charge of Dinah when one of us is around or nearby? She can hold her, feed her, rock her to sleep, and we can do our work within hearing range."

Naomi nodded at that, a deep appreciation in her eyes. "A *gut* plan."

Hopeful, he went on before Raesha could shut him down. "When I am working at the old place, Raesha will be in charge. Whether here or in the shop. I will help set up a baby area in the shop, wherever you want it."

She nodded. "Much appreciated. I will have lots of help. Susan comes from a big family. She is good with babies."

"And you have others who come and go," Naomi added. "This will be the most loved and cared for *bobbeli* in all of Campton Creek."

"How should we explain this?" Josiah asked, concerned that rumors would continue to fly. Used to people staring, he only smiled and nodded a greeting now. But he did not want these two women to bear the brunt of the rumors.

"We tell the truth as we have from the beginning," Naomi said without preamble. "We are helping our friend and neighbor with his little orphaned niece. That is all anyone needs to know."

"That is all," Josiah said, "but they will find out more and they will add to what they hear."

"We'll deal with that one day at a time," Raesha said. "We have to come up with a suitable and safe area for Dinah, and most have already heard that your sister is missing."

"I think so," he agreed. "I haven't offered much but people know and some have been kind. Others, not so much. But that is the way when we do not understand the situation."

Naomi watched them with her shrewd gaze. "We will continue to help you, Josiah. Rest assured on that. We are learning as we go, however. It's been a long time since I held such a sweet little girl."

Raesha shook her head and smiled at Josiah. "So many details in raising a baby."

"That is true." He took a bite of his sandwich and washed it down with tea. "Josie gave her up for all the right reasons. She knew the child would be safe and loved here." Putting down his sandwich, he said, "I cannot imagine what she must have gone through. I knew she was troubled, but Josie would never give up a child without a *gut* reason."

"Now we hope we can find her and bring her here, too," Raesha said, her eyes holding his. "Wouldn't that be a joy?"

"It would," he admitted. "But what if she wants nothing to do with me…or her daughter?"

Standing, he stared down at Raesha. "If I never see my sister again, what will I tell that sweet little girl?"

Chapter Nine

The more he was around Raesha Bawell, the more Josiah realized she was different from any woman he'd ever known. In addition, she was smart, determined, faithful to a fault and outspoken on most subjects. Maybe this was what kept her single. Did most men scratch their heads and walk away?

He, however, found her candor refreshing. She wasn't disrespectful to anyone but she was firm and kind, with a no-nonsense attitude. He watched her now as she talked with the girl she'd introduced as Susan Raber. Susan held Dinah, her dark eyes bright with interest, while Raesha and Josiah moved an old bassinet they'd cleaned and polished into a cozy corner behind the long wide desk of the shop.

Dinah would be warm and safe here and away from the customers who would come and go. Even now, two Englisch women were admiring the *bobbeli*'s pretty eyes and bright smile. Susan handled them with expert ease, allowing them to look at Dinah but not touch her. Germs were everywhere. He did not want his niece to get sick.

"I'm ready to purchase my items," one woman said, her big coat flapping dangerously close to some trinkets on a nearby table.

"I can help you with that," Raesha replied, turning from where she'd placed a clean blanket into the bassinet. "We are sorry for the distractions today. But we have a little one to consider."

"She's adorable," the blonde woman said with a smile. "It's nice that she can be here with you while you work. You and your husband are truly blessed."

Raesha shot Josiah a glance while Susan's eyes popped wide.

"Denke," Josiah said. To explain more to a stranger would only make matters worse, but Raesha would have his hide since he didn't correct the woman.

The smiling lady glanced from Raesha back to him. "You two seem so perfect together."

Her tall friend gave her a stern warning glance. "Let's finish up here. We still want to tour the covered bridges."

Raesha rang up the shawl, gloves and candles, and then took the woman's money. Placing all of the items into a handmade bag with the shop's logo on it, Raesha thanked the customers and remained silent until the bell on the double doors chimed as they left.

Susan didn't waste a minute. "Are you two...?"

"No," Raesha said. "No, nothing is going on between us."

Josiah bobbed his head, suddenly too warm. "I did not correct the Englisch woman because then I'd have to explain the whole situation."

"You only had to say we are taking care of her for a friend," Raesha replied. "Or... I could have at least said that."

"Well, that's over now," Susan said to the smiling baby in her arms. "That woman will forget all about us when she sees our beautiful bridges. But if you ask me, I think these two do make a good match."

"Did little Dinah ask you anything?" Raesha asked, her eyes full of aggravation and mirth.

"No, not exactly," Susan retorted. "But she is a very wise young girl. She's smiling her agreement."

Josiah couldn't hide his own grin. Raesha's disapproving gaze moved to him. "And you were worried about rumors, so why are you trying not to laugh?"

Josiah couldn't explain it. "I don't know except that when you are all in a flutter you make me smile."

Susan giggled and then straightened her expression to look more somber.

Raesha turned back to spreading blankets and checking the bag of baby things she'd brought from the main house. "I am not all in a flutter. We will get adjusted to this but we don't need to give the impression we are more than friends. We have enough explaining to do as it is."

Josiah turned serious. "If this is too much for you, I can make other arrangements."

"Neh," Raesha and Susan said in unison.

"I like Dinah," Susan said. "I'll help out."

"I agreed to this," Raesha said. "There is no need to change our plans."

Josiah glanced from Raesha's stubborn face to Susan's watchful one. "Then I will return to my work. I'll come by later to pick her up."

"Pick her up? For what?" Raesha asked.

"To take her to the *grossdaddi haus* with me as usual."

"Oh." Raesha's eyes filled with acceptance and disappointment. "We did agree to that."

"*Ja*, and we've been doing that very thing for days now. Are you all right?"

"Of course. I just got busy and didn't know where you aimed to take her."

Susan's eyes went so wide, he was sure the girl was going to pop them right out of her head. "You're the person living in the *grossdaddi haus*?"

"*Ja*. I'm a paying customer and it was cleared with the bishop."

Susan glanced at Raesha. "This is so much better than chasing my brothers and sisters around."

"He's to take Dinah home with him at night, so they can get acquainted and he can learn how to take care of a *bobbeli*. Because he plans to sell his place and take her away to Ohio one day soon."

"Well, that's too bad," Susan replied, taking the now-sleeping Dinah to the fresh crib. "Because whether you two know it or not, things might not work out the way you've planned."

"What does that mean?" Raesha asked, her hands on her hips.

"That is between Dinah and me," Susan said on a giggle. Then she added, "God might have other plans for you two."

"When did you become so know-it-all?" Raesha asked with a mock tartness.

Josiah shook his head. Women and their riddles. A man could never guess what they truly were talking about. No wonder he was still single. He didn't know how to deal with all the emotions and unspoken expectations that came with women. He'd watched his *mamm* cower and give in to his forceful father, never knowing how she really felt. He had not learned the proper cues and warnings, or the proper courting tactics, with a woman.

But he'd spoken the truth earlier. Raesha made him laugh. She made him wonder. She made him happy. The kind of happy he hadn't felt in a long time. She didn't do many riddles but her bluntness was refreshing.

And yet she scared him. In that place in his heart, the place he'd boarded up and forgotten, she scared him.

"I must get to work," he said in way of an escape. "I will take Dinah this evening. I have her bed ready and I'll need you to show me how to wash diapers to get them…clean…again."

"That's my task," Raesha retorted, affronted.

"I'm willing to learn," he replied.

Susan seemed to be enjoying this too much. "I have never heard that said before."

Raesha nodded and straightened her *kapp* strings. "Very well. We will have a lesson in diaper cleaning and washing."

Josiah went out the side door to the yard, the crisp morning air bringing him relief. Inhaling deeply, he took off toward the old farmhouse, glad for something to take his mind off the woman who had somehow broken a seal inside his heart.

And yet, even in his angst and clumsiness, he couldn't help but smile. Maybe young Susan was right. Maybe he and Raesha could be a good match. But a lot would have to happen before that came to pass.

First being, the woman in question would have to show some interest in him.

* * *

Raesha knocked on Josiah's door, a plate filled with fried ham, two biscuits, and some rice and gravy in her hand. He had come to the shop to take Dinah for the night, but he didn't come over to the kitchen for dinner.

Not that she'd invited him or expected him. After Susan's pointed observations regarding both of them, she had decided to keep her distance from the man.

Then why was she standing here at his door?

When she heard Dinah crying, Raesha's heart leaped. She couldn't stop her need to protect the little girl. Josiah would take good care of her, but most men left childcare to their wives.

But you are not his wife.

The door swung open. He held a crying Dinah in a blanket, his face flushed and with worry in his eyes. "I'm not sure what's wrong with her."

Raesha stepped inside the cozy little house and put the food on the table. "Let me see."

Josiah gladly handed the babe to her. "I fed her and did a fairly *gut* job of changing her but now she's fussy."

Raesha shifted Dinah against her shoulder and started patting her tiny back. "Did you try to burp her?"

Josiah's confused stare was almost comical. "Burp her?"

"This," she said, still patting the baby. "You only need to gently pat her back so she can expel some air from her feeding."

Josiah watched silently as she calmed Dinah. "You seem so natural at this."

Raesha hummed a soft tune, one of her favorite hymns—"Precious Memories." She knew she had people praying her through the overwhelming events of the last week.

Father, I pray I do the right thing for all.

"You have calmed her," Josiah said, his hair mussed and his sleeves rolled up. "Clearly, I do not know what I'm doing."

Raesha's heart went out to him. He tried so hard to please everyone. She wondered again what he must have gone through in the house across the way.

"If it becomes too much, we are here to help," she said. She wouldn't push him to let the child stay with Naomi and her all the time. He needed to learn how to be a good guardian to Dinah.

"*Ja*, and I am forever grateful for that."

"But you want to do your part?"

"I have to do my part. For Dinah, for Josie. But I have never raised a child. I want to do the best job I can. I had to take care of Josie after my parents died, but she was older and I had help in Ohio. This is different. Dinah needs constant care."

"I've not been blessed with children," she admitted. "Aaron and I wanted children and we thought…" She stopped, thinking this conversation had become inappropriate. "He blamed himself but…cancer took over our lives."

"I'm sorry for your loss," Josiah said. "But you seem to know what to do with children. I'm sure helping others has taught you to nurture."

She smiled at that and kept moving around the room until Dinah became groggy. "As we told you, we've housed a lot of people over the years. Family members who come and go, searching for something in their lives. Some come to visit and find their own homes here, some come for a few days or weeks and then go back home. Naomi came from a family of eight children, much like Susan."

"And you?"

"My parents have passed and my younger twin sisters, Emma and Becca, are both married and live right next to each other in another community about an hour or so from here. My older brother, Amos, also lives there but across the valley from them. When they come to visit, they usually stay for a few days. I get to spoil my three nieces and two nephews."

Josiah smiled at the sleeping baby. "This place seems to draw people in need. You and Naomi are kind and you have a successful business. I've dreamed of much the same. But I don't think it's in my future."

She listened and saw the anguish mixed with hope in his eyes. Taking Dinah back to her crib in the corner, she asked, "So you plan to go back to Ohio, *ja*?"

"I had planned to but now I don't know. If Josie is nearby, I need to stay close." Giving her a measured glance, he said, "I owe my *onkel* some money he loaned to me when I first went to search for Josie in Kentucky. One of my cousins is not happy about that and accused me of taking advantage of his *daed*."

After tucking the baby in, Raesha turned back to Josiah. "Ah, so that explains your need to sell out and go back to Ohio. You want to take care of things with your relatives."

"*Ja*, of course. I pay my debts."

"That is noble and shows you have integrity."

"Integrity but I need a steady income. I'm good with the land so I know I could make it here. I'm waiting to hear from Josie. She might show up back in Ohio or go back to Kentucky but I feel she's somewhere nearby."

The worrying about his sister had to be taking its toll on him. "I'm so sorry, Josiah. I can't imagine what you have been dealing with, searching for her, not knowing where she is or what might have happened to her."

"I know I should leave it to God but... I worry."

"That's a natural reaction, considering Josie could be alone and frightened."

He rubbed his eyes and nodded, his head down. "But God has sent us a gift, Raesha. Surely finding Dinah here is a sign to me, *ja*?"

Raesha couldn't speak. The agony in his words struck her to her core. "I believe so, Josiah." She couldn't ask him to stay simply because she loved little Dinah. That would be selfish and unkind. "You have to decide what is best for you and Dinah because you might not ever find your sister."

His head came up. "I won't stop looking. I can't. Josephine has suffered enough in her young life. I fear she got herself into some kind of trouble, based on how we were raised."

Raesha waited, hoping he would tell her.

But he turned away. "I've said too much. *Denke* for settling Dinah. I can take things from here."

"Eat your dinner while you can," Raesha replied, disappointed that he didn't want to talk about his childhood.

He nodded. "That and then I am going to sleep."

She went to the door but turned, her hand on the doorknob. "I pray you will find a restful sleep, Josiah."

He didn't speak. He stood staring over at her, his

eyes dark with a whirl of emotions. Finally, he said, "The same to you."

Raesha went back to her side of the house and found Naomi sitting in her favorite chair by the warmth from the heater.

"Are you not ready for bed?" she asked.

Naomi patted the chair across from her. "I wanted to talk to you, daughter."

Raesha smiled. Naomi had called her daughter since the day Aaron had brought her here. "What is on your mind?"

"You and Josiah," Naomi replied, her hands folded in her lap. "That is what is on my mind, daughter."

Chapter Ten

Raesha's heart bumped. "What about Josiah and me, Mammi Naomi?"

Naomi slowly sipped her tea and took her time forming her words. "I've watched you two all week, with the *bobbeli*, with each other and even when you're not near each other."

"You don't have to worry," Raesha said, hoping to reassure her mother-in-law that Josiah was being a gentleman, proper and polite. "He's a kind man and he respects the boundaries that we abide by."

"I wasn't talking about propriety, Raesha," Naomi responded with a knowing smile. "I do not doubt you are beyond reproach."

Raesha shook her head. "Then what are you trying to tell me?"

Naomi shrugged her shoulders. "I think you two make a good match."

"What?" Raesha shifted in her chair. "Are you serious?"

"Very," Naomi said, her hands tucked against her lap

shawl. "You need to find a *gut* man and I believe God has sent you one, and a babe to go with him."

Shocked, Raesha stood up and paced in front of the old propane heater. "It's a little too early to think such things, if at all, don't you think?"

"Never too early to find a soul mate." Naomi's kind eyes held hers. "But it will become too late one day."

Raesha had an image of herself, sitting in that very rocking chair, alone. Would anyone come to check on her?

Of course they would. She might be lonely but she'd never really be alone. Would she?

In her defense, she said, "But Josiah and I barely know each other and besides, he is determined to go back to Ohio to pay his *onkel* the money he loaned Josiah to search for Josie."

"That shows integrity," Naomi replied, as if she hadn't heard the rest of what Raesha had said. "But he can easily mail a check or some cash to his *onkel*. He might decide to stay here if he thinks you are interested."

Raesha sat back down on the chair across from Naomi. "I'm not interested."

Naomi didn't say a word. She was very clever, knowing when to stay silent. It made others tell her everything on their heart. Raesha wouldn't fall for it.

But the silence in the big room and the quiet contentment in Naomi's expression made her twitch. "Okay, I might be interested."

"Just as I thought."

"But… I can't be interested. He has so much to do and he is concerned about Josie and Dinah. Josiah will do what's best for both of them. He put Josephine first when he took her to Ohio, thinking she'd be better off with family. But I wonder if his uncle and cousins treated him badly. He had no money and no hope when he left Campton Creek. He became indentured to them in a way, I believe. Now his guilt over all of it is eating away at him. He came back here to fix the place up and sell it, but I think he also came back here to put an end to the past and move on with his life. Only now, he has hope that Josie is still somewhere nearby."

Naomi's old rocker squeaked and creaked. "For someone who says she does not know this man, you sure seem to have learned a lot about him."

Wishing she'd stayed silent, Raesha gave Naomi a tight-lipped stare. "We've talked to each other, *ja*."

"Do you think he is interested in you?"

"No. I mean, I don't know. He could be but it can't come to pass."

"Why not?"

"I explained," Raesha said, thinking her mother-in-law could be very persistent at times. "He is going to sell out and leave and he'll take Dinah with him. End of story."

"And what about you?" Naomi asked. "Why are you holding back?"

"For one, I only just met the man a week ago, and you know I'm not interested in remarrying."

"Aaron would want you to do just that. You can still love and mourn my son, but you could also honor him and be happy in this life, too."

Naomi tried to stand and Raesha rushed to help her. "I am fine in this life. I am blessed and busy with work I love. I'm content."

Content. There was that word again. Raesha had never doubted that contentment and happiness went hand in hand. But now she doubted what true happiness really meant.

"I think this is the beginning of a new story," Naomi said with her serene smile intact. "Give it some time. You have to admit finding the babe and the *onkel* in one week has to be God's doing."

"Yes, but I don't think God wants me to rush his doings," Raesha said, her words calm while her mind raced with embarrassment and annoyance. Josiah was a handsome man with his broad shoulders and dark curly hair. How could she not notice him? He filled any room he came into, especially her kitchen.

But why did everyone think she needed to be married to be happy? She'd been content…

Raesha stopped short, a new realization causing Naomi to glance over at her. Yes, she'd been content. But happy went deeper than content.

She could see that now and she felt that difference each time she looked at Dinah or saw Josiah walking across the footbridge between their homes.

"We will let nature take its course," Naomi said, her tone soft, her smile full of assurance.

Raesha turned back Naomi's bed and then gave her a kiss on the cheek. "*Gut* idea."

Naomi wasn't finished. "But remember, do not let me stand in the way."

"You are not in the way," Raesha replied, love pouring over her heart. "This is between Josiah and me and… God will show all of us the way."

She wouldn't leave Naomi alone no matter that any number of people would gladly move in here with her mother-in-law or take Naomi in. Raesha couldn't bring herself to leave. She'd built a life here and she loved the

Bawell property, the hat shop, her workers, her friends and this community.

"*Denke*, for caring about me," she told Naomi. "Now you need to rest."

She helped Naomi into her nightgown and gave her the pills the doctor wanted her to take each night, and together they said their nightly prayers, which now included praying for Josiah, Josephine and little Dinah.

Naomi finished the prayer. "*Im Namen des Vater, des Sohns, und des Heiligen Geistes.*"

In the name of the Father, the Son and the Holy Ghost.

"Amen," Raesha said in unison with Naomi.

Then she turned down the lamp, tucked the blankets tight and left the door slightly open. She'd listen in for Naomi while she finished up some knitting and mending in the parlor. Because she knew sleep would not come to her right away.

She couldn't stop thinking about what Naomi had suggested earlier and she couldn't stop thinking about the man and the baby so nearby and yet so out of her reach.

September moved with the swiftness of a reckless wind toward winter. The woods had changed to a more barren landscape and the trees were beginning to shed their various leaves. Snow would come soon, and with it the busy Christmas season at the shop.

For now, Raesha and Josiah settled into a daily routine where he brought Dinah over early each morning and Raesha and Naomi watched her during the day while he worked on the old place next door. Raesha took Dinah to the shop with her on most days, but Susan had become so efficient, Raesha had begun to go in later and come home earlier.

"I don't mind," Susan kept insisting. "I love my work here and I'm helping support my family. Besides, you need time with the little one away from all the fuss here in the shop. We're all right here, doing our jobs, like clockwork."

Of course, Susan got to see Daniel a lot more at the shop, too. It seemed to be a winning situation for all and Raesha expected to be making another wedding bonnet soon.

But she gave another young girl who lived around the curve some extra hours to help Susan.

"I'll figure something out before we get too busy," she'd promised Susan.

Raesha had to admit she enjoyed seeing Josiah every day, too, and on the occasional night when he needed help learning how to handle a baby. But she tried not to show how Josiah made her heart leap or that her head got all befuddled.

Naomi watched them together with unabashed pleasure and Susan kept her keen eyes on them whenever Josiah came into the shop to check on Dinah. The employees had gotten to know him and appreciate him. Especially when he would lend a hand here and there, always inquisitive about hat-making.

Then he'd come back to pick Dinah up just as the sun was slipping away over the tree line. Somewhere in there over the last couple of weeks, he began staying for dinner, rather than taking a plate to the house he rented.

Probably because Naomi had said one rainy night, "Why don't you just eat here, Josiah? It's the practical thing to do."

Naomi was all about being practical.

Raesha couldn't protest. That would be disrespecting her elder. And what would it hurt to have Josiah share a hearty meal with them while they all spoiled Dinah? It saved her having to walk it over since he couldn't carry a plate of food and Dinah and all her supplies, too.

She had to admire the way he'd taken to his niece. Most men would frown on such hands-on helping with childcare. But Josiah had experienced taking care of his young sister. He didn't seem to mind middle-of-the-night feedings and changing diapers.

Raesha washed most of the baby clothes and hung them to dry even if he insisted on washing his own clothes, and he'd given his best to scalding and bleaching diapers, too.

A stubborn, proud man who didn't want to seek help from anyone.

A knock at the door brought Raesha out of her musings. Some friends were gathering here this afternoon for a frolic—quilting, baking and making plans for the fall festival that would take place in town near the Hartford General Store. Campton Creek held a spring mud sale and a craft festival each year and managed to squeeze in a couple of fall and harvest festivals and, sometimes, mud sales before winter set in.

Susan grinned when Raesha opened the door. "I brought apple fritters and oatmeal cookies from Mamm. She let me escape!"

"I'm so glad to see you," Raesha said, tugging her inside the warm house.

"As if you didn't just see me earlier at the shop," Susan replied, glancing around. "Where is my wee friend?"

"Dinah is sleeping," Raesha replied with a finger to her lips. "And so is Naomi."

"*Gut* to have an afternoon off," Susan mock-whispered. "Wednesday is always a slow day for the front."

"While the back of the shop is steady with work," Raesha replied. "Daniel is getting very good at being the boss back there."

"He loves his work," Susan said with a soft smile. "And he appreciates that you trust him."

Susan went about helping her set out refreshments: coffee, lemonade and tea, along with fruit and nibbles. Then her young friend whirled to stare at Raesha.

"Do I have a bug on my nose?" Raesha asked, waiting patiently for Susan to spit out whatever was going through her always-bubbling head.

"Was it hard for you to take over the business? I mean, as a woman?"

Raesha put down the folded yellow cloth napkins she'd taken out of the cupboard. *"Ja,"* she admitted with a sigh. "The men who work in the hat shop were used to taking orders from Aaron and his *daddi* before him. At first, they refused to even acknowledge me. I had to keep smiling and giving out orders."

"When did they come to respect you the way they do now?" Susan asked, her eyes wide with curiosity.

Raesha thought about it. "Ah, that happened a few months after Aaron had died. I needed a rush order for a client two counties over. They were lollygagging about and I came into the shop and stood with my hands on my hips."

"You were perturbed?"

"Slightly." Raesha smiled now, but she remembered how her heart trembled that day. "I told the foreman to shut down the machines and then I announced that the Bawell Hat Shop was my world, because it had been my husband's world. I told them I now had to take care of Naomi—that sweet old woman who had no one else to help her. I didn't want to let her down and I reminded them of all she'd done for them, too."

Susan burst out laughing. "You shamed those young men."

"I did and I'm not ashamed to admit that. Slackers are not welcome in my shop."

"You know, Raesha, we all admire your spunk."

"Who is *we all*?"

"My friends and I, Mamm, everyone I know. They respect Naomi and admire you for staying by her side. Is that why you've not married again?"

Shocked at that question, Raesha shook her head. "I am fine with my work and my home. I fell in love with Aaron and I also fell in love with this place. I could never leave it for anyone."

Susan's impressed smile changed when she looked past Raesha to the now-open side door.

Raesha turned to find Josiah standing there with a confused, disappointed expression on his face.

Had he heard her declaration?

Chapter Eleven

Josiah couldn't get Raesha's words out of his head.

She'd never leave her home. Her words had burned through him hot as a branding iron. *He'd* left his home without even bothering to rebuild it. Up and left it gutted and charred and abandoned, thinking he'd had no other choice. After the horrible fire and his parents' deaths, he'd only wanted to get as far away from the farm as possible.

Why hadn't he waited and let the community help him rebuild way back then? If he had, Josie might be happily married by now and living at the old place with her husband. Or he might have found a wife here and could have made a life working the land.

At the time, he wanted his sister to never have to see that house again. And he did not want to have to explain to everyone how the fire had happened either. Had he been wrong to guard so many family secrets?

Now he regretted his hasty decision to uproot Josie and start over fresh somewhere else. But at eighteen, he hadn't known what to do or where to go. His mother's people had long ago moved on and most had died. His father hated his family and talked badly about them, but Ohio had seemed the only place left for Josiah and his traumatized little sister. Even though they had not been welcomed with open arms, his *onkel* had taken them in. Only to work both of them so hard, Josie rebelled and took off.

But something else about Raesha's words had grabbed at him.

She'd never leave this community. Now as he worked on the old barn, tearing away vines and weeds, knocking down charred boards and broken windows, he had to admit it had crossed his mind a time or two that she would make a good wife.

But would she follow someone like him?

Would she give up her life here to go to Ohio?

No. He had to quit thinking that way. She was firmly settled and had a thriving business, something unusual for a widowed Amish woman. She was good at her work and good with little Dinah. What if she wanted both? Her work and a family?

Could he handle that?

He'd been handling that.

Raesha's work ethic impressed him. He'd been inside the back of the shop and watched how Daniel King and her other workers took extra care to create handmade products. Raesha and Daniel had guided him on steaming brims and measuring felt to match the patterns and the sturdy paper hat forms. He'd seen the women sewing away on treadle machines, their hands moving the materials to make the stitches perfect. Daniel and Susan had told him all about straw suppliers and how to wet the straw and weight it down with bricks or rocks to shape it.

So many sizes and shapes. He'd worn hats all of his life and had never given a thought to how they were made. For a brief moment, he thought he could be content learning that trade.

But he didn't know if he'd stay here.

Father, I need to turn this over to You. I need to focus on what needs to be done now.

A lot still needed to be taken care of with this farm. The Fisher farm covered only a few acres but they'd managed to eke out a living here. Or so he'd always believed. His mother, Sarah, had somehow made money on the side to help feed her family. Until Abram Fisher had discovered she'd been hiding money from him.

Josiah stopped, took a breath, inhaling over and over. The memories of the fire always disturbed him even though he'd been away at the time. But Josie remembered what she could and had mentioned details at the oddest moments. What must those same memories have done to her? She'd been only nine and she'd witnessed the whole thing. He feared those memories had driven her to destruction.

She'd had a child. Josie wouldn't give away her own child unless she'd had no other choice. Obviously, she had not married Tobias, the boy she always spoke about in her letters.

Telling himself he wouldn't leave until he got word from the lawyer lady or Mr. Craig regarding Josie's whereabouts, Josiah felt caught between a rock and a hard place. Stay here and hope his sister would return home? Or go back to Ohio and bear the brunt of his cousin's wrath and his *onkel*'s grudging kindness?

As hard as this work was, here was the best place right now and maybe for the rest of his life.

But where would that leave Raesha and him?

There is no Raesha and you, he told himself. *She has everything she needs right here. And you have nothing to offer her.*

He stopped hammering at the old wood and turned to stare over at the Bawell place. The two-storied house shone a clean white against the October sunshine. A warm spell had hit and the temperatures were crisp but pleasant. The house seemed to glow against the golden-and-russet leaves of the trees. The big barn stood solid and tall behind the house. The mums lining the porch welcomed people to the big door and the fall garden grew hardy and bright.

Then he looked back around at his place. Forlorn and torn, half-broken and withered, half built back to new. He'd had only half a life here anyway and not a very good life after he'd left.

Left his mother and sister without anyone to defend them. Would he ever get over the guilt of that, so he could finish rebuilding his life?

I have failed, Father. I don't know how to make it all right again.

He wasn't good enough for the likes of Raesha Bawell.

He'd never been good enough for his father or his extended family and he'd failed his sister miserably.

Deciding he'd get this place ready to sell as he'd planned, Josiah accepted that if he couldn't find Josie, he might have to move on. But where? Did he go back to Ohio to stay? Or did he find another community and start all over again?

Father, what am I to do?

His life seemed so overwhelming at times. How

many walls would he have to tear down to find peace and contentment?

Josiah went back to his solitary work, his thoughts and prayers on how to find true redemption. He'd have that only when he knew Josie was safe.

Much later, he heard a buggy approaching and turned to squint into the late afternoon sun. Jeremiah Weaver waved to him and hopped down to hurry toward him.

"*Gut* day, Jeremiah," Josiah said, nodding. He and Jeremiah had met at the general store and gotten to know each other when Jeremiah had come to help Josiah with rebuilding the house. Jeremiah had been a prodigal who'd returned to his faith and was now happily married and had a baby boy to add to his new wife's two older children.

"Morning, Josiah," Jeremiah said, glancing around. "You've made progress here."

Josiah dusted off his hands. "*Ja*, but more is needed."

Jeremiah nodded and stared out toward the woods. "Listen, I was doing some work at the Campton Center and…a phone call came in for you."

"For me?" Josiah put down his tools. "Who would be calling for me?"

"Alisha Braxton got a call on your behalf. It's about your sister, Josiah. Mr. Craig has located her. But she's sick and in a hospital about thirty minutes away."

Shock coursed through Josiah. Josie! Dropping his toolbox, he said, "I must get to her."

"*Kumm,*" Jeremiah said, his blues eyes full of urgency. "I can take you to the Campton Center. We have a driver there who volunteers to taxi Amish as needed."

"*Denke,*" Josiah said. Then he looked toward the Bawell place. "I have to tend to Dinah."

"I'm sure the Bawell women will take care of her."

"I'll tell them I have to go," he said, his mind full of questions. "Josie needs me."

Jeremiah touched his arm. "I'll drive you over to get whatever you might need."

Together, they headed to the waiting buggy.

Josiah couldn't speak. Josie was alive but ill.

He had to get to her right away.

This could change everything and very quickly at that.

What if Josie wanted nothing to do with him?

Raesha waved to the last of her friends, her mood upbeat in spite of their teasing her about the new developments in her life. She couldn't let their pointed suggestions sway her in any way.

"I've heard he's handsome," Deborah Troyer said with a knowing smile. "And available."

"I saw him in town," Beth Weaver added. "Jeremiah said if he's rebuilding the old place, he might consider sticking around?"

"He plans to sell it." She tried to explain. Several times.

But the women were off and running on a thread of speculation that moved as quickly as their nimble fingers against patterns.

Beth went on. "He can't take care of sweet Dinah alone. He's blessed that you are being so kind, Raesha."

Deborah smiled over at the crib. "Dinah is such a good *bobbeli*. She needs a mother."

Another friend added, "Yes, Raesha, she needs a mother."

"Time will tell what Josiah decides," Naomi said in

her best commanding voice. "Until then, enough. We are here to work, not to make idle assumptions."

She sent Raesha a serene smile and then winked at her.

That shut everyone down on that subject. The women moved on to children and housework and what they planned on bringing to the Campton Creek Fall Festival next weekend. They quilted and mended and crocheted and knitted, the tightness of their teasing, well-meaning love as strong as the threads they wove.

But Raesha had seen the sweet concern behind the comments. They wanted her to have a family of her own.

Tired now and still smiling about their comments, Raesha turned to go and check on Dinah when the back door burst open and Josiah stood there, his expression full of shock, his eyes wide.

"What's wrong?" she asked, her heart jumping with dread.

"They've found Josie," he said, his hands on her arms. "I must go to her."

Josie. "Where, how?" Emotion crashed through her in great waves. She didn't even mind that he'd grabbed her arms.

He named the hospital toward the west. "Jeremiah came to tell me. There is a taxi waiting at the Campton Center."

"Go," she said. "Go to your sister. Dinah will be fine with us until you return."

"I don't know how long I'll be gone."

Seeing the struggle in his eyes, Raesha held his gaze. "Go to your sister, Josiah. I promise Dinah will be taken care of until…" Stopping, she inhaled a breath. "Until you bring her *mamm* home."

His eyes filled with gratitude and surprise. "If I can bring her home. You do not mind? She can stay with me in the old house. It's put together enough—we'll move over there and make do."

No, they wouldn't make do. The house needed furniture and lamps and heat, not to mention a new stove and all sorts of other things. Raesha knew she wouldn't send them away. Especially not with little Dinah. She couldn't be sure if Josie would be able to take care of her own child.

"We will discuss that later," she replied. "Right now, go and see what is wrong with her. And stay as long as you need to do so."

He held her arms and then realized what he was doing. Dropping his hands away, he kept staring at her. "You are a kind woman, Raesha."

"Your sister will need a lot of time and quiet to recover. We have the room available. And Josiah, we will pray for you to bring her back and soon."

He nodded and whirled to hurry to the *grossdaddi haus*.

Raesha watched him go inside and then turned and held her hand to her heart.

What if Josie wanted her baby back? What would happen then?

Chapter Twelve

Josiah walked up the long hospital hallway, the sound of machines beeping and voices calling urgently overhead jarring him. Somewhere a phone rang. A nurse answered it, her tone calm and professional. Then in another room, a well-dressed woman wept while she held a sleeping man's hand.

All of this was foreign to him but the kind nurse at the big desk had told him he'd find his sister in room 102.

"At the end of the hallway."

Josiah stopped when he saw Josie's full name on the sign by the door. *Deidre Josephine Fisher.*

Their father had not approved of the names. He'd wanted his daughter to have a more humble name. But she became Josie and that seemed to fit.

Taking a breath, Josiah pushed at the door and silently peeked inside. Josie lay sleeping, her dark hair long and thick but not as shiny as it once was. Her skin, always pale, now looked washed-out and she had dark circles underneath her eyes.

When a doctor came toward him, Josiah glanced around.

"Could I have a word with you, Mr. Fisher?" the young doctor asked, his voice low.

Josiah looked at his sister again and then came back out into the hallway. The doctor motioned to two chairs by a large window with a view of fall across the hills and mountains.

"I'm Dr. Caldwell. Your sister has been through a lot."

Josiah glanced to the partially opened door. "She ran away and I couldn't find her. But I had reason to believe she was nearby." He didn't plan on mentioning the baby.

"She's very sick," the doctor replied. "She had pneumonia and honestly, if she hadn't come to us when she did, I don't think she would have made it."

Josiah absorbed that information and then asked, "How did you find her?"

"We didn't," Dr. Caldwell replied. "She stumbled into the ER about four days ago. She's been in ICU and we just now moved her to a private room. She was so sick and she was hallucinating."

"How so?" Josiah asked, knowing what that word meant.

"She kept talking about her baby."

Josiah closed his eyes and felt a pain so deep, it took his breath away. "She had a child," he finally said. "I now have the child, a baby girl, with me."

The doctor nodded. "We discovered that she'd given birth from examining her but we couldn't be sure when. So you knew?"

"Not until recently," Josiah said. "I came back here to search for my sister and take care of some property. She had left the baby with my neighbors."

"How long ago was that?"

"A couple of weeks now," he admitted. "After hiring

an investigator, I learned the child was related to me. She will grow up Amish."

The young doctor glanced around and then said, "Your sister won't be able to leave the hospital for a few more days and then she'll need a safe, comfortable place to rest and recover. Can you provide that?"

Josiah nodded. "*Ja*, I have kind neighbors who are helping me with the child and they have offered to let Josie stay with them, too. Two widowed women who are experienced in fostering."

The doctor nodded, seemingly satisfied. "When you go in to see her, don't ask a lot of questions," he suggested. "She's not only physically frail but…whatever happened with her has left her shaken and frightened. She might not be ready to talk about it."

Josiah nodded and then asked, "So has she mentioned a husband?"

"Your sister told us she is single," Dr. Caldwell said, standing to check his pager. "But she did ask for you. She asked for her brother and told us she thought you were in Campton Creek. We called the Campton Center, hoping someone would find you. A man named Nathan Craig verified you were in the area."

"He has been searching for her," Josiah explained. "And now, I have found her. *Denke*, Dr. Caldwell."

Josiah watched the doctor hurry to his next patient. But he had to wonder—how did Josie know he was back in Pennsylvania?

Josiah went back into the room and sat down beside his sleeping sister. He took Josie's hand, noticing how skinny it felt inside his bigger one. Her skin seemed to droop around her. She'd always been healthy before, robust and all girl. Now she'd become a shell of herself.

Josie moaned in her sleep, her head moving as if she were denying something. How he wanted to take away all of her pain.

She let out a soft cry and then opened her eyes wide. "Josiah?"

He heard the plea in his name.

"I'm here, Josie. I'm here," he said, his hand squeezing hers. "It will be all right now."

A single tear fell down her face and she looked away, out the window toward the hills. "It's fall."

"*Ja*, did you not remember?"

"I don't remember a lot of things," she admitted.

Then she went back to sleep.

Josiah held her hand, his head down while he prayed. Not knowing what to pray for, he only asked God to guide him. He had to take her home and nurture her and watch over her. He wouldn't let her out of his sight this time.

He had other concerns now, however.

His sister had a baby out of wedlock and then left that baby abandoned on a porch.

Would the Campton Creek Amish community accept her with open arms or would they shun her and make her life hard to bear?

He knew his people back in Ohio wouldn't want her there.

But what about the people here? They had once belonged to the Campton Creek community. He'd have to clear all of this with the bishop, of course. Josie would have to confess before the church and turn her life back over to God.

Was that why she'd come back here? Was that why she'd called out for him? Would the community shun her?

So many questions. If she couldn't live among the Amish here, he'd have no choice but to take her away. Again.

So he prayed and sat with her, talking gently about all he'd done to the house and how kind the neighbors had been, until the nurses came in and told him he'd have to leave. The sun was setting over the trees and hills.

"I'll come back tomorrow," he said to her, over and over. "I won't leave you again."

Giving her a gentle kiss on the forehead, Josiah turned to the nurse. "You will let me know if anything happens, if she has a change?"

"Yes. I promise." She took the number to the hat shop, smiling and nodding her head. "I'm familiar with the Bawell shop. Such a nice place. I shop there for Christmas and birthdays a lot."

"I'm renting from them," he explained. "I can be reached through that number and the one at the Campton Center."

"We'll put that information in her charts," the nurse replied. "Go home and rest, same as your sister. She needs that more than anything else right now."

"Will she be all right?" he asked as they walked to the door together.

"In time, I hope," the nurse said. "In God's own time."

Josiah left with a heavy heart and found a taxi outside to take him home. The thirty-minute drive seemed like a lifetime.

After the driver dropped him off, he stood outside the Bawell place and stared over at the home he'd left. It looked better now, thanks to the help he'd received from this giving community. But the new facade couldn't hide the pain his family had suffered inside that house.

Would that be the best place for Josie right now?

Before he could form a thought on that issue, the front door of the Bawell house opened and Raesha came hurrying toward him.

"Josiah, you're back."

He walked to meet her by an ancient oak tree in the front yard. "*Ja.* They wouldn't let me stay. Said she needs her rest."

"Will she be all right?"

Seeing the concern in Raesha's pretty eyes almost undid him. "With time, the nurse said." Then he told Raesha what the doctor had reported.

"Pneumonia. That's serious," Raesha replied. "I'm thankful she went for help." She glanced into his eyes. "She must have been so afraid. God's grace has brought her back to you."

He nodded. "The nurse told me she was in a homeless shelter, freezing and sick. One of the volunteers there is a nurse and she told Josie she needed to go to the hospital. Josie refused but then sometime in the night, she left the shelter and found her way to the hospital down the street. Collapsed inside the emergency room doors."

"Oh, my." Raesha held her arms against her stomach. "Have you had supper?"

"*Neh.*" He'd forgotten to eat and he wasn't sure he could do so now either.

She took his elbow. "*Kumm*, Josiah. You need nourishment and you can visit with Dinah. She's awake."

Exhausted, Josiah followed her inside and took off his hat.

"You can wash up. We have pot roast, rolls, and carrots and peas."

Suddenly, he was starving. "*Denke*, Raesha."

Naomi came out of the bedroom, holding Dinah close. "She has been changed and bathed. I'll put her in her little crib and she can sit with us during supper."

He saw the glance that passed between the two women but tried not to speculate on what it meant. After washing his hands and running water over his face at the sink, Josiah dried his hands and rolled the crib close.

"She looks so much like her mother."

Naomi motioned for him to sit across from her and Raesha. "Tell us about Josephine."

And so he did. In between bites of the delicious roast with potatoes and buttered rolls, he described his beautiful little sister, comparing the way she looked today with the way he remembered her. "She deserves better than this," he said. "She deserves some happiness."

Raesha shot a glance to her mother-in-law again.

"You do not want her here?" he asked, dropping his fork.

Naomi shook her head. "No, no. You misunderstand our concern."

"And what is your concern?"

Raesha sipped her hot tea. "We wonder if she'll be capable of taking care of Dinah."

"Ah." Now he understood, a sweet relief washing over him followed by a deep concern. "I don't know the answer to that question yet. She is weak in body and spirit, according to the doctor. He advised me not to pester her with questions. She slept while I talked, but I did not mention the *bobbeli*. Will it be a problem if she doesn't take to Dinah right away?"

"No," they said in unison.

"No," Raesha repeated. "We only want both of you to know that we are here and we will help however you need us."

Satisfied, he nodded. But then, he'd seen a shard of relief in Raesha's eyes, too. Did she want Josie to be a real mother to Dinah or was she afraid Josie would take the child away?

Finishing his meal, Josiah took the fresh coffee Naomi brought to him. "I'll have to go back and forth to the hospital until she's better," he said. "I think it might be best if Dinah stays here in the house with you until I can bring Josie home." Then he added, "And maybe even after."

"We'd be happy to have her," Raesha said, smiling at Josiah's wide-eyed expression.

Josiah decided Raesha would be happy to have his niece for a very long time to come. Was he right in letting her spend so much time with a child whom she might not be able to keep with her?

But what other choice did he have? He trusted Raesha with Dinah and until he knew how Josie would react to the baby, he couldn't ask for a more perfect substitute mother.

Then something hit him in the gut, making his stomach roil. He couldn't imagine any other woman in his life either.

But how could he even think about these new feelings now, when his life was in such an uproar?

"You must be so tired," Naomi said. "Would you care for some apple pie?"

Josiah looked up to find the older woman smiling at him. Did she know he'd just been hit with a lightning bolt of shock?

"I'd enjoy that, Mammi Naomi," he said, his gaze shifting to Raesha.

"Gut," Naomi replied. "Raesha will be glad to slice you a piece. I'm tired myself. I think I'll go on to my room."

Raesha and Josiah looked at each other. The expression on her face showed the same fear and awe that went swirling through his stomach. Would he be able to eat pie?

"She rarely goes to bed this early," Raesha said after handing him a slice of cinnamon-infused apples inside a flaky crust. "But this has been a trying day."

"You don't want to be alone with me."

His statement brought her head up. "Why wouldn't I want to be alone with you?"

"It's not proper?"

"We have two very capable chaperones—my mother-in-law and your niece. One refuses attention and the other one needs it constantly. I don't think we'll be alone at all."

"Gut point."

They both burst out into giggles.

"Shh," Raesha said, her grin glowing. "She can hear very well for her age."

"Which one?"

More giggles and then somber expressions as they studied each other. Really studied each other.

"Your pie is growing cold," she finally said, dropping her head.

"So it is." He ate in silence, the day's events caving in on him. "Do you worry that bringing Josie here will cause concern in the community?"

"We will not turn her away."

"But…she is not well and…something happened to her. Something that I fear to even voice."

"We will help her heal. She will be left alone but surrounded with love. I promise you that, Josiah."

"What if she is shunned?"

"We'll consult the bishop. I pray there will not be a ban put on her, and I hope he'll understand she needs shelter now and she needs to heal."

"Don't we all?"

Raesha lifted her head, her eyes on him. "Will you tell me one day?"

"Tell you what?"

"About what really happened in your house? What caused that fire?"

Did she know the truth?

"What do you mean? Have you heard something?"

"No. But I wonder. Josie was a young girl and she watched her parents perish in a horrible way. That has to change a person."

"It did," he finally said. "But I don't know what happened, exactly. She only told me she was playing outside and saw the fire."

"Your parents were there?"

"In the house." He took a breath, hating to even think about that horrible day. "She said that she ran in to tell my folks and they both hurried to the barn. That's the last time she saw them. She never talks about it beyond that."

Raesha nodded and got up to remove their dishes. "This place has a way of opening up our hearts to reveal all of our secrets. I think Josie needs that kind of healing now."

"Will you be all right if she wants Dinah back?" he asked, needing to know.

She placed the plates in the sink basin but she didn't turn around. "Why do you ask that?"

He came close but refrained from forcing her to look at him. "I can see how much you adore my little niece. And I thank God each day that Josie left Dinah with you. But I worry that you'll become too attached to Dinah."

She whirled then, her eyes bright with a mist of fear and resolve. "I'm already attached to Dinah," she admitted. "But I know that God's will has to be accepted, no matter my pain."

Staring out the kitchen window, she said, "I had to watch my strong, proud husband die and I accepted that. I had to learn to run a business on my own, in spite of the odds, and I accepted that. I think I can handle it if Dinah has to leave us…but it will take a while to get her sweet presence out of my heart."

Josiah didn't move. "What if you didn't have to let her go?"

Pivoting back to face him, she asked, "What does that mean?"

"What if you and I—"

Dinah let out a wail, causing them both to jump.

"I'll attend to her," Raesha said. Then she glanced at him over her shoulder. "Go and get some rest, Josiah. You'll want to get back to the hospital early in the morning. Your sister needs you."

He'd been dismissed. He'd misread her.

She didn't really want *him* in her life. But she did want Dinah.

He left, his heart heavy with worry and wondering.

What would Raesha have said if he'd finished his question?

Chapter Thirteen

The next morning Raesha went into the shop early. The Harvest Festival would be held the third week of October and she had several tasks to complete before a stream of tourists arrived at her place of business.

"Daniel," she said, calling into the back where the quiet would last only a few more minutes, "did we get that shipment out to New York?"

"Yes, Mrs. Bawell," Daniel replied, his smile soft and full of respect. "All loaded and boxed and Ben delivered one hundred winter hats to the shipping store. We left the receipts in your box on the desk."

"That's a relief." She checked the long shelves lining the wall inside the organized shop. "We have a fair amount of inventory in both summer and winter hats. I think we're on schedule."

She'd been concerned since her life had changed so drastically in the last few weeks. A baby and a handsome renter, and related to each other at that. Feast or famine around here.

Lord, You do challenge me but I'm thankful for the opportunity.

Her life had been less than challenging lately. Almost stagnant and too still. She'd become complacent. Not anymore.

Nodding in approval to Daniel, she said, "What would I do without you?"

Daniel shrugged. "You know I love working here. Considering I've been doing it for two years now, I hope you know you can depend on me for anything."

Trying not to read too much in her young friend's declarations, Raesha knew the whole community must be abuzz with the happenings in the Bawell house.

"You are kind," she replied. "Things have changed in my life, for the good I think, and I am grateful that you were able to step up and keep the shop running smoothly for me."

"My job," the young man replied, his smile beaming. "I'll get the festival booth set up out front. Susan and I will man it and we have people scheduled to help."

"Susan and you." Raesha watched him blush. "She is a *gut* girl, Daniel. I'm happy for both of you."

He looked so confused, she almost laughed. Maybe he didn't realize he was in love. "You do care for Susan, *ja*?"

Gulping in air, he bobbed his head. "*Ja*, but I didn't think anyone noticed, especially her."

"Oh, trust me, she has noticed," Raesha replied. "I can vouch for that."

The man grinned from ear to ear.

Raesha went through the mail, laying aside anything that wasn't urgent. Then she saw an official-looking envelope from the country records office. The birth certificate?

When the back door to the shop opened, Raesha expcctcd to scc another employee. But Josiah walked in and gave her a nod.

"Excuse me, Daniel," she said, hurrying away.

Daniel's eyes held amusement mixed with questions.

Maybe her workers *had* noticed something between her and Josiah, too. She needed to be careful in how she acted around him. While they'd done nothing inappropriate, rumors could still fly. The man had enough to deal with already.

"Josiah, I think this is the document you've been waiting on."

"The birth certificate?" He took the envelope and tore it open. Then he nodded his head. "Deidre Josephine Fisher—*Mudder*. Baby girl—Dinah Charlotte Fisher. Born on July 18 of this year." He shook his head. "She loved that book, *Charlotte's Web*." Looking back at the paper, he said, "No one listed as the father."

"Then that is final proof," Raesha said. "Josie is truly your niece."

"I already knew it, but yes, this is official proof."

He stood for a moment, his head down.

"Did you need me?" Raesha asked, thinking that was a loaded question. "You came in here for something?"

"I only wanted to let you know I'm leaving for the hospital. I saw Dinah and helped feed her a morning bottle. I thank you for calling your friend to come and be with Naomi and her."

"Beth Weaver loves babies," Raesha said, thinking what woman didn't. "You know Jeremiah is her brother."

"Yes. He's been a comfort to me."

"He was a prodigal but he is home and fully committed to Ava Jane and their children now. His best friend,

Jacob, was her first husband. She already had a boy and girl when Jeremiah came back into her life."

"There is hope," Josiah said, his always-tumultuous gaze moving over her face. "I didn't sleep very well, but I pray that my sister did."

"Go and be with her." Raesha heard doors opening and people chattering. "My staff is arriving for the day. I have to go over some of the things we need to get done before the Harvest Festival."

"I'd forgotten that is approaching. Maybe I can do more if Josie is feeling better."

"Do not think about it," Raesha replied. "You've done enough by helping with our ornery machines in the shop and fixing our rickety booth for out front."

"I've always been handy with contraptions," he admitted. "I had to learn a lot on my own, growing up."

Raesha saw a shadow fall across his face. He went dark each time he mentioned his childhood. She wished he'd talk to her but only when he felt sure enough to do so. Letting it go for now, she watched him leave and hurried about her business.

But she couldn't deny what that birth certificate had proved. Dinah belonged to his sister.

She prayed his sister would be able to talk to him when he got to the hospital and that the girl would turn out to be a mother to her child.

"She had a rough night," Nurse Ruthie told him in a whisper. "She's frightened and physically weak. Maybe you can get her to eat some pudding and broth."

"I'll do my best," he said. "Josie can be stubborn."

"So we've noticed. But that stubbornness is what made her seek help. She wants to live."

"I hope so," Josiah replied. "I want her well."

Nurse Ruthie guided him into the quiet room. "Josiah, she might need some counseling once she's better. Someone to talk to about her fears and emotions."

He understood what the nurse was saying. "The lawyer lady suggested that, too. I will seek that help at the Campton Center."

"A great place to start," the nurse agreed. "Judy Campton and her volunteers have great resources and they come without a bill to pay."

Josiah wondered about his sister's hospital bill but he'd deal with that later.

When they went inside, Josie was sitting up but staring out the window. The sunny day should brighten her mood, even if the view couldn't.

"Hello, Josie," he said.

She didn't even look around.

"I see you didn't prefer your oatmeal," Nurse Ruthie said. "Josie, you need to eat to gain your strength. Would you allow your brother to help you try a bite or two?"

Josie turned her head, her gaze catching Josiah. The fear and shame in her expression broke him. She shook her head but didn't speak.

The nurse took the tray and left the room, shutting the door behind her.

Josiah took off his hat and pulled a chair up close to the bed. "How are you today?"

His sister's big eyes widened. "Why are you here?"

"Because I love you and want to bring you home. They said you asked for me."

"I don't remember asking for you. I can't go home. That part of my life is over."

"I'm staying near the old place," he said, careful not to upset her. "If you'd like, we could live there again."

She twisted away, a hand going to her heart. "You left me there before."

Josiah lowered his head, her cold words burning through him. "I did and I regret that."

"I don't know where I should be."

"You should be with me. I won't leave you again."

Josie stared down at her hands. "I can't go back to Kentucky."

"Would you want to one day?"

She shook her head, tears forming in her eyes. "I can't, Josiah. I just can't."

Then she slid down and pulled the covers up. "I'm tired."

"You should rest. I'll be here when you wake up."

Josie watched him with somber eyes. "Why did you come back here?"

Glad she was asking, he nodded. "I heard you might be back in Campton Creek. I've been searching for you since…since I got word that you had left Kentucky."

Josie closed her eyes. "You should leave me alone and get back to your life."

"You are a part of my life. I shouldn't have let you go to Kentucky."

Her eyes opened wide. "Why do you say that?"

"Because you ran away and—"

He stopped, unable to say the words.

"And had a child," she finally said, each word a whisper. "You know, don't you?"

Josiah didn't say anything at first. Then he gazed at her, his heart bursting with agony. "Josie, you left her on my neighbor's doorstep. Did you hope I'd find her there?"

His sister clammed up and turned away. "I don't want to talk about that."

Josiah stayed with her another hour while she moved in and out of sleep. The nurses and doctors made their rounds, checking her vitals and encouraging her to eat and rest. He watched as they forced her to take breathing treatments to keep her pneumonia from coming back.

"She needs to get up and move about," Nurse Ruthie told him. "She's weak but exercise will give her strength."

He needed to get back to work, but before he left, he touched his sister's arm, knowing she wasn't really asleep.

"Josie, will you let me help you take a short walk in the hallway?"

"I don't feel like it."

"If you don't move around, you could become ill again."

"I'm better."

"*Kumm* now. One turn up the hall and back and then I must get back to Campton Creek."

She lifted her head to stare at him. "You should have stayed away. I had a plan and you messed it up."

"Was that plan to leave your child with strangers and never let me know?"

She bobbed her head, looking every bit the humiliated little sister he remembered. "She is better off with them."

He lifted Josie up and coaxed her to stand. She wobbled and he held her. "Why do you think that?"

"You know why."

"No, I don't. I do not know what happened to you."

He had her up. But when he offered her a robe she shook her head. "I'm not going to walk with you. Because you want information and I have none to give."

Pulling away, she turned back to the bed and almost fell. Josiah helped her back in and covered her. "Tomorrow, we walk. Be ready."

"You don't need to come every day."

"And what will you do when they release you? You can't stay here forever."

"I'll go back to the shelter."

"You will not."

"You sound a lot like *Daed*, you know."

That statement, said with such malice, floored Josiah.

"I am not my father, Josie."

"I hope not," she retorted. "I'll figure this out, Josiah. The way I always have."

He wanted to remind her of where that had gotten her but she looked exhausted and, as the nurse had told him, his sister was fragile. So he touched a hand to her arm and then turned and left the room.

This would be a big battle. His sister had always had a mind of her own. He'd tried to bear the brunt of their father's wrath but Josie saw it and had to have heard it. At times, she ran from the fights to hide away in the barn.

Now the past surrounded them in bitter memories.

Did he try to keep her here, with those memories?

Or should he take her away to try to help her heal?

He couldn't leave Campton Creek right now. Josie would have to accept staying with the Bawells for a while.

But he wouldn't break that news to her until the doctors released her and she had no other choice.

Raesha took the clothes off the line and carried them inside, the clean scents of sunshine and fresh air surrounding the sheets and towels. She placed little bags of dried lavender in the linen cabinet that stood in the big upstairs hallway. It made the sheets smell as fresh as a garden.

Taking a set of sheets to the *grossdaddi haus,* she opened the unlocked door and went inside. Josiah kept the place clean. No dust anywhere and no dirty dishes in the sink. The man was so self-sufficient she could hardly believe her eyes.

He was a bachelor but he didn't act like one. But then, he'd mentioned having to learn things on his own growing up.

Did his father not teach him about life?

Again, she had to wonder what he and his sister had suffered. For years, she'd glanced over at the old place but the trees between the properties had kept most of it hidden from her. When she came out of the little house behind her home, she took a deep breath and decided she'd go for a walk after she put away the rest of the sheets and towels. Just over to the Fisher farm. Maybe if she stared up at the house long enough, she'd find some answers.

When she came through the back door, Naomi stood to meet her. "We have a visitor," her mother-in-law said, giving Raesha a pointed warning glance.

Raesha looked past Naomi to find her sister Emma standing there. "Emma, is everything all right? Is someone sick?"

Her sister, so young and vibrant, smiled and shook

her head. "*Neh*, silly. Can't I take some time to *kumm* and visit my older sister?"

"Yes, but where is Becca? You two always come together." The better to gang up on her.

Emma's gaze moved around the room and landed with such accuracy on the crib in the corner that Raesha immediately understood. Her sister had come snooping.

"Where is Becca?" Raesha asked again, her gaze moving from Naomi back to Emma.

Naomi remained as cool as a cucumber, her smile gentle, her eyes piercing with subtle warnings.

"Becca has two sick *kinder*," Emma said, her green eyes bright with questions. "What's going on with you, Raesha?"

"What have you heard?" Raesha asked, cutting the chatter. "Because I know you didn't drive all this way just to be chatty."

Emma shrugged. "Well, since we live near Goldfield Orchard, word got out that the hatmaker in Campton Creek had found a baby on her porch. Then we heard two men had come asking about a missing Amish girl who'd been seen in our area."

"So you put two and two together and decided to come and check on me?"

Emma held her hands over her white apron. "David brought me, *ja*. We took a taxi into town and then borrowed a horse and buggy from David's cousin to ride over here."

David's cousin lived away from town in a small isolated house to the west. He wouldn't have known much about the happenings in Raesha's life since he ignored most people anyway.

So she couldn't blame him. Word had traveled and

her curious, concerned sisters would want answers. So here stood Emma, lovely and fresh faced, a happy mother come to see if her older sister was up to mischief or doing good.

Or rather, she'd talked her loving husband *into* bringing her, Raesha decided. Well, it was inevitable. She'd been so preoccupied she'd neglected to head this off at the pass.

Since she had not done anything wrong, she stiffened her spine and smiled. "What would you like to know, Emma? I'll give you a thorough report so you can explain all the details to Becca and Amos."

Raesha suspected her brother would be curious and furious. He tended to control the family, of course.

Emma moved farther into the room and then stopped at the crib. "A little girl?"

Naomi made a face and shrugged. "She knows this already. Your sister has a way of pulling the truth out of a person."

Emma grinned. "But Mammi Naomi has a way of not really answering any questions."

Raesha joined Emma, her gaze moving to the crib, where Dinah slept. "So now that you are here, it is *gut* to see you."

Emma hugged Raesha tight. "We were only worried about you."

"I understand and appreciate that," Raesha said, holding no ill will.

"I couldn't help it," Emma said. "When people started talking, I knew I had to come and check on you. David took Sara and Lara to see the covered bridge so we could visit. I hope you don't mind if we stay overnight."

"Of course not. You must have a lot of questions,"

Raesha replied. Then she tugged her sister close again. "You know you are always *wilkum* here."

Emma smiled and said, "I'd love to hold her when she wakes up."

Raesha's eyes got misty. Her sister loved her and had come to see if she was all right. But the family would want the truth.

"I should have contacted you sooner," she admitted. "Josiah, this little one's *onkel*, was the one asking about the missing girl. The man with him is an Englisch private investigator."

"Josiah, is it?" Emma replied, her hands on her hips. "Why don't you start with him?"

Chapter Fourteen

Josiah knocked on the back door, weary from seeing his sister so despondent and sick. But he needed to give Raesha a break and he figured holding little Dinah close would make him feel better.

When Raesha opened the door, her expression held apprehension and concern. "Josiah, you're here early today."

He stood as usual with his hat in his hand. "I came straight from the hospital. I'll take Dinah with me for the rest of the day."

Raesha cast a glance over her shoulder, her actions full of hesitation. "That would be fine. Can you come inside for a while? She's awake now and…we have company."

Wondering what was going on, Josiah stepped inside to find a petite young woman holding Dinah but staring up at him.

"I'm sorry," he said. "I can come back later."

Raesha looked from the woman back to him, trepidation in her eyes.

"Josiah, this is my sister Emma. Her twin is Becca

and I have an older brother—Amos. Emma lives in Williamson Way, which is near Goldfield Orchard, but she and her husband have come to visit."

Suddenly, Josiah understood. Raesha's sister must have heard something. She might even remember seeing Josie. He wanted to ask but stopped himself.

Instead, he nodded and smiled. "It is nice to meet you, Emma."

The woman stared at him, assessing him with bright green eyes. "It is *gut* to meet you, too, Mr. Fisher. My sister had been telling me all about this new development in her life."

"That would be my niece and me," he admitted. "Raesha and Mammi Naomi have been kind to me." His gaze touched on Raesha, who stood solid and tall, her chin up and her gaze on Dinah. "I will never forget their generosity."

Raesha's eyes lifted to his with a sweetness that took his breath away.

But Emma's eyes widened. "Dinah is a sweetheart. I can understand why my sister is so smitten…with her."

Josiah heard the little gasp Raesha tried to hide. "I can come back later since you two are visiting," he offered, nervousness overtaking him.

He'd never been good at conversation and especially conversation with a woman. Besides, her sister was eyeing him with way too much interest. Would he pass the test she obviously wanted to give him? Did she think he'd take advantage of the young Widow Bawell? Never? Or had he already?

Confusion made him break out in a sweat.

"So you live on the property?" Emma asked while she swayed back and forth, smiling down at Dinah.

"I've told you—he lives in the *grossdaddi haus*," Raesha said, shooting her sister a daring glare.

"I wanted to be sure I understand," Emma replied. "I'm surprised the bishop allowed that."

"The bishop approved it because I'm here," Naomi said with a slight lift of her voice. "I make a fine chaperone and nanny."

"I wasn't implying anything was wrong," Emma said, looking just a little chagrined. "But... I have to consider my sister."

Raesha motioned Josiah out of the spot where he stood frozen. "Sit down at least. I'll get you some spice cake and tea."

Emma placed herself at the table, too, her smile light and her mood chatty. "Spice cake and tea sounds great. I'll have some, too, while I get to know Josiah."

He looked up at Raesha, wanting to shout for help. But he wouldn't be a coward. "What would you like to know?"

Emma's smile never wavered. "So you once lived next door? I suppose you'd already moved on and never even knew Raesha when she married Aaron and moved here."

"I left when I was eighteen," he replied, the memories of taking Josie away tearing through him.

"And went to Ohio, I hear."

"Ja."

"And now you're back because your sister went missing and you have realized Dinah is her child, but you're also here to sell the farm next door. Then you'll take off again?"

Josiah glanced at Raesha. "I...uh..."

Raesha hurried over and set a plate full of chunky

cuts of spice cake on the table. "Eat your snack, Emma. Because you can't ask questions with your mouth full."

Her sister chuckled and held tight to Dinah. "Okay, I know I'm being nosy. I'll hush now."

"You know about as much as anyone," Naomi said, shaking her head. "And maybe more than most."

Josiah and Raesha both looked at her but she only smiled and reached for her own slice of cake. "What a nice time we'll have at supper tonight. We have much to catch up on, don't we, Emma?"

Emma's amused gaze swept the room. "We do at that. David should be along soon with the *kinder*. They will love seeing a baby in the house."

Josiah saw a flash of hurt passing through Raesha's eyes. He wanted to tell her well-meaning sister to form her words more carefully. She meant no harm and yet he could almost see the bit of smugness in her words. Why did everyone think a woman had to be married with children and that she should not go against her husband at all?

His own mother had tried to please his *daed* over and over. Until the bitter end. They'd died together trapped in that barn.

Or maybe only one of them had been trapped. Maybe the other one had wanted to die there. But not alone.

"I must go," he said, getting up so fast he almost knocked over his tea glass. "I'll come back to get Dinah later."

Raesha sent her sister a warning glance and walked him to the door, a perplexed expression on her face. "Will you take supper with us?"

Josiah didn't think he was up to any more questions.

"*Neh.* I just want my niece with me tonight. I'll make myself a sandwich at home."

She looked disappointed but didn't press. "I'll see you in a little while, then."

Josiah nodded and slapped his hat on his head. He had some thinking to do. He'd felt this way before, torn and hurting and wondering what to do. But those times had involved Josie and what might be best for her, or trying to please his strict uncle and resentful cousins.

These feelings rushing through him now were new and different. He cared about Raesha and wished he could do something nice for her, to show her.

But that would be wrong on his part. He'd already taken up too much of her time, and each day she grew closer to Dinah.

Torn between wanting to make Raesha happy but wanting to help his sister heal so she could raise her own child, Josiah started walking. He kept walking until he came upon the big covered bridge that spanned the deepest part of the creek.

The bridge seemed to be holding this community together, a strong backbone that supported anything that put weight on its sturdy cross-beamed structure. The bright red of the wood had faded to a mellow pinkish patina, worn in places and rich in other places. Life. This was a place that followed life while the creek flowed and moved and filled up during floods and went shallow in dry times. The gurgle of the water below only highlighted his thoughts and brought him a measure of peace and relief. Who could predict life anyway? He'd tried to live a good life, but he'd failed over and over.

He couldn't dream about a woman who had everything except the one thing she longed for and she

couldn't leave her happy life here to follow a vaga-
bond such as him around the country, searching, always
searching, for his own happy ending.

*Gott, am I not worthy of a happy life? Could You
show me how to be a better man so I can work on my
flaws?*

Maybe this bridge would be a good spot to ask the
Lord for help. Josiah stood there, watching the creek
flow, seeing fish jumping here and there. A hawk flew
over, curious. Some squirrels frolicked in the trees along
the shore. Birds chirped and fluttered. Life continued,
no matter the currents hidden underneath the surface.

He heard laughter and turned to find a beautiful
woman walking toward him, two older children by her
side. She held a dark-haired baby in her arms. They
looked so perfect, it pained him. Would he ever have a
family of his own?

When the woman drew close, she smiled and waved.
"Hello."

The boy ran ahead and nodded to Josiah. The girl
glanced at the water and back to him. "Can you swim?"
she asked.

"Sarah Rose, what a question to ask," her mother
admonished. "Can you at least say hello?"

"Hello," the pretty girl said. Then she ran toward
her brother.

The woman shook her head and shifted the giggling
baby onto her shoulder. "She learned to swim two years
ago, after she almost drowned right down there. We are
thankful but now she wants everyone to know how to
stay safe around the water."

"I'm so sorry," Josiah replied. Then it hit him.
"You're Jeremiah's wife, *ja*?"

"I am," she said, her blue eyes bright. "Ava Jane Weaver. I see you've heard that story. He saved Sarah Rose's life and now he's a part of our lives." Then she looked Josiah over. "And I'm thinking you're Josiah Fisher. My husband goes on and on about you. He considers you a new friend."

"That's me," he said, taking off his hat. "Jeremiah has been a *gut* friend to me."

She beamed with pride. "He has a way with people. Maybe because he's been on the other side of life out there. He's more dedicated to his life here than ever before. But it took us a while to find our way back to each other."

"I can see he's happy," Josiah said, his tone wistful.

"But you are struggling?"

"In so many ways. I won't bother you with my problems."

"Nonsense," she said. "Why don't you walk home with us and stay for supper."

"I…uh… I don't know." He had Dinah to consider.

"You look like you need a friend," she pointed out.

Josiah did need a friend. Someone who wasn't so pretty she made his eyes hurt or so kind she made him want to be around her all the time or so funny he couldn't stop laughing. He needed a friend who could listen, just listen, and then give him a knock on his noggin and tell him to do what he had to do, not what he wanted to do.

"I'd appreciate having supper with you and your family, Mrs. Weaver," he said.

"Call me Ava Jane," she replied. "Now I have to corral those two before they go looking for tadpoles."

She called to the two older children. "Eli, Sarah Rose, hurry along. We have a guest coming for dinner."

The *kinder* rushed up and surrounded Josiah, asking him rapid-fire questions. He started laughing while he tried to answer.

"See, you're feeling better already," Ava Jane said.

When they came to the yard, Jeremiah turned from drawing water at the well and waved. "What have we here?"

"We found him on the bridge," Sarah Rose explained with her hands on her hips. "I think he's staying for supper."

Jeremiah laughed. "Then I'd better finish washing up."

As they approached, he reached for his son, his eyes on his wife. "I see you've met JJ and his *mamm*."

Josiah nodded. "You said you were a blessed man. Now I can attest to that. You have a wonderful family."

"I do," Jeremiah replied. "I do." Then he clapped Josiah on the back. "And did I tell you she's a great cook at that?"

"Raesha, why are you so restless?" Emma asked after they'd cleared the supper dishes. "Are you worried he won't come for the *bobbeli*?"

Raesha glanced to where David sat with their twin girls, talking quietly with Naomi while she rocked Dinah.

"He'll be here soon. He's usually not this late. Most nights he has supper—"

"Here with you," Emma finished, her expression knowing.

"Here with Naomi and me," she replied, tired of trying to cover. But she had done nothing wrong. "Not every night."

"But a lot of nights," Emma said.

"Okay, most nights."

"This is about more than helping a friend, isn't it?" her sister asked.

"Why would you say that?"

"I see the way he looks at you, sister," Emma replied. "And I see the way you look at him. Do you have feelings for this man?"

"I like him," Raesha admitted. "He is a *gut* man."

"That may be so but he comes with a lot of baggage."

"I can't believe you said that," Raesha replied. "He's had a hard time of it most of his life. He's trying to raise his little niece and he just found his sister. She almost died and she has a long way to go in healing properly, in both body and spirit."

"I'm sorry for all of that," Emma said. "I have to worry for you, though."

"I will be fine. I'm always fine."

"*Neh*, you are not. You weren't fine when you had to watch your husband die a horrible death."

"Are you trying to help me or make me feel worse?" Raesha asked, her voice raised enough to make David and Naomi glance up.

"I'm trying to figure out what you expect from this man. Do you plan to be his nanny for the rest of his time here? Or do you want more?"

Raesha couldn't tell her sister she wanted more. So much more. What could she say?

A knock at the back door brought her up and out of her chair. "That must be Josiah now."

"Saved by the knock," her sister teased. "But this conversation isn't over."

"I figured as much," Raesha said with a twisted smile.

But it was over for now. She wasn't ready to share her feelings with anyone, not even herself. Right now, she only wanted to help Josiah take care of Dinah and accept that the child might not be with her always. The baby belonged to another woman, a troubled, fragile woman. Josie could recover and demand her child back. Then they would all probably disappear right out of her life just as quickly as they'd come into her life.

But how could she watch them go now that they were embedded in her heart?

She opened the door, her emotions boiling over, her soul pierced with a dull ache that she so wanted to fix.

Josiah stood there, his dark eyes holding hers. "I'm sorry I'm late. I had supper with Jeremiah and his family."

Something in his words touched her. "You needed to get away from all of this, right?"

He nodded. "I had a lot on my mind."

"I never asked you how Josie was doing today."

"Not so *gut*," he admitted. "I'm worried for her."

He glanced into the room. Emma had joined her family with Naomi. His gaze fell on Dinah. "I can see that my niece is safe and being spoiled."

"It's hard for anyone to resist her sweet smile," Raesha said. "Do you want to come in and meet David and the twins?"

"Your sister, a twin, has her own twins, too?"

"She does. God has a sense of humor, I do believe."

They laughed together, easing the tension.

Then he came farther into the room. "Before I meet them, I wanted to ask you a favor."

"What is that?"

Leaning in, he said, "Would you mind going with me to see Josie? I thought if she had a woman to talk with, she might respond better."

Surprised, Raesha wasn't sure what to say. She glanced back at her family and then looked up at him.

"You don't want to do this?"

"It's not that, Josiah," she said. "I'm just wondering how she'll react to the woman she left her baby with coming to visit her, how that might make her feel."

"I think you could bring her comfort and reassure her," he replied. "And maybe that will help her to decide to come home."

Raesha's heart pulsed with pain. Did she have the courage to help this troubled young girl? The girl who had the power to break her heart if she took her baby back?

"I will be glad to talk to Josie," she said, knowing she had no other choice. "I'll make arrangements to go with you to visit her as soon as my sister leaves tomorrow."

"*Denke*, Raesha," he said. "Now let me meet your brother-in-law and those pretty little twins."

Chapter Fifteen

The next afternoon, Raesha hugged her sister good-bye. "*Denke* for coming to check on me. Will you give a good report?"

They'd enjoyed supper last night and after her sister had spent some time with Josiah, Emma seemed better assured. Josiah had a way of conversing with ease even if he did seem so shy at times.

Emma grimaced and then nodded. "I'll tell the truth. You are helping a neighbor. It's not as if you and Naomi haven't done this before. You took Becca and me in for a while, hoping to make a match for us, remember?"

"How could I forget?" Raesha replied. "Neither of you liked our choices. But you went on to find wonderful husbands on your own."

Emma's smile said it all. "Ja, and even though I should pay you back by messing in your business, I am not going to do that. This is too personal and too close to your heart, ain't so?"

Tears pricked Raesha's eyes. "It is too much, too soon. I have much praying to do. I read my Bible and wait for answers but… I have to abide by the will of the Lord."

"I think the Lord's hand is all over this one," Emma said, her gaze gentle. "He has placed a wonderful man and a sweet baby right in your hands. But I will keep your secrets close, sister. You know, though, Becca will want details and Amos will be all gruff and demanding. I'll stand firm and tell them you are fine and you are doing what you do best—helping another human being."

Relieved, Raesha held Emma's hands in hers. "I can only pray you don't cave and blurt out everything. Because I'm not so sure what the truth is right now. My heart is all mixed-up."

"I still don't know your true feelings either," Emma admitted. "But I'm pretty sure everyone else who sees you two together has it figured out."

Raesha slapped at her hand. "No one has anything figured out. We're all just spluttering along, trying to find our way."

"Emma?"

They turned to find David waiting with the buggy. "We have to go. Now."

"I'm coming," she called. Turning back to Raesha, she said, "We don't want to miss our taxi home."

Raesha hugged her sister again. "Love to all. I wish you could stay for visiting Sunday."

"I have to get back," Emma replied, waving as she hurried to the buggy. "Becca will be frantic and frazzled. I'm sure she'll need help with the *kinder*. I hope they are all feeling better now."

"So do I," Raesha said. "Give them one of those snickerdoodles we made this morning."

"If I can keep David and my twins from eating all of them."

She waved them away and then turned back to go

inside, but stopped in the yard to take a look across the way. Toward Josiah's place.

The house looked fresh and new, rebuilt and painted a clean white with stark black shutters. It wasn't a large house. Built on the foursquare model from what she'd heard, with the small front porch added later. But it seemed to be sturdy again. She wondered if the man rebuilding the house was also trying to rebuild himself and his faith, piece by piece.

Isn't that what we have to do, Father? I pray You will help all of us rebuild, especially Josie.

Raesha had tried to readjust her attitude toward the wayward girl who'd left a baby at her door. She did not know what Josie had been through, but who was she to judge?

So she'd prayed a lot, read the Scriptures and consulted Naomi while they were alone after Emma and David took a walk with the girls earlier.

"You are wise to pray about this," Naomi said, understanding in her eyes. "It's difficult, either way."

"He wants me to visit her. I told him I would but I can't see how I'll help."

"She needs a woman's counsel."

"But me? I have her child in my home."

"She made the choice to leave the child here."

"What if she gets angry, or worse, goes all silent on me?"

"We keep trying," Naomi said. "Shunning is one thing and we will deal with that if it happens. But forgiveness is always the best first step to finding true peace. For you, this means you have to accept that this girl has suffered some sort of trauma and she had good reason to leave her child in a safe place."

"I also have to keep telling myself that no matter what, Dinah is not mine to keep. I might have to let her go, whether she lives next door or in another community far away from me."

Naomi took her hand. "I'm praying about this situation as always. The Lord will show us the way."

"*Gott*'s will."

"It is the only way to accept things we have no control over."

Now as she gathered her things to make the trip to the hospital with Josiah, Raesha steeled herself against what might come. Glancing toward the shop, she missed the days when she had gotten up, had breakfast with Naomi, then walked to the shop door to get down to business. While she'd never worked full days since she had responsibilities in the house and in the fields, too, she still loved the energy of being in the shop, helping customers and talking to always-curious tourists.

She felt as if she were neglecting the very business that had kept her going. Busying herself with work kept her mind off losing Aaron and not having a family of her own.

That constant, steady routine had been shattered and shifted but in a way that also brought her a new kind of happiness. And the worst kind of pain.

I will get through today, she told herself. Then she'd bring in reinforcements to set up the tents in front of the shop so they could show off their wares during the festival next week. She and her staff had everything in order—the quilts, knickknacks, pillows, shawls, artwork and hats, of course. Along with baked goods and jams and jellies. They always had a large booth with plenty to display.

That she could deal with.

Her task today would be difficult.

But when she turned and saw Josiah coming toward the back door, she knew she had to be doing the right thing. He looked so lost and forlorn, her heart beat harder for him.

"I will do my best, Father."

She only prayed her best would be good enough to help Josiah and his sister.

"I appreciate you doing this," Josiah said as they headed to the Campton Center to catch the taxi they'd reserved. "You are busy with the shop and the festival… and helping me. I will find a way to return the favor."

"You've already done enough," she reminded him. "Fixing up the creaks in the house and putting new hinges on the squeaky doors makes my life easier."

"Creaks and hinges, my specialty," he teased. "I'm also *gut* with a hammer and nails and with tearing out old boards. I have the cuts and bruises to prove it."

She laughed at that. The weather today was clear with a crisp chill. Early fall weather. Tugging her lightweight black cloak closer, she took in the fresh air. "When will you have your barn building?"

"I don't know," he said. "Samuel suggested after the festival. More manpower then."

"I will plan out the meal schedule," she said, already seeing it in her head. "We can line up tables near your property and I'll have the women bring food for dinner. You'll all be hungry and we'll all get to visit."

"You take on anything, don't you?"

"I take on what needs to be done, *ja*."

"I've never known a woman like you."

She glanced over at him, trying to gauge if that had been a compliment or a complaint. Maybe a little of both.

"What kind of woman am I?" she asked, needing to know.

Josiah sent her a quick glance. "The truth?"

"I want to hear the truth."

"You are kind, loving, encouraging and you work hard."

"I think I can live with those descriptions."

Clicking the reins, he added, "This might be too forward but you are also very pretty."

She blushed and tugged her cloak close. "I am plain and simple but that's a nice compliment."

He looked at her in full then, his eyes holding hers. "You will never be plain and simple, Raesha. You have a sweet soul."

"Denke." She had to look away. The man had a way of making her feel all warm and cold at the same time. "Is it my turn to compliment and critique you?"

Lowering his head, he said, "What do you think of me?"

She watched the road, seeing other Amish buggies passing and checking when a vehicle honked at them, afraid of what he might find in her eyes. "You are a *gut* man who is trying to do his best. You work hard for yourself and anyone in need. You want to do right by others even when it's uncomfortable or not in your best interest."

"You have me figured out, I see."

His tone indicated disappointment. "Does that upset you?"

"No. You got it right. But… I've changed so much in the last few weeks. I realize I've made mistakes that I might not be able to repair."

"God's grace will sustain you, Josiah."

"I'm leaning on that." Then he gave her another quick glance. "Do you find me...appealing?"

Raesha knew they were stepping into dangerous territory. "You are a nice-looking man."

"Nice looking?" He grinned and tugged at his hat. "I would hate to turn your face sour each time you look at me."

"You do not turn my face sour," she said on a giggle. "Seems when I'm with you, I laugh more than I normally do."

"And that's what I admire about you. You make me laugh and you laugh with me. It is *gut*, ja?"

"It is *gut*," she replied. "But we have much between us that we cannot laugh about."

"I will try to remedy that."

They arrived at the Campton Center and after he had secured Chester in a fenced area with water and food, they found the waiting taxi. Soon they were on their way to the hospital.

Sitting in the back seat next to Josiah in the comfort of the fast-zooming automobile only made Raesha more aware of the man. This morning, he smelled clean and fresh, like the air around them. His dark, shiny hair was combed but still untamed. It curled and flipped around his collar and ears. His clothes were clean and tidy.

Touching her *kapp*, she thought of how she'd been so careful in picking her own clothes today. A maroon dress pinned with a clean white apron, dark hose and sturdy walking shoes. Her hair secured in a bun beneath her *kapp*.

She'd dressed to look nice for Josie, to show the girl that she meant no harm. But she'd also dressed to make Josiah proud, to look special in his eyes.

Am I wrong, Lord, to think such thoughts? Am I following Your will or trying to bend things toward my own way?

When they reached the hospital and entered through the busy, sterile main lobby, Raesha held her breath and prayed for guidance and clarity.

She was afraid of what she might find.

She was afraid the woman lying in that hospital bed had the power to break her heart. And so did the man who'd asked her to come here.

Josiah knocked softly and then pushed at the partially open door, then entered Josie's hospital room. The room was quiet and dark, the bed empty. At first he was afraid Josie wasn't inside.

His sister was sitting in a chair by the window. When she heard the door open, she turned to look up but she didn't smile or acknowledge him. She wore a pink robe, her dark hair braided down her back.

"Hallo," he said, wishing he could find his sister somewhere underneath that shell. "How are you today?"

"I'm okay," she said. "One of the nurses brought me a robe." Then she looked beyond him, her eyes widening in fear at the sight of an Amish woman standing in the doorway. "Who is this?"

Josiah tugged Raesha into the room. "This is Raesha Bawell. The woman who is caring for your daughter."

Josie gulped a breath and put a hand to her mouth. "Why did you bring her here?"

Josiah now wished he hadn't asked Raesha to come with him today and that he hadn't blurted that out. Nervous and unsure, he couldn't bring himself to speak. He didn't want to upset his sister but she needed to see that she would have a peaceful place to stay when she came home. And that her baby was safe and well.

Raesha pushed past him and slowly sat down in a chair across from Josie. "I insisted he bring me here. I wanted to let you know that Dinah is healthy and thriving and that we are so blessed that you chose us to take care of your baby. She will be loved and cared for until you feel up to taking her back. I promise you that."

Josie's eyes boiled over with tears. She gripped the arms of the chair, her knuckles turning white, and began to shake her head. "*Neh*, I can't take her back. You must understand, I cannot raise her. I do not want to be with her. I left her with you for a reason."

Raesha lifted her gaze to Josiah, shock in her expression. "Why don't you want her back?"

Josie kept shaking her head. "I can't take her back. I won't. If you came here to make me, well, then I'll have to leave again."

Josiah stepped forward. "Josie, do not do that. It's not safe and you are still not strong. You will come and live with me until we can figure this out."

"I won't do that either," the girl said. "I left her for Miss Naomi. I want Miss Naomi and you to take care of her. She's better off with you both. Not me."

"Naomi loves Dinah," Raesha said, bobbing her head. "But she is concerned that you left the child with us. We wish you'd come inside with Dinah. You would have been *wilkum* in our home."

"I couldn't stay," Josie replied. "I… I don't belong with the Amish anymore."

Josiah stepped forward. "Josie, don't say that. You can find your way back to your faith."

"You don't understand. It's too late for that." She

lifted her eyes to Raesha. "Promise me you will let Dinah stay with you."

Raesha sent Josiah a worried glance. "We will take care of her for as long as needed but…she is your child."

Even as she said the words, Raesha knew it was the truth. She wouldn't hope to keep a mother from her child. But she had to understand. "Why did you decide Naomi should raise Dinah?"

Josie heaved a sob, her eyes on Raesha. "She was kind to our *mamm*…before. She would help us when she could and she always hugged me and told me I could come to her for anything. Always. I knew she'd take care of the baby. I want Dinah to stay with her. I didn't know you were there. But I'm glad now."

Josiah shot Raesha a confused gaze and touched his sister's arm. "Are you saying you don't want your own child, Josie?"

Josie's sobs escalated. She buried her face in her hands and heaved. Then she looked at Raesha, terror in her eyes. "Don't make me take her back. You can love her and care for her. Please don't make me take her back. I know I'm horrible and I can never return to my home but don't make me do this."

Raesha pulled the girl into her arms and held her there, her hand moving down Josie's hair. "Shh. It will be all right. I will take care of Dinah, I promise." Then she lifted up to face the girl. "And you are *wilkum* to come and stay with your *brudder* in the *grossdaddi haus*. When you are able. We will not disturb you there."

Josie held tight to Raesha, soaking her dress with tears. "I don't want to see the *bobbeli*. I can't see her. Ever."

Josiah looked defeated, his hat in his hand, tears in his eyes. "What can we do?"

Raesha didn't let go of the heartbroken girl. She held tight and looked up at Josiah. The agony she saw in his face only reflected the agony she felt in her heart.

Her gaze holding his, she said, "We will do what we can, when *she* is ready. But, Josie, we are not going to let you go back out there alone, do you hear me?"

The girl nodded, her head on Raesha's shoulder, her sobs slowly turning to silent weeping.

Raesha lifted Josie's chin. "Let's get you back into bed so you can rest. I will sit with you for a while and we'll see if you feel up to having a light meal."

Josie didn't argue. She crawled into the bed and let Raesha put a blanket over her.

"Rest," Josiah said, his hand stroking her arm. "I'm so sorry, Josephine."

Raesha touched Josie's forehead. "No matter what, Josie, your brother loves you and wants you well. And I do, too."

The girl closed her eyes and went silent.

Raesha walked with Josiah out into the hallway. "I will stay with her. Why don't you go and find something to eat."

"What is going on?" he asked, his eyes bright with unshed tears.

"I don't know," Raesha admitted. "But whatever it is, your sister is in no shape to take care of a child right now."

After Josiah walked away, his shoulders down, Raesha went back inside and sat down in the chair by the bed, her eyes on the frail young woman who slept there.

But she had to wonder.

What had happened to Josie to make her so afraid of her own child?

Chapter Sixteen

Josiah saw the doctor out in the hallway.

"Dr. Caldwell, do you have a minute?"

The young doctor turned and greeted Josiah. "Mr. Fisher, good to see you again. Did the nurses tell you Josie can go home tomorrow?"

Josiah shook his head. "*Neh.* We went straight to her room. A friend came with me today. Raesha Bawell, the woman who found Josie's baby."

"Ah, I see. A woman's touch."

"I think I made things worse by bringing her. Josie wants nothing to do with her baby."

"I wanted to talk to you about that, since Josie gave us permission to share her medical files with you."

"Is there something else wrong with my sister?"

"Yes, I'm afraid so. She's healing physically but she'll need to eat good hearty foods and try to exercise and get fresh air. That's not what I'm concerned about."

"What should I know about?"

"Your sister needs some counseling to help her emotionally."

"I can see that. She's upset about something."

Dr. Caldwell pulled him aside. "I don't know for sure since she won't talk about it, but I believe your sister suffered an assault. I think someone forced her."

Josiah appreciated the doctor's discretion. "I thought so, too, but I was afraid to even ask."

"Don't mention it to her," the doctor replied. "But she refuses to name the father of the baby and she told us that he's not in the baby's life."

"And she doesn't want the baby," Josiah said, dread filling his heart. "Maybe because the child reminds her of what happened to her?"

"I think so." Dr. Caldwell touched Josiah's shoulder. "I hear the Campton Center has resources for the Amish. We have their pamphlets here at the nurses' station. You can probably find a counselor there."

"I'll do that," Josiah said, weary with all the responsibility falling on his shoulder, but glad to accept it. "The center helped us with all of this so maybe they can help Josie, too."

The doctor went on to explain her medication and her follow-up visits. "Make sure she stays on course. We don't want her pneumonia to return."

Josiah thanked the doctor and then turned to go back to the room. He wasn't very hungry anyway.

When he opened the door, Josie was awake and Raesha sat smiling at her. Both women looked up when he came in.

"*Gut* news," he said. "You are being released tomorrow."

Raesha's smile brightened. "That's wonderful."

But Josie looked frightened and tearful. "Where will I go?"

Josiah wanted her with him but before he could mention that, Raesha spoke up. "You can stay with your brother in the small house he's renting from us if you want. It has a back porch that faces away from the main house. It's private there and you'll have a view of the covered bridge off in the distance."

Josie didn't look so sure.

"Or there is the Campton Center."

"What's that?" Josie asked.

Raesha rushed on. "It's a huge estate house that is now a place where we can go and get advice without having to pay much or nothing at all. They have rooms there for just such circumstances."

"I'm a circumstance?" Josie said, reminding Josiah of her old spunk.

"You are a sick young woman who is afraid to return to her people," Raesha said, reminding him of *her* spunk. "If you stay there, you'll have a staff around the clock to...help you."

"And it's close to us," Josiah added, hoping Josie might consider that and then maybe later, she could move in with him. "I can visit you every day."

Josie slipped down, the covers almost touching her chin. "I don't want to see the baby."

"You won't have to do that until you're ready," Raesha said, her hand tight over Josie's. "You'll be in a safe, beautiful place and you can come and visit Josiah or he'll come there to see you. I'll visit you as often as I can."

Josie lay there staring up at the ceiling tiles. "I just want some peace. I'm not ready to face anyone."

Nor was she ready to face what had happened, Josiah decided. The Campton Center could be the one place where she'd be able to open up and get this terrible burden out of her system so she could heal.

Because right now, she wasn't herself and the community would consider her an outsider who'd left on her own. Left and had a child without a husband to stand by her. She might be shunned and never welcomed back.

"I think the center is the best solution for now," he said. "You'll be nearby and with people who can help you, people you can talk to."

"I don't have anything to talk about," Josie replied, fear back in her eyes.

"Then don't talk," Raesha said, shooting Josiah a warning. "Just rest and read and take your time. You are always welcome in our home but if you won't feel comfortable there, I understand."

"Denke," Josie said. "I mean, thank you."

Her words tore at Josiah. She didn't think she could return to her Amish roots. But she could. He knew she could if she tried hard and asked for forgiveness. But maybe his sister didn't want to try. She seemed to have given up.

"I'll go and check with the desk," he said, "about getting you home tomorrow."

"We can stop by the Campton Center, too," Raesha said. "We'll reserve you the best room in the house, Josie."

Josie smiled at that. "A real room. That will be a blessing."

Josiah smiled for the first time since they'd arrived. Raesha had a way about her that made anyone feel better about things. He wondered how much she'd had to sacrifice by taking his sister under her wing. How much it must have hurt to know the woman she was now nurturing could one day take the baby she loved right out of her arms.

* * *

"It's all arranged," Raesha told Naomi that night. "Josie has room at the center for the next two weeks. We've set up time for counseling, too. Mrs. Campton wants to meet with Josie."

Naomi nodded. "Ah, you know she was a licensed counselor for many years before they both retired. She still helps out now and then. She was a tremendous help to Jeremiah Weaver when he came home."

"And look at him now, married with a new baby boy, happy and a strong member of our community," Raesha said.

"The Lord's work. Jeremiah did his part. He dedicated his life to his faith and his *Gott*."

Raesha moved about the kitchen, her mind on Josie coming home tomorrow. "Josiah is beside himself about what to do. I think she needs time to heal in her soul, too."

"This baby," Naomi said. "I take it she did not love the father."

"I don't think she knew the father, to be truthful," Raesha said. "I think someone took terrible advantage of her and now she has to be the one to pay for that person's sin."

"This man forced himself on her?"

"I think so. She is not ready to tell us what happened."

"I hope it wasn't the man who wanted to marry her."

Raesha stopped stirring the soup she'd made. "I don't think so. Josiah said she was happy and in love with Tobias and that he loved her, too."

Naomi's eyes went wide. "That is why she left Kentucky, then. She is ashamed of what happened to her and she felt she could not marry the man she loved."

"That is heartbreaking," Raesha said. "I resented her, you know. For deserting her child, for not taking responsibility. But after meeting her today and seeing her agony, I only felt sympathy for her and now I truly want to help her."

Naomi buttered rolls they'd baked yesterday. "That is why *Gott* allowed her to leave Dinah with us. The baby is being cared for, but the mother is in need of our prayers and forgiveness. We can help bring this girl back to her faith so she can have a *gut* life, here or somewhere far from here."

"You always see things in a different light," Raesha said, understanding that this task would not be easy.

"I see what the Lord puts before me," Naomi replied. "So many things."

Raesha felt the imprint of that last remark. Her mother-in-law thought she and Josiah made a good match. They were friends and now they were being pushed together even more.

But her heart wasn't ready to explore her feelings for Josiah. So much between them, so many things to overcome.

The Lord will see me through as He always has, she thought.

"The soup is ready," she announced. "I'll go and find Josiah."

"And I'll check in on Dinah," Naomi said, going over to the baby's crib. "Awake and alert. What a sweetheart."

Raesha thought about the baby they'd come to love and she also thought about the man she was beginning to care a lot about. It seemed so simple. They could make a perfect family and yet, there was no perfection here. Only the Lord held perfection.

For so long now, she'd dreamed of a family, of children laughing and her husband coming home to give her a presupper kiss. Aaron had done that. He'd loved her and cherished her and tried to be the best husband possible.

Not perfect but the best.

Now she could see a new future just out of her reach.

She wouldn't look past today. She wouldn't try to second-guess the Lord's plan for her.

But she sure would like to know what else could change in her life.

When she knocked on Josiah's door, she was surprised to find Nathan Craig standing there with him. "Mr. Craig, it is *gut* to see you again."

"Hello, Mrs. Bawell," the Englischer said. "It's good to see you, too. Josiah is getting me up-to-date on Josie."

"Yes, we're thrilled she is leaving the hospital."

Josiah looked sheepish but nodded. "I wanted Mr. Craig to find out about the father of her child."

Raesha understood. "I see. Do you think that is wise?"

"I only want to know his name," Josiah replied. "I will not tell him about Dinah."

"I think that's best for now," she replied. "He might force the baby away."

"Or he might not want any responsibilities," Mr. Craig said, his eyes going dark.

"I want to know who he is," Josiah said. "Amish or Englisch."

"What will that help?" Raesha asked.

"It will help me," Josiah replied, his tone firm.

She wouldn't question him further. This was his business, not hers. But she was caught in the middle of it so she was glad he'd confided in her.

"Supper is ready," she announced. "Mr. Craig, please come and have some beef-and-vegetable soup with us."

Nathan Craig looked surprised. "You know, that sounds good on this bright, chilly night. Thank you."

"You are always *wilkum*," she replied.

She wished she could hear this man's story. He wore his troubles as a map on his face. But a map that had many roads.

So much was changing in her world, but Raesha decided she'd stay steadfast and lean on the Lord.

And she'd stay busy. She had much to do over the next few days. Too busy to worry about what she could not control.

Josiah smiled at her as they made their way to the house. "Josie will be nearby this time tomorrow. I hope she won't leave us again."

"I hope that, too," she replied.

She did not want the girl to come to any more harm and she couldn't bear seeing the man she cared about being in such agony again.

"This is a *gut* day," Josiah said the next afternoon, looking so young and relaxed Raesha couldn't help but feel the same way. Josiah needed something uplifting to boost his spirits, and getting Josie settled at the Campton Center had done just that.

"We give thanks to the Father," she replied, knowing that God had provided for little Dinah and now for Josie, too.

Now they had to do the same.

"Do you think Josie will be okay here?" he asked, taking in the big room and attached bathroom. "This is much more than we are used to." He motioned to the bathroom where Josie had gone.

Raesha wondered how Josie would react to meeting Judy Campton. The elderly woman made quite a statement in her quiet, dignified way. Because her assistant and lifelong friend, Bettye Willis, had Amish roots, Mrs. Campton had made it her business to always support the Amish of Campton Creek. And they all returned the favor by watching out for her and this stately old mansion.

Taking in the big bed with the ornate headboard and the comfortable floral chairs near a bay window that overlooked the pool and sweeping backyard, Raesha realized Josie's life would never be the same. But then, neither would Josiah's. She would help him take care of his little family, but what would she do if he took Josie and baby Dinah back to Ohio?

When Josie came out of the bathroom, walking slowly and looking pale, she stood and took in the room. "I... I don't know what to think. I have lived in many places since I left Kentucky but this one reminds me of a castle."

"Do you like it?" Josiah asked, worry in his words.

"What's not to like?" his sister said. Dressed in jeans and a too-big blue sweater that Raesha had found on sale at the general store, she moved around the room. "I need the privacy and I love looking out at the garden."

"You have a couple of weeks here," Josiah said. "So you can heal and talk to people who understand."

"Do you think I've lost my mind?" Josie asked, her tone bordering on harsh.

"Neh," he replied. "I think you've lost your way."

Josie walked to the window and stared out.

A knock at the door brought her head around.

Raesha moved to answer and found Bettye pushing Mrs. Campton in a wheelchair.

"Hello," Bettye said. "Mrs. C wanted to meet all of you right away." She nodded to the white-haired woman in the chair.

"It's so nice to have you here, Josie," Mrs. Campton said, her gnarled fingers touching her pearls. "And Mr. Fisher and Mrs. Bawell, so good of you to help Josie through this."

Josie stared at Judy Campton, fear in her eyes. "I'm not sure what I'm doing here, but this is a lovely place."

"It's a healing place," Judy said after Bettye left. "You have been through a lot and now your only task is to rest and talk to me."

"So you think there is something wrong with me?" the young girl asked, defiance in her eyes.

"I think there is something wrong with a world where a young girl thinks she can't come home again," Mrs. Campton replied without missing a beat.

Josie didn't smart off at that remark. "I guess I can tolerate it for a few days."

"I think you will find our place very reassuring and safe," Mrs. Campton said. "Let's all sit down and I'll explain how this works."

Raesha sank onto a brocade footstool, feeling small and out of place. But she listened as Judy Campton told Josie about the rules—curfews and no wandering away. She was free to come and go, but she had to let someone know at all times and she had to be back by eight each night.

"Do you think I'll run away again?" Josie asked.

"Do you want to run away again?" Mrs. Campton countered.

Josie glanced at her brother and then to Raesha. "I don't think so. But I won't stay where I don't belong."

"Then together, you and I will figure out where you do belong," Judy Campton replied.

Raesha could see why this woman helped people get their lives back together. She smiled without judgment and listened without condemning. A lesson for anyone.

Josie sat back in her chair. "I'm tired."

"Then you must rest," Mrs. Campton said. "Supper is at six thirty sharp." She looked Josie over. "Do you prefer Englisch clothing or Amish?"

"Englisch," Josie blurted out. Then she hastily added, "For now."

"For now, it is," Judy replied. "I'll have one of our volunteers show you the clothing room."

Soon after that, Josie curled up in the comfortable bed and closed her eyes. Josiah wheeled Mrs. Campton to the elevator she'd had installed.

"Bettye will meet me upstairs," she said after thanking him. "This takes me to the hallway and then to the garage apartment. Very convenient."

"We appreciate what you are doing," Josiah said.

"We have a lot to work through with that one," Judy replied, her words kind. "But we will get there."

On the ride home, Josiah turned to Raesha. "Do you think she'll stay there? Maybe I should have insisted on bringing her home with us."

Raesha didn't have the answer for that. "You have

to decide where home is, I think. And then you must convince Josie that she needs to be with family, wherever that might be."

He sent Raesha a perplexed glance. "*Ja,* I wish I could figure that out."

"Give it time," she replied. Because she wished he could figure that out, too.

But she wished he'd pick here for his home.

Chapter Seventeen

Festival day dawned chilly and windy, but soon the sun was out and the crowds started pouring through. Vehicles parked in designated fields along the main road and filled up parking spaces in town. Neighbors lined up with their wares, some in booths and some with long tables near the road.

Josiah met up with her at the double tent the Bawell Hat Shop had set up in the yard near the dirt driveway. "This is a big event," he said, taking in the buggies and cars lined up along the yard and road. "You have a large selection of things to sell."

"We work toward this all year," she explained with pride. "Spring and fall." Lifting a basket of jellies and jams, she started toward the booth.

"Here, let me," he said, taking it from her to walk with her. "Do you enjoy this?"

"I do," she admitted. "I love talking to neighbors and selling them things they need—quilts, canned goods, crocheted items, and hats and bonnets, of course. Some save up just to buy a good hat."

He tugged at his own. "I think I need to get a new one."

Raesha smiled at that. He didn't know she'd already been working on a new winter hat for him. She'd sneaked the measurements from one of his old hats she'd found on the *grossdaddi haus* porch.

"We'll see what can be done," she quipped after he'd handed off the basket to Susan. "After this, we get ready for the Christmas season. The Englisch love to buy Amish gifts for friends and family. So it never ends."

"How do you do it?" he asked, admiration in his gaze.

Raesha stopped in a spot away from the action beneath the shade of an old oak by the shop's porch. "I told you, I love this. I know I'm different from most and some of the men here frown on me being a businesswoman, but… Aaron never minded. He relished the way I took charge and helped him out in the shop. He always wanted to be outside doing farmwork so when I slowly started taking over, he got to do more of what he truly loved."

"And you discovered you enjoyed being the boss?"

She saw the amused smile that came with that question.

"I had to learn to be the boss, *ja*. But I also realized I have a good head for business and what I didn't know, I learned. I can make a hat from start to finish because I want to know what my employees go through each day. I've learned every aspect of hat-making and running a gift shop."

"You are amazing," he said, his eyes full of a warmth that took away the chill of the wind. "Mr. Hartford said you plied him with questions about such things. He's very proud of you."

"He understands how business works," she replied, happy to hear that news. "He works hand in hand with all of us and provides us with specialty items that we use and need."

"I'm impressed," Josiah said, glancing around. "You managed to find help with Dinah today and yet, you keep checking on her and me. Thanks to you and Naomi, my niece is growing strong."

"She is so precious," Raesha said. "I get a burst of joy each time she smiles at me."

"I do, too."

It had been two days since they'd left Josie at the center. "Have you heard from your sister today, Josiah?"

"Not yet," he admitted. "I invited her to the festival when I was there yesterday but she said no. She seems to prefer sitting by the window and watching the birds in the garden."

"Time spent in quiet is always healing," Raesha replied. "I hope to visit her Sunday afternoon, if that's okay."

"You can go with me," he suggested. "If that's okay with you, that is."

Raesha laughed. "We need to stop being so polite about things. You know I'll do whatever I can to help."

His eyes held hers, and all the commotion around them seemed to slip away. "And you know that I want you with me."

Raesha's heart fluttered against her apron.

Looking away, he added, "I mean, when I visit Josie."

Disappointment stopped her heart and settled her. "Of course. I'll plan on it."

She turned to get back to work, but Josiah stopped her. "Raesha…"

"I understand," she said, not wanting to hear any explanations or excuses. "I have work to do."

Hurrying away, Raesha stiffened her spine and concluded that Josiah Fisher was off-limits to her. At least until he could decide whether he wanted her in his life or not. But then, she had to decide the same about him, too.

Josiah helped where he could and tried to stay out of the way. The Bawell Hat Shop was a popular destination. The booth had stayed busy all day and the door to the shop jingled in a constant melody. No time to track down Raesha and try to salvage the connection they'd almost made earlier.

Now as the festival drew to an end, the afternoon sunshine waned and the air grew cold. Time to finish up.

He did his part by carrying tables and chairs back to the storage area in the big barn, putting away tent canvases and taking up stakes. This work didn't require much thinking, so he stayed silent and hurried along.

But Raesha had extra help and she had everything under control. While he admired those traits in her, he also wished she'd open up to him and let him get a little closer to her.

He wanted to know her heart. Did she have feelings for him? Or was he imagining what could never be?

Now he stood on the tiny porch of the little house that had become his home, his mind on going to see Josie tomorrow. His sister's smile had returned but she still had that dark, faraway look in her pretty hazel eyes.

"I can't discuss what she and I talk about," Judy Campton told him yesterday. "But I will say that she is blessed to have survived all she's been through. She hasn't told me everything but I can tell from her silence that she is suffering greatly."

Josiah left it at that, his many questions still unanswered. He wanted the truth but he had not heard from Nathan Craig so now he waited, his patience running thin and his heart growing weary with doubt and apprehension.

Deciding he'd go and get Dinah early, he came around the house and saw a group of men finishing up with removing some of the other tables and booths along the road.

Samuel Troyer waved him over. "Josiah, what have you decided about setting up your barn raising?"

Surprised, Josiah shook his head. "I hoped to get the house finished up but a new barn is in my plans."

"Winter is coming," Samuel replied, his tone calm. "Need to get it up in the next few weeks or you'll have to wait until spring."

Josiah thought about that and then he considered his limited budget. "I can't afford a big barn. I'd thought to build a smaller one with a loft and room for a horse and buggy."

"We can get that done," Samuel replied. "Talk to Mr. Hartford. He has discount lumber lying around everywhere but it's good wood. We can add in the rest."

"I'll do that," Josiah said. "Then there is the matter of my sister. She is improving but I'm not sure what to do when she is ready to leave the Campton Center."

"Can the girl stay with you?" Samuel asked.

Josiah thought this man would give him the answers he sought. "I hope so. But...will she be shunned?"

"We will discuss this with the bishop," Samuel suggested. "Bishop King has noticed that you and Raesha seem to be close."

Who hadn't noticed that?

"We are friends. She is a big help to me with the little one."

"You have a lot going on," Samuel noted. "I pray you can do what needs to be done."

"I am trying my best."

"I'm here if you need advice."

Josiah nodded. "*Denke.* I want my family whole again. I'm praying toward that end."

Samuel looked toward the house. "Well, you have two very strong champions on your side."

"You mean the Bawell women."

Samuel smiled. "You could do worse."

"I could," Josiah admitted. "But I'm not sure what to do about that. The one I'm interested in might not feel the same about me. Besides, I've always shied away from marriage."

"And why is that?" Samuel asked.

Josiah had never voiced it before. "I don't want to wind up like my *daed*," he said, the admission lifting a great weight off his shoulders.

If Samuel was surprised, he didn't show it. "What makes you think that could happen?"

"I don't know. I've heard bad traits can be inherited."

"Not if you ask God to give you a pure heart and grace to get on with your life," Samuel replied. "I've seen that heart in you, son. And that grace. Don't let something good slip away because you can't forgive the man who brought you into the world."

Josiah didn't know what to say but his brain brightened as if a gas lamp had been lit inside his head. "I'll let you know about the barn raising, Mr. Troyer."

"Ready when you are," Samuel replied. "As for your sister, I hope she will turn back to her Amish family and find her faith again. Part of letting go of the past is looking to the future with hope."

Josiah wanted to have that kind of hope. But he was afraid it would be an uphill battle.

Visiting Sunday always brought Raesha a sense of excitement. Sometimes, friends would come by and sit with Naomi and her for the afternoon. They'd talk about life, read a bit of the Scriptures and sing favorite hymns.

Today, she would be doing the visiting. As planned, she was going to the Campton Center with Josiah to see his sister. Dinah was all tucked in while some of Naomi's friends came to sit with her and watch over the baby. By now, the whole community knew about little Dinah and anyone who saw her fell in love with her.

But they still weren't sure about Josiah and how much time he was spending with Raesha.

"Are people talking?" he asked now as he helped her up onto the buggy, Chester lifting his hoofs in impatience.

"People always talk," she replied. "If you're worried about the three women who are probably staring out the kitchen window at us, let them stare. We've done nothing wrong."

"We are friends," he added, sounding as if he were trying to convince himself of that status.

"*Ja*, friends who are trying to take care of a child and a troubled young woman."

"Do you ever wish I'd not come into your life?"

Glancing over at him as Chester took them up the long drive to the road, Raesha shook her head. "Why would I wish such a thing?"

"Because Dinah and I have interfered in your life."

"Dinah is not an interference," she retorted, clearly appalled. "But you on the other hand…"

Josiah shot her a frown only to find her smiling.

"You are a cruel woman, Raesha Bawell. You tease because you like me, right?"

"I like you well enough," she admitted, trying to keep things light.

"You know, a lot of people have hinted to me that you and I…would make a good match."

Shocked, Raesha ignored the heated blush moving down her face. "People should mind their own business."

Josiah looked frustrated and tried again. "But they make a *gut* case. We are both single and… I need a woman's touch."

Raesha almost gulped in fear but that comment brought her back to reality. Was he about to propose? "Are you serious?"

"I'm contemplating," he said, the look of utter confusion in his gaze making her almost laugh. "I'm trying to be logical but I know you don't want to leave Naomi."

"And you're not sure you will stay in Campton Creek."

He clicked the reins and got a snort from Chester. "Then there is Josie to consider."

"You want her with you, but she doesn't want to be around her own child."

The playful mood shifted at about the same time the wind blew cold across Raesha's burning skin.

"It's something to consider," he said on a deflated note.

"Why don't we take this one step at a time," she finally replied. "Josie needs to get well, in both mind and body, and you still have to fix up the farmhouse and barn to sell."

"You're right. Logical at that."

"The one constant is Dinah. She is not a burden, Josiah. I love her."

Josiah gave her a look that said nothing but told her everything. She'd made it sound as if she cared for only the *bobbeli*.

Raesha wanted to shout to him that she cared for him, too. Too much. But she wouldn't give him false hope. She could not up and move to Ohio or anywhere else. Josiah had a lot of decisions to make, and most of them involved keeping his sister and her child with him.

Which meant Raesha might be left out, even if she wanted to be with him and his little family forever.

They sat with Josie in the big sunroom where they could see the old camellias in the Campton Center garden.

"I made cookies," Josie said when they arrived. "And I can make hot tea for us."

They both asked for tea since she seemed so eager.

"She looks better," Josiah said when she hurried away to the kitchen on the other side of the house.

"I think being here has helped her," Raesha replied, glad to see him relax a bit.

Glancing around, she took in the white wicker furniture and the lush ferns on each side of the big room that was mostly windows and doors. Other exotic plants sat here and there, reminding her of the opulence of this huge house.

"I can see why Josie might love it here," she whispered to Josiah. "It's very relaxing and…beautiful."

"This community is blessed to have such a place," he replied. "The Englisch here seem to accept us."

"That has never been a problem," she assured him. "We work with them, side by side."

He looked over at Raesha, his dark eyes full of hope. "We could make it work, I think. Bringing her back to your place, with me. I hope since she was never baptized, the bishop will allow that."

Raesha wanted that, too. "What if she gets upset about Dinah?"

He mulled that over. "We'll keep them apart."

Raesha wondered if that was any way to live but she'd cross that bridge when she came to it. Josie didn't seem in a hurry to leave the luxury of Campton House. Raesha had a feeling the girl might want to stay out here in the world, but that could be because she was ashamed to return to her roots.

"Only if you feel comfortable with that," he said in a hurry. "The old house is ready but I don't know how she feels about the place."

Raesha wanted to respond but Josie came back in, carrying a silver tray with a teapot and cups on it.

After she served tea and cookies, she sat down. Today, she wore a pretty button-up sweater and a flowing floral skirt over some sort of boots, her hair pulled back in a stern ponytail.

"I might get a job here," she announced. "Mrs.

Campton needs someone to help with the baking and kitchen work."

"Do you want to work here?" Josiah asked, concern marring his earlier happiness.

"Yes," Josie said, her tone firm. "I don't think I want to return to the Amish, brother."

Josiah looked at Raesha, the hurt inside his heart shining brightly in his dark eyes. She gave him an encouraging stare.

"There is plenty of time to consider that," she said, hoping to diffuse the situation.

"I don't need time," Josie retorted. "No one will want me back and... I'm okay with that. I can work here and stay in an apartment here in town."

"It seems you've thought this out," Josiah said. "I only ask that you consider this very carefully before you make a rash decision."

"It's my decision to make," Josie said. "Have another cookie."

Josiah took a sugar cookie but held it in his hand. "I'm glad you're feeling better," he told his sister. "But I think we need to head back. The weather is getting worse."

With that, they left after visiting his sister for only a few minutes.

"You're right," he told Raesha once they were in the buggy again. "I have a lot to work out before I can even consider getting on with my life."

Raesha didn't know what to say. But a future with him seemed impossible at this point.

Chapter Eighteen

October turned the fields fallow and the trees golden and burgundy. A soft rain covered the countryside this morning.

Josiah stood on the little porch of the place he had come to think of as home and stared across at the house where he'd grown up. He had two days to decide where Josie would live. There with him or here with him and the Bawell women.

And Dinah.

She still wanted to live in town and work at the Campton Center. He'd talked to the bishop Samuel Weaver by his side to guide him and vouch for him.

"Your sister can return but she will have to accept the tenets of her faith—our ways—Josiah. If she fails again, she will not be able to come back."

Samuel nodded. "You must make her understand that she will not be shunned as long as she confesses all and gives her life back to *Gott*."

"But she was attacked," he explained. "This is not her fault."

"We understand that," Bishop King said. "Still, she left

the child here and ran away and she's been through things we don't know about. It's best for her to start fresh."

"I will explain all of this to her," Josiah promised. "I cannot predict if she will accept or not."

He knew if Josie decided to stay with the Englisch, he'd have limited contact with her. But he would not give up on his sister.

He hoped to convince her to come home with him.

But he wasn't sure where his real home might be.

The rain increased but he stood still, his heart hurting for the life he'd had inside that house. He should have stayed and protected Josie. That regret would stay with him until his dying day.

Then the door behind him opened.

Raesha stood there, wet and shaking. "I looked all over for you. Everywhere."

"What's wrong?"

"The shop— I got a call that you need to go to the Campton Center. Mrs. Campton said Josie has had a breakthrough and she's asking for you."

Josiah remembered other phone calls. "This could be good news, then."

Raesha bobbed her head. "It could be. Or…it could mean she's not coming back to us. Ever."

"I'll go and see what has happened."

She nodded, so used to this. So used to having to tell him bad and good news and then take care of Dinah for him.

He loved Raesha. He could see that now, here in the cold rain. She had run through that rain, searching for him because she always did the right thing. Even if her heart was breaking.

He wanted to say so much to her.

But he had to go.

"I'll be back soon, I hope."

"Take your time. We'll be right here."

Waiting.

She would wait.

But one day, she'd get tired of waiting.

"She has told me everything," Judy Campton said when Josiah came into Alisha Braxton's office. "Now it's time for her to tell you. She realizes that and is willing to be honest with you." Mrs. Campton sat in a chair across from Alisha, weariness showing in her sagging shoulders.

The lady lawyer's eyes held sympathy. "After you talk to Josie, if you need me for anything, Mr. Fisher…"

"Denke," Josiah said, already heading out the office for the stairs to Josie's room. Then he turned back to Judy Campton. "And *denke* for working to heal my sister. Go and rest now."

"I think I shall do that," Judy Campton said, her expression serene now. "I'm getting too old for this, I think."

Josiah decided he'd aged ten years himself.

But he took a deep breath and prayed for strength. Because he didn't know what his sister would say to him. Then he knocked on the door.

"Come in."

Her voice sounded strong but when he saw her, he could tell she'd been through the wringer. Josie looked wiped out and so tired.

"Josie?"

"Let me talk, brother," she said. "Let me get it all out, please."

"All right."

He sat down across from her and remained silent.

"In Kentucky, we hung around with some Englisch kids who were the same age as us. Tobias—the man I was to marry—knew one of them. They were good friends."

She stopped, stared out the window, her hands clutching the bright fabric of the chair. "Drew seemed so nice and I tolerated him because Tobias admired him. They worked the land together."

Josiah wanted to hit something or someone. He hated the terror that edged her calm words. "What happened?"

She lifted her head. "Drew drugged my drink one night and…took advantage of me. I woke up in a room in his house and… I knew something bad had happened. But I went home to the place where I stayed with some other girls. I told them I'd spent the night with an Englisch girl at her home. But they knew. They had to know."

Josiah had so many questions but he stayed still and silent.

"I never told Tobias the truth but I stopped going to Drew's house after that. I told Tobias it didn't feel right. He never questioned me but I did notice he didn't go there as much after that either."

Holding a hand to her face, she went on. "We were planning our wedding. Two months until I'd become Tobias's wife."

The sobs came softly but she kept talking. "I started feeling sick all the time, throwing up. One of my friends asked me if I could be pregnant.

"I tried to deny it. Told them I had a stomach virus. But I went to the midwife and she confirmed it. I was pregnant and… I knew Drew had to be the father."

Josiah sat up, his hands falling against his knees. "I'm so sorry, Josephine. So sorry I wasn't there to watch out for you."

She wiped at her eyes. "Tobias loved me. He watched out for me but…he didn't know that his best friend had done this horrible thing. I panicked. I was so embarrassed and afraid and ashamed. I ran away and found work and a room and when I had enough money, I tried to get to Ohio but then I realized I'd be shunned there."

Standing, she paced before the window, her arms held against her stomach, a solid shield. "I managed to catch a bus to Pennsylvania and… I think you know the rest."

"You stayed in a small settlement not far from here," Josiah replied. "Had your baby at the hospital and then tried to take care of Dinah on your own."

"But I was too sick, Josiah. I was too sick and… traumatized. I remembered Mrs. Bawell. How kind she was when we were living next door."

Josiah stood and stopped his sister's pacing. "You did what you had to do, Josie. But what about Tobias? You could have explained to him."

"No, I could not." Pulling away, she shook her head. "I could not tell him what his friend did, Josiah. I was too ashamed. I was afraid no one would believe me."

"That boy needs to be punished."

"He has been," she said. "I got word from a friend who didn't know about what he'd done to me. She was just gossiping but she wrote to me and told me he'd been arrested for doing the same thing to another girl—this one Englisch and with a powerful father. He went to jail. He will be there for a long time. I don't want you to do anything, hear me?"

"I hear you," Josiah said, thankful for justice. "Still I'd like to pummel his head."

"You don't mean that."

He did but he'd pray on that matter.

"Do you believe me?" she asked, her voice wobbling. "I need you to believe me."

"I believe you," he replied. "And I'm sorry, so sorry. But you can come home now. You can come back to your faith."

"I don't know if I can do that," she said, anger coloring her words. "Do you see what I have become?"

"I see my sister and I love you."

"I'm flawed, damaged. I'll never be well."

"I will help you. We will all help you."

"You and Raesha Bawell. The woman who wants to keep my baby?"

"She wants what's best for Dinah. We all do."

"Well, I'm not what's best for Dinah. I can't bear to look at her."

"She is an innocent child, Josie."

"I was once an innocent child, too. But not anymore."

"Josie, you can be forgiven and accepted again. It's different here. People are less strict. Not like—"

"Not like our father?" She looked surprised.

"I'm telling you, the Bawells won't judge you."

"But the rest of them will."

"I don't think so. I will protect you."

His sister gave him a look that chilled him. She didn't believe him because he had already failed her.

Raesha waited by the window, watching for Josiah. Would he bring Josie back here or would she stay at the center and find a job in town?

"My life used to be so simple."

"You know you are way too young to be talking to yourself," Naomi said from behind her. "Talk to me instead."

"This man," Raesha said, lifting her hands up. "He's so hard to understand. I can't decide if he likes me or hates me or wants me in his life or just needs me to take care of his niece."

Naomi stood by the kitchen table, steady as a rock. "I think he likes you, a lot. I think he wants you in his life. And I think he needs you to help with his niece but he feels badly about asking."

"You're taking his side?"

"I didn't know there was a side."

Raesha pulled out the frying pan to make a light supper. "Scrambled eggs and biscuits."

"Perfect," Naomi replied. "But you hate scrambled eggs."

"I'll eat biscuits. With ham."

Naomi went to her chair and smiled and talked baby talk to Dinah. "Hard to believe she's been with us for one month now."

"She's growing up fast."

"She's already trying to roll over. In a month or two, she'll be so proud of herself."

Raesha stopped beating eggs and walked over to look down at the gurgling, smiling infant. Dinah had been gifted with so many girlie baby gowns, the child would never get around to wearing all of them. Today, they'd dressed her in a blue broadcloth dress with smocking across the front and a white crocheted bonnet that couldn't contain her brown curls. Her little feet were covered in dark blue bootie socks.

Touching on one of her kicking feet, Raesha said, "She is so beautiful. Why does she have to be so beautiful?"

"*Gott* made her that way."

Pulling her hand away, Raesha backed up. "I can't keep doing this. I'm going to tell Josiah he needs to hire someone else to be his nanny."

Naomi's rocking chair creaked. "He'll have to take the money he's saving to buy lumber for the barn."

"He'll manage. He works hard and he's always picking up odd jobs to make ends meet." Raesha went to the pantry closet and uncovered the leftover biscuits from breakfast. "He helps Mr. Hartford around the store and then comes back to work on the house and tear down what remains of that barn. It's a wonder he ever gets to spend time with Dinah or Josie."

"He is industrious in that way. He wants that old farm to shine so he can get the best price for it."

Raesha buttered the biscuits and checked on the oven. "I could wait until after the barn's done, I suppose."

"It's your decision."

As usual, her astute mother-in-law had let her talk herself out of a rant. And out of finding a nanny for Dinah at that.

"I'm going to finish supper now."

"I'll sit here and chat with Dinah."

Raesha made the eggs and browned the biscuits, adding some preserves and some ham slices. It was that kind of night.

Then she heard the buggy jostling up the lane and all of her anger and frustration went right out the window.

Josiah was back. But he wasn't alone.

His sister, Josie, was in the buggy with him.

* * *

"How did you convince her to come?"

Raesha sat with Josiah at the kitchen table. Naomi had gone to bed and now he was holding Dinah and feeding her a bedtime bottle. They'd agreed that the baby would stay with Raesha and Naomi for now since Josie refused to see her.

"It wasn't easy. She thinks she can't come back but I told her this place is different."

"We are very forgiving around here."

"She is ashamed and frightened so she uses a bad attitude to cover that up."

"I can understand that. What she must have gone through. I wish this man could be taught a lesson."

"I wanted that, too. But he is behind bars. I'll have Nathan Craig confirm that for our peace of mind. And so I won't go and find the man and kill him with my bare hands."

"Josiah, you know that is not our way."

"It's *my* way," he retorted with such anger, Dinah's eyelashes fluttered up from dozing.

"You can't go after this man. That won't change what has happened."

"I want to teach him a lesson but that might upset Josie even more." Carefully passing Dinah back to Raesha, he said, "I'd better go and check on her. She was worn-out when we got home."

"Take her some food," Raesha said, indicating the plate she'd made up for both of them. "She needs nourishment."

"She needs a lot of things but Mrs. Campton thinks the worst is over. She told me to just love her and let her be."

"*Gut* advice."

Taking the plate, he stared over at Raesha, his brown eyes burning coals. "I'm going to give you extra rent money to cover Josie's upkeep and to show you how much I appreciate your help with all of this."

"Don't insult me," she replied on a loud whisper. "I don't mind you paying honest rent but I refuse to charge you for taking care of Dinah or helping Josie. Stop that nonsense."

"Why are you so stubborn?"

"Why are you so dense?"

Raesha held Dinah close but he inched forward. When the baby let out a soft whimper since they'd scared her awake, Josiah shook his head and backed away.

"We will discuss this more later."

"You don't owe me any money, Josiah."

"I owe you everything," he replied. Then he turned around and stomped to the door. "And I have nothing to give you."

After he left, Raesha sat down in the rocker and held Dinah close to lull her back to sleep. "He has more to give than anyone I've ever known," she whispered to the drowsy little baby. "I just need to convince him of that."

Chapter Nineteen

Raesha braced herself. She wanted to go and see Josie but she had to tread lightly here. The girl had been with Josiah for three days now but Raesha had not seen her. She'd tried to give Josie the time and space she needed. But now, the girl needed some clothes.

Josiah had gone to meet with Bishop King, Samuel and Jeremiah going with him to offer support and assure the bishop that Josie should find her way here, not out there alone.

And while he was off doing that task, Raesha had left Dinah with Susan's younger sister Greta and Naomi cozy inside the big house. One thing about this community—everyone truly pitched in to help, especially when it involved children.

Now she had an hour to talk to Josie.

Knocking on the door of the *grossdaddi haus*, Raesha held a basket of clothes and shoes for the girl. And a plate of blueberry muffins she'd made earlier.

"Who is it?" Josie called from behind the door.

"It's Raesha. I came to welcome you to our home."

Josie opened the door and stared at the basket. "I have clothes."

"You need these clothes," Raesha said, trying to keep her tone neutral. "May I come in? It's a chilly morning."

Josie opened the door and let her inside. Raesha set the basket on the small kitchen table and turned around. The place was clean and smelled of lemon furniture polish. Josie had rearranged a few things to make it cozy.

A good sign.

A hand on the basket, Raesha said, "There is a wool cloak and new bonnet in here and some sturdy winter shoes that should fit you. Everything you need in twos, so you can wash and change often."

"That's nice of you," Josie said, touching a finger to the wool cloak. "And I love blueberry muffins."

"Then sit and have one."

Josie grabbed a muffin and moved to the sofa by the woodstove. "This is a cozy house."

"It's a strong house," Raesha said, sitting down across from her in a high-backed oak chair with ruffled cushions. "Many people have stayed here."

"My brother says you take in people."

"When we need to, *ja*."

"I didn't want to come here."

"I know, but I'm glad you did. Your brother needs you."

"Josiah? He's never needed anyone."

"You don't really know your brother, do you?"

"Do you know him?"

"I think I'm beginning to," Raesha said. "He works hard and tries to take care of things. He wants to make everyone's life better. Meantime, he barely has time to live his own life."

"He's had plenty of time," Josie said, putting her muffin down on the table. "He went away and left me… in that house."

"He was young and he wanted a better life."

"I wanted that, too, but I didn't get to leave. And when I did have to go away, I messed up."

"Josie, you didn't mess up. Someone else is to blame for what happened to you."

"I shouldn't have been at that party that night. Tobias was there but he was downstairs in another room." She stopped, broke off some muffin. "I… I remember trying to call his name."

Every time Raesha wanted to be angry with this young woman, Josie said something that broke her heart. "You could get in touch with Tobias. I'm sure he's concerned about you."

"He's probably married now," Josie said, her voice cracking. "I should have stayed away but it was tough out there on my own. I really tried to make it. I don't want to be a burden."

Raesha saw the truth in the girl's whispered words. "Josie, do you want to be Amish again? Or would you rather stay out there in the world?"

Josie shook her head. "I don't know. I feel safe here and I miss my Amish friends. I miss Tobias. But there is no place for me now."

Raesha touched her hand to Josie's. "You have a place here, whether it's in this house or the house your brother had rebuilt. Remember that. You will always be safe here."

Josie's eyes went wide. "I don't know. I need to be alone now. I don't want to think about this."

"I'll leave you alone, then," Raesha said. "Josiah should be back soon."

Josie nodded, tears in her eyes.

"If you need me, come to the front door of the hat shop. You don't have to go through the house."

The girl didn't say anything. She sat with her hands crossed in her lap, her hair falling across her face.

Raesha hated to leave her, but what else could she do? Pushing would only make Josie bolt. And she did not want that to happen again.

She went to the door but turned when Josie called out.

Josie stood and rubbed her hands down her sweater. "Is she happy?"

"You mean Dinah?"

The girl nodded.

"She is a sweet, pleasant baby. She is growing strong. Other than a little colic now and then, she is a fine girl."

Josie's eyes watered, tears spilling over like a current on the creek. She didn't speak but she nodded.

Raesha wanted to rush back and hug her close but she didn't do that. Josie was so fragile, one sudden move could crush her.

"I will check on you later," Raesha said.

Josie nodded and turned toward the smaller of the two bedrooms.

Raesha shut the door and left, her prayers focused on this girl's healing.

"Josie doesn't know if she's ready to seek forgiveness," Josiah told Raesha later that day. "But the bishop is willing to see this through."

"I'm thankful for that," Raesha told him, her eyes

warm. He loved this time of day when they usually sat with Dinah for a few minutes before he took her across the way.

Now he couldn't do that. Josie was there.

"She should be with her mother," he said, then after seeing the hurt in Raesha's eyes, wished he hadn't.

Lowering her head, she replied, "Maybe one day."

He stared down at Dinah. The baby gurgled and kicked. Raesha had managed to find several bibs and gowns for his niece and they all made her look even more adorable.

To break the silence, he said, "I think she recognizes my voice."

"And your presence," Raesha replied, her face blank now. "She knows who you are."

"She smiles more at you, though," he offered, hoping to salvage their precious time together.

"Do you think so?"

"I do." He held Dinah's chubby fingers. "She has a firm grip." Then he looked over at Raesha. "Where is Naomi?"

"She decided to meet Josie. She went over about an hour ago to sit with her."

Seeing the fatigue in her eyes, he said, "I have burdened both of you so much."

"Do not say that again," Raesha replied, getting up to check on the pot roast cooking on the stove. "We have helped many people but we've both been blessed having Dinah here."

"People will talk and think I'm shirking my responsibilities."

"People will always talk. I know your heart."

"Do you?"

She whirled at his question, her eyes vivid with surprise. "I hope so."

Tugging up from where he'd been kneeling next to the crib, he came to stand by Raesha in the kitchen. "I wish that we could have met in a different way."

"I do, too."

"I'm not good with courting or making conversation," he admitted. "I think that is why I'm still alone. But with you, I feel *gut*. I get terrible nervous around you, but… I like being around you."

Her eyes went soft, her smile quiet. "I feel the same, Josiah. I loved my husband so much but…you have added a bit of happiness to my life."

"So it's not just about Dinah?"

"*Neh*. Dinah is a precious child. But if I'd never held her in my arms, or never known her sweetness, I'd still care about you. You are the kind of man any woman would be proud to call her own."

His heart lifted, hope flowing like a river. "Could you call me your own?"

Raesha went back to stirring the pot. "The question is—can you ever call me your own? Or will you soon go away forever?"

Josiah didn't know the answer to that question. But he did know one thing. He could so easily love this woman.

How could he reconcile that realization with what lay ahead for him?

Before he could answer that question, Naomi entered the back door and smiled at them. "Josie and I had a wonderful time getting to know each other. She invited me back."

"That's nice since it's your house," he said, misery

settling over him. "How does she seem to you, Mammi Naomi?"

"Confused and shattered," Naomi replied without batting an eye. "We give her love. Lots of love. It's a cruel world and she has seen that cruelty firsthand."

"Will she ever heal?" he asked, hope hinging on the question.

"With time, maybe," Naomi said, her gaze moving over his face and then back to Raesha. "But she might not ever accept this baby."

He shook his head. "I can't leave one and take the other. They should be together."

"We will take care of Dinah until she is able," Naomi reminded him.

"And if she never can be able?" he asked, raking a hand down his face. "Does that mean I leave my niece here with you two and take my sister to be with family?"

"That is a question that you and Josie need to ask each other, I suppose," Naomi replied. "The child was left at our door. We won't turn her away."

"But I can be turned away. My sister and I?"

"She is not saying that," Raesha told him, her tone stern. "You are a grown man. You can go wherever you please. That baby doesn't have a choice."

So he went across the way, still wondering if Raesha loved Dinah and only tolerated him. If he had courage, he'd ask her outright. But he didn't think he was worthy of even that question.

Touching the door handle, he wondered what he'd do about Josie. He wouldn't leave her again. Maybe it would be better to leave the *bobbeli* and take his sister away from all the pain and memories.

Was that God's plan for him? For Raesha? For Josie?

Josiah said a prayer for patience and understanding and…for acceptance. He'd never been good at the acceptance part. He wanted to argue with the Lord and convince Him that Josiah knew best. But he knew nothing.

"I leave it in your hands, *Gott*."

No matter, he'd have to accept that in order to take care of his sister, he might have to leave Raesha and the child behind.

"I want to go home," Josie told him a few days later.

Surprised since she'd been venturing out to visit with Naomi on the porch, he studied his sister. The color was back in her face and she'd gained some weight back.

"Home? You mean to Ohio?"

She nodded. "That is the best place for us, don't you think? But we don't have to live with *Onkel*. I don't want to live with the family again."

Josiah felt the punch of a thousand fists inside his chest. So this was his answer, then?

"Why do you want to go back there?"

"I can't live here."

"What are you afraid of, sister?"

Josie stood and went to the kitchen window to stare across the way. "That house over there," she said.

So that was it. He'd have to sell the place and move on, just as he'd planned. He'd never have a life with Raesha.

"And what about your child?"

"My child has found a home, Josiah. I am at peace with that."

Peace? She was at peace with that?

How could she be so cold, so detached?

Did that man do this to her? Take her soul?

He tried to think, tried to focus. "I still have to get the barn built. Men are coming in two days to do that."

"Don't rebuild the barn," she suggested.

"Why wouldn't I?" Josiah replied, tired and dejected.

Josie whirled to stare at him, her eyes bright with fear and anger. "Some things can't be rebuilt, Josiah."

And some things couldn't be forgiven, he decided. His sister would never forgive him for leaving her all those years ago.

"Josiah, I heard you're not rebuilding the barn," Raesha said the next day when he came to visit with Dinah.

He'd been quiet the last few days, in and out without eating or staying to visit. He hadn't gone to church last Sunday, citing he needed to stay with Josie.

People were beginning to take it for granted that Dinah would grow up in the Bawell house. But they weren't so sure about Josiah and his sister. What was their story?

Raesha wanted to know the rest of that story, too.

She loved the man. She'd fought against it but now she could feel it each time he entered a room. That image of having him and Dinah with her didn't go away easily.

Now he gave her a glance that told her everything.

"You're leaving," she said, glad that they were alone. Naomi had taken Dinah out in the new stroller they'd found at the general store. Just for a brief walk along the drive.

He took her hand. "Josie wants to go back to Ohio."

"Does she, now?" Raesha tried to stifle the resentment she felt toward the girl. "I thought she didn't like it there."

"She likes it there better than here," he said. "I'm putting the place up for sale as is. I'll take any offers."

"And then you'll just go?"

"No. We leave next week. I've worked out the details through a real estate agency."

"I see." Angry that he hadn't explained any of this to her sooner, she nodded. "So just like that, you leave and go on with your life. Have either of you considered Dinah?"

"Yes. We want to leave her with you if you don't mind. You love her and she will be safe and happy here. I will send money to provide for her."

Pulling her hand away, Raesha asked, "So you will just walk away from her and me, Josiah?"

He looked up at her, his eyes as dark as a storm. "I have no other choice."

"Because Josie doesn't want her baby?"

"She is my sister and she has suffered enough."

"She might leave again."

"*Ja*, she might. But I have to do this. I wasn't here for her before and she has not forgotten that."

The pain tore through Raesha. The unfairness of it all crashed over her. She loved this man and she loved this baby.

But she had promised to accept what came. "How can I love Dinah without you here, Josiah?"

"You love her already," he said. "More than you will ever love me."

"You have no idea," she retorted, tears streaming down her face. "No idea at all about how much love I have to give."

"I want to stay," he said. "Raesha, I want to stay but I can't do it…and you can't leave."

"You never asked me."

"Because I know the answer. I heard you say it myself."

"You have a choice and you've made it. I understand." And because she was angry and hurt, she added, "You run away from the truth, Josiah. The truth that is right in front of your eyes."

He took her arm again, his eyes misty, his breath rising and falling with each word. "Do you think this is an easy choice? I want more than anything to be here with you and Dinah and take care of both of you. But Josie needs me."

Raesha was about to tell him to go, but a crash on the porch caused both of them to run to the back of the house.

Naomi lay on the porch floor, panting. "I'm sorry. She took Dinah. Josie took the child out of the stroller and ran away. I tripped over the steps. Had to alert you."

Raesha fell down beside Naomi and shouted at Josiah. "Go to the shop and call for a doctor. And then go and find you sister and Dinah."

She held her mother-in-law and prayed. For all of them.

Chapter Twenty

Josiah heard the siren coming up the road but he kept running, searching, calling out for his sister. He looked in the barn and the yard, around the closed shop. He peeked in windows and opened doors.

The stroller lay on its side in the driveway, just a few feet from the house. Why had his sister taken the baby she wanted no part of?

He kept searching. The whole community would be alerted soon and they'd help. Then they'd tell Josie she had to leave. He'd take her and go. He should have never returned to Campton Creek.

Running again. Raesha thought he was running but this time he was trying to do the right thing.

He looked over at the old place, the cold late afternoon dark with gloomy clouds making the house look broken and forlorn. Could she have gone there?

Hurrying across the arched bridge, he gulped in the chilly air and kept praying. *Why now, Josie? Why?*

Then he heard a baby crying inside the house.

"Josie?"

Josiah hurried up onto the porch and shook the door

open. Then he followed the cries upstairs to the room that used to be Josie's.

And found her in a corner, holding Dinah tight, both of them crying.

"Josie," he said, sliding down on his knees. "Josie."

"I'm so sorry," she cried out. "I'm so sorry. I love her. I love my baby. But I can't take care of her."

"Why did you take her?" he asked, pushing at his sister's hair, checking to see that Dinah was all right.

"I heard you fighting with Raesha. She loves you and she loves Dinah. And I'm forcing you to leave both of them. I panicked. I thought if I took her away again, you could be with Raesha."

He sank down beside his sister and put an arm around her thin shoulders. "Why did you refuse to even look at the baby before?"

"I couldn't take it anymore," she admitted. "She reminded me of that night, that boy. I tried not to love her, brother. But I do."

The relief he felt swept through Josiah with a river-swift clarity. "I prayed that you would come to see that, Josephine. It will be okay. We will take Dinah with us and go home."

"No," Josie said. "*I* will go. Alone." Looking down at Dinah, she whispered, "But you need to stay. You belong here and so does she."

She handed him the baby and he cuddled Dinah close, his eyes on Josie. There had to be another reason she wanted to leave again. "Tell me what happened here, sister. Before I came back home."

Josie scooted toward the corner of the wall, sobbing. "I didn't mean to cause a fire, Josiah. I didn't."

"What?" Josiah calmed Dinah and then touched a hand to Josie's sweater. "What are you saying?"

"They were fighting. He…he hit Mamm. I was lighting lamps and I turned and ran to the barn, still holding a lamp." Gulping, she wiped at her eyes. "I was so scared I fell and dropped the lamp. It spilled onto a hay bale. The barn caught on fire."

Josiah closed his eyes, the horror of what had happened cloaking him in darkness. "But you ran out? You didn't stay in the barn."

"I screamed and tried to get out," she said, her voice going calm now. "He came running and jerked me out of the way, threw me to the ground and told me I was stupid. He went inside."

Josiah could picture his angry father, pushing his child away, shouting his wrath. "Then what happened, Josie?"

"Mamm came running, her face all bruised. She went in after him, Josiah. She went in and I heard her scream. They never came out." Burying her face in her hands, Josie sobbed. "It was my fault. All my fault."

Josiah let out his own sob. All these years, his sister had carried a guilt far greater than anything he'd ever known. She believed she'd killed her parents.

"Josie, listen to me. This was not your fault, you hear me? This was an accident and not your fault."

His sister looked up at him, the little girl he remembered gone now. "But that's why God punished me. That's why I couldn't marry Tobias or take care of Dinah. *Gott* punished me and now I'll never be able to get married and have another child."

Josiah held his sobbing sister close and wished he could take on her pain. "You are safe now. Gott loves you. He has brought you home, sister. And you are strong enough to tell the truth of all you've been through. Did you not know? He was there with you all along. For He has brought you home to heal."

"I don't believe that," Josie shouted. "I want to go away."

"Sister, listen to me," he said, seeing the path ahead in a new light. "We have both been running away from the truth. It's time we stop that. We don't have to live in this house but we have found a wonderful place where we can all live."

"You mean with Raesha and Naomi?" she asked, her voice cracking, her eyes full of uncertainty.

"They love us. They want us there. If you can't raise Dinah by yourself, they will gladly take on that task."

"They don't want *me* there."

"Yes, they do. They both do. Have you not seen what those two women have done for us?"

Wiping at her eyes, Josie bobbed her head. "*Ja*, I've seen it and felt it and cried because they have been so kind. But I'll be shunned and…no one will ever want me."

"*Gott* wants you," Josiah said, his hand rubbing Dinah's soft curls. "*Gott* wants us here."

"How can you be so sure?" she asked.

Josiah held Dinah close as he lifted up and reached out his hand to his sister. "Because here we are, back where we started, the truth between us clear. This is our opportunity to start over again with people who love us. That, sister, is *Gott*'s doing."

She shifted away, buried her face against her knees.

"Josie, we can stop running now."

Josie lifted her head and glanced around the empty room. "It's just a house, isn't it? A lonely old house."

"*Ja*, that is all—just wood and beams. But across that little bridge out there is a home. And it's waiting for us. Will you go there with me so I can tell Raesha how much I love her and want to marry her?"

Josie's smile started out small and then brightened to a big grin. "I never thought I'd hear you say such words."

"Neither did I," he admitted. "But no truer words have ever been said."

"And what if she refuses?"

"I'll keep hanging around until she sees the light."

Raesha sat by the bed, her hand gripping Naomi's. Her mother-in-law had finally dozed off to sleep. The doctor had deemed her fine and dandy after she'd insisted she had only a sore foot, bruised knee and some bruised pride.

"I made it to the porch but that crooked step got me," she kept saying. Followed by, "Have they found the children yet?"

"Not yet," Raesha had said fifteen minutes ago. Over an hour had passed and several people had gone off searching.

She did not know where Josiah, Josie and Dinah had gone.

Had he taken both of them away?

A knock at the front door caused her to drop Naomi's hand and stand up. Hurrying to the parlor, she closed the door to Naomi's room, then took a deep breath. Good news or bad? She didn't know how to pray.

When she opened the door, she found Ava Jane

Weaver standing there. *"Kumm,"* she said, wondering if the woman would tell her the worst.

Ava Jane came inside and then turned toward Raesha. "They are all found," she said, her blue eyes full of understanding. "They will be home shortly."

Raesha sank down on the nearest chair. "I was so worried."

Ava Jane got her some water and then pulled up a kitchen chair to sit with her. "Jeremiah decided to check the house."

"You mean, Josiah's house?"

Ava Jane nodded. "He found them upstairs, talking. They were on their way back here but my *daed* and Jeremiah talked to Josiah about a lot of things."

"Will they have to leave?"

"I don't know but I hope not," Ava Jane said. "Jeremiah sent me to sit with you and Mammi Naomi."

"But you have the *kinder.*"

"My sister is with them. She was staying over since we have baking to do early tomorrow. She helps me a lot these days."

"You have a *gut* sister."

The small talk calmed Raesha while her heart exploded with both despair and hope. What could they be discussing?

After a cup of tea and more talk, the door finally opened and Josiah walked in holding Dinah, his sister trailing behind him. Raesha glanced over at Ava Jane and then back to Josiah.

He looked frazzled but he also looked hopeful. Almost at peace. Then he looked at Ava Jane. "Your husband is waiting outside. *Denke* for staying with her."

"I'll go, then," Ava Jane said, getting up. She touched Raesha's arm. "If you need anything—"

"I appreciate you," Raesha said, hugging Ava Jane.

After her friend left, she stood near the kitchen table, her hand on a chair. "Are you all right?" she asked, her gaze moving over all of them.

Josiah brought Dinah to her, and leaned close. "We are better than all right."

Raesha took the baby onto her shoulder, her hand holding Dinah against her heart. The baby cooed and settled her head against Raesha's neck, the sweet smell of her bringing tears to Raesha's eyes.

Josie stepped forward. "I am sorry, Raesha, for taking Dinah. I thought if I took her back, you and Josiah could…make a life together. Without worrying about me."

Raesha's anger and fear disappeared. Josie looked as if she'd cried a flood of tears. "But you didn't do that."

"Neh," the girl said. "I went to the old place and prayed. Josiah found Dinah and me there."

"We had a long talk," he explained. "About a lot of things."

Raesha held steady, her backbone straightening, her head up. "So you're all going. Is that it, then?"

Josiah shook his head. *"Neh,* we are not going. That is, if you are willing to let us stay."

"But I thought—"

Josie came closer and touched her fingers to Dinah's unruly curls. "I can't raise her alone. I need my brother to help me."

"Of course you do," Raesha replied, her heart careening out of control. "I understand."

"*Neh*, you don't understand," Josiah said, smiling for the first time. "We need you with us."

"I can't go—"

"We want to stay," he said. "Raesha, will you listen and let me say what I need to say?"

"Well, get on with it, then."

Shaking his head, he took Dinah from her and passed her to Josie. The girl took the baby and smiled.

Raesha gripped the chair back so tightly, her knuckles were going stiff. She couldn't speak.

Josiah pried her hand from the chair and then took her other hand. "What I'm trying to say is that we want to stay here and… I want to marry you and raise Dinah with you."

Dizziness took over. She thought she might be floating on a cloud. "What?"

"He wants to marry you," Josie said. "And I talked with Mr. Troyer and his son-in-law and told them I want to stay here and I'm willing to confess all and be baptized. For life, Raesha. No more running. We want to call this our home."

"Yes, what she said," Josiah added, grinning from ear to ear. "Please, Raesha, will you say something?"

"She'd better say yes" came a steady voice from the other room. "Don't make me have to get up and come in there and talk some sense into all of you."

Raesha burst into laughter and then she burst into tears.

"I say yes," she told Josiah. "I say yes."

He pulled her into his arms and swung her around, laughing, crying, smiling. "I love you. I could never leave you."

Josie cried, too, soft, healing tears. "Can we stay, Raesha?"

"Yes," she said. "I want all of you here with me."

"I feel the same," Naomi called. "But will you please bring the celebration in here. I am missing out."

Josiah gave Raesha a quick kiss and then set her down. "Let's get in there before she hurts herself again."

He took Dinah back and then urged Raesha and Josie forward. Josie took Raesha's hand, her expression full of joy.

Together, they trooped into Naomi's room and found her wide-awake and sitting up. "Tell me everything," she said. "I know the Lord had a hand in all of this and I need details."

Josiah and Josie sat down in chairs by the bed while Raesha sat in a rocking chair and held Dinah close. Then they explained what had happened when Josiah found Josie inside the old house.

"I'm so sorry," Josie kept saying.

"You are forgiven," Naomi replied. "And now, you two must forgive your father. You've paid the price of growing up in that house. Time for a new start, with us. We have so much to celebrate. Life, happiness and two of our own returning to the fold."

Dinah giggled and clapped her hands together.

"I agree," Naomi said, clapping her hands, too. "We've taken in many people in this old house, but you three have been the most challenging. And the most loved."

Josiah reached a hand out to Raesha. "I can't wait for the rest of the challenges. We are home at last."

Raesha's contentment turned into such joy she

thought her heart would burst. "We are all home," she said, gratitude coloring her world.

A month later, Josiah Fisher married Raesha Bawell in a service held at the Bawell house. Bishop King listened to them as they promised to love, cherish and care for each other through sickness and health, troubles and joy. Then the bishop held his hand over theirs and told them to go forth with the Lord's blessing and in his name.

Later, they hosted a barn raising across the way and a feast for the whole community, then sang hymns to celebrate their life together.

Raesha wore a new *kapp* stitched with delicate embroidery with one pink rose hidden in the stitches. For Dinah and for Mrs. Fisher. They would never forget.

Later, she and Josiah stood on the front porch, braced against the November chill.

"Thanksgiving is coming," he said, his arm around his wife's waist. "I am thankful for so many things."

"So am I," Raesha replied, her heart happy as she stared at the woven brown basket that now held pumpkins and mums, the basket that had brought her a child, a new family and more love than she could have ever imagined.

It would forever be her cornucopia, overflowing with blessings.

* * * * *

AMISH HIDEOUT

Maggie K. Black

With thanks to my wonderful agent,
Melissa Jeglinski, for her enthusiasm and support,
and to my editor, Emily Rodmell, for entrusting me
with this story and always pushing me to become
a better author. Thanks also to Debby Giusti and
Dana R. Lynn, who are writing the next two books
in this series. I can't wait to read them.

Finally, thank you to the friend who recently
told me off for ignoring who I was with
and texting at the dinner table. You were right.
Thanks for helping me think about my relationships
and how I use my phone in a new way.

He hath made every thing beautiful in his time:
also he hath set the world in their heart, so that
no man can find out the work that God
maketh from the beginning to the end.
—*Ecclesiastes* 3:11

Chapter One

Time was running out for Celeste Alexander. Her sneakered feet tapped on the floor beneath the desk. Her fingers flew over the keyboard so quickly it seemed more like a rapid dance than typing, knowing each keystroke could be her last before US Marshal Jonathan Mast arrived to escort her to her new life in the witness protection program. The early-morning sky lay dark over wintery Pennsylvania farmland outside the safe house window. She knew she should sleep. After all, she had no idea how long the journey ahead would be until she finally reached the small apartment in Pittsburgh that would be her new home for the months until she testified at Dexter Thomes's trial.

It had been almost two weeks since an evil but genius computer hacker, who went by the online handle "Poindexter," had stolen tens of millions of dollars out of the bank accounts of thousands of ordinary Americans in one of the largest bank heists in history, without even leaving his chair. But she'd found him and now he sat in a jail cell, thanks to a single curious thread that Celeste had started following online. When she'd gathered all the evidence she could, she'd tipped off the feds, and Dexter had been arrested. News had quickly spread through the online community that a self-employed computer programmer—a blonde, twenty-six-year-old woman, no less—had uncovered the true identity of the criminal the feds' best minds hadn't been able to find.

But the stolen money still hadn't been recovered. The thought of letting a single one of those people wake up one more day with an empty bank account was unthinkable. Not while there was something she could do about it. She frowned. The battery was down to less than 10 percent and she'd forgotten the charging cable in the room upstairs where she'd slept last night.

"You gave her a laptop?" The voice of US Marshal Stacy Preston came sharply from somewhere behind her. "Please tell me you didn't let her go online. The last thing we need is another misguided Poindexter fan trying to come after her and keep her from testif—"

"Really? You think I joined the service yesterday?" US Marshal Karl Adams shot back even before Stacy had finished her sentence. From what Celeste had seen, those two didn't talk so much as volley sentences back and forth like some kind of verbal tennis match. "Of course not! She had a basic tablet with the internet capability disabled, and after scanning it for bugs, I let her borrow a keyboard."

"And you didn't think to check with me?"

"You were asleep!" Karl said. "Do you check every decision you make with me while you're the one on lookout? It's got zero internet capability. It's not like I gave her a cell phone."

Celeste gritted her teeth, blocked out the verbal sparring of the two US marshals in the room behind her and their sporadic walkie-talkie exchanges with the other marshals positioned around the remote property, and focused her eyes on the text streaming down the screen. Dexter might be in jail. But this would never truly be over. Not until the stolen money was found.

She breathed the prayer and kept typing, ignoring the red low-battery warning. Three days ago, she'd been seconds away from alerting the feds of her crazy suspicion that the unemployed college dropout she'd been digging into online was in fact Poindexter himself, when she'd felt what she thought was God prompting her to first download a complete backup copy of every line of code of his she could see. It had been the right move. By the time the feds broke down his door, Dexter's machines had been wiped clean. But if the feds had found anything in the data she'd recovered, she hadn't heard. Already she could see patterns in the data, though. Many sequences were eight or nine numbers long. Maybe phone numbers and social security numbers? If almost fifteen years of computer programing had taught her anything it was that nothing was ever truly random, no matter how it seemed. In the same way, there was always method and order in what God called her to do. At least, that was how she chose to see it and that was the hope she'd clung to when her apartment went up in a ball of flames.

She'd had no idea just how high a price she'd end up paying when Dexter had shot her a single flippant and cocky message on an online forum about Poindexter's crime. She'd almost ignored it. The online world was a minefield filled with the kind of rude men who seemed to like insulting women for kicks. But something about the glowing way he'd referred to Poindexter in his posts made her suspect he was more than just an admirer of his. So, she'd figured out a way to track him down and followed the right lines of code to prove her hunch was right.

Finding him was the easy part. Getting over her own doubts had been harder. After all, she was a nobody—a freelance computer programmer living on her own in a tiny downtown Philadelphia apartment, taking on small projects while she looked for a full-time job and saved up her pennies to one day move out to the country and have a house of her own. The feds had promised her that she could remain anonymous. But even from behind bars, Dexter had other plans. Within hours of his arrest, her identity had been posted online and her entire nest egg had disappeared from her bank account. Two days later her apartment had exploded just as she'd been steps away from walking through the door. Now, less than twenty-four hours after losing everything but the clothes on her back and the contents of her purse, she sat in a Pennsylvania safe house, clinging to her belief that this was somehow still all part of God's plan for her life.

The two US marshals behind her seemed to be fiddling with their walkie-talkies. Not that she could make out much of their actual words, just the clicks of them fiddling with the dials and switching channels, and a low murmur of concerned conversation.

"Is everything okay?" Celeste turned and looked over her shoulder, suddenly feeling very aware of her long blond hair as it brushed against her neck and shoulders. Would they make her cut it? Would they make her wear colored contacts to hide the natural green of her eyes? Would she ever be able to go back to writing computer code? Just how much about her life was going to change?

Stacy and Karl exchanged a glance. The pair had been the ones who'd picked her up from the Philadelphia police station and brought her here. Ginger-haired with a lazy grin, Karl's more laid-back attitude had seemed to balance Stacy's more focused approach, despite the fact the there was an odd tension between them, like cats with static electricity. Right now, both of them were frowning.

"Marshal Mast is running late," Stacy said. She brushed her fingers along her temple and tucked a wisp of chestnut hair back into her tight French braid. "We haven't been able to reach him. But at last check-in, Marshal Cormac, who's patrolling the perimeter, reported that nothing seemed off."

"Jonathan's phone probably died." A professional smile brushed Karl's square-jawed face, and Celeste had the distinct impression he was doing it to be reassuring. "He's technophobic, by the way. So whatever you're working on, you'd better get it done before he gets here, because it's possible he'll make you give up the tablet."

He couldn't. Could he? She'd disabled its internet capability herself, and no one had touched it but her and the feds. It was as harmless as a piece of technology could be. The walkie-talkies crackled again. The marshals went back to talking in hushed whispers. She blocked them out, along with that old familiar nagging headache that always started in her temples before slowly spreading through her shoulders and arms until the very tips of her fingers seemed to ache. If US Marshal Jonathan Mast was technophobic, then she'd just have to outrace him and find where Dexter had hidden the money before he got there.

The battery died. She groaned. Well, that was that.

"You guys mind if I go upstairs and get my charging cable? The battery's dead."

The room went black. Then she heard the distant sound of gunfire erupting outside.

"Get Celeste away from the windows!" Karl shouted. "I'll cover the front."

What was happening? *Lord, help us!* Prayers and panic battled in her heart as she felt Stacy's strong hand on her arm pulling her out of her chair and pushing her toward the hallway.

"Stay low and stay close," Stacy said. "We're going to get you out of here."

"No, wait!" Celeste pulled away. "I need the tablet."

The data had been scrubbed from the internet, and the feds were stumped. Leaving without it would mean giving up any hope of finding the money. Wrenching her arm from the marshal's grasp, she reached up and grabbed the tablet, yanking it from the cord and stuffing it inside her sweatshirt.

"Come on!" Stacy shouted. "We have to hurry—"

Her voice was swallowed up in the sound of an explosion, expanding and roaring around them, shattering the windows, tossing Celeste backward and engulfing the living room in smoke. Celeste hit the floor, rolled and hit a door frame. She crawled through it, trying to get away from the smoke billowing behind her. Her eyes stung. The sound of gunfire grew louder. Stacy yelled something about gunmen in the yard. Karl's voice sounded from the darkness telling Celeste to find cover. Her heart beat so hard in her chest she could barely move.

Dexter had found her. Somehow he'd found her in a witness protection safe house. And now he was going to kill her.

Suddenly a strong hand grabbed her out of the darkness, taking her by the arm and pulling her up to her feet so sharply she stumbled backward into a small room. The door closed behind them. She opened her mouth to scream, but a second hand clamped firmly but not unkindly over her mouth. A flashlight flickered on and she looked up through the smoky haze, past worn blue jeans and a leather jacket, to see the strong lines of a firm jaw trimmed with a black beard, a straight nose and, finally, deep and dark, serious eyes staring into hers.

"Celeste Alexander?" He flashed a badge. "I'm Marshal Jonathan Mast. Stay close. I'll keep you safe."

Huge green eyes looked up at him, framed with long dark lashes and wide with fear. Blond hair fell in thick waves around a heart-shaped face. A sweatshirt and faded jeans fell loose over her slender and unmistakably shapely form. He was thankful to see she was wearing shoes and clothes that she could run in. The panicked breath that brushed hot and fast against his palm began to slow. Something stirred deep inside his chest. This was Celeste Alexander? This was the brilliant computer expert that Dexter Thomes would seemingly stop at nothing to keep from testifying at his trial? Of course Jonathan had seen her picture when he'd read her file and picked up the basics: twenty-six, only child, orphaned in college, freelance computer programmer. But somehow it hadn't prepared him for just how beautiful and vulnerable she'd seem.

Help me protect her, Gott.

A prayer crossed his heart so instinctively it shocked him. He couldn't remember the last time he'd prayed for anyone or anything, let alone using the old Pennsylvania Dutch word for "God" from his Amish childhood faith. He and the God of his childhood had been on strict nonspeaking terms since he'd been eighteen, his mother had died and the pain of losing his *mamm* had made him realize he had to choose between the community he came from and the call to serve and protect as a cop. Somehow it had just welled up inside him, taking both his heart and mind by surprise.

He eased his hand away from Celeste's lips. "Are you all right, Miss Alexander?"

"I'm okay, and please call me Celeste," she said, taking a step back and shaking off his hand. Faint tears glittered in the corners of her eyes, and he suspected she was "okay" mostly because she'd decided to be. "Can I call you Jonathan?"

"Sure thing." He nodded, appreciating her directness.

"How did you even know how to find me?" she asked. "I couldn't see a thing."

"I helped my dad evacuate a major barn fire when I was a child," he said. "People and animals. Guess some of it stuck with me."

He wasn't sure why he'd told her that. His childhood was about as comfortable a conversation as his faith was. He'd loved everything about growing up *plain* except for the fact the *Ordnung* guidelines that ordered society made it clear that being Amish and a cop were incompatible. Not that he expected a city-dwelling computer programmer to feel anything but disdain or amusement at a life without technology. But, judging by the way her shoulders relaxed, it seemed to set her at ease. "Did everyone make it out alive? From the barn fire?"

"Yes, they did." A slight and unexpected grin brushed his lips. "Even the barn cats. And I'm going to get you out of here alive and safely now. When did you get here?"

"Last night." Those compelling eyes grew wider.

He frowned. He disliked informing a subject of too much of an operation, but the walkie-talkies were down and she had information he needed. Hopefully, she was as levelheaded as her file had led him to believe.

"On my way here I got an email from Marshal Karl Adams telling me that there was a change of plans and you weren't arriving until tomorrow," he said. The rise of her brows told him in an instant how right he'd been to suspect something was up. "It told me to turn around and go home. But I decided to proceed. As I got closer, I saw a black SUV parked by the road ahead and no one was answering the walkie-talkie. So I called for backup and hid my vehicle, then cut through the woods and came in through an underground tunnel entrance. How many hostiles have you seen?"

"None," she said. "I just saw the explosion and heard gunfire. I was with Stacy and Karl in the living room and then the windows exploded. There was just so much smoke and gunfire I barely knew which way was up. We need to make sure they're okay. I really don't think Karl sent that email. He seems pretty straight up. They both do. I suspect someone hacked his email and also jammed the walkie-talkies."

She was probably right about Karl. In fact, Karl's casual openness about his Christian faith had the irritating habit of reminding Jonathan how much he missed his own.

"Well, if you can get me to the walkie-talkie jammer, I can disable it so you can be back in communication with your team."

Her chin rose. He blinked. He was here to protect her. She was the one in danger and she was offering to help him?

"Agents Preston and Adams are well trained and dedicated, as are the other marshals on-site," he said. Without a doubt they were all currently risking their lives to find and protect Celeste. "Contacting them and letting them know you're all right will be my top priority, once I've got you to safety. Right now, all that matters is getting you out of here alive. Follow me and I'll take you out the way I came in."

He switched off the flashlight and waited for his eyes to adjust. One of the benefits of growing up *plain* was that he'd always known the darkness as a friend to be embraced and not an enemy to be combatted with a glare of electric lights. Sunrise was less than twenty minutes away. He needed to get her into his truck before then. He eased the door open a crack and listened. Gunfire sounded in intermittent bursts from somewhere else on the property. Smoke seeped down the hall, but he neither felt nor heard flames. It had been a small explosive device, he imagined, just intended to take out the front door and windows, making it easier to breach the building.

He steadied himself to lead her down the hall to freedom, but instead felt the furtive brush of her hand on his arm. "I need to go back to my room. It's upstairs."

"I'm sorry, there isn't time." He didn't turn. "But there's a bag of spare winter clothes hidden in the passage and more necessities in my truck."

"But I need a charger for my tablet—"

"No, you don't. You shouldn't be on the grid at all."

Again Jonathan readied himself to go. This time her hand tightened on his arm.

"I wasn't planning on going 'on the grid.' I need to review some of Dexter Thomes's data while completely off the grid, and until I can get my tablet charged, it's dead."

Something as strong as iron moved through her voice. Even in the dim light he could see the firm jut of her shoulders. He remembered looking at her file and wondered how anyone—let alone a well-meaning citizen—could possibly have the patience and determination to sit at a computer for eighteen hours chasing down a criminal hacker. Now he was beginning to see. "The feds have people chasing the money. All you need to focus on is staying alive long enough to testify."

Gunfire erupted somewhere to their right. He could hear the voices of US marshals shouting. Sounded like hostiles were about to breach the house. Then he heard a familiar voice coming down the hall. He stepped through the door, keeping Celeste safely behind him.

"Karl!" he called, relief filling his chest as his eyes fell on the familiar form. "I have Celeste! I'm taking her out through the underground passage. I've called for backup and I'll get in touch once we're safe."

"Thank You, God," Karl prayed. He said, "You're a sight for sore eyes. We have four hostiles on the perimeter. Stacy is holding down the front door. Communication's down." Gunfire grew louder. Stacy's voice echoed through the darkness, calling for Karl. "Stay safe."

"You, too."

Karl turned and ran toward the front of the house. Jonathan reached for Celeste's hand, enveloped it in his and ran down the hallway. They pushed through a door into a large country kitchen. He closed the door behind them, then glanced down at the woman whose small hand had slid so naturally into his. He dropped her hand, an odd heat rising to his face. Now why had he done that? They started across the kitchen floor toward the cellar. Suddenly the door behind them flew back. A thin man in a dark ski mask burst through with a gun in his grasp. Celeste screamed. The man set her in his sights and fired. But Jonathan had thrown himself between Celeste and the gunman before the bullet could meet its mark. They tumbled to the ground as he heard the bullet strike the wall behind them.

Jonathan rolled up to one knee and returned fire. The gunman fell back behind the door. "Celeste! Get behind the counter and stay low!"

Jonathan gritted his teeth and braced his hand against the wooden floorboards. There was no way to reach the cellar now, not without running straight into the line of fire. Even if they managed to make it, they'd tip the criminal off about where they were going and there'd be nothing to stop him from following. He'd spent the first eighteen years of his life in a huge country kitchen like this one and now he was going to die in one, trying to protect a woman he'd barely met and yet who had already managed to tug at strings he hadn't even known he had. Another bullet flew through the kitchen door, shredding the corner of the countertop and sending wood chips flying. Suddenly he knew their way out.

"Celeste! There's a pantry behind you. Crawl inside and wait for me there."

"Got it!" She started crawling, and he followed, keeping low to the ground. They reached the pantry and slipped inside. He closed the door behind them and pushed a shelf against it.

"Now, stand back," he said. She pressed her back against the wall, whispered words tumbling from her lips. The tension in his heart tightened to realize she was praying, and when he spoke again his voice felt oddly husky in his throat. "Don't worry. Everything's going to be okay. There's more than one way into the cellar."

He holstered his weapon, bent down and felt with his fingers along the floorboards. Then he pulled out his pocketknife and slid the blade between the head of one of the loosest nails and the well-worn wood. Within moments he'd worked it free. He moved on to the next. All he had to do was remove two boards and that should be enough for them to slip through. Voices shouted in the kitchen beyond them. Sounded like the gunman had been joined by a second. He worked the board loose and pried it back. Then he grabbed the one beside it and yanked it off, as well. A hole lay at their feet. It was a crude means of escape and once someone checked the pantry it would be clear where they'd gone, but hopefully it would buy them enough time to get a head start.

"I'm going to jump down now," he said. "It's only about eight feet. When I call you I need you to jump in after me and I'll catch you. Okay? Trust me. I'll keep you safe."

He reached for her again. He felt her fingers slide between his and squeeze. Then he pulled away.

"Ready?" he asked. She nodded. He dropped through the hole and tumbled into darkness.

Chapter Two

Celeste crouched by the hole and waited for Jonathan to give her the all clear. There was a scuffling sound beneath her like something falling. Then there was silence. The kitchen door slammed back on its hinges. Loud footsteps sounded as a second person stormed into the room.

"She ran in here!" It was a male voice, raspy and hoarse.

"And you opened fire?" A second male voice let out a string of swear words. This voice was cold and sharp, like the sound of a knife slicing through wood. "What are you doing? I need her alive!"

Alive. Something about that one simple word and the menace with which it was delivered made her limbs shake. She bent down lower, bracing her quaking hand against the wood, waiting for the sound of Jonathan's words telling her it was safe to jump.

Lord, You've been my light and my guide no matter how rocky things got. Please guide me now.

"Where did she go?" The commanding voice was back.

"I don't know!"

Then came the sharp beam of light swinging back and forth in the dim kitchen, sending sudden bursts of glaring white light shining through the gap between the door and the door frame, blinding her eyes for a moment before swinging around the kitchen again. She peered out through the tiny gap. The man who'd been shooting at them had rolled up his ski mask. Not much, but enough for her to see he was grizzled, probably in his early sixties, with the kind of broken nose that had been punched more than once and a scar down one side of his jaw, breaking up the gray-and-white stubble.

"Well, find her! I'm not paying for nothing!"

Paying? Who was this second man? Why did he need her alive? What did he think he was paying for?

"I'm ready for you! Time to jump." Jonathan's voice floated up through the hole.

She hesitated. She needed to see that man's face. Just for a moment. She needed to know who was giving the instructions and who Dexter Thomes had sent after her.

"Come on!" Jonathan's voice grew firmer. "We've got to go."

She stretched her legs slowly, her hand inching up the door frame as she slowly got to her feet. She could see the man's legs now, clad in jeans and a dark jacket. Shaggy brown hair fell around his shoulders. He wasn't wearing any kind of mask, almost like he wanted his face to be seen.

Just one glance. That was all she needed. Just a little bit more data to complete the picture.

"Celeste!" Jonathan hissed. Urgency strained the marshal's voice. "Hurry up!"

The figure turned. She recoiled, wondering for a moment if he'd somehow managed to hear Jonathan's whisper above the ruckus of gunfire and shouting outside. The man's eyes seemed to lock on her hiding place and suddenly she saw his face, with its shaggy beard, blue-tinted glasses and squinting eyes.

She stumbled backward. No... No, it couldn't be.

He raised a finger, then started toward the cupboard. She took another step back. Her foot slipped and she fell. She bit her lip and barely kept from screaming as air rushed past her.

Then she felt the strength of Jonathan's arms around her breaking her fall. She gasped a prayer of thanksgiving. Darkness filled her gaze. The smell of damp earth and old brick rushed in with each breath. For a moment silence fell, punctuated only by the sound of Jonathan's ragged breath. "Are you all right? What happened?"

No, she wasn't all right and she couldn't begin to make sense of what she'd seen.

"Do you know if they saw where you went or where you were hiding?" he asked. But somehow her mouth couldn't form words. It was like her brain was stuck on just one thought. Dexter Thomes. She'd seen Dexter... Jonathan's hand brushed her elbow and steered her down the tunnel. "We've got to move. Come on."

He marched her down the hallway. Her footsteps faltered beneath her.

It couldn't be Dexter. He'd been arrested—he was behind bars awaiting trial, and if he'd escaped or been released someone would've told her. If he was on the run, would he actually be brazen enough to walk into a witness protection safe house without even covering his face? There was something chilling about the arrogance of a man who'd go by a moniker Poindexter that was so close to his own first name. But all of her research had shown he was an only child. He didn't have a twin...

She opened her mouth, but no words came out, and, instead, a long shiver spread through her body.

"Don't worry, I have a bag of warm clothes and supplies hidden up ahead," Jonathan said.

Her limbs were shaking all right, but it wasn't from the cold. She had to tell him what she'd seen. "Listen, after you jumped through the hole in floor, I heard the gunfire stop and two men talking. I listened to what they were saying and tried to get a look at them—"

"That's not your job," he said. "Your job is staying alive, and when I give you an instruction, I expect you to follow it. Now come on."

"Wait, it's important..."

"Tell me later. When we're out of this tunnel and somewhere safe."

Yes, but if it really was Dexter in the kitchen and he came after them, shouldn't Jonathan arrest him? Shouldn't someone do something?

"Wait, I think it was Dexter!" If he heard her, he gave no indication, and he was propelling her at such a brisk walk that she was almost jogging to keep up with his long stride. "He said he wanted me alive."

"It doesn't matter if Dexter sent him or not." His pace didn't even falter. "All that matters is that I'm going to keep you safe."

She nearly growled. Was he always this pigheadedly focused? She stopped so short he seemed to barely catch himself from tripping over her. "No, listen, I mean, I think it was literally Dexter Thomes. I just saw

Dexter Thomes—Poindexter himself—or a very good lookalike standing in the kitchen, barking orders and talking about taking me alive."

Jonathan felt his mouth open and shut like a trout. He wasn't used to being caught off guard and didn't much like it. He ran a hand over the back of his neck. "That's impossible. Dexter Thomes is in jail. I don't know how you could even tell in the ski mask."

"He wasn't wearing one and the other man pulled his up while they were talking." Even in the dim light he could tell her arms had crossed. "And I'm telling you that either Dexter, or a doppelgänger who looks remarkably a lot like him, is barking orders upstairs."

Right. Well, he didn't know what that meant, but thankfully it didn't sound like anyone was coming down the tunnel after them, at least for now. Had they not checked the cupboard? Had they been distracted by something?

"I know Dexter Thomes better than anyone," she continued. "I did my homework before reporting him to the feds. He's an only child. He doesn't have a sibling or a twin. He shouldn't be out on parole…"

Her words paused as his hand brushed her shoulder. "I hear what you're saying and as soon as we're safe and clear I'm going to call my boss, Chief Deputy Louise Hunter, for an update and I'll tell her what you said."

"I want to tell her myself."

"Fine." He hadn't expected someone who sat behind a computer all day to be quite so driven and tenacious. "Now we need to keep moving."

He pulled a flashlight from his belt and switched it on. His eyes didn't exactly need the light to see and it ran the risk of alerting anyone who was following them, but for now they seemed to be alone. Celeste was clearly rattled, and he had a hunch it would make her more comfortable. He swung the beam over the old red-and-orange brick walls and then tilted it down to illuminate the path ahead of their feet. He started jogging again, fast enough to keep moving but not so fast he couldn't detect any danger ahead. She kept pace.

"You said it didn't matter if he wanted me dead or alive," she said, after a long moment. "But of course it matters. When you're analyzing data you can't ignore anything. Not the fact he wanted me alive. Not the fact one of them looked exactly like Dexter Thomes and the other like a sixty-something criminal enforcer."

Wow, she didn't let up, did she? Her legs might be struggling to keep up with his long strides, but that was nothing compared to what she was doing to his brain. "So, you heard a man who looked like Dexter Thomes tell a violent thug in his sixties that he wanted you alive?"

"Correct."

"And I'm telling you, it doesn't matter what he said."

"How can you say it doesn't matter?"

"Because who's to say he was telling the truth?" His voice rose, and he winced as he heard it echo off the tunnel walls. Thankfully, it seemed they weren't being followed, because if the flashlight hadn't alerted them the sound of their voices would have. "He's a criminal! He might've said he was going to keep you alive and then kill you anyway. You can't predict what a monster like that is going to do."

"Dexter Thomes isn't a monster—he's a man," Celeste argued. "A very smart, evil and cunning man who spent years planning his heist. Everything he does matters. Even the fact that either he didn't check the cupboard to see if I was in there, or he saw the hole and decided not to come down after me." Huh. So she'd noticed that, too. "My life is staring at tiny pieces of code and lines of text, looking for the patterns. That's how I found him and that's how I'm going to find the money he stole. That's who I am. I'm a computer programmer."

Something almost like understanding flickered in the corner of his mind, but he didn't let it take root. A chill brushed his skin. Cold air was seeping in from somewhere. Was the door to the entrance open?

"And I'm a US marshal with the Federal Witness Protection Program," he said. "I place witnesses into new lives and keep them safe. Maybe one day you'll go back to being a computer programmer again, but right now, you're a witness. Now, we need to stop talking, and if anything happens stay behind me."

His footsteps slowed. He needed to figure out where the cold was coming from. Celeste fell into step beside him and he had the unexpected and ridiculous urge to slide his arm around her shoulder. Instead, he switched off his flashlight, keeping one hand on it and the other on his holstered weapon. Their feet moved without making a sound. He'd never minded quiet. In fact, he preferred it over noise. But there was nothing comfortable or peaceful about the bubble of silence that surrounded Celeste. She was on edge and uneasy. It was like her mind was a whirling machine, spinning and turning so quickly her entire body radiated tension. His hand twitched with the desire to brush his fingers reassuringly across her shoulder blades and tell her that she had nothing to worry about, because he was here and he would keep her safe.

Faint and pale light trickled through from the end of the tunnel.

"Stay here," he said. "As close to the wall as you can get. I mean it. Don't move. Don't go anywhere."

"Got it! I'll stay right here with my back against the wall." Her voice was almost defiant, then suddenly her tone dropped and he felt a hand brush his arm. "I'm sorry about what happened earlier. I didn't mean to make your job any harder that it already is."

He swallowed. "It's okay. It can't be easy to go from being a folk hero to thousands of people to taking orders from someone like me. Now, wait here. I'll be back in a second."

He pulled away from her and walked slowly and carefully down to the end of the tunnel. Something lay across the doorway. His heart stopped.

It was the body of a US marshal.

Chapter Three

"Stand back!" Jonathan's voice echoed down the tunnel ahead of her. Celeste's heart pounded hard in her chest as she heard the worry moving through his deep voice.

Dear Lord, was I wrong to stay up above in the kitchen and listen? Did I really see who I thought I saw? What can I do? How can I help? I feel so helpless.

She'd felt almost fearless days ago when she was sitting in her living room, alone with her laptop searching for Poindexter. She'd never expected to be able to find him. Not really. She'd just started pulling one thread that led to another thread and then another, until they reached deeper and deeper into Poindexter's online web to the man in the center of it all. But no, she hadn't felt like a hero. She hadn't even figured out where he'd hid the money. Besides, all she'd been doing was using her talent to the best of her ability and counting on God to guide her.

"What's going on?" she called.

At first there was no sound except the beat of her own heart. Then she heard a deep, long sigh moving through the darkness.

"Hang on one second," Jonathan said. "There's a body here. It's another marshal by the look of it. I need a moment to check it out and also do a visual sweep for any hostiles. I need you to stay there and don't move until I give you the all clear. Please confirm that you've heard me."

"I've heard you," she said. She pressed her back against the wall, feeling the cold of the bricks seep into her limbs. She wasn't cut out for this. She didn't hide in dark tunnels. In fact, she rarely even left her little rented apartment in the city, not that she didn't love the thought of country living. In fact, thanks to the internet she'd been able to shop for handmade clothes and blankets from self-employed seamstresses, handmade soaps from home-based artisans and order everything imaginable—from fresh vegetables grown on farms outside the city to homemade soups to cheeses, breads and even pies. Before someone working for Dexter had emptied her bank account and wrecked her credit, she'd been saving up for years to buy an actual house of her own, somewhere outside the city, where grass and trees would fill her view from the window beside her desk instead of buildings and buses. She'd lost all of that; she was trapped. She pressed her hands to her eyes to keep sudden tears at bay.

Lord, I know I should trust You have a plan in all this. I've trusted You to guide me this far. I need to believe You won't abandon me now.

Then she heard Jonathan's voice again, deep, comforting and as solid as steel.

"Celeste? A US marshal has been shot and killed. His name was Rod Cormac. He was a good man. My guess is he was shot at a distance and tried to make it to the safe house to warn the rest of the team before he died. He didn't look like he was followed. Now I need you to come to me, nice and slow."

She took a step forward and saw them. Jonathan was crouched down on the ground beside the body of a man, lit by the soft gray light of the approaching dawn. The man's hair was blond and his limbs were curled up like he'd just lain down to have a nap in the snow. Her body froze. She couldn't move. She couldn't do this. She wasn't cut out for any of it.

"Look at me, Celeste," Jonathan said firmly. "Don't look at him. Look at me."

His voice was a soft-spoken command, snapping her eyes back to his face, and if she was honest with herself, there was something almost kind of comforting about it. He held her gaze every bit as firmly as if it was her hand inside his. "It's going to be okay, and I will keep you safe. Just trust me and do what I say. Okay?"

She nodded. He broke her gaze and reached for something in the shadows by the wall. It was a large black bag. He pulled out a gray wool blanket and laid it carefully over the body. Then he knelt for one long moment beside the fallen marshal. Jonathan's head bowed, his eyes closed and his lips moved in what she could only guess was silent prayer. A shudder moved through his limbs. Then he stood and wiped his hand over his eyes.

He pulled out a thick coat and tossed it to her as he stood. "Put this on. There should be gloves and a hat in the pockets. We'll find you winter boots as soon as we can. We need to hurry. It's only a matter of time before someone finds the blood trail and follows him here."

Celeste looked down at the coat in her hands but somehow couldn't get her arms to move. Then her gaze rose to the snow-covered trees beyond the doorway. What if the person who'd shot Rod was still out there? What if they got shot the moment they stepped through the door? A man she'd never met was dead. And why? Because she'd hacked some lines of computer code and was going to be a witness at the criminal's trial? Right now, Stacy, Karl and several other marshals were fighting for their lives because of her. Someone had already died because of her, and there was no way of knowing how many more would before this was all done. The horror of that welled up inside her.

Jonathan stepped forward, gently took the coat from her hands and held it out for her to slide her arms into. Her eyes met his for one long moment, and her breath caught to see the depth of sorrow echoed there.

"What was he like?" she asked. She let him ease her hands into the sleeves.

"Rod was a good marshal and a good man." Something in the tone of his voice made her think this wasn't the first colleague he'd lost in the line of duty. "He had a wacky sense of humor. I liked working with him."

She felt him slide the coat up over her shoulders. She didn't know why she was so frozen or why her body didn't want to move, only that asking questions somehow helped. "Did he have a family?"

"He had a very large black dog and a very nice long-term girlfriend who he never tied the knot with because this line of work involves a lot of travel and doesn't lend itself to relationships."

He nudged her shoulder. She looked up into his face.

"How exactly did he die? Don't just say he was shot. I want to understand."

"He was shot twice in the abdomen," Jonathan said.

His tone was steady and without a hint of uncertainty. There was something comforting about it. "He lost a lot of blood and passed out."

She bit her lip. "Did he suffer?"

He paused, then reached down and slowly helped her do her zipper up.

"I won't lie. He would've been in a lot of pain. But he also used his dying breath and the last ounce of energy he had to get here. My guess is that he was trying to warn us about what was happening and tell us there were hostiles on the property. When backup arrives they'll retrieve the body and notify his family. He died a hero's death and will get a hero's funeral. Now we have to move. Come on."

Still, she was hesitating. She needed more answers.

"I don't understand why the person in the kitchen looked like Dexter—if he's really in jail," she said. "Or why he wants me alive. Or why the walkie-talkies were down or how anyone could find a WITSEC safe house. I don't even know if Karl and Stacy and all the other US marshals protecting me are going to be okay. What if there are more shooters in those trees? What if they shoot at us? What if they kill you and take me?"

Her voice rose to a wail, and as much as she hated it she didn't know how to get control of it again. Her hands began to shake, a harsh uncontrollable quivering that moved up her arms and into her body.

"Celeste!" Jonathan's voice grew urgent. "Focus. Look at me. You're in shock. It's totally understandable, but you've got to fight through it. Now I don't know how computers work. I've never opened one up and looked inside, and you could definitely say I didn't exactly grow up in a technologically advanced house.

But I'm guessing that in computer code every character or number has a purpose, right? Every part has its own thing it's doing? Right?"

She blinked and a smile crossed her face, which was so unexpected it shocked her. What an odd way to explain it. He wasn't right, but kind of close. "Something like that."

"Okay," he said. "Well, each of us has a job to do. Rod's was to watch the perimeter. Karl and Stacy's job is to hold down the fort and give us a chance to get out of here." He took another step toward her. His hands rested on her shoulders. "Your job is to testify against the man who's ultimately responsible for Rod's death and make sure he faces justice for stealing all those people's money. And my job is to keep you safe until you do."

He stood there a moment with his hands on her shoulders, and something inside her wanted to step closer, to lean into his chest and let his strong arms envelop her, in a way no man had since her father had died. Even though she barely knew Jonathan Mast, and he didn't seem like the type who was into hugs. She closed her eyes and felt her lips move in silent prayer. The she opened her eyes, swallowed hard and stepped back. "Okay, I'm ready to go."

She grabbed a pair of leather gloves from the pocket of her coat and pulled them on. He did the same from his. He reached for her hand. She took it and he quickly yet carefully led her around the body and out into the cold predawn air. They ran, pressing through the thick trees as their feet pounded down the snow. The ground sloped beneath their feet. Gunfire echoed in the distance. The sun was starting to rise as the faintest pink sliver of light along the gray horizon. The trees parted and she saw the road.

Jonathan dropped her hand and led her along the tree line to where a large and tough-looking truck lay hidden in the trees by a camouflage cover. "Stand way back. I need a minute to uncover the truck, do a quick sweep to make sure no one tampered with it, and get it back on the road. Then we're good to go."

She crossed over to the other side of the road and waited as he started the engine and slowly pulled the truck back onto the road. A small battered-looking car flew down the road to her left and fishtailed to a stop. A tall heavyset young man behind the wheel held a cell phone.

"Hey! I think we've found her! Start recording!" a shorter and stockier young man called, leaping out of the passenger side. Celeste turned and ran, sprinting in the direction of Jonathan's truck. A blast sounded in the air behind her. She stopped and turned back. The young man's shoulders rolled back in a swagger as he pointed a handgun sideways at her. "Yo, you're Celeste, right? Celeste Alexander? You're that hacker chick that Poindexter's got a bounty out on? I'm Miller. That there with the phone recording, this is my buddy, Lee. Get in the car now! Or I'll kill ya!"

Jonathan shifted into Drive and was about to punch the engine when one word he'd heard the thugs shout a split second earlier finally caught up with his brain. *Recording.* The brazen thugs now pointing a gun at Celeste weren't just announcing their crime like a bad online video—they were recording it, too. Just like whoever Celeste had seen in the kitchen they weren't wearing ski masks. No, these two wanted to be both seen and known.

Thankfully, Jonathan was wearing civilian clothing. He shoved a hat down hard over his head and wrapped a scarf around his face. Then he gunned the engine. The truck shot out of the woods and straight across the road, swerving to a stop behind Celeste so that the driver's side door was directly behind her.

She spun back, her eyes wide. Her hand rose to her lips.

The gun-wielding showman jumped back in shock with a shout that turned into a nervous laugh. "Whoa! Lee, you getting this? Make sure you're getting this!"

Jonathan unholstered his weapon. Disgust whelmed up inside him. These criminals were threatening Celeste at gunpoint and treating it as some kind of game, when a good man had just died protecting her. He leaped from the truck and raised his gun high with both hands. "Celeste! Get behind me!"

She ran for him, darting behind him so quickly she nearly slid and fell. Miller turned back.

"Who are you?" Miller shouted. Jonathan didn't answer. No, he wasn't about to announce who he was and flash his badge on camera until he found out what exactly they were caught up in. For now, being undercover suited him just fine. Miller jabbed the air with the barrel of his gun. "Look, I don't want trouble. I just want the hacker girl. Let me take her and go."

His voice shook. There was a whole lot of nervousness hiding behind the bravado, and desperation, too. Not that it made anyone safer. A determined and reckless amateur was every bit as dangerous as a professional.

"That's not going to happen," Jonathan shouted. "Put the gun down."

Miller waited a long moment, eyeing him as if weighing invisible options. Jonathan stared him down and didn't blink. The US marshal had no doubt what would happen if it came to a shoot-out, but still he was going to do anything in his power to stop it from happening. He could still remember vividly what it was like to fire a gun for the first time. For a young man coming from an Amish background, there'd been something so foreign about it. Now, as his eyesight narrowed, his shoulders relaxed and his fingers prepared to fire, it was as comfortable as if the weapon was an extension of him. He just prayed that today wouldn't be the first day he took a life in the line of duty.

"Whatever, man!" Miller threw his hands up like an exaggerated shrug. "You win this round. I don't care. I'm just in it for the money, and Lee here's just got us probably a grand's worth of footage. Poindexter's got everyone with dark web access and the willingness to step up and make a few bucks out looking for her. So, you can take her now, but someone else is going to take her back from you later. That's just how the game's played."

"What game?" Celeste's voice came from behind Jonathan. "Tell me! How did you know where I was? Why does Poindexter want me taken alive?"

Miller didn't answer. Instead, he turned back toward the car, gun still dangling from his fingers as he had a quick word with Lee outside of Jonathan's earshot.

"Get in the truck," Jonathan said without turning. "Keep your head low. The keys are in the ignition. If bullets start flying, gun the engine and don't stop driving until you reach a police station."

Please, Celeste, don't argue with me. He heard the scuffle of her footsteps on the snow and the slam of the door closing. *Thank You*, Gott!

Miller nodded to Lee. Then he swung back. The gun rose in his hands. His finger flicked over the trigger. Jonathan dropped to one knee and fired, hearing Miller's bullet fly past him into the trees a millisecond before his own bullet ripped through the arm now pointing a gun at him. Miller dropped the gun, grabbing his arm and collapsing to the ground as a scream flew from his lips. Lee turned his camera phone toward his writhing partner.

Jonathan bounded into the driver's side as Celeste moved over to the passenger side to make room for him. He holstered his weapon, shut the door and slammed his seat belt on in one seamless move.

"Fasten your seat belt and hang on tight!" He glanced at Celeste. "It's going to get rough."

Chapter Four

He heard her seat belt click. Jonathan's truck surged backward, coming within a foot of hitting Miller before swerving sharply off the road to get around the criminals' car. For a split second the entire scene played out before him in a glance. A howling and angry young man was down on the ground beside the car. Another bullet ripped from his gun that once again failed to meet its mark. The second young man bounded from the car and ran toward Miller, filming the scene with his phone as he did, and somehow Jonathan's eyes managed to meet his and hold them for a split second. They were devoid of emotion. This wasn't personal. It was just a payday for whatever criminal found her first. How was he supposed to protect Celeste against that?

Then he threw the truck into Drive.

"Hold on!" he shouted. "We're about to spin!"

He hit the gas and yanked the steering wheel hard to the right. The truck spun. Its wheels skimmed over the ice. He waited until the final moment, and tapped the breaks and yanked the wheel back. The truck righted. They sped forward, down the road as trees and the early-dawn sky flew past them in a blur of white, pale purples and grays. Gunshots faded in the distance. The sun crept over the edge of the horizon. He pulled off the scarf and hat, then glanced at Celeste. "Are you okay?"

Her smile was weak, but she seemed to be giving it her best shot. "That was some driving. Guessing you must've been tearing up the streets when you were a teenager."

He shifted his gaze to the windshield ahead. The road spread ahead of him in an endless line of white. "Actually, I didn't get my license until I was twenty."

Before then it had just been horses driving the family buggy. It was funny. As a teenager, he couldn't wait to get behind the wheel of a car and drive. But when he had, he'd been surprised how impersonal it felt. It didn't listen or respond. It was just a machine, like any other.

"Speaking of vehicles, our first stop is going to be switching this truck out for another one," he said. "I do use the other truck when I can because it drives better. But the fact Lee was recording all that makes it more important that we do. Then it's about a five-hour drive to the new safe house, which, as I believe you know, is set in an apartment complex in the suburb of Pittsburgh. We'll stop for breakfast in about an hour, but there are some granola bars, apples and bottles of water in the cooler behind your seat. I've got to call my supervisor and let her know where we're at."

He reached for his earpiece, clipped it to his ear and turned on his phone. Celeste's fingers brushed his arm.

"Wait, aren't we first going to talk about what happened?" she asked.

He sat back. "I don't know what went wrong, how those criminals found you or what they're really after.

Clearly, someone's out to get you and trolling to rope in any criminal element they can find, from people with tactical weapons and smoke bombs, to idiots with cell phones. Hopefully, talking to my supervisor will help."

He dialed the number.

"Louise Hunter." His supervisor's voice came on the line, crisp and clear. He had no idea how old Chief Deputy Hunter was, but both the streaks of gray in her jet-black hair and the stories she told led him to believe she was probably hovering somewhere on either side of sixty. She was the kind of woman who'd been married to the same man for forty years, had fourteen grandchildren and a career that spanned countless escaped convicts, national manhunts and hundreds of lives saved.

Jonathan gave her a heads-up that Celeste was sitting beside him in the truck and then filled her in on Rod Cormac's death and the ambush at the safe house. As much as he hated briefing his boss in front of the person he was assigned to protect, time was of the essence and there weren't that many options. Then she confirmed what he'd feared—this was the first update she'd received about the situation at the safe house since he himself had called for backup before going to find Celeste. Communications were still down at the farm. He could only hope Stacy and Karl were okay.

"Rod was a dedicated marshal," Hunter said. "He'll be deeply missed." There was a pause, long enough to let him know she felt the sudden loss every bit as hard as he did. "Unfortunately, we haven't been able to confirm anything about the situation or the safety of the other marshals on-site. But we have a team currently moving into formation. I will make sure you are updated as soon as we have more information. How is Miss Alexander doing?"

Jonathan glanced over at Celeste. Her head was turned away from him. The morning rays caught her golden hair.

"Miss Alexander is safe and well. She was thankfully unharmed and has come through her ordeal with remarkable resilience," he said. Was *remarkable* too strong a word? Perhaps. But it was true. "She'd like to speak to you personally about the man she saw in the safe house. She said he looked like Dexter Thomes."

"I'd like to speak to her, as well," said Hunter.

He reached to turn off his earpiece, then paused. "Are we certain that Dexter Thomes is still behind bars?"

"Last I heard," she said. "But I will be confirming that immediately."

"Thank you." He kept one hand on the steering wheel. With the other he switched off the earpiece and then he held out the phone toward his passenger. "Celeste, my supervisor, Chief Deputy Louise Hunter, would like to speak to you. I've switched off my earpiece, so her voice should come through the phone's speaker now. But if not, I'm sure you know how to change that in the settings."

"Thank you." Her fingers brushed his, just briefly, as he handed her the phone and he felt something like electricity rush through him.

What was it about this woman that had this strange impact on him? Her file had been thin. Her parents had died when she'd been just nineteen, and had no siblings and no significant romantic entanglements. She'd taught herself programming in elementary school and won several computer, electronic and robotic awards in high school and university. She'd started getting a master's degree but had to drop out for financial reasons and had made her own way as a self-employed computer programmer after having been turned down for way too many tech jobs that she was clearly overqualified for.

Brilliant and attractive, not to mention tenacious, it was no wonder he was attracted to her. He could rationalize that much at least. But, even if circumstances had been different, she deserved better than a man like him who, when faced with a choice between the career he felt called to and his own family and Amish heritage, had walked away and chosen work because the call on his heart to serve his country had been too loud for him to ignore.

Yes, he'd been eighteen, Mamm had just died, his older *bruder* and only sibling had told him he had to make a choice, and his *pa* had never been someone he'd felt like he could talk to. But it had been his choice and one he could never undo. He shuddered to think what a woman who had no family would ever think of a man who'd walked away from his.

He took a deep breath, pushed aside the unwanted thoughts and listened as she talked to Hunter. Truth was, he wasn't sure what to expect. After all, she'd been pretty stubborn back at the safe house and dug her heels in pretty hard. To his surprise she was crisp, polite and thorough, going through exactly what she'd heard and seen without any embellishments or exaggerations.

"The man I saw looked exactly like Dexter Thomes," she told Hunter, "even though my vantage point was obscured by smoke and low light. Clearly, if Dexter is still in prison, he must be a doppelgänger, but the similarity was uncanny. I researched everything I could find about Dexter Thomes before I contacted the feds and told them my suspicions he was Poindexter. His mother is deceased, his father is not listed on his birth certificate and he has no known siblings. If he had a secret twin I should've uncovered it."

The women exchanged a few more words, and he noticed Celeste made a point of asking his boss to please let them know when the safe house had been secured and if the other marshals were all right. Then she handed the phone to Jonathan. He switched his earpiece back on.

"I'd like you to take her to the central Pennsylvania safe house outside of Altoona for one night," Hunter said, "while we do another sweep of the Pittsburgh apartment and also confirm that Dexter Thomes is really still behind bars. Barring any unforeseen difficulties, she can move into the Pittsburgh apartment tomorrow."

"Understood," he nodded, feeling the lines of a frown wrinkle his forehead. The plan would add extra travel time and delay the start of her new identity and life. Not to mention the diversion would take them right through Amish country and painfully close to the family farm he'd left behind. He thanked his boss and they ended the call.

"Everything okay?" Celeste asked.

"I hope so," he said. "She'll keep us posted. We're going to take a brief detour to another safe house for one night and then head on to your new apartment in Pittsburgh tomorrow." He paused. Worry hovered in the depths of her eyes. "I have faith that Stacy and Karl will be okay. They're very good agents. They know what they're doing. And don't worry. We'll be at the temporary safe house later today, and if all goes well you'll be in your new life tomorrow."

They lapsed into silence as the truck drove through the winter morning. The sun rose higher. They passed farms with rolling fields and empty roadside wooden fruit and vegetable stands that reminded him of those his mother had expected him and his brother, Amos, to help out with during the summer.

"Did you grow up in the city or the country?" Celeste asked after a pause so long he wondered if she'd fallen asleep.

He guessed she was trying to change the subject away from Dexter, the fallen marshal and what had happened at the farmhouse. He was thankful for it. He pressed his lips together for a long moment and debated how to answer. He didn't talk about his past for a very good reason. Most people knew nothing about the Amish, and the last thing he wanted was to listen to someone else's uninformed opinion about the world he'd grown up in or answer questions about why he'd left. But maybe Celeste wasn't like most people. "The country."

"I always wanted to live in the country," she said. "I don't know why, but even though I'm a born-and-bred city girl, I always felt like something—God, maybe—was calling me to live in the country. When I was little, my parents used to rent this summer house, surrounded by nothing but trees and fields. I loved it. Then my parents both got cancer and we couldn't afford it anymore. There were a lot of medical bills. I always told myself that one day I'd save enough to buy my own place outside the city, but Dexter Thomes took all that." She looked up at him. "You know he stole all my money, too, after I turned him in? Took out multiple loans in my name, stole my identity and utterly destroyed my credit."

He didn't know what to say. "I'm sorry."

"At least I knew the risk I was taking. I chose to hunt him down and tell the feds what I found. I put myself in his crosshairs. All the other people who had their life savings, college funds and retirement nest eggs stolen didn't do anything. They just woke up one day to find their lives ruined. I just wish I'd found where he hid the money." Her hands clenched into tight fists on her lap. "Not to mention it looks like he's now using his stolen money to pay criminals to come after me."

Instinctively, his hand reached out and brushed her arm. Her muscles were so tense she might as well have been carved from stone. "Don't worry. I'll keep you safe no matter how many criminals he throws at you."

Something fierce flashed in the depths of her eyes. "And who's going to stop the next Rod Cormac from dying? Or get those people their money back?"

He didn't have an answer to that. Then again, he wasn't sure she was expecting one. After a while, he saw her eyes close and her lips move in silent prayer. He found prayer filing his own core, too.

God, I don't reckon You and I are on speaking terms. But, please be with Rod's family and friends right now. Comfort them in their sadness. Please, may no one else die because of Dexter and his crimes. And be there for Celeste, too. Help me keep her safe, protect her from anyone who would want to hurt her and make her dreams for the future still come true.

He'd seen the size of the new apartment he'd be moving her into tomorrow, and it was a long way away from a house in the country. He could still remember the day he'd stopped believing that God called anyone to anything. He'd been eight and had excitedly told his brother, Amos, who was then seventeen, that God had called him to be a cop. And Amos had told him that it wasn't God—it was his own stubborn willfulness, because he couldn't be both a cop and Amish.

He turned off the small rural highway onto a larger one. After a while, a large, expansive truck stop came into view. It was teeming with vehicles and several big chain restaurants. He pulled to a stop in a row in the back beside the big blue pickup. He cut the engine. "Now we grab our stuff, switch vehicles and get back on the road."

They hopped out of the black truck and into the blue one, after he'd done a complete sweep of the vehicle for tracking devices or anything so much as a speck of dust out of place. Thankfully, it was clean. A moment later they were weaving their way back through the crowded parking lot.

The smell of doughnuts and coffee wafted toward them. Normally he'd have taken her in to grab a quick bite before hitting the road again. It was easy to be anonymous in a crowd, and there was no way any criminal organization could have eyes on every single rest stop of the highway, even if they happened to either figure out or guess what direction they were headed. After all, WITSEC expected their marshals to spend just a couple of weeks with witnesses helping them integrate safely into a community and letting them know where to reach help before leaving them to live their new lives. Starting over safely was the goal—not spending the rest of their lives hiding behind a closed door.

Still, something about this particular case and this particular witness gave him pause. If Dexter Thomes had been able to find a WITSEC safe house, was it possible he'd be able to find her in Pittsburgh? It wasn't like hunkering down behind her computer screen and cutting off all contact with the outside world was going to be an option for Celeste. Hunter had been very clear the plan to ensure her safety involved keeping her off-line. Yes, they'd stop for food, and he'd use that opportunity to introduce her to the idea of watching her own back when he wasn't going to be there. His gut told him to find somewhere much smaller and more remote. Fortunately, he knew just the place.

Suddenly her fingers grabbed his arm and squeezed so tightly he almost winced.

"We need to go—now." She pointed with the other hand out the window at what looked like a remote-controlled helicopter hovering behind them. "Because I think we're being watched by that drone."

Chapter Five

The small skeletal machine hovered around the parking lot like a wasp looking for a place to land. She couldn't spot the person who was controlling it.

"It just looks like a toy." Jonathan shrugged.

The small device flew until it was almost parallel to the back window. It was only then she realized her fingers were still latched onto his bicep. She let go and pulled her hand back. "It might be a hobby drone, but that doesn't change the fact people can use them to take video and pictures."

"You think that toy helicopter is spying on us?" he asked. "Trust me, we weren't followed and nobody knows we're here." Well, when he said it like that she sounded ridiculous. But he didn't understand technology the way she did. "Don't worry, we'll be back on the highway in half a second, and if it follows us, I'll shoot it out of the sky."

Was he joking or trying to reassure her? Maybe both. His voice was so dry she couldn't tell. Moments later they were flying down the highway again. The drone didn't follow.

"Should we be worried that we haven't heard from anyone on your team yet?" Celeste asked.

"Not necessarily," he said. "We're talking about securing a sprawling location with multiple hostiles and possibly multiple casualties. It will take time. Hunter will want to get all her facts straight before she calls, including confirming Dexter Thomes is still safely tucked away behind bars. Not that I think it's remotely possible he could've broken out of prison without us knowing."

"So you're convinced we're dealing with a Doppelgänger-Dex?" she asked.

He chuckled. "Doppelgänger-Dex is what we're calling him now?"

"Unless you can think of a better name," she said. "Though maybe Doppel-Dex for short."

He laughed again. It was a comforting sound that rumbled from somewhere in the back of his throat. "Well, when the safe house is secured and someone on the team gets in touch, hopefully, they'll confirm that the real Dexter is still in jail, the man you saw will have been apprehended and we'll know who he is."

"Hopefully." She leaned back against the seat. Her eyes closed. Jonathan Mast seemed to be a good man, and she had to admit there was something about him that made her feel safer than she'd ever imagined being able to feel under the circumstances. But between Doppel-Dex and the hobby drone, it seemed that the US marshal assigned to protect her probably thought she was crazy or at least seeing things.

The tablet full of data she'd gleaned from Dexter's website sat like a dead weight in her pocket. Were there answers on it? Something that would tell her where the stolen money had gone? If so, she had no idea when or how she'd ever be able to access it.

She hadn't been online or even been able to check her phone in almost three days and it irked her, like she'd lost a part of herself. She couldn't remember the last time she'd gone this long without scrolling through the news or logging into chat groups. She stared out at the endless countryside streaming past her window. All the plants and animals living on her virtual farm would probably be long dead before she could ever log back into it.

Yes, she'd chased down a criminal online and didn't regret it; however, she'd never imagined the cost would be getting cut off from technology and losing her ability to still do her job. And then there was her money being stolen, and the explosion in the apartment where she'd grown up with her parents, taking with it a lifetime of memories. She'd been left with nothing but borrowed clothes, a tablet full of data that she couldn't read and the protection of the man sitting beside her.

She cast a sideways glance at him. There was something about him that she just couldn't put a finger on. It was like some invisible piece of coding had created a glitch in the circuits in her brain. Or a kind of connection that drew her in and made her want to find out more, while also feeling the irksome urge to prove herself to him and to make sure he knew she wasn't just someone in need of rescuing. She couldn't begin to identify it or figure out the source code. Maybe it was because her entire life was in his hands. It couldn't just be how good-looking he was. She'd never thought herself shallow about people's looks. Although he was definitely handsome.

There was a strength to his body and form that made her think he should be tossing heavy bales of hay into a wagon or a barn, or herding cattle. Yet, whenever his hickory-brown eyes had fallen on her face, there was something protective and hardened in their depths that was all cop. Or if not a cop, then some other profession like a soldier, firefighter or paramedic, who ran into chaos and put their life at risk to rescue others. There was something sad about him, too, and a severity to the lines of his jaw that made her suspect he didn't smile enough and was in need of a good home-cooked meal.

His hair was properly black, not one of those shades of dark brown that people sometimes mistook it for. It curled slightly, down at the nape of his neck and on top, and she suspected that if he ever let it grow out it would turn into a full head of curls. His trim black beard swept down the strong lines of his jaw and under his chin, like an artist had defined them with charcoal. The eyes that scanned the snowy vista outside were dark and rich brown with black rings around the iris. If someone had ever asked her what she thought of brown, she'd have said she figured it was the least interesting color there was. But not this shade. Not his eyes. No, these eyes seemed to contain a depth that made her think of rich, dark earth.

His gaze snapped to her face as if realizing she was analyzing him. One eyebrow rose. "Everything all right?"

A flush of heat rose to her face. She'd always been awkward and never exactly good at small talk, which was probably why she'd never had so much as a successful date with a man, let alone an actual relationship.

"Sorry," she said. "I was just thinking that you know a lot about me and I know practically nothing about you."

He waited a very long moment, then asked, "What do you want to know?"

She bit her lip. What did she want to know?

"How long have you known you wanted to be in law enforcement?"

There was another even pause. A look moved across his gaze that was somehow deeper than sadness or even regret. Then when he spoke, she wasn't quite prepared for what came out of his mouth.

"Was I right in thinking you were praying back at the farmhouse?" he asked. She nodded. He turned away from her and stared straight ahead through the windshield, with one hand on the wheel and the other lying in the space between them. "Then I'm guessing you're familiar with the biblical stories about David and Jonathan. That's who I was named after, Prince Jonathan, son of King Saul. I couldn't get enough of those Old Testament battle stories as a child. There was nothing I wanted more than to be one of those heroes of old, the kind with a shield and sword, who worked together with others to save my country and the people in it from evil and tyranny."

A grin crossed his lips. It was unexpected, cute and infectious, and it somehow softened his face. She liked it. Then the smile faded again. He shifted his hand on the steering wheel.

"I didn't see my first cop until I was eight. My parents had me late in life and mother always had health and mobility issues, with her joints mostly. She had early onset of arthritis and some kind of nerve damage when she'd given birth to me. Her mind was really sharp, though, and she had the best sense of humor. Anyway, the summer when I was eight I was in town with my seventeen-year-old brother and my mom, and these tourists started bullying us. They yelled at us mostly, but also threw some trash and pushed my brother around a bit." He swallowed hard. "My mom fell."

She reached for his hand without even thinking and squeezed it. He squeezed her back for one long moment. Then he pulled his hand away.

"Then this man and woman in blue uniforms showed up and told them to leave us alone," he continued. "I knew then that's what I wanted to be. Then when I was twenty and studying criminology I realized that what I really wanted to be was a US marshal. Specifically I wanted to work in the protection side of law enforcement, as opposed to the detection side. I wanted to help catch fugitives. I wanted to transport prisoners. I wanted to protect endangered witnesses. I wanted to be out there, like Prince Jonathan from the Bible, with my shining shield and sword literally and physically protecting people every day. I wanted to protect people and keep them safe." A glimmer of a smile brushed his lips again. "Plus, I still really want to go out and fight the Philistines."

A laugh slipped from her lips, taking her by surprise. Her fingers rose to her lips as she felt her smile spread into her cheeks, and as his eyes turned to her face there was something new there, a glimmer of something that again she couldn't define. All she knew was that she'd never seen it before. For a long moment neither of them said anything.

"Are the stories of David and Jonathan still your favorite part of the Bible?" she asked. "I've always loved the Psalms, Proverbs and Ecclesiastes."

"My father loves those, too. It's funny. You almost talk like him." Just like that the smile fell from his face and his hands snapped back to two and ten on the steering wheel. "I haven't picked up a Bible in years."

There was a tone to his voice that made her think of a book slamming shut or a door being locked. US Marshal Jonathan Mast was done sharing. Silence filled the car again. The longer it drew out, the colder and thinner the air felt and the more her chest ached.

Lord, I don't know why he opened up to me like that or what the pain is in his heart that pushed him away from You. But if there's anything I can do to help him, anything You want me to say, please let me know.

The truck slowed and it took her a moment to realize why. There was a horse-drawn buggy on the road ahead. A young man in a large brimmed hat held the reins. Jonathan gave him a wide berth, nodding to him as he passed.

"He's Amish, right?" Celeste asked.

Jonathan's gaze stayed fixed on the road ahead. "Yes, most of these farms are."

She glanced out the window, looking anew at the large beautiful farms with barns and silos. "I haven't driven through the Amish countryside since I was a child. I always assumed my memories were larger than life. But it's every bit as beautiful as I remember."

"You should see it in late summertime," he said, "when the fields are full of flowers and the crops are almost ready to be harvested. There's no place more beautiful on earth."

She blinked. Had he really just said that? See, that was why he confused her. He could be so open and real one moment, and then shut off and closed the next.

Another buggy loomed ahead of them on her side of the truck. This one had a couple in the front, her large black bonnet tilted toward his bearded face as if whispering a secret in his ear. Six little heads, in hats and bonnets, bounced up and down in the back.

"It's funny," she said. "When we used to drive through the Amish country as a kid, all I wanted was to get out of the car and ride in a buggy. Now, I just wonder how they do it."

"You mean, how does a family take their kids out in a buggy in January?" he asked. "With a whole lot of blankets and warm clothing. What kid would want to be stuck sitting in the back of a car with seat belts on when they could be outside with the horses, and their cousins, brothers and sisters piled around them?"

She laughed. Yes, when he put it like that it definitely sounded better than being in a car. "No, I meant I can't imagine how people live entirely off the grid. No car, cell phone, internet or electricity."

"It's peaceful," he said. His voice dropped. "It's not right for everyone, but I have a feeling you're the kind of person who'd like it. Well, if you weren't a computer programmer."

She had the odd sense that he'd given her a bigger compliment than she'd realized. They lapsed back into silence after that, but somehow it was a more comfortable space than before. It reminded her of the kind of comforting quiet that surrounded her when she curled up with a good book or spent hours happily typing lines of code. Something about the faint glimmer of a smile on his face led her to believe he understood those kinds of silences, too. She wondered if he'd ever had anyone to share them with.

He turned onto a smaller rural road, passed a smattering of stores and then she saw the wooden sign for a diner ahead. He pulled in. It was a low and long building, with a spacious parking lot and a smattering of picnic tables. He parked in a wide open spot near the front of the lot.

"Hope you're hungry," he said. "The food here is great and the owners are really friendly."

"I'm guessing this place is part of some kind of witness protection network?" Celeste asked. "Cops on the door? Security measures?"

"Nope." He cut the engine.

"But Dexter Thomes has goons out to kill me! I can't just waltz into a diner and order scrambled eggs like a regular person."

"You can, and sooner or later, you're going to have to." He undid his seat belt and turned to face her on the seat. "Yes, we're taking a risk—a calculated one. Witness protection isn't about locking people away in a secure facility with guards on the door, and my job isn't just to watch your back 24/7. Not after the initial stage. Part of the purpose of witness protection is to equip you to live a fairly normal life and still keep yourself safe. There are people in witness protection who haven't actually seen an agent in months or even years, and just check in by phone regularly. After the initial transition and adjustment phase you're going to find you don't want to hide in your apartment with the door locked and the blinds down. Over time, you'll learn how to make friends, go shopping and live a fairly normal life. Starting with eggs."

Her head shook. "What do you mean some people spend months or years in witness protection without seeing a marshal? The trial is just a few months away. It's your job to protect us."

It's your job to protect me! I thought you'd be there for me as long as I was in danger!

"One thing I've learned about this work is that it's unpredictable," he said. "Last I heard the trial was scheduled for March. But trials get postponed for all sorts of reasons. I've seen trials get delayed for years because of appeals, charges get suddenly dropped over technicalities and people who've expected to be in witness protection for a few days end up in their new lives indefinitely. I won't always be able to be there every moment of every day to have your back, unfortunately. And you might have to hide from Dexter, and whoever he sends after you, for the rest of your life."

She looked away, but not before he could see the look of fear that washed across her face. Her gaze rose to the sky. Somehow he knew she was praying and couldn't shake the feeling he'd be the one breaking it to her that her prayers weren't going to be answered as she'd hoped. He'd hated telling her the truth about how long and lonely a life in witness protection could be.

She turned back. Her arms crossed and her chin rose. "Okay, so where do we start?"

Did she have any idea how extraordinary she was?

"Step one is only frequenting locations that you know are safe," he said. "Places with good lines of sight and good exits, that are run by honest people who aren't likely to be involved in anything illegal on the side or pry into your business. Once we get you settled into your new home, I can help you identify those. Step two is learning to fly under the radar."

He reached around into the back seat, opened his duffel bag and pulled out a baseball cap and shapeless black sweatshirt and handed them to her. "I'm hopeful we won't need to look at any drastic changes to your appearance. Still, the last thing you want to do is draw attention to yourself. Put these on."

He waited as she fished an elastic band out of her jeans and tied her hair back into a bun. Then she put on the sweatshirt and pulled the hat down over her head.

"I've never been into clothes or worn makeup," she said. "I've always been pretty plain and nobody much cares what the person hiding on the other side of the computer screen looks like."

Plain? As in unattractive? Who was she kidding?

"Well, your new life isn't about hiding so much as being inconspicuous," he said, trying not to notice how beautifully the wisps of blond slipping out from under the hat framed her heart-shaped face. "It's about being the kind of person who doesn't get noticed. Which is hard for someone with looks like yours."

She blinked so hard her entire body sat back. Heat rose to the back of his neck. Had he really just said that out loud?

"What do you mean looks like mine?" she demanded. "You think I haven't heard enough men online and in person take potshots about my weight or my shape, or how thin my hair is, how funny-looking my nose is or how my eyes are too far apart?"

Wow, so she'd come across a lot of jerks in her life. She honestly didn't know that she was an attractive woman? How could anyone that exquisite go through life thinking they were funny-looking or plain?

"Well, despite what idiots might have told you, you're kind of a head turner." His neck grew hotter. What was he saying? "Your hair is fine. Your face is fine. Everything all looks fine. Come on, let's go eat."

He pushed the door open and half stumbled out, like he'd spent too long on a boat and gotten sea legs. By the time he'd made it around to her side of the truck, she'd already hopped out and closed the door behind her. They walked over to the diner. His hand brushed her shoulder as they reached the door, and even through her jacket and sweatshirt he could tell she was shaking.

"Don't look so nervous," he said with a smile that he hoped was reassuring. "Compared to what you've been through in the past week, getting coffee and eggs should be a breeze."

He pushed the door and held it open for her, then followed her in and couldn't help but notice she was scanning the room the same way he would. He liked this diner. It was a long building and wider than someone would've expected from the outside, with two rows of tables. Chairs instead of booths made it easier to jump up at a second's notice, and along with the front door there was a large emergency exit at the side, not to mention a third exit through the kitchen. Two of the tables were occupied with elderly couples.

"Where do you want to sit?" he asked, tilting his head close to hers.

"I don't know," she said. "I'm just stuck thinking I'm going to have to walk into every building from now on wondering who's out to hurt me and how to escape."

"Trust me, it's not as bad as all that, and soon enough it'll be second nature. Now let's go eat."

He reached for her shoulder, but somehow as she stepped forward he found his hand sliding down to the small of her back, his fingers fitting so comfortably there it surprised him. He led her over to the table by the window and pulled a chair out for her, noticing the slight shake in her limbs as he did so. He understood why her legs were wobbly. Not as much why his were, too.

A middle-aged woman with spikey blue hair and a name tag reading Missy arrived almost immediately with menus, mugs and a pot of hot coffee. He thanked her and she left.

"It's a pretty simple menu," he said, sliding one of the two laminated sheets across the table to her. "I hope you like eggs."

A gentle smile lit her face.

"I like simple," she said. She looked down at the menu. "There's nothing worse than those fancy coffee shops with hundreds of ways to order coffee. I always feel so awkward and uncomfortable and like I'm holding up the line."

"I like things simple, too," he said. There was a comfort in simplicity and that was part of what he liked about this place. There was one egg, or two or three, with bacon or sausage. There were pancakes and syrup. There was hot brewed coffee being poured into chunky and solid white mugs. Celeste chose two eggs with fruit. Jonathan went for three eggs with bacon. And they sat mostly in comfortable silence, exchanging simple furtive glances while they waited for the food. The late-morning sun sent dazzling rays bouncing off the blanket of crystal-white snow.

They finished their meal and sat for a long moment, just enjoying the coffee and the sunshine.

"How was it?" he asked.

"Amazing," she said. "I can't remember when I last

had a meal that wasn't on my desk wedged beside my laptop."

The sound of children laughing dragged their attention to the door. A girl of about three charged into the room, followed by a young boy, a teenager and two tired but smiling parents. Missy met them at a table with menus and coloring pages. He guessed they were regulars. He watched as the mother pulled electronic game devices out of her bag and slid them in front of the younger two even before they'd settled into their chairs and wriggled out of their coats. Her own phone came out, too, and the father checked his before he examined the menu. The teen boy curled into a corner chair with headphones in and some kind of device Jonathan couldn't see hidden in his hands. He sighed.

"You don't like kids in restaurants?" Celeste asked.

"I love kids in restaurants," Jonathan said, turning back. "I love kids, period. I just don't like that they're so focused on their devices that they're totally ignoring each other. I don't doubt those parents love their kids. But I don't get the point of spending time with another human being only to ignore them."

"So, you're a 'no phones at the dinner table' kind of guy?" she asked.

He paused. How could he possibly explain to a computer programmer how he sometimes missed living in a home with no electricity?

"I'm a 'no electronic devices during family time' person," he said finally. "Anytime family members are gathered together, whether sitting in the living room, eating at the dinner table or curled up in bed at night, then the point should be to be together, not stare at flickering screens."

"Why Marshal Mast!" She tilted her head. "I didn't imagine you were old-fashioned."

"Well, if there's something old-fashioned about wanting to pay attention to the person you're with, then I don't much want to get with current fashion."

She laughed, then leaned forward. "Do you have any?"

"What, kids?" He blinked. Had she really just asked that? "No. No kids, no wife, no pets and no family. Family just isn't something that tends to happen easily when you're in a career like mine. I take it from your file you have no significant relationships? It's something we look into, because the last thing we need is some ex-boyfriend suddenly deciding to track you down."

"No, no relationships." A sad smile crossed her face. "I'm not for small talk, or dating, or any of that. The closest I've come is a very small handful of people I met online, who either turned creepy or disappeared suddenly without notice. Every date I've been on has been a disaster. It's hard to find someone looking for anything real, but so very easy to find men who want female attention. Dexter was one of those."

He leaned forward. "You had a relationship with Dexter?"

"No, he was fishing around online looking for female attention on some message boards I frequent. Any female attention. It wasn't personal. I didn't give him the time of day. But something about how he was talking about how brilliant Poindexter was got me thinking. It was an anomaly in the pattern. Men like that usually only talk about themselves."

His phone started to ring. He glanced at the screen and his heart leaped with joy.

"It's Karl!"

A smile broke across Celeste's face. Her gaze rose to the sky outside. "Thank You, God."

Thank You, indeed. He shot Karl a quick text telling him he'd call back in a second. Then he stood. "I'll go take it outside the back door while you go freshen up."

The emergency exit was right by the washrooms. Plus, the cold air might help snap his head back in the game. Something about being around Celeste made his head spin. She agreed. He left some money on the table to cover the bill, then walked to the back of the diner. He waited until she'd slipped into the ladies' room, then stepped out the back door and called Karl.

"Karl Adams."

"Hey, man, you have no idea how good it is to hear the sound of your voice!"

"About as good as I imagine it was to see your face in the hall." Karl's voice boomed down the line. "Hunter tells me you got Celeste out safely?"

"Absolutely. We just stopped for food, but you and I have a moment to talk without being overheard. What's the word?"

"The farmhouse is secured. Three hostiles were taken into custody. There were several minor injuries. Only one casualty."

"Rod Cormac," Jonathan supplied.

"Yeah." Karl let out a sigh. "Stacy is talking to his girlfriend and family now."

"He was a great marshal."

"He was the best."

A long pause spread down the phone as the two friends shared a silent and unspoken moment of grief. He was sure Karl was silently praying.

The easy way Karl talked about God jarred him somehow. He envied it. He missed the way his family had talked about God so easily around the farm, as if God really was, as his *mamm* put it, "the unseen guest at every meal." He admired the way Celeste kept turning to God for help and fully believed He had a plan for her life.

I miss talking to You, Gott. *But I don't even know how to come back to You.*

Karl went back to briefing him, this time in more detail and flavor. Jonathan held tight and listened. Only two hostiles in combat gear had breached the safe house. One, a career criminal who was already well-known to the feds, had been arrested, and one had escaped the net. Two more criminals, much younger and far less experienced, were picked up on the road shortly afterward. They'd been identified from the description Jonathan had given Hunter. Footage of Celeste had turned up on one of their phones. Karl had no way of knowing whether it was already uploaded to the dark web.

"I want to give you a heads-up," Karl said. "Chief Deputy Hunter has told Stacy and I to be prepared for a potentially quick assignment change. We were supposed to be doing a prisoner escort in Philadelphia tomorrow. But Hunter has said there's a possibility she might pull either Stacy or I to take over escorting Celeste. It's just a precaution. In case you've been identified. It happens to the best of us."

"I know," Jonathan said. He ran his hand over his beard. As much as something inside him hated the thought of Celeste being transferred to another marshal, he wasn't surprised.

"Is it true Celeste thought she saw Dexter Thomes in the safe house kitchen?" Karl asked.

"It's true that's what she thought she saw. She calls him Doppel-Dex. She also thought a remote-control helicopter was watching us when we stopped to switch trucks. I don't know what to think." He glanced back. Celeste was standing inside the diner with her back to him. He shifted his gaze. His heart stopped. She was scrolling through data on some kind of small electronic device. *What was she thinking?* "I gotta go. I'll call you back."

He hung up, slammed the phone into his pocket and yanked the door open. Celeste spin toward him. He snatched the device from her with one hand. The other hand grabbed hers and pulled her close enough that they could whisper. "What do you think you're doing?"

Chapter Six

Conflicting emotions surged through him. Where had she gotten an electronic device? Yes, she'd told him she had a tablet with some of Dexter's data on it, but she'd also told him it was completely dead. How had she been foolish enough to use an electronic device when her life was in jeopardy and she was being hunted online by people who wanted to take her life? Why had he trusted her out of his sight for so long? What was it about her that had made him drop his guard like that and think he could trust her?

Yet, as he opened his mouth, it went dry, and all the questions that filled his mind died on his lips. Finding no words to say, he stood there, with his hand holding hers and her wide eyes looking up into his. Her lips were parted, half gasping and half panting in shock. Her body was so close anybody looking on would've been forgiven for thinking he'd spun her around to kiss her. He let go of her hand and looked up, breaking their gaze. No one else in the diner had seemed to notice their pirouette and he was thankful for that. He looked down at the device in his hand. Letters and numbers filled the screen. "What is this?"

"I told you, I had a tablet full of data that I downloaded from Dexter before he blew up my apartment." Her voice barely rose about whisper, but the frustration of her tone was unmistakable.

"You told me it was dead."

"I borrowed a charger from the mother of the device-addicted children," she said. "Don't worry. Like I told you, this device is perfectly safe. It can't connect to the internet. And I think I'm on to something with my hunch about number patterns. I think Dexter tried to track down someone specific. I think if I could just figure out who he was looking for, where he was looking for them, and why, I might have a lead on finding where he hid the money."

"How can you possibly know that no one is using this device to track you?"

"Because I know how electronic devices and the internet works."

"What if you're wrong?"

"I'm not!" Her voice rose for a moment. Then she seemed to catch herself and lowered her tone. "It's extremely unlikely. Extremely. But if there's even the possibility I could find that stolen money, it's a risk I'm willing to take."

"Well, I'm not, and it's my job to keep you safe."

The teenage boy at the table glanced their way, and even though Jonathan was confident he wasn't able to overhear them, he still held up a hand warning to Celeste to stop talking. Then Jonathan moved closer and dipped his head slightly. "Let's take this outside."

She pressed her lips together. He could tell there

was more she wanted to say. Well, she'd have to wait. Clearly, something about her had distracted him so much he'd fallen off the ball. He turned the electronic device over in his hand. It was the size of the notebook that the waitress had taken his order on. He frowned and turned it around looking for a switch to turn it off. As if reading his mind, Celeste reached over, slid her finger along the side, her hand brushing against his for a fleeting moment as she pushed a button so tiny he couldn't even see it. The power light turned off.

"Thank you," he said. He slid it into his inside jacket pocket. He reached down, unplugged the cord from the wall and rolled it between his fingers. His hand rested on Celeste's back just between the shoulder blades as they walked to the family, returned the charging cable with an exchange of polite smiles and then headed out the front door.

They'd gotten about five paces away from the door when Celeste stopped and turned toward him. Her arms crossed. "So why is it okay for you to take the risk of us stopping at a roadside diner, but it's not all right for me to take the risk of combing data on an off-line electronic device?"

Because it's my job to determine which risks to take. I'm the experienced US marshal entrusted with your safety, and you're the witness.

The answer snapped to the front of his tongue, but he held it back and instead took a deep breath. Celeste wasn't just any other witness. There was something special about her that he couldn't put into words.

"You're right," he said. "I took a risk in stopping here for food. Because despite what happened at the farmhouse, I'm still working on the presumption that my goal is to help you learn to live an independent life. There's a world of difference between walking into an out-of-the-way roadside diner and using an electronic device to track down a dark web hacker's stolen money. Especially since I'm guessing the feds already have the exact same data you have."

"They don't know Dexter like I do," Celeste said. "He wasn't even on their radar."

He scanned the parking lot. A small red car was parked near the front entrance with the hood up. It was only a few feet away from his truck. A couple seemed to be arguing over it. Looked like someone was having car trouble. He steered Celeste away from them and picked a safe middle ground where they couldn't be overheard by either the people taking care of the car or anyone coming out of the diner.

"But what if no one ever finds the money?" she pressed. "Dexter Thomes stole millions of dollars."

"From a bank," he said.

"No, from people who deposited money in the bank," she countered. "From parents, families, students, people living on their own and the elderly. He dipped his greedy hands into thousands of bank accounts."

She stepped toward him until they were almost toe-to-toe. He reached out, his gloved hand hovering just inches from her shoulder. Then he pulled back. Something weird seemed to happen whenever he even barely brushed against her. Instead, he crossed his arms across his chest. It was a stance and a gesture that usually intimated people and made them step back. Instead, she took another step forward, closing the remaining gap between them until she was almost stepping on his toes. "What's your point?"

"That I need to finish the job I started. I found the trail of bread crumbs. I didn't find the money. If I found the money and traced it back to him, they might not even need me to testify at trial. All this would be over. And all those people's lives would be changed."

"I get it," he said. "I really do. I just don't know what we can do about it."

Out of the corner of his eye, he was aware of movement behind them. It seemed the woman from the duo having car problems was coming toward them.

"Hey!" a female voice called. "You guys couldn't give us a jump, could you? I think the battery's dead."

He turned around, feeling Celeste one breath behind him. Normally the possibility that this obscure pair at a random country road diner would have anything to do with the witness he was protecting would've barely been a fleeting thought in his mind. It was just too unlikely. Yet, so much of what had happened since Celeste had been placed in his care made so little sense at all. The woman was younger than he'd realized at first glance. She was barely more than eighteen, with dark curly hair and baggy jacket. She looked more like the kind of person he'd expect to find trying to sell individual joints or small amounts of drugs outside a club than working for the world's top computer hacker. The scowling man standing beside the car looked at least ten or fifteen years older, with a large nose that had once been broken and scar on his neck from what Jonathan guessed was more likely a broken bottle than a knife. Whatever kind of relationship they were in, it probably wasn't a positive one.

"Sure thing." He smiled, putting a bit of extra drawl into his voice and dropping his law enforcement stance and posture in an instant. He glanced back at Celeste. "Honey, I'm just going to grab my jumper cables from my truck and give these two a boost. Then we're going to get back on the road."

While I make careful note of both these two, and then run them and their car through the system as soon as we hit the road.

The look of utter relief that flooded over the young woman's face was so palpable it made his senses tense up even more. Okay, whoever she was she was definitely in trouble. She was also walking back to the car.

"Good news, Fisher!" she called. "This nice man is going to give us a boost!"

The man turned. A grimace crossed his face and his lips contorted into what Jonathan could tell was supposed to look like a grin. "Well, that's mighty kind of you."

Jonathan knew his own fake smile was a whole lot more realistic than this man's, but still he could feel his jaw tighten as his gaze swept over Fisher's form. Everything about him smelled trouble.

"Oh, no trouble at all," he said. "Just let me get my cables and—"

The soft yelp of fear and pain and danger that slipped from Celeste's lips was enough to make his own words stop in an instant and every nerve in his body leap to attention. He spun.

The young woman had pressed a handgun into Celeste's side.

Chapter Seven

It only took a fraction of a second's glance back to the sneering man to confirm what Jonathan's gut already knew. He'd pulled a gun, as well. *And I apparently totally underestimated the resources Dexter Thomes has and the lengths he will go to in order to hurt Celeste.* Two criminals, two guns, Celeste's life in the balance— and he was trapped in the middle. He let his eyes linger on Celeste's, hoping she was praying and that God was listening to her prayers. Then he glanced at the girl holding her at gunpoint. She was shaking like a rabbit. Fisher noticed it, too.

"Gina!" Fisher snapped. "Wake up! Put her in the car and don't let her move or I'll kill ya when we're done with her."

Gina hesitated. Her hand shook so hard he knew that if he spooked her she'd probably shoot Celeste by mistake. And Jonathan didn't doubt she was terrified enough of Fisher that she'd probably kill Celeste to save herself. Gina's fear shook something inside Jonathan. The criminals who'd breached the farmhouse had been well armed and focused. The kidnappers with the cell phone camera had been brash and arrogant. These two were a whole different breed of criminal. Edgy and not well armed, with more than a whiff of desperation. The worst part was that he had no idea how they'd found them. His truck was clean of tracking devices, and even if Celeste had been right about that toy helicopter taking pictures of his truck, how would it have possibly found them all the way out here?

"Gina!" Fisher barked. "Move! Now!"

How long would they have until someone in the diner noticed? How soon until someone came out the back door? How soon until someone new pulled in? What would happen if Gina and Fisher opened fire?

Oh Gott, *I don't know what to pray. I don't know if You're listening. Just please, help. For so long I've felt like the fact I walked away from my family and Amish life meant I've lost any right to call out to You for help. But, please, don't punish Celeste for my mistakes. Save her, Lord. Help me save her.*

Fisher was snarling now, barking orders at Gina in a stream of swear words and threats. Jonathan blocked them out. Instead, his eyes focused on Celeste. She'd told him that Doppel-Dex had made it very clear he wanted her taken alive. He hoped that was true.

"Do what he says," Jonathan told Celeste. "Just go with her to the car. Trust me."

Because I'm going to take out Fisher, and then I'm going to come rescue you. But Gina needs to calm down first before she accidentally kills you, and I need you out of the line of fire.

He didn't know what he expected to see in her face in that moment. But through the fear that filled her eyes, he could see something deeper, something he hadn't been able to detect back in the darkened farmhouse safe house, but which now shone clear and vibrant in the light of day—determination. She was a fighter. She was determined to stay alive. And it strengthened his resolve not to let her down.

"Get down!" Fisher snapped. "Or I'll shoot!"

Sure thing. Jonathan crouched low, raised his hands and gritted his teeth. Through his peripheral vision he watched Gina and Celeste walk around to the side of the car.

"Hey, we don't want any trouble!" Jonathan called. "Just tell me your price and maybe we can work something out."

"You want to know my price? Fifty thousand." Fisher aimed the gun between Jonathan's eyes. "I want all 50K and not a penny less."

50K? As in fifty thousand dollars? Gina opened the back door.

"Really? Wow, that's a lot of money," Jonathan yelled. *Come on, man, focus on me. Don't look at the women.* "Who's willing to pay that much for her? How do you expect to collect?"

Gina's hands shook as she nudged Celeste in the side with the gun. They climbed into the car.

"Shut up!" Fisher shouted. "Kneel down and put your hands on the top of your head!"

Jonathan stayed crouched and did none of the above.

"Look, let me give you a hot tip. Dexter Thomes, aka Poindexter, is still locked away behind bars. So whoever you think is going to pay you isn't him."

The man laughed. It wasn't pretty. "Do you think I'm an idiot?"

Yup. An evil and deadly one, who wasn't about to tell me anything I needed to know.

Gina climbed into the car and shut the door. Jonathan charged and threw himself at Fisher. He stayed low, letting Fisher get a round off that flew over his right shoulder. Then, with one hand, he grabbed the gunman's wrist and yanked the gun up over his head. With the other he leveled a strong blow to Fisher's face. The gun flew from Fisher's grasp as the man crumpled against the hood, unconscious but breathing.

Jonathan glanced up at the faces of the two women sitting in the back seat of the car. Two pairs of wide eyes met his through the windshield, one terrified and one trusting.

He shoved Fisher's gun in his pocket and pulled his own trusty service weapon.

"Listen, Gina," he said, keeping his voice low like he was dealing with a spooked and frightened animal. "I don't want to kill you, and I don't think you want to kill her. I think you're just doing what you were told to do. Drop the weapon and get out of the car, nice and slow, and nobody needs to get hurt."

The young woman's head shook. "I can't... Fisher..."

"Fisher is unconscious, I have his gun and I can take you somewhere he'll never find you." Jonathan stepped closer and raised the weapon. He had a clear shot now, just past Celeste's shoulder. One shot and Gina would be dead. But he really didn't want to take it.

Please let me help you.

A flurry of activity yanked his attention to the diner. The family was bursting through the door. The little girl screamed. The father shouted. Jonathan raised his badge and yelled.

"I'm a US marshal! Everyone get inside, lock the doors, stay away from the windows and call 9-1-1!"

A gun fired inside the car, sending glass flying as a bullet exploded through the windshield. Celeste tumbled backward out of the car and onto the ground, leaving Gina moaning and doubled over in the back seat. He blinked. Celeste looked up at him.

"She was going to shoot you," Celeste explained. "So when she turned and aimed at you, I grabbed the gun and kicked her with both feet."

The hat had fallen from her head. Her blond hair fell loose and wild around her shoulders. Gina's gun was clenched in her hand. Looking down at her, Jonathan felt like he'd lived a thousand lives in one instant. *You're the most incredible person I've ever met. If I feel all this for you after less than a day, how will I ever let you go when all this is done?* She handed him the gun. He took it with his left hand, then reached for her hand with his right and pulled her to his feet. Behind her, he could see Gina sobbing hysterically in the back seat of the car.

"Come on!" He squeezed her hand and felt it tighten in his. "We've got to run."

They ran for the truck. He threw the door open, and practically lifted her up into the passenger seat. He closed the door behind her the moment she was clear, then ran around to the other side, allowing himself one glance back. Fisher had roused and was groaning. Gina was crying so hard she her body shook. The diner's blinds had closed and the lights went off. He prayed for the safety of those inside.

"What were you thinking, fighting her for the gun?" he demanded. They peeled out of the parking lot. One hand was clamped on the steering wheel, the other dialed Chief Deputy Hunter. "Don't get me wrong. It was impressive. It was incredible. I can't tell if I should be in awe or infuriated. But you also should've trusted me to handle it. You could've gotten yourself killed."

"The gun wasn't pointed at me!" Celeste spluttered. "It was pointed at you. I'm not an idiot. I waited until she was distracted, I was out of the line of fire and then I fought her for it. It was smart."

"It was risky!" His head shook. The phone rang. He couldn't figure out if he wanted to yell at Celeste or kiss her right now. But neither was an option and neither urge made his job any easier. "Yeah, it was brave. You've got guts. I'll give you that. But if I die they'll just find another marshal to protect you. If you die, there'll be no one to testify against Dexter Thomes at his trial! Remember that!"

"Chief Deputy Louise Hunter." His boss's voice filled his earpiece.

"There's been an incident," Jonathan said. He filled her in quickly and gave her the location, a description of Fisher, Gina and the vehicle in rapid fire. "The diner seems to have gone on lockdown. Hopefully they've called 9-1-1."

"I'll make sure the 9-1-1 call went through and that authorities are on the way," Hunter said. "Where are you now?"

"We're back on the road and headed west. We're still en route to—"

The phone clicked. Celeste had hung up his phone.

"What are you doing?" he demanded, and the determination and fire in his face nearly shook her resolve.

Instead, her fingers tightened over the phone.

"What are you doing?" She threw his words back at him. "You wanted to get rid of my tablet, but you're still using a cell phone?"

"It's my work phone!" His voice rose.

"It's traceable and hackable!" Her voice rose to match it. "Do you think the fact I logged into the tablet is what made two random criminals show up at the diner? Well, I'm telling you it probably wasn't. Because it's not putting out a signal. Your phone is."

"You honestly think these criminals are sophisticated enough to hack a government-issued cell phone?"

"Yeah." Her chin rose. "I do!"

She could feel her feet digging into the floorboards beneath her feet. He was wrong, and she was right. She knew it. Problem was she had no idea how to convince him of that. He was the most stubborn man she'd ever met. And while she kind of admired his resolve and found it attractive, right now it was infuriating that he wasn't respecting her expertise.

"Look," she said. "I don't know how to convince you. I can't prove it to you without access to the right tools, and I might be wrong. Maybe both of our devices are clean and they found out we were there another way. But it's important you know that it's a possibility."

Jonathan's jaw set. His hands tightened on the steering wheel. He made a sharp turn to the left. The truck sped away from the highway and toward a strip of buildings.

"Let's set up a test of some sort," she said. "We put my tablet in one location and your cell phone in another. Then we wait and see if criminals show up at either place."

A run-of-the-mill truck stop was coming up quickly on their left.

"Can you wipe it?" he asked. "Quickly. Erase everything on it."

"Yeah, of course."

"Do it," he said. "Now."

He swiftly shifted into the left-hand lane. Her finger fumbled with the buttons. Was he really asking her to wipe a law enforcement cell phone clear? She took a deep breath and wiped it.

"Done," she said. "But a really tech-savvy person with the right skills and tools might be able to reconstruct some of it."

"Give it to me." He stuck his hand out and she dropped the phone into it. He pulled a hard left, crossing the highway and swerved into a truck stop. He rolled the window down, then as she watched, he smashed the cell phone hard against the side of the truck over and over again, until all that was left in his hand were cracked and mangled pieces. With the quick flick of his hand he tossed the pieces into a dumpster. Then he pulled back onto the highway. They sped in the opposite direction.

Her lips fell open. "I can't believe you did that."

"You made a good point," he said. "If you were wrong, I lost a cell phone. If you were right, my phone was putting us is danger. Now, can you give me your word that it is completely impossible we're being tracked through your tablet?"

No, she couldn't. Someone could have remotely re-enabled the internet after she'd disabled it, or the device could've been infected with some kind of virus. But she was 99 percent certain and it was a risk she was willing to take. Did he have any idea how important the data on the tablet was? Or how impossible it would be for her to ever get her hands on it again? Frustrated tears pressed against the corners of her eyes. "No, I can't. It's very, very unlikely, but not impossible."

An access road lay ahead on the right. He slowed the truck and turned into it. Thick trees surrounded them on all sides. He pulled to a stop, turned and looked at her.

"Do you agree that our location is being tracked, somehow?" he asked. "We can agree on that, right? Because while there's no logical reason those criminals should've been able to find the location of the safe house, even if there was a leak within the US Marshals office—unlikely though that is—or they somehow hacked into somebody's emails, that still wouldn't explain how they found us at a random diner I told nobody we were stopping at."

"Agreed. Could they have tracked your truck?"

"Possibly." He stroked along the edges of his beard. "But that means they tracked both trucks, somehow, without knowing I was going to change vehicles, and decided to attack us in a public place instead of all the much more convenient and more remote places on the roads we've taken to set up an ambush. And between the clear blue sky and empty roads I definitely would've noticed if we were being physically followed."

She pressed her lips together. He was right.

"Please," she said. "Don't destroy this data. It's my only hope of ever finding where Dexter hid the stolen money. We can save it to a memory stick. Or even just print it! Paper is better than nothing. It doesn't have to be on an electronic device. I just don't want to lose it."

His eyes closed and for a long moment he almost wondered if he was praying. Then his dark eyes were on her face again. A smile crossed his lips that warmed every corner of her heart.

"I just remembered I have a memory stick that nobody's touched but me. Got it years ago and it's been on my key chain ever since. What if we transferred the data onto the memory stick and I promised to hold on to it until I find another option. Okay?"

She nodded. She didn't like it, but he'd smashed his phone because he'd trusted her. She could do the same and trust him. "Okay."

"Deal." He reached into his pocket, pulled out the tablet and gave it to her. Then he slowly worked a small, flat and bright yellow bobble off his key chain. "I got this years ago at a youth conference I went to as a teenager at a church that wasn't mine. The speaker talked about God having a plan for our lives and it was just so inspiring that I picked up a copy of the talk on the way out. I can guarantee that unless someone broke into my home and pilfered it from my bedside table while I was sleeping, or literally picked my pockets, stole my keys and slipped them back without my knowing, nobody has touched this but me. Is there any way people can trace the data itself?"

"Not if I save it as a plain text file." She plugged it into the side of the tablet, turned it on, converted the file to plain text and downloaded it to the memory stick. The whole thing took less than thirty seconds. Then she gave the tablet back to Jonathan. "Thank you."

"No problem."

He slid the memory stick back onto his key chain. Then he drove back and forth over the tablet until it was nothing but a collection of shards he then collected up and threw in a trash can. They kept driving. She leaned

back in her seat and watched the memory stick swing
as it dangled from the keys in the ignition.

*Now what, Lord? I'm trying so hard to believe You
have a purpose for my life. But I feel like I've just lost
the last sliver of who I was.*

"What do we do now?" she asked.

"I call my boss, fill her in on everything that's happened, make sure we're still on track as per our destination and get someone to meet us there with a new
cell phone for me. I'm still not happy with the idea of
you using an electronic device, not until we know more
about what's going on. But I'll ask if somebody can
bring us something we can use to print your data out on
paper so at least you have something to go over it with.
Oh, and also to bring you a box of pencils."

He cut her a sideways glance. A grin crossed his face
and it was definitely growing on her. She felt a smile
twitch at the corner of her lips. Had she ever smiled this
much before? In school, she'd always been accused of
being too serious and not knowing how to lighten up.
Since then countless men in stores, coffee shops and
the street had accused her of not smiling. Now somehow, in the middle of everything that had gone on, this
one equally serious man was making her smile. It was
an unfamiliar feeling. She liked it. "Don't forget a pencil sharpener."

He guffawed like a clap of thunder disappearing into
the rain. "Deal."

The smile faded and a darker look moved through
his features. He looked straight ahead again. "There's a
town about thirty minutes east from here called Hope's
Creek. It's pretty far off the beaten path, but it has public

phone booths in the center of town. I can call Hunter's secure line from there."

"Public phones?" She couldn't remember the last time she'd seen a phone booth anywhere—at least one what was functional and not covered with graffiti. "What kind of small town still has public phone booths?"

"It's near a large sprawling Amish community." He still wasn't meeting her gaze.

"But the Amish don't believe in telephones! Just like they don't believe in electricity or cars."

A totally different laugh left his lips now. It was a bitter one that emanated from the back of his throat, and it was almost like he'd tried to bite it back and failed.

"You make it sound like they don't believe they exist," he said. "Of course they do. They just have a very different relationship with technology than the *Englisch*. That's the term they use for the outside world, and people like you and me. A lot of them hire cars, use electricity in their businesses or use public phones when they need to. They just don't believe in letting technology take over lives and ruin relationships. If you don't have a phone in the home, then you pay more attention to the people you're with. If you don't have electric lights you get better sleep at night and wake up ready to face the day. If you don't have a car…" His voice trailed off into a sigh. "If you don't have a car you never move too far away. Living by the *Ordnung*, which I guess you'd call the rules the Amish live by, is not about hiding from the world. It's about having everything in the correct balance, in relationship with others and *Gott*."

"Well, I didn't know that," she said. It was one of the longest monologues she'd heard come from his mouth.

"But I like learning, and I've always wanted to know more about the Amish. The thing I'm going to miss most about the internet is the ability to find out about things I don't know much about."

He released a long breath.

"I'm sorry," he said. "That came out stronger than I intended. I just don't like anyone judging people by their appearances. And in my experience, too many people just see a beard or a bonnet, and don't even try to see the person underneath."

"Hey, I get it," she said. She reached across the center of the truck. Her hand brushed his sleeve and she felt the strength of his arm under her fingers. "It's okay. I'm a female computer programmer. I was the only woman in some of my university classes. I get horrible messages from strangers online when they realize I'm a woman. I get what it's like when people judge based on appearances." He smiled. It was a good smile and a relieved one, like he was worried that he'd somehow offended her and was glad to know he hadn't. They lapsed into silence. The sun rose even higher. Bright blue filled the sky above them. Then she saw a buggy out her window. It was driven by an older man with a long white beard. Then there were more buggies with the young and old, men and women, families with kids, and groups she guessed were friends. She glanced at Jonathan. "I can see what you meant earlier. It does look like fun."

But his face was as serious as a man driving to his own funeral. She frowned as an uncomfortable thought crossed her mind, one that had been nagging at her for a while.

"Can I ask you a question?" she asked. "Why didn't

you kill Gina? You had the shot. Instead, you showed mercy."

He ran his hand over the back of his head. "I didn't need to kill her."

"You didn't kill Fisher, either," she said. "Or Miller. Or Lee…"

"I haven't killed anyone," he said. "I'm not in the business of going around killing people I don't have to kill. Whether I'm escorting a prisoner who's trying to escape or part of a manhunt scouring the countryside for a criminal or putting my life on the line to protect a witness like you, if there's a way—any way—the criminal I'm up against can end up in court, facing justice instead of dying by my bullet, I will always choose justice and mercy."

"Have you ever taken a life?" she asked.

"No," he said. "A few times I've shot someone so severely I honestly believed the wound would be fatal. But each time, thankfully, they'd been saved by paramedics."

She paused, pondering her next question. Instead, to her surprise, his hand reached for hers and she felt the warmth of his fingers brush her skin.

"Trust me, Celeste," he added. "I believe in you. You stopped a criminal no one else could, and if anyone can find that missing money it's you. If I'm ever faced with a choice between pulling a trigger and letting somebody hurt you, I will save your life."

Chapter Eight

Not much had changed, Jonathan thought, as he slowly eased his truck toward Hope's Creek. It was a small town, with an official population of just a couple of thousand but many more living in the sprawling Amish farms spread out through the countryside, including his own family and people he'd grown up with. The ice-cream store was closed for the winter, but the faded sign was the same. The florist had a new name, but the hardware store looked exactly as he remembered it. Amish community, at least as he'd known it, had centered around family and friends. Even church had been held in the people's homes. Hope's Creek used to be his entire world. Yet, he couldn't say he had ever expected this to be his world forever. No, something inside him had always prompted and pushed him to go out into the world and make a difference.

As a child, he'd believed with his whole heart it was God. But his *bruder*, Amos, had told him in no uncertain terms that it couldn't be, and his *pa*'s quiet and stubbornly simple faith had made him feel impossible to talk to. Something defiant inside Jonathan had decided his only option was to leave. He'd been eighteen, mourning the loss of his mother and like a horse with blinders on. But now that he'd chased after that calling and become the man he'd thought he was supposed to be, where was he? The two parts of him were like oil and water, or two magnets repelling each other. Amos was right. He could never be both Amish and a cop. And now he was back, for the length of a single phone call, just a short buggy ride away from the only place he'd ever considered home.

He pulled into the center of town, near where the outdoor community phone boxes were or, at least, had been. A park bench sat where the community phone booth once had. But before he could worry about that a storefront caught his eye: Miriam's Second Hand Thrift Store. Handwritten signs in the window, in both English and Pennsylvania Dutch, told him they only took cash, all proceeds went to charity and that free clothes and food were available to those in need. More importantly, a large sign on the door mentioned there were community phones for free use within.

He pulled to a stop out front. Through the window he could see a striking woman in her late thirties in an Amish prayer *kapp*, dress and apron behind the counter. Beside her was a fresh-faced young man he guessed was probably no more than eighteen. He paused. Women running businesses in the Amish community were rare. At least in his experience. Was Miriam a young widow who'd started her own business after her husband's death? Was it a family-run business?

"I'm going to go in there and use the phone," he said.

"Can I come, too?" she asked.

He paused. His eyes scanned the street. Yes, she'd

probably be safer in the store than she would be sitting out in the truck. "Sure, but hide your hair under the hat and stay close."

He walked around to her side of the truck, opened the door and reached for her hand. She took it, hopped out of the truck and gave him a weak but honest smile. They started across the frozen ground toward the thrift store and it wasn't until they pushed through the door that he realized he was still holding her hand.

The store was brightly lit and larger than he'd expected from the outside, with neatly arranged racks of *Englisch* clothes, displays with beautiful quilts and blankets, beautiful displays of secondhand furniture, and tables selling Amish preserves, jams, jellies and breads. A large display on one wall, with a world map covered in pins, outlined the charitable work in both the United States and overseas that proceeds went to funding. A sign above it in English and Pennsylvania Dutch read Be a Light in the World. His heart warmed.

Celeste read a large sign surrounded by smiling daisies and sitting on the front counter: Questions about Amish life? Please Ask. She pointed to it. "I guess that's one way to deal with ignorant people like me."

"I never said you were ignorant." And never would.

"Maybe not, but I know I have a lot to learn."

A light shone in Celeste's eyes as she scanned the store, full of curiosity and inquisitiveness, and it almost reminded him of the spark he'd seen in her eyes when she'd talked about the data.

"Can I help you?" the young Amish man called.

He stepped out from around the corner and crossed the floor toward them. The teenager's voice was polite, but his blue eyes were guarded in a way that made

Jonathan remember how he and his brother had been harassed by tourists when they were younger. His name tag read Mark. A second slightly larger badge read Feel Free to Ask Me about Amish life, and Jonathan felt the odd impulse to clap Mark on the shoulder and tell him in Pennsylvanian Dutch that he knew firsthand that took courage.

Instead, all Jonathan said was, "We're looking for a phone."

Mark pointed to two stalls near the back, each with a small chair. "This way."

"Danke." Jonathan nodded and Mark withdrew.

Jonathan scanned the space between the phones and the front door. The lines of sight were clear. There was only a smattering of other customers in the store. He'd be able to get from the phone to anywhere on the floor in about two seconds flat. Besides, he really didn't want her listening in on his next conversation with Chief Deputy Hunter. Karl's warning that he and Stacy had been told to be ready for a potential assignment transfer irked him at the back of his mind. There'd been multiple attempts on Celeste's life. Fisher and Gina had definitely seen his face. A transfer was the logical next step.

But somehow I'm not quite ready to say goodbye.

He glanced at Celeste. "I'm going to need a moment of privacy. Are you going to be okay if I leave you? Don't go out of the store. Stay within eyesight of the phone booth. Browse and if you find any clothes you want or things you'll need, feel free to fill a basket or two. I think I even saw some luggage and toiletries, and I'm sure you'd appreciate getting some new stuff."

Not to mention he'd like to give this business a large donation when he left.

His hand slipped from hers, but she squeezed his fingertips tightly before they could fully let go. "Thank you."

He pulled away and then watched as she walked over to the woman with auburn hair behind the counter. A wide and welcoming smile filled her face as she came around the counter to greet Celeste, and Mark stepped behind the till to take her place. Sure enough, the woman's name tag read Miriam.

He left Celeste in animated conversation with the other woman, went into the phone booth and dialed his boss's number. She answered immediately.

"This line isn't secure." Had the last line been?

"Understood."

He briefed her quickly, filling her in on how they'd destroyed their electronics because Celeste had been concerned they could be hacked. It was odd, as he said it, how he'd trusted her implicitly, like she wasn't the person she was protecting but a partner or a member of the team.

He watched as she and Miriam were joined by a younger Amish woman he guessed was Mark's sister and a year or two older. She led Celeste through the store, their heads bent together like old friends. He couldn't look away from the smile that brushed Celeste's lips.

She's extraordinary, God. She's like nobody else I've ever met. She's this exquisite combination of beauty, brains and heart that just tumbled into my life, for a short period of time, and knowing me I should be irritated or annoyed at knowing it can't last. But instead I'm just too amazed that she exists at all and happy that I ever got to meet her. So please, I'm asking You,

*watch over her, protect her, guide her, keep her safe
and make all her dreams come true.*

"Under the circumstances we think the best course
of action is a transfer of marshals," Hunter said. "I'd
like you to head to south. P. will meet you and take over
your current assignment. You'll be temporarily assigned
to work with A. for the time being."

In other words, he was to head to the southern Penn-
sylvania safe house, he'd be reassigned to work with
Karl Adams and Celeste would be transferred into Stacy
Preston's care.

He gritted his teeth. He wasn't surprised. He'd seen
this coming. The only thing that mattered was Celeste's
safety. Yet, somehow, the words still landed like a little flurry of punches knocking the air from his lungs.

"Understood." He knew the place. They'd be there
in half an hour. Then Celeste would disappear from
his life, he'd be on to a new assignment and he'd never
even know for certain where she'd gone or how to ever
contact her again.

He ended the call, but instead of crossing the floor
to find Celeste, he found his footsteps taking him to a
secluded part at the back of the store that he guessed
was the processing center for donated goods. Twin boys,
with auburn curls like Miriam's were playing on a car-
pet with a pile of colored blocks. He guessed they were
about four or five.

A stack of Bibles and prayer books, in English and
Pennsylvania Dutch, sat on a wide wooden shelf next
to a sign reading Free! Take One! Something inside
him itched to reach for one. Instead, he leaned his back
against the wall and pressed his hands over his eyes.

I feel so lost. I don't even know why I keep crying

out to You when I'm sure You've given up on listening to me. But something about Celeste keeps pushing me here, to this point. So, I'll ask, what was the point of all this, Gott? Celeste is so certain that You have a purpose for people's lives? But what could the purpose possibly be to bring her into my life only to disappear again?

He took a deep breath and wiped his eyes. He'd barely taken a step when he felt a hand, heavy and strong, land on his shoulder. Somehow he knew who it belonged to even before he turned to face to see the cinnamon-brown beard and dark piercing eyes awash with confusion, sorrow and anger.

Amos.

"Pa!" the boys cried, leaping to their feet and running toward Jonathan's older brother.

"Bruder." Amos shook his head. "What are you doing here?"

"It's simply beautiful," Celeste murmured, letting her fingers brush over the intricate quilt patterns. The stitches were so neat, even and precise. It was hard to believe they'd been done by the young woman standing beside her.

"Do you sew?" Rosie asked. She had said she was eighteen, Mark's older sister and Miriam's daughter. A strawberry blond wisp of hair slipped out from under her white cap.

"No," Celeste said. "I always wanted to learn, but I never had the opportunity. I did teach myself to knit off an internet tutorial once. I made myself a sweater." She shook her head. "I'm sorry. You probably don't know what the internet is."

Rosie laughed. It was a soft, kind and inclusive laugh

that seemed to pull Celeste in instead of making her feel like she was getting mocked. "Yes, I know what the internet is. We just don't use it. When Mamm doesn't need me in the store, I teach school."

"You're a teacher?" Celeste felt her eyebrows rise.

"I am," Rosie said. "My mother was a teacher before she married my *pa*. When he died, she moved here with my *bruder* and I, and started this store. Then she found love again and now the family is larger."

There was a twinkle in her eye that told Celeste there was a story there. She glanced at Miriam, who now crouched down, arms wide, to welcome two small boys charging through from the back of the store. She couldn't believe the courage of a woman who had started her own charity, helping others, as a widow in a new community, with two small children. "God always has a plan."

"*Yah!*" A wider smile burst across Rosie's face. "*Gott* is always *gut!*"

"I believe that, too," Celeste said softly. Or at least she always had. Unexpected tears rushed to her eyes and she wasn't quite sure why. She blinked them back. "I'm sorry, I'm afraid I don't know much about Amish life, but I really enjoy your patience in answering my questions. I feel like I've asked so many so far."

"It's okay," Rosie called. "As Grossdaadi says, the purpose of a light is to shine."

Grossdaadi. Would that be grandfather, Celeste guessed? She'd been able to piece together the little bits of Pennsylvania Dutch that Rosie slipped into conversation, like *yah* for yes, *Gott* for God, *mamm* for mother and *gut* for good.

"I was wondering how you sew your dresses," Celeste admitted. "The folds are so neat and precise, but I don't see any zippers or buttons."

"We use pins," Rosie said. "Would you like me to show you?"

"Please."

A shadow moved past the door. She looked up. A man was standing outside by the truck. He was heavy-set, with broad shoulders, tinted glasses and an un-kempt shaggy beard.

And my eyes are telling me it's Dexter Thomes, even though my brain is telling me that it can't be.

He was here. Somehow, he'd found her. But how? They'd gotten rid of the cell phone and the tablet. They'd changed trucks. But here he was, scanning the streets of the small town like he was looking for something, and she knew without a shadow of a doubt he was looking for her. Through the gap in his open jacket she could see the handgun concealed just inside his jacket.

"Excuse me," she said. She turned and started through the store toward the bank of phones. Her heart stopped. The phone sat there in the cradle and she couldn't see Jonathan anywhere. Her heart pounded hard in her chest.

Help me, Lord. Where is he? Where has he gone?

She glanced back to the street. The doppelgänger Dexter was looking in the window. She quickly shielded her face and turned away.

"Everything all right?" Rosie asked.

Celeste's head shook. "No, it's not. I came in here with someone. A man. And now I can't see him any-where."

She scanned the store. Panic, swift and sudden, rose upside her chest like a wave. Where was he? He wouldn't just have disappeared or left the store without telling her.

Help me, Lord! I don't know what happened to Jonathan!

The front door jangled. She looked up and her heart stopped as Doppel-Dex walked through the door. She dropped to the floor, behind the rack of dresses, and hid, peering through the fabric at the same hulking form she'd seen back in the farmhouse kitchen. Whoever he was, he looked enough like Dexter Thomes to fool the average person. Especially if they'd only seen him through a video screen.

"I'm looking for this woman!" He slapped a cell phone down on the desk in front of Mark and Miriam with the screen up. "Her name is Celeste Alexander, and I'm offering a lot of money for anyone who tells me where she is. You people understand money? You tell me if you see her. I will give you money."

Miriam's eyes dropped to the picture on the screen. Her lips moved in what Celeste guessed was silent prayer. But Mark's young eyes seemed to cut straight across the room in her direction as he called out something in Pennsylvania Dutch that she didn't understand. *Help me, Lord!* A hand brushed her sleeve. She clamped her hand over her lips to keep from screaming. Then she felt the rustle of fabric and realized Rosie had dropped down and crept over beside her. The younger woman's eyes met hers, wide and filled with a fear that mirrored her own. "Are you in trouble? Do you need help?"

Celeste nodded. "Yes. Please hide me."

Chapter Nine

Jonathan stood in the back of the shop and just listened as Amos told him how much his absence had hurt him and their *pa*, and how his father's health had declined in his absence. How Amos's heart had been swallowed up in anger for a long time until a beautiful widow named Miriam, who was a couple of years older than he was, had moved to town with her two young children. She had challenged him to open up his heart to God and the world again. What was there to say? He was guilty of everything Amos was accusing him of. And his brother wasn't even yelling. Instead, his older brother's voice was every bit as level and calm as their *mamm*'s used to be. There was a softness to his brother's eyes, too, and a slight graying of his hair at the temples. He was a father now, a husband, and he'd taken care of everything on his own after Jonathan had left.

How will he ever forgive me?

"Talk to me, bruder," Amos said, his arms crossed. "You disappear for years and then I see you standing here in my family shop dressed like an *Englischer*?"

Where did he start? There was so much he wanted to

say. So much he wanted to ask. He wanted to tell Amos he wasn't sorry he'd become a marshal, but he was incredibly sorry for how he'd left, and he wished there'd been a way he could go back in time and do it all better. He wanted to ask the names of his sons and what it was like to become a father. He wanted to explain just how strongly he'd felt called to protect others and how deeply it had hurt when he felt Amos had rejected him.

But all the words fell silent on his lips as he stood face-to-face with the brother he'd fought with, lost, missed and regretted hurting.

"I was wrong," Jonathan said. "Forgive me."

Before Amos could respond, voices rose behind them. Up to this point he'd been able to tune out the sounds of conversation coming from the store behind him. But now someone was yelling, his voice bellowing and echoing as swear words poured from his lips. Amos's head turned sharply at the sound of raised voices in the store. Jonathan followed his gaze. A large bearded man with long shaggy hair and tinted glasses was standing at the front desk, pointing his finger at Miriam and Mark. And as Jonathan watched, all the doubt he'd been feeling disappeared from his mind in an instant. While his brain knew this man must be imitation, he looked exactly like Dexter Thomes. Celeste had been right.

Celeste!

Desperately he scanned the store for her. Where was she? Where had she gone? *Help me find her, Lord!* He'd lost sight of her for only moments and now she was gone. Amos turned to go, but Jonathan clasped a hand on his shoulder.

"I'm sorry," he said quickly. "You deserve an explanation and my time. But it has to wait. I am a US marshal with witness protection. I am here guarding a woman whose life is in danger. That man wants to hurt her. We came in here together, and she is now missing."

The hostility faded in an instant from Amos's face. No matter how he felt about Jonathan and no matter how deep the rift they needed to mend, he understood.

"Where was she?" Amos asked.

Relief filled Jonathan's core. Amos was a better brother than he deserved right now.

"She was there," he pointed, "talking to the young Amish woman."

"Miriam's daughter, Rosie." Worry floated deep in Amos's eyes. Then he glanced at Jonathan. "This man is looking for you, too, yes? Stay here."

Amos strode across the store floor, his shoulders back and his head held high, radiating the strength and confidence that Jonathan as a child had both admired and been intimidated by. Jonathan watched as he exchanged a few brief words with Doppel-Dex, then the man stormed outside. Amos locked the front door behind him and switched the sign in the window to Closed. Mark moved immediately to shut the blinds. As the young man did so, Amos waved Jonathan to join them. Jonathan glanced out the front window through the gap in the closing blinds. Doppel-Dex was standing on the sidewalk outside the store confronting people with Celeste's picture.

"What did you tell him?" Jonathan asked.

"The truth." Amos's strong arms crossed his broad chest. "That I have not seen the woman he is looking for and we are closing for a family emergency." Then he turned to Miriam, and an unexpected sweetness filled his gaze. "Miri, this is my brother, Jonathan, the *Englischer* US marshal."

Jonathan turned to Miriam and nodded. "It is very wonderful to meet you. I'm sorry the circumstances are not better. I'm looking for the woman I came in the store with. Have you seen her?"

She nodded and pulled the two small boys closer to her.

"It is a joy to meet you," she said. "You have already met Mark. These are our other boys, David and Samuel." Her eyes darted to the sidewalk, then back to Jonathan. "Come."

She led them through the store to the display table and pulled up the cloth. Two women in Amish clothing hid under the table, their white starched prayer caps close together as if in prayer.

"You can come out," Miriam said softly. "It's safe for now. He's gone. But stay low."

The young woman Amos had called Rosie slipped out first. But it was the second woman who seemed to catch his very breath in her hand and hold it. A long gray cape was draped around her shoulders, a white cap sat pinned over her blond hair. Green eyes met his.

Celeste! Thank You, Gott!

He crouched down, reached for her hands and helped her up. "Are you all right? What happened?"

"Doppel-Dex." The name slipped from her lips in a gasp of fear. Her hand tightened in his. "I saw him outside. Then he walked through the doors and Rosie hid me."

"And the quick change into Amish clothing?" he asked.

"That was Mark's idea," she said. "Mark said something in Pennsylvania Dutch about how my clothes looked exactly like the picture. Dexter didn't understand him, but Rosie did. She grabbed clothes and helped me get changed as best as we could in hiding."

He glanced from his brother, Amos, to the family that he didn't know he had. Gratitude filled his heart.

"You saved her," he said. "Thank you."

Celeste turned to Jonathan. "We need to get out of here and fast. These lovely people have done more than enough, and I don't want them in danger."

She was right. True, Doppel-Dex was gone and Amos had locked the door behind him, but he was still between them and the truck and there was no telling what he'd do. He turned to his brother. Conflicted feelings churned in Amos's eyes, as if his heart was being overwhelmed by more emotions than he knew how to process. Miriam's hand brushed her husband's arm. His touched her shoulder protectively. Her hands slid gently to her stomach.

"This woman is in trouble," she said gently. "We must help her escape."

Amos reached for his wife's hands, enveloping them in his own.

"My responsibility is to protect you," Amos told his wife in Pennsylvania Dutch, his voice husky in a way Jonathan had never heard before.

"And you always do," his wife replied. "Now God is calling us to help them."

As Jonathan watched, he saw an understanding dawn in his eyes that he knew an hour-long conversation of his most persuasive arguments could never have accomplished.

"Jonathan," Celeste said softly. "We can't let them help us."

"Trust me," he whispered, knowing those words were far too little and yet all he could say. "Please."

He could tell by the fire that flashed in her eyes that trusting him was the last thing she wanted to do right now, and while normally he admired her tenacity, right now her patience was what he needed most of all. How would he ever explain to her what was happening? Not just that as soon as they were safe she was going to be transferred to Stacy's protection. But that he had an Amish family he hadn't told her about and hadn't seen in almost a decade due to his own stubborn heart? He'd never opened up about his home life or past to anyone, and now he needed to in order to keep her alive.

Amos's hand landed protectively on Jonathan's shoulder. "Tell me what you need."

He turned to face his brother. His eyes were serious, kind and strong.

"I need a way out of this building and this town," he said, "where Celeste can't be spotted or traced. I need to get to a new vehicle that hasn't been seen by the criminals who are after her and a way to get my truck out of town."

His brother ran a hand over his long beard.

"Go with Mark," Amos said. "He will find you clothes to change into so that they do not recognize you. There is also a basket of food in the back room I packed for lunch that you can take. You need to make a phone call and tell your people about the criminal here, *yah*?"

"Yah." Jonathan nodded. Doppel-Dex was still pacing outside, showing people Celeste's picture. They had to hurry.

"Okay," Amos said. "I will take Celeste with me and the family now to the buggy. The *Englischer* will not look closely at one Amish woman among many. Once I have left my family at a friend's house where I know they will be safe, I will come back with the buggy and meet you and Mark outside of town. I will then drive you to the home of an *Englisch* mechanic we do business with who sells old vehicles. He will have something that you can use to continue on your journey."

There was a finality to the way he said the word "journey." It implied he knew his brother was passing through, and Jonathan couldn't say he was wrong. He swallowed hard.

"Mark has many good friends at the *Englisch* church," Amos added. Something flickered in his eyes, making Jonathan suspect his brother was conflicted about how close Mark was to the *Englisch*. He wondered if his father was, too. "I am sure one of them can take your truck when the criminal has gone and leave it parked somewhere out of town."

His brother had always warned him of the evils of the outside world, and here Jonathan had come home, bringing that evil with him. He glanced from his brother's face to the members of his family searching for words to say. Then he turned to Celeste and took both of her hands in his as a thousand unspoken words bubbled up inside him. Instead, he said, "Amos is my brother. These people are my family. Go with them. They'll keep you safe."

He turned to go, trying to pull his hands from her grasp. Instead, she held on tight.

"You have to tell me something more than that."

"I know," he said. "But it's going to have to wait."

He broke her gaze. There was a very real possibility that Celeste might never forgive him for not telling her that he was Amish, he thought as he followed Mark quickly through the store and into the back room. After all, in the conversations they'd had about the Amish, he'd never once told her that he'd grown up Amish or they were in his own hometown. And he knew, if he was honest, that telling himself that it was just because he was the US marshal assigned to protect her wasn't good enough. As it was, leaving Celeste's side had felt not unlike tearing the thin roots of something just beginning the sprout out of the soil.

Mark led him through back rooms, full of donated clothes to be sorted, used furniture and discarded electronics. The sheer number of old televisions and computers was staggering.

"Nobody will take them," Mark said, as if clocking Jonathan's gaze. "They never do. Mamm has gotten people to come in and fix them, but everybody wants something new."

Mark pulled a white shirt out of a bag and fished a pair of suspenders out of another one. Then he handed him a coat and hat off a set of hooks by the door.

"Thank you," Jonathan said, quickly trading his clothes for the ones Mark offered.

"No problem." Mark shifted his weight from one foot to another like he wanted to ask a question but didn't know how.

Jonathan slipped his apartment key and the memory stick of data off his key chain, slid them into his pocket and handed Mark the truck keys. "You'll find it out front. Blue Ford. Dented back fender. Hershey plates."

Mark nodded and took the keys. Jonathan watched

as deep worry and pain filled the young man's eyes. He suspected the person Mark was worried for wasn't himself.

"You look like you want to say something," Jonathan said.

"Your brother is a very good man," Mark said. "So is your father. They took very good care of us and welcomed us into their family."

A family that Jonathan had abandoned.

"And I hurt them very much," Jonathan supplied. Mark nodded. "I was angry about my mother's death. Amos and I were fighting about everything. He wanted me to step up and get baptized. I couldn't talk to my father. The way he talked about God made no sense to me. I thought God wanted me to be a cop. Maybe He did. But I went about it the wrong way."

"Amos will forgive you and help you," Mark said. He shifted his weight from one foot to another as if weighing his words. "Because he is a good man. When he tells your father, Grossdaadi Eli will forgive you for being so close to the farm and not visiting."

His words cut Jonathan deeper than Mark would ever know.

"Do you think that they are wrong to forgive me?" he asked.

"No, I am worried you will hurt them even more," Mark said. "Especially Grossdaadi Eli. He is growing old. When Mamm and Amos married, he was slow. Now he is much slower. You have to sit, then wait and wait for him to say anything. Then when he does talk it's all from the Bible and you have to guess what he means. It's like he knows the scripture so well that whenever his brain is slipping and can't find the words he wants, *Gott*'s words are what his mind reaches for."

Something caught in Jonathan's throat. Was his father slipping into early onset Alzheimer's or dementia? Or just slowing with age? His father had always been a very quiet man and slow to speak. He'd gotten married later in life, had Jonathan when he was nearing forty and was now in his midsixties.

"How do they feel about you having friends at the *Englisch* church?" Jonathan asked. He didn't know how his father would have felt with him going to an *Englisch* church when he was Mark's age, but he would've expected Amos to have a problem with it. Maybe Amos had changed or Jonathan had been wrong about him. Or both.

"They know that I want to follow *Gott*, but don't know yet if I want to be baptized," Mark said. "They think I should. But I feel like *Gott* wants me to wait."

"I'm sorry," Jonathan said. "I know how hard that can be."

"Do you?" Mark asked and Jonathan could sense genuine questioning in his voice. "Every time I try to talk to them about the *Englisch* church and baptism, I think they're afraid of losing me like they lost you. And I could never imagine leaving my family."

These people were Jonathan's family? The thought rattled in her mind as she quickly followed Amos out of the store and onto the street the moment he gave the all clear that Doppel-Dex had gone. Rosie flanked her on one side and Miriam on the other, holding each of the boys' hands in one of hers. Conversations she'd had with him in the diner and on the road flickered through her mind. He'd had so many opportunities to tell her about his family and hadn't. Maybe because despite whatever warm feelings he'd kindled inside her, they weren't actually friends or had any relationship besides the fact he'd been assigned to protect her. She'd been foolish to even imagine for one fleeting second it had been any other way.

She scanned the street. The blue truck was still there where they'd left it. Doppel-Dex was nowhere to be seen.

"Keep your head down," Rosie said softly. "Amish women don't greet strangers on the street."

She followed them along the street and then behind the store. There stood a magnificent dappled horse and simple black buggy sitting outside under an overhang.

"Is the horse out here all day?" Celeste asked.

"No," Amos said. "Thankfully, I had just come to the store to bring my family lunch. We always pause to have a meal together."

She watched as he helped the boys scramble into the back of the buggy, followed by Rosie.

Miriam smiled kindly at Celeste. "Now, watch what I do and I'll show you how to climb up."

"Hey! You!" A voice, loud and vulgar, seemed to shake the quiet laneway. Her heart stopped. Doppel-Dexter charged down the quiet road toward them. "Stop!"

Fear poured over Celeste like cold water.

Help me, Lord. Protect me. Protect these kind people who've helped me.

"Go," Amos said quietly. "Get in the buggy."

But she couldn't. Instead, her feet seemed rooted in place, just like they had back in the farmhouse tunnel. Jonathan had called it "shock," but it felt more like she'd suddenly turned to ice, both shaking and immobile at once.

Miriam climbed into the buggy and settled on the seat. Without a word, she reached down for Celeste's hand.

"I said stop!" Doppel-Dex raised his hand, brandishing a handgun. He pointed it at them like he was punctuating the sky. "Somebody said they thought they saw the girl I'm looking for go into your store."

Amos turned to face him. She realized Jonathan's brother was positioning himself between her and the man who was willing to risk so much to get his hands on her.

"My store is now closed," Amos said. "If there was a girl in there, she is not there now."

Doppel-Dex stopped just feet away from them. He was so close that Celeste could smell the stench of cigars on his clothes. Who was this man? Why was he hunting her? Was he using the money Dexter had stolen to hunt her? Why did he look almost exactly like the criminal who was now in jail waiting for the day she would testify against him and put him away for good?

And, above all, one question burned larger and larger than the rest—how had he found her?

She kept her eyes on the ground, fighting the temptation to look up in his face and search his eyes for answers.

"You have a very nice family here," Doppel-Dex snarled. "You really want to risk something bad happening to them by protecting some woman you don't even know?"

Amos didn't answer. Instead, Jonathan's brother just stood there, a pillar of silent strength and resolve in the face of the criminal's taunts.

Doppel-Dex swore at him. Ugly words and threats poured from his lips, and as they stood there silently in the face of his vulgar onslaught she suddenly remembered the story Jonathan had told her about the bullies they'd faced when they were children. For a second, standing there, it was like her heart was split in two thinking about the two very different brothers they'd been. One brave enough to stand strong and resolved in the face of bullying. One equally brave feeling called to fight back.

Lord, please, save and protect this family! I don't know what the hurt or pain was that drove Jonathan and his brother apart. But, please, keep them safe. Heal their brokenness and pain. Don't let them get hurt because of me.

"How about you, girlie?" Doppel-Dex focused his attention on her. He held his cell phone up. "You seen this woman?"

Her chest tightened. She locked her eyes on the ground and tried to breathe.

Please protect me, Lord.

Doppel-Dex walked up to her. Beside her, she could feel Jonathan's older brother step protectively toward her.

"Hey! Girl!" His voice rose. "You speak English? You know I'm talking to you, right? Do you have a tongue in your head?"

Her body shook. The prejudice in his voice stung like a whip. He was so close now she could smell the stench of his breath. A gun waved in front of her field of vision, then a large hand with fat fingers, and for a moment she thought he was going to grab her throat.

She looked up, her eyes scanning his face. Suddenly she was staring through the tinted glasses at the ugly eyes beneath, face-to-face with the man who would stop at nothing to hurt her. The gun tightened in his grasp.

Save me, Lord. I'm about to die.

Chapter Ten

"You see this girl, you call me," Doppel-Dex snapped. "Okay? Or I will find you and kill you slowly. I'll kill all of you."

Her breath caught. He didn't recognize her. They were inches away. How was it possible that he didn't recognize her?

Too many people just see a beard or a bonnet, and don't even try to see the person underneath. Jonathan's words floated in the back of her mind.

Her gaze dropped back to the ground. Doppel-Dex swore at them and walked off. *Thank You, Lord!* Suddenly she felt she was able to breathe again.

"Come on," Amos said softly. "Let's go."

Amos offered an arm to steady her and help her up, as Miriam grasped her hand and helped her the rest of the way. Amos climbed up into the buggy and they drove in silence through the small town. He dropped the family off at a small farm on the outskirts of town, where a large, bearded Amish man promised Amos he'd keep Miriam, Rosie and the twins safe until he returned. Celeste hugged each of the women in turn, wondering how she could feel so much care and admiration for people she'd only just met.

"Travel safe," Miriam said, embracing her with the kind of protective hug that she hadn't felt since her mother had died. "May God go with you."

"And with you," Celeste said. She looked from mother to daughter. Words that she didn't know how to say filled her heart. "Thank you!"

She and Amos returned to the buggy and started driving back toward town. As they drew toward the shop, she saw an Amish man, tall with broad shoulders and a straw hat, standing by the road, holding a large picnic basket. Amos slowed to a stop. The man looked up. Dark eyes met hers and she felt something surge in her heart. It was Jonathan, and for the first time the reality of what he'd said hit her for real. This was his past. These people were his family. He climbed into the buggy.

"I called my boss and the police," he said. "They know the criminal who looks like Dexter is here and are converging to find him. Hopefully, he won't slip the net this time." He looked over at his brother. "Thank you for keeping her safe," he said.

Amos simply nodded. He flicked the reins, and the horse started trotting. "There was some trouble, but thanks to *Gott*, we were safe."

"What kind of trouble?" Jonathan's worried eyes searched Celeste's face.

"We saw Doppel-Dex," she said. "He confronted us as we were getting in the buggy."

"I'm so sorry," Jonathan said. His hand took hers and squeezed it. "Are you all right? Is everyone okay?"

Tears swamped her eyes. She'd barely been managing to hold them back, but the concern in his voice and the touch of his hand had somehow let them flow. She nodded. "He said someone had seen me go into the thrift store. He threatened us. But he didn't recognize me! He was right there. In my face, waving a gun at us, and he didn't recognize me. It's like he didn't look close enough. It was like he couldn't see beyond the bonnet."

"Thank You, *Gott*..."

The prayer moved simply and quietly over Jonathan's lips, like hidden water moving beneath the rock. They lapsed into silence as the buggy left town and pulled out onto the highway. She felt Jonathan beside her on one side and his brother on the other, two such different but similar pillars of strength. She had so many questions. She didn't even know where to start asking any of them; all she could do was pray.

The journey took longer than she'd expected. Despite the fear burrowing inside her and the odd tension between the brothers, after a while she found herself settling into the rhythm of the buggy and the soothing clop of the horse's steps in the snow. It was peaceful in a way she couldn't place, and again she felt the odd longing for a place she'd never known or seen move through her. She found herself very aware of the sound of the horse breathing and the way its flanks rose and fell. Despite everything that had happened, for the first time in as long as she could remember, she felt at peace.

Would there be any of this in the place where Jonathan was taking her? Would there be trees and rolling hills? Or would she be in a square of concrete walls, looking out through her window at more buildings and concrete?

Lord, I know all that matters right now is my safety

*and I don't even know what I'm asking. Please just re-
assure me that You still have a plan.*

After a while Amos flicked the harness and said
something in Pennsylvania Dutch. The buggy turned
right and went down a long driveway. A smattering
of buildings appeared at the end, what seemed to be a
house, a couple of barns and a garage. Then she saw a
few vehicles gathered around it.

"Wait here," Jonathan said. "I'll only be a moment."

"Okay." She nodded.

She searched his face, her eyes seeking out his for
reassurance. But he didn't meet her gaze. Jonathan and
Amos walked side by side to the farmhouse with the gait
of two men who were each inside his own world. She
was left alone with the horse, standing there quiet and
content, as thick flakes of snow swirled down around
them. She tucked a warm blanket around the soft fabric of her skirt, finding the clothes much warmer and
more comfortable than she'd expected.

*I feel so lost and confused right now, Lord. Am I still
within Your hand? How is all of this part of Your plan?*

After a while, she heard Jonathan and Amos exit the
farmhouse, followed by an elderly man clad in a large
overcoat and hat. Jonathan opened the door of a truck
and started the engine of a rusty maroon double-cab
pickup truck. When it was cleared of snow, Jonathan
walked over to the buggy. He reached for her hand and
helped her down. She turned to Amos. His shoulders
had sagged and there was a sadness about him that
made her thankful he'd be back with Miriam and the
children soon. She walked over to him and reached for
his hand. He smiled and didn't take it, but the kindness

in his eyes dispelled every fear she had that she'd committed a social faux pas.

"Please thank Rosie, Mark and Miriam for their kindness," she said. "I cannot thank you all enough for what you have done to help me. I will be praying, every day, that God blesses you and keeps you all safe."

"And we will pray for you," he said. "Travel safely."

She walked to the truck, climbed inside and then sat there with the engine running, watching through the window as the two men paced around each other and shared an awkward goodbye. Jonathan walked back to the truck, and Amos left in the buggy. Jonathan pulled the truck down the driveway. They drove for a while, then stopped at a small gas station and changed back into their everyday clothes. When they got back in the truck, Celeste opened the picnic basket and ate the simple meal of bread, jam, meat and cheese. But when she offered some to Jonathan, he waved her off. His dark brows were knit. The truck shuddered and shook beneath them and for a moment she almost felt the familiar tension headache threatening to creep back.

"It was very kind of the farmer to let us have this truck," she said, grasping for a topic of conversation when she could no longer take the silence.

"He didn't. I bought it," Jonathan said. His voice was clipped. He stared straight through the windshield. His thoughts, his feelings, everything about him seemed locked somewhere far away where she couldn't reach it. "Two thousand cash. More than it's worth but it'll last long enough to get us to the drop-off point."

"Drop-off point? What exactly are we dropping off?"

But if Jonathan heard her question he chose not to answer it. They kept driving. The tension in both her heart and her body grew stronger with each jarring shake and bump. The sun crept down toward the horizon.

"Talk to me, Jonathan, please," she said. He'd done so much for her. He'd saved her life time and again. And what had she done for him? Nothing. There was nothing she could do for him. Even though something about him drew her heart, the same way the breeze rustling in the trees tugged at a deeper longing somewhere inside her.

"Talk to me," she said. "Are you okay? Because you can talk to me, you know. I know we haven't known each other very long, but I'm here and I'm willing to listen."

He hesitated. She waited.

Then he shook his head. "Don't worry, I'm fine."

No, he might want her to think he was fine, but clearly he wasn't.

She took a deep breath.

Lord, I'm really not good at this. I've never been good at small talk or getting people to open up. But I promised You I'd always try to listen to Your prompting even if I didn't understand it.

"What happened between you and Amos?" she asked.

"I left," he said, so quietly she almost didn't hear him. "I was eighteen. We fought. I stubbornly thought I was right and he was wrong. I left and never came back."

Her hand rose to her chest. He'd walked out on his family?

"But Miriam and the children…"

"I never knew they existed until today," he said. "When I chose not to be baptized and to become a cop, I lost everything."

"Is that why you didn't tell me you're Amish?" she asked.

He bristled.

"I'm not Amish," he said. "I was raised Amish but I was never baptized. Being Amish isn't something you're born into. It's something you choose, and not something you choose lightly. It's a commitment between you and God, in relationship with the community. I deeply love and respect the *plain* life. But I've always felt something inside me telling me to work in law enforcement."

She waited, letting the silence—uncomfortable as it was—fill the space between them, with the rattle and shake of the vehicle. She didn't understand how he'd grown up, what he'd gone through or how he could've walked away from his family. She didn't understand what it was about Jonathan that kept pushing her out and pulling her back in again like the beating of a heart or waves gently lapping a shore. But she could listen.

"The story I told you about the day I knew I was meant to be a cop was true," he said. "Every word. I was in Hope's Creek with my mother and my brother when I was about eight and he was seventeen, when some tourists started hassling us because we were Amish. They followed us and threw things at us. They knocked my mother down and gave my brother a bloody lip..."

His voice trailed off. He ran his hand over the back of his neck.

"I was scared," he said. "I was really scared. I was little, and the most important people in my life were being hurt. I balled up my fist and punched back as hard as I could. And they laughed at me and I fell down. Then this car was there, suddenly, beside us with flashing lights and noise. This man and woman stepped out in uniforms with badges and they made the bullies stop." His voice rose. "They protected us. They rescued us. They defended us."

He paused. Silence filled the truck again. The rattle of the ancient vehicle shuddered beneath them.

"That was it," he said. "That was the moment for me. That was when I knew who I was meant to be and what I was meant to do. I was supposed to be there to protect people who couldn't defend themselves. The police had rescued us, and I was going to spend my life doing just that. Rescuing others. But Amos didn't see it that way."

No. From the little she knew of Amos, she imagined he wouldn't.

"How did he see it?" she asked.

"For Amos it was an important lesson that being called to live for God means that sometimes we face persecution," Jonathan said, "and that sometimes walking in God's path for us isn't easy. It was the start of a major fight between us that neither of us could back down from. Maybe we were just too stubborn. Or maybe it mattered so much to each of us that we couldn't see it any other way. But it was a barrier between us that just grew and grew until I didn't know how I'd ever be able to tell him that I felt called to leave. How could I? It was a reminder that we would never see things the same way. See, he didn't blame the bullies for being ignorant or having evil in their hearts. In his mind, they didn't know any better. Still he blamed me for getting angry and losing my temper…" His voice broke. "Or maybe he didn't. But it felt to me like he did. But they were threatening and hurting my mother. What else could I do?"

His voice trailed off again. Suddenly she could see

him, in her mind's eye, standing there with his small fists raised. Sudden and unbidden tears filled her eyes.

"I know you don't seem to believe that God calls people to things or that God has His hand on your life," she said. "But I've lost track of the number of times I've seen you call out to God to help us through. I believe, or at least I think, that maybe God was calling you to do exactly what you're doing. Maybe God called you to protect people. Maybe God really did want you to become a US marshal in witness protection. You just tried to go about it in the wrong way."

She didn't know much. She didn't know this man and couldn't begin to pretend she understood his story. But she knew the God he'd read about in the Bible as a child. She knew the God he'd prayed to and called out to. She knew what she believed.

"Do you miss the Amish way of life?" she asked.

He glanced at her sideways. "With almost every beat of my heart. But that doesn't change the fact I know who I am and what I'm meant to be doing."

Okay. Then didn't he hear what he was saying? How couldn't he see what was so clearly in front of him?

"I don't believe God would put a calling on your heart if it wasn't God's plan for your life," she said.

"I know that's what you believe," he said. "But do you think it was God's plan for your apartment to blow up? Or for you to be on the run from killers? Do you think any of what you're going through is bringing you closer to that house in the country? Because I'm telling you that's not what life in witness protection is like."

Something bristled at the back of her neck.

"Hope doesn't make a person weak, Jonathan. Neither does faith."

"I wasn't meaning to imply it did," he said, then he sighed. "I'm sorry, I'm not good at this. I'm a very private person and I don't like letting people in. So I'd appreciate it if you didn't tell anyone about what happened today. Not about my brother. Not about my past. None of it."

There was something final about the way he said it, like a door had closed somewhere in the air between them.

"Of course not," she said. "I don't know when or how I even would."

"You've been reassigned to US Marshal Stacy Preston," he said without looking her direction. "In a little over an hour we'll reach the drop-off point, meet up with her and go our separate ways."

She sat back on the uncomfortable vinyl seat, sucking in a sudden shallow and painful breath like she'd just had the wind knocked from her.

She was being reassigned to Stacy? Why? How? What did this mean? A dozen questions filled her mind, but only one escaped her lips.

"Will I ever see you again?" she asked.

He shook his head. His shoulders dropped as sudden sadness seemed to sweep over him.

"No," he said. "Probably not."

Oh. She leaned back against the seat, trying to ignore the prickling of tears at the edge of her eyelids and the pain of her breath as it rose and fell in her chest.

God really was closing a door, then. Whatever it was she felt, whatever it was that had nudged her toward Jonathan, God was closing a door, changing her path, and there was nothing she could do about it.

The late-afternoon sun flashed against the windshield, blinding her eyes and pushing the tears closer to falling. She closed her eyes and turned her head away, suddenly feeling too tired to keep them open. She couldn't remember the last time she'd slept, really slept. Jonathan didn't speak. Neither did she. She just sat there with her eyes closed and her head leaning against the vinyl headrest, feeling the uncomfortable springs pressing against her. She wasn't sure how long she drifted in that uncomfortable space between being neither fully awake nor asleep. She felt she'd been fighting sadness, doubt and fear for so very long, and it had finally caught up with her, lapping at her heels, sweeping her over, pulling her down.

Lord, what's going on? Why did You bring this man into my life and why am I feeling drawn to him if he's about to leave?

No, she wouldn't give up hope. She couldn't. Somehow this was all going to work out according to God's plan. Stacy was a wonderful agent and she'd connected really well with her. Stacy would keep her safe. Everything was going to be okay. It had to be.

A car filled her eyes in an instant, small, black and seeming to come from nowhere. Then it hit them with a bang, hard and deafening, seeming to shake the truck and throwing her hard against the passenger door.

"Hang on!" Jonathan shouted. The truck swerved. "Help us, Lord. Save us, *Gott*."

She held on tight as the world shook. They were spinning, flying off the road. Metal screeched. The truck crashed, cutting off Jonathan's prayers in an instant. She looked up.

There was a web of broken glass. Beside her, Jonathan was slumped over the steering wheel. "Jonathan!" Her hand fumbled for the seat belt.

Help us, Lord! Please help us, Lord.

She released the seat belt and turned toward him. The door fell open beside her. Hands rushed in, dragging her backward, clamping a rag over her face and stifling a scream as it tried to escape her lips. Something sickening and sweet filled her senses.

She tumbled backward, feeling herself being yanked roughly from the truck.

Her body hit the ground. Darkness swirled around her, threatening to pull her under.

Jonathan's head ached. Stars filled his eyes and pain pulsed through his body. He slumped forward and the long, loud, wailing sound of a horn filled his ears and echoed through his head. Celeste's muffled scream still hung in the air. They'd been in a car crash, a direct collision with a vehicle that had shot out of a side road, rammed into them and forced them off the road, like someone on a near suicide mission. They'd been thrown into a wild spin as the old truck's brakes had seized. His eyes refused to open. His body refused to move.

Save me, God! I'm helpless! I know I tried to push You away. I know I've stubbornly thought I could live this life on my own. But right now, I can't do this on my own. I need Your help. I need to save Celeste.

Her face filled his barely conscious mind. Those beautiful green eyes huge with curiosity and intellect. The way her hair fell in soft blond waves around her face. The way her fingers felt when they slipped in between his. The way she pushed and challenged him, chipping away at the walls surrounding his heart until he feared they just might swing open. No, he couldn't let the pain win. He had to fight back. He had to push through. He had to save her.

"Help me, God! Help me save Celeste!" His eyes snapped open as the prayer left his lips. He peered through the windshield, watching through the cracks as a young man half carried and half dragged Celeste toward it. He popped the trunk and pulled Celeste toward it.

No! He would not take her.

Jonathan yanked the seat belt away and tumbled from the truck, landing hard on one knee.

"Stop!" Jonathan pulled himself to his feet and raised his hands with his service weapon clutched steadily in his grasp. "Put her down! Gently! Then get down on the ground! Hands in the air!"

The man froze. He was maybe in his late twenties, with a thin face that had seen more than his fair share of beatings. Jonathan didn't want to shoot him, especially not while he was holding Celeste, but he was prepared to if that was what it took to save her life. Jonathan steadied the gun.

"Don't be a fool," Jonathan said. "You have nowhere to go and I'm not going to let you take her. I really don't want to kill you. Please, don't make me."

Seconds passed. The wind brushed the trees. The setting sun blazed across the horizon. Then the young man crouched slowly and set Celeste on the snowy ground. She groaned softly, stretched and curled up into a ball. *Thank You, God!*

"Hands up!" Jonathan barked. "Step away from her! Now! What did you do to her?"

But as he stepped closer, one whiff of the sweet scene in the air told him even before the criminal did.

"Just chloroform!" The man's hands shot straight above his head. "Small amount! Just so she'd come easy."

"You mean, just so she couldn't fight back!" Jonathan gritted his teeth. Okay, it would take a while to wear off, but she should be okay. The way the man's eyes darted to the skyline and back told him everything he needed to know. "You're a coward. You could've killed all of us, and for what?"

"Look, I don't want any trouble!" The man's voice shook. "I just really, really need the money. And I wasn't going to hurt her. I promise!"

The money. Again, this promise of money had criminals taking foolish risks to hurt her. How could he or Stacy or any US marshal ever hope to protect her from something like this? From desperate people taking foolish risks from every corner to get their hands on her?

"Tell me, how much money is her life worth?"

The man didn't answer.

"Fifty thousand dollars?"

"I wasn't going to hurt her. I promise."

"You drugged and tried to kidnap a woman for fifty thousand dollars!" Jonathan barked.

The man's eyes grew wide. They were glassy and bloodshot. Pity stabbed Jonathan's heart. He was probably an addict. "Yes…sir… I wasn't going to hurt her. I promise! Nothing bad was going to happen to her!"

He wasn't sure who the man needed to convince more, Jonathan or himself. He'd had enough of this. He was going to get his answers right here, right now. "Where were you going to take her? Who were you taking her to?"

"Nobody! I wasn't taking her anywhere!" The man's eyes grew wide. His arms began to bend, but Jonathan's weapon twitched in his hand and the man's arms shot back up again. "I was taking her to a motel room, but not to do anything bad! I promise! All I needed to do was what the website said. I needed to take a video of her, showing I had her, and upload it to Poindexter's website. Then I'd get the money sent to me. Anonymously."

"Then what?"

"Then nothing!" he stammered. "Once the money was in my account, I was going to leave her there, call 9-1-1 and then the police would come get her! Promise!"

No, whoever was behind this would've made him give them his address and wait there until they arrived. Then they'd have killed him. He didn't even want to imagine what they'd have planned for Celeste. He allowed himself one quick glance at her, curled on the ground, sheltered by the warm cloak Rosie had given her.

Hang on, please. Just one moment longer.

His heart ached between the desire to do his job and the need to sweep her up into his arms. Instead, he steeled his resolve. He'd been chasing his tail like a barn cat ever since he'd rescued her from the farmhouse.

"Is it true the same website that has people trying to kidnap her is giving out rewards for taking her picture or posting video of where she is?" Jonathan asked. "And who's behind this? Who's giving the orders?"

The man blinked. "Poindexter!"

"Poindexter is in jail awaiting trial!" Jonathan shouted. "His real name is Dexter Thomes!"

"No, the feds arrested the wrong guy! Celeste was wrong. Dexter Thomes isn't Poindexter. The real Poindexter is out there! He keeps posting updates and instructions!"

That may be what the man believed—Jonathan didn't

for an instant. Celeste was convinced that the man she had tracked down, Dexter Thomes, was Poindexter and that was good enough for him.

"Besides!" he added. "Some people online are saying that not only is Dexter Thomes not Poindexter, he isn't even in jail! Police are covering up the fact he escaped! It's all over the dark web!"

How do I protect her from the enemy when the enemy is the internet itself and its ability to exploit people's greed and their willingness to spread lies?

"How did you know where to find us?" Jonathan asked. The man's hand flinched toward his pocket. "Hands up!"

"I was just reaching for my phone!" he said. "I was going to show you! Poindexter's set up a new portal on the dark web for people wanting to win money by helping him find her. Cell phone pictures, video clips, traffic cameras and store security footage. From there it's really easy to triangulate possible locations and hope you get the right one. You know, the typical scavenger hunt stuff!"

How was a US marshal ever able to protect a witness from the entire electronic world?

Jonathan walked forward. "Put your hands on the hood of your car and keep them there. Don't even think about moving."

He advanced slowly, thankful to see the criminal back up as he did so. He waited until he saw him place his hands on the car, then he reached Celeste and crouched on one knee beside her. While he allowed himself only a quick glance at her from his peripheral vision, it was like every synapse in his brain and fiber in his body was keenly focused on her. He brushed his fingers along her face, felt her shudder against his touch and the warmth of her breath. He swept her up into his arms and cradled her there with one hand, while the other kept the gun trained on the criminal.

"Don't worry," he whispered. "I'll get you out of here and somewhere warm soon. I promise."

"Please!" The man shook. "Don't kill me! I just wanted the money."

Him and how many others? And if this man had found them, how soon until the next one did?

"Throw your phone and your driver's license down on the road," Jonathan shouted. He had no choice but to let him go. If he made him walk or handcuffed him in his car, he could freeze to death before anyone found him. And taking him with them where he was going was definitely not an option. Hopefully, he wouldn't make it too far with his car dented and wrecked from the collision. Jonathan had only one priority and she was currently nestled securely in the crook of him arm.

The man peeled out so quickly Jonathan was afraid he was going to spin out again. He fishtailed, righted himself and sped off.

Thank You, Gott.

He holstered his weapon and pulled Celeste deeper into his arms. Her eyes fluttered. Her body was limp in his arms, but her pulse was strong.

"Just give me one moment, and then I'm going to take you to the safest place I know."

He steeled his heart. He was going back to Amish country. He was going to take her home.

Chapter Eleven

Celeste seemed to be drifting between awake and asleep, from what he could tell. He kept talking to her as he carried her to the car, promising her that when she woke up he'd make sure she was somewhere safe. He laid her carefully in the back seat of the truck long enough to kick the windshield out from the inside. Then he sat beside her in the back seat, cradling her face and neck with one arm while he checked the man's ID.

Steven Penn, aged twenty. What a mundane name and a young age for someone to be in such a bad and desperate place. Poindexter's page was open on Steven's phone, open to a gallery of pictures. He scrolled. There it was, all of it. The location of the farmhouse safe house. Lee's video phone footage of Miller's attempt to kidnap her. Drone photos from the lot where they swapped out the trucks. Cell phone pictures from the diner, which he guessed were taken from the teenager of the electronics-addicted family. Then, finally, the traffic camera where he'd slowed to a stop outside Hope's Creek. No wonder they'd known how to find her. He talked the photos through with Celeste out loud as he looked at them, describing each one in turn. Could she hear him? He hoped so.

"You were right," he said. He stroked her head. Her blond hair tumbled through his fingers. "The diner wasn't as safe as I thought it was, and you were right about the drone. I should've listened to you. I should've told Hunter that you needed to be involved in setting up your own protection plan. We've never faced an enemy like this before. It's not a person—it's a swarm of enemies all connected by one unknown spider manipulating them through the web. I don't know how to fight this. All I can do is run."

He placed a quick call to an encrypted mailbox where he knew he could leave a message for Chief Deputy Hunter undetected. He told her there'd been another attempt on his assignment's life and gave her Steven's full name, social security number, driver's license and license plate. He told her they were going dark, he'd call as soon as he could and he'd keep Celeste safe.

He left her buckled safely in the back seat of the truck, as far away from the missing windshield as possible. He placed the phone under the wheel of the truck and backed over it. Then he turned the truck around and drove back toward Hope's Creek, sticking to back roads and inching along, feeling the cold breeze whipping at him over the dashboard and through the empty hole where the windshield had been.

His eyes cast constant glances in the rearview mirror. He watched as Celeste dozed, lying curled up sweet and peaceful, in the back seat of the truck, her chest rising and falling, and her eyes fluttering, as if she was in a restful sleep just awaiting someone to wake her. He kept talking to her as he drove. Not about anything important. Just stories from childhood, about barn cats and rabbits, and how he'd run down the hill with his brother and twisted his ankle, but stubbornly walked home on it anyway. As sun was setting low beneath the sky, he crested a steep hill and stopped at the top, looking down at the frozen lake that lay below.

"Okay, Celeste, this is where we get out," he said. He put the car in Neutral, pulled the emergency brake and hopped out. Then he opened the back door and pulled Celeste into his arms again. "We need to ditch the vehicle. I suspect Steven is going to get picked up pretty soon and I don't think anybody's going to trace this old truck. But we can't risk it. The last thing we want is someone spotting it on a traffic camera or drone."

"Mmm-hmm," she murmured softly.

She nestled closer to him. The scent of her filled his senses. Protecting her was hardest thing he'd ever had to do in his life, but he wouldn't have traded the assignment for anything in the world. He cradled her to his chest, popped the brake and leaned hard into the truck with one shoulder. The truck rolled slowly down the hill and out onto the ice. The tires skimmed across the surface for one brief moment before crashing through and sinking slowly under the water.

He waited. The wind shook the trees and buffeted his body. He held Celeste tighter.

She whimpered in his arms. "Jonathan? Where are we? What's happening?"

"Shh, it's okay," he whispered. "You're safe. I've got you. We've just got a little bit of a walk ahead of us."

He bent down and pressed his forehead against hers, feeling the softness of her skin and the warmth of her breath. Their lips were so close that all it would've taken was to let himself move just an inch and their mouths would've touched. Instead, he pulled back, feeling something stir inside him, like something long dead coming to life.

Eventually the truck disappeared under the surface. His eyes rose, watching as the setting sun spread long lines of endless pink and gold along the darkening sky.

Help me, Lord, I can't do this without You.

He started walking, trudging across the fields in knee-deep snow, taking one step at a time, with nothing but the bag over his shoulder, the clothes on his back and the woman he was bound to protect held in his arms.

"I'm taking you home, Celeste," he said, not knowing if she could hear him, but that talking to her helped more than she'd ever know. "Back to the house where I grew up. You get to meet my father, Eli, and see the rest of the family again. I'm really very scared about it, honestly. Terrified. See, knowing you've made a mistake is a whole lot different than knowing how to fix it or what to say. I mean, how do you apologize for leaving home for years? What do you say? My father and I have always struggled to communicate. He really likes his silences. And now Mark says his health is failing. My brother put his life and his family's lives on the line to protect us? How could he ever ask them to risk their lives again?"

The sky was an inky wash of dark purple and blue as the farm where he'd grown up in came into view. He'd always heard that things from childhood looked smaller than adults remembered. But somehow it was even bigger—a large farmhouse in the middle with its snow-covered roof and huge white porch, framed by a barn for the horses and another for the buggy and wagon, a hutch for the rabbits and chickens, and fields on the other, ringed by fences and trees. A second, smaller house not much larger than a cabin, had been built beside the main house since he'd left. That would be the *grossdaadi* house where his father lived.

His footsteps slowed as he carried her across the fields, down the long drive and to the front steps.

I'm not even sure how or why I started praying to You again, Gott. *It kind of snuck up on me, but somehow I don't know how to stop. There are so many ways this can go wrong. But Celeste said that if I trusted You that You would guide me. Please help me protect her. I need You now.*

He knocked on the front door. It swung open. There stood a bearded man, with hair white from age and piercing blue eyes. Jonathan felt his head bow.

"Pa, forgive me." He choked on unshed tears he'd never let fall. "I was wrong to leave and I am sure it hurt you to hear I came to town today and did not visit. I don't know the right thing to say to heal what I did. But I'm here for your help. I need sanctuary. I need your help to protect this woman's life."

His father nodded. There was a long pause in which Jonathan could only guess what he was thinking. "*Gott* heals all things in His time." He turned and looked over his shoulder, and it was only then that Jonathan saw Amos, Miriam, Rosie and Mark watching in a silent tableau from the kitchen doorway. "Come quickly. Your brother and this woman need our help."

The smell of something warm and delicious and comforting roused Celeste slowly. She stretched to find she was lying on a bed that was so impossibly soft her body seemed to be sinking into the quilts. She opened her eyes, and it took her a long moment to adjust to the darkness. Then she saw the light of the moon, silver and simple, shining down through a gap in the curtains.

"How are you?" a woman's voice asked. Then the golden glimmer of lamplight moved through the darkness. She rolled over and saw Miriam sitting on a chair by a low table.

"I'm okay, thank you," Celeste said. She sat up slowly, feeling the grogginess that had kept pulling her under time and again recede to the edges of her mind.

She remembered everything that had happened since the car crash, and yet the memories were fuzzy, like dreams she'd kept drifting in and out of.

The car accident. The abduction attempt. Being chloroformed. The long cold drive before abandoning the truck and continuing on foot. And the stories Jonathan had told her. Dozens of them, it felt like, all about his childhood, his life and his childhood faith, as if the closed book of his life had suddenly opened up and spilled out when she was her weakest and needed something to hold on to in order to keep the fear at bay. Sudden emotion swelled in her chest. He'd been struggling so hard with coming back home, and yet he had, for her, to keep her safe.

Lord, whatever he's doing now, wherever he is and whatever's happening, please guide him and be with him.

"How's Jonathan?" she asked. "Where is he? Is he okay?"

"He's asleep in the chair by the fire," Miriam said. She stood slowly. "He stayed up sitting with Eli, his father, for a long while."

Yes, she vaguely remembered the old man with the white beard and kind eyes who'd greeted them.

"What did they talk about?" Celeste asked.

Miriam smiled softly. "I don't think they talked much at all. Sometimes it is better to sit and be silent with someone when you don't have the right words to say. The Lord moves in silences just as well as He does in words. Now, I brought you some stew, along with some fresh bread, a glass of cold water and another of milk. Jonathan said you would be hungry."

"Yes, I am, thank you." Celeste swung her legs over the side of the bed and was grateful to feel they weren't as wobbly as she'd feared they'd be. "How long have I been here?"

"A couple of hours," Miriam said. "You woke up a bit and I helped you walk upstairs. I made sure you were okay and then told Jonathan to let you sleep."

Miriam set a lamp down. She pulled a small table over beside the bed and placed the tray holding the simple meal on it. As Miriam turned and picked up the light again, the glow cast gentle shadows along her form, highlighting the tight, round curve of her belly, through the thin, soft fabric of her home dress. Miriam followed her gaze, and there was a sweet, almost dreamy quality to her smile. One hand slid protectively over her stomach.

"Yes, Amos and I are having another child this spring," she said. "He always wanted a large family. Rosie and Mark's father died when they were very young, and Amos was so happy to become their *pa*. Then came David and Samuel. Now *Gott* is blessing us with one more."

Celeste swallowed hard. This woman was pregnant, had been threatened by a criminal in front of her children and still had the grace and courage to welcome her into their home. Jonathan had been so right when he'd reminded her not to judge someone by appearances.

"I don't know how to thank you for protecting me," Celeste started. Her head shook. "You don't know me and have no reason to help me. And you've done so much…"

Her voice trailed off.

"Hush now," Miriam said firmly, "and eat, then sleep. We can talk more about your situation in the morning."

Celeste nodded. She started to eat. The food was warm, hot, soothing and delicious, with tender chunks of beef, along with carrots, potatoes and another root vegetable she couldn't place. There was a quiet to this place and to Miriam that she appreciated. She'd never been good at small talk and always felt socially awkward around strangers. It was nice, somehow, to be able to feel it was okay to just sit there in the peace and not try to find the right words to say.

"This is really good," she said after a long moment. "I've never tasted anything like it."

"It's Amos's favorite," Miriam said. "The baby's, too."

"How did you two meet?" Celeste asked.

"At my shop," she said. "The building belonged to Rosie and Mark's father. His name was Isaac. He said he always felt that God wanted him to use it to help others. He wanted to take things that were unwanted, unused and damaged, repair them, and give them to others who needed them. He wanted to raise money to help people doing God's work overseas. He believed in healing broken things."

Her eyes glanced past Celeste to the window, as if looking at something very far away.

"We moved here as a family, following his dream,"

she continued. "But he died before the store was open. I was alone with nothing, in a new community and a widow with two small children. Many people were very kind to us. Then I met Amos. He was carrying a lot of hurt and a lot of anger."

"I know Jonathan regrets hurting him very much," Celeste said.

"Three stubborn men living under one roof, all of whom lost the woman who held them together." Miriam shook her head. "Like bulls knocking around hurting themselves and each other. When I met Amos he had such a deep need to love and be loved." Her smile deepened. "We healed each other's hearts. Two months after we met, we were married."

"So quick?" Celeste felt herself gasp and then felt guilty almost immediately. "I'm sorry. I shouldn't judge anybody else's relationship. I've never had what you and Amos have. I wouldn't know what it's like."

A chuckle slipped Miriam's lips, but not an unkind one. It reminded her of the way her mother would laugh under her breath when Celeste complained she would never solve a computer problem just moments before she invariably did.

Instead, all Miriam said was, "Get sleep while you can. I'll make sure Rosie comes in to wake you in the morning and helps you get dressed. In the meantime, there is a nightdress for you at the end of the bed. Sleep well."

"Thank you."

Miriam slipped out of the room, with a rustle of fabric and skirts.

Celeste waited until the door was closed, then set the tray back down on the table and changed into the nightgown. She guessed it was Mark's room she'd been

given and wondered where the young man was sleeping.
Miriam had taken the lamp with her, but dim moon-
light filtered through the window and slowly her eyes
adjusted. She crawled under what felt like a mountain
of blankets, pulled them up around her chin and curled
into a ball. There was something soft and gentle about
the darkness and silence that surrounded her.

What time was it? She had no way of knowing. It
could be after midnight. It could be as early as nine.
Whatever time it was she doubted somehow that she'd
have been in bed if she was back home in her old apartment. No, she'd likely be reading a book on her tablet,
surfing the internet on her laptop, clicking through social
media on her phone or streaming something on her tele-
vision. Doing anything other than lying still and letting
the darkness enfold her. She took a deep breath and let it
out slowly, feeling an odd sense of peace spread through
her limbs. It was only then she realized with a start that
her usual tension headache and the nagging pain she was
so used to feeling in her limbs was gone.

Despite the chaos, despite the fear, despite the un-
certainly, there was a deeper, more enveloping peace
that surpassed her understanding.

*Thank You, Lord. I don't know what You're doing.
I don't know why I'm here or what happens next. But
thank You for bringing me here. Please be with this family and in this home. Help me share this sense of Your
love and peace with Jonathan...*

She drifted off to sleep with the US marshal's dark
eyes filling her mind and his name on her lips.

Celeste was awoken by the morning sun spreading
across the floor and onto her face. Then came the sounds

of birds chirping, animals baying, the twins running up and down the hall, and dishes clattering from the kitchen below her. She sat up and looked out, feeling her breath catch in her throat at the beauty that spread out beneath her. Prayers of thanksgiving surged through her heart that her mind couldn't even begin to find words for.

A gentle knock brushed the door frame.

"Hello?" It was Rosie.

"Come in." A smile crossed Celeste's lips as the door slid open and the young woman's face filled the doorway, her arms filled with brightly colored fabric. She slipped from between the covers and gave the young woman a hug. "It is so wonderful to see you again."

"You, too." Rosie smiled. "Mamm thought you might like some help getting dressed."

Three dresses hung loose and soft over her one arm, one in peach, one in a bright green and one in the faintest yellow. In the other she held a small white prayer *kapp* and box of pins. She laid the dresses down on the bed. "And our last lesson in how to pin a dress was rather rushed."

Hidden behind a curtain while a criminal came looking for her. Yes, it had been.

She giggled. Celeste laughed.

"Well, I'm very happy we have more time now," Celeste said. Her hands ran over the fabric and let it fall through her fingers. She couldn't believe how good the fabric felt or how lovely and delicate the colors were. She'd always assumed that the fact Amish clothing was plain meant it couldn't also be pretty. But the simple colors and the way the fabric flowed was more beautiful than anything she was used to.

She chose the green dress, and then paid close attention to every tuck, fold and pleat as Rosie helped her pin it on. After that the younger woman waited while Celeste brushed her hair and curled it into a bun, and then helped her pin her white starched *kapp* in place.

They walked through a hallway and down the stairs to the kitchen. Warmth and clatter rose to greet her, with the smells of sizzling bacon and eggs. They stepped into the kitchen. It was the largest kitchen she'd ever seen, with drip coffee brewing on the wood-burning stove and a long wooden table that she imagined would sit at least fifteen. It was laden with breads, jams, preserves, fruit compote and skillets of eggs and cheese.

Amos, Mark, David and Samuel were so engrossed in their breakfast and happy conversation that they didn't seem to have noticed her. But her eyes were drawn to one man, sitting tall and strong at the side of the table, in a simple white shirt and overalls, his dark hair with a touch of curl bent low over his food. Jonathan turned and looked up at her with a look so simple and honest that it stole her words from her lips.

She then realized the only one missing was his father, Eli.

"*Gude mariye!* Good morning!" Miriam's voice turned her attention to the sideboard, where Miriam stood with a frothy pitcher of milk. "How did you sleep?"

"Very well," Celeste said, her voice sounding more relaxed than she was used to. "I think that was the best night's sleep I've ever had."

All forks dropped and conversation stopped. The men rose, but Jonathan was quickest to his feet.

"Welcome," Amos said. "We apologize for starting to eat without you, but Miriam said we should let you

sleep and that you'd probably prefer a more relaxed start
your morning."

Celeste felt a smile cross her lips. "Yes, she was right,
thank you."

There was a slight pause, then Amos waved his
hands and people sat down and went back to eating. All
but Jonathan, who stayed standing, his eyes locked on
her face with a look so genuine and raw that it was like
they were the only two people in the kitchen. Maybe
even in the world. He pulled out the chair beside him.
She walked over to him. He waited.

"We'll talk later, after breakfast," he said quietly.
"How are you?"

His hand brushed her back as he pulled the chair out
for her. They sat. She turned to look at him. How was
it possible this extraordinary man was just inches away
from her, sharing a meal with her in his family home?

"I'm very good," she said. And she was, in a way
she didn't know how to explain or put into words. Here
in this kitchen, with people she barely knew, she felt at
peace in a way she couldn't ever remember feeling before. That longing in her heart had returned, tugging her
toward the place where it belonged. Could it be something like this? A large, warm kitchen with a table full
of food? A married couple in love with four children
and another on the way? A space filled with people who
clearly cared about each other and God?

Conversation flowed cheerfully and happily around
the table. David told her that he'd found three eggs the
day before and wondered how many he'd find today.
Samuel wanted to go sledding. Rosie was excited her
favorite horse was going to have a foal.

They lingered over the meal, sitting and talking

long after the food was done. When the meal was done, Amos rose to help Miriam and Rosie clear the dishes. When Celeste tried to join them, Miriam waved a hand in her direction, with a smile on her face that was inscrutable yet sweet. "Why don't you get Jonathan to show you around the farm?"

"I'll help you!" David shouted, rising to his feet.

Samuel was only a moment away on his heels. "I'm coming, too!"

Celeste glanced at Jonathan. He looked at the boy's eager faces. A smile beamed across his face and set something alight in his eyes, as if he was seeing for the first time something he'd thought he'd lost.

"I'm sure your uncle Jonathan and Celeste would like a quiet walk…" Amos started.

But Jonathan held up a hand. "I'd love for David and Samuel to show us around. If that's all right with Celeste."

"It's very all right," she said.

The boys yelped and ran for the door, only remembering to pause and clear their dishes when their father waved his hand ever so slightly in their direction. The boys wriggled into their boots and put their hats on. When they dashed outside, two farm dogs raced up to greet them.

"There are a couple pairs of boots by the door," Miriam said. "Take whichever pair fits you best, and we'll pick up some that are the right size from the store later today. There are mittens on the bench. The cloak and bonnet closest to the door are for you."

"Thank you," Celeste said, realizing she'd said the words more in the past few hours than she'd said in her life. "How do I say that in Pennsylvania Dutch?"

"Danke." Miriam smiled widely.

Celeste felt her own smile grow in response. *"Danke."*

She slid her feet into a pair of soft brown boots and slipped the cloak around her shoulders. It was warm and comforting. A gentle blast of cold air made her look up. Jonathan was holding the door open. A warm brown jacket sat around his shoulders, and a wide-brimmed hat covered his head. He reached for her arm.

"It's pretty icy," he said. "Let me help you. The paths can be kind of tricky until you get used to them." Her hand slid neatly into the crook of his arm. She followed him outside. The farmhouse door slid closed behind them.

"I want you to wear a cloak and bonnet whenever you're outside," he said. "I don't think we have to worry about aerial drones here. We'd be able to see them a mile away. But I will feel better knowing that you're as un-recognizable as possible."

She nodded. "Agreed."

Her eyes scanned his form. The simple coat high-lighted the muscles of his broad shoulders and chest, tapering down to his abs. Then she blinked as something hit her.

"You're not carrying your gun! Where is it?"

"In a locked box in the shed," Jonathan said. A frown creased the lines between his eyes. "It was the condition my *pa* set. We are welcome in his house and he will protect us. But all weapons have to stay outside."

Chapter Twelve

"Come on!" David yelled, scampering ahead toward the barn.

"I'm coming!" Jonathan replied, and tilted his head toward Celeste. "It's still very hard for Amos and Pa to accept that I went into law enforcement. They are very conflicted." He ran his hand over his beard. "As am I."

He guided her up the path, through the snow and toward the barn, holding her as tightly as he dared. The memory of how they'd arrived, cradling her in his arms and to his chest, filled his mind. If he was ever close to her like that again one day, under better circumstances, he might be tempted to ask if he could kiss her smiling mouth. He knew, though, that having any kind of relationship with her was impossible.

"Why wasn't your dad at breakfast this morning?" she asked.

"I saw him early this morning," Jonathan said. "He said he needed time alone with *Gott* to think and pray. We shared a cup of coffee before he left. We talked a bit last night. Well, less talked than sat beside each other in silence and watched the fire. He is a good and a very

Godly man, but has never been one to talk or say those words of reassurance I needed. When I was younger I couldn't handle how quiet he was, how he was drawn into long silences and never answered my questions. How could he work for hours in a field without talking, especially when my mind was full of conflicting thoughts? It wasn't until I'd lived in the *Englisch* world, with its oversharing on social media and its need for instant gratification to every nosy impulse for information, that I began to understand the value of being quiet and keeping some things inside. Now that he is older and his mind is slower, he talks even less. But he has welcomed me home. And I am not about to change the personality of a sixty-five-year-old man. I guess I will get used to sitting in silence and waiting."

"Do you think he's forgiven you?" Celeste asked.

"He forgave me years ago, even as I was storming out the door."

He waited for her to pry, to ask more questions and to dig away at the broken parts of him he wasn't ready to reveal. Instead, she said, "I'm glad it went well. If there's anything more you want to tell me, I'm happy to listen."

Gratitude flooded his heart, followed by a wordless longing to have this woman by his side, protecting her and caring for her.

The boys reached the barn, pushed the door open and tumbled inside, leaving the door open.

"Wait right there!" David called. "We have a surprise!"

"We'll wait!" Jonathan chuckled, then he turned to Celeste. "How much do you remember from the pursuit last night?"

"It's kind of jumbled," she said. "I remember the crash and the man who chloroformed me. I remember you took his phone but let him live."

"I couldn't hold him," Jonathan said, "and wasn't about to let him freeze to death. So I let him go and called Deputy Chief Hunter from his phone. Then I disposed of both the truck and the phone."

"I remember all that, but it's cloudy," she said. "He had pictures of me, right?"

"Someone calling themselves Poindexter has set up a website collecting pictures and videos of you," he sighed, wishing he could spare her this. "He's paying for each tip he gets. He's offering fifty thousand to anyone who kidnaps you. I don't know why."

"I do," Celeste said. "Dexter doesn't know how I found him. He doesn't know how I beat him and how he was hacked. If he kills me and I don't testify at trial, he'll get away with the theft. But he'll always know he lost to me and he'll never know how. If you let me create an encrypted server and go online, I could review the website data and tell you who's running it and who's behind it."

He shook his head, watching the light dim in her eyes as he did so.

"I'm sorry," he said. "I wish I could. I really do. But it's not safe."

Her gaze dropped to the snow beneath their feet. "I wish you believed I could do it."

"Oh, I do believe in you, Celeste." His voice dropped. His hand brushed her chin and tilted it up, until her eyes were looking into his. "I have complete faith in your abilities and I wish I had believed you sooner. I know if anyone can figure out who's running Poindexter's website, why we have Dexter Thomes's doppelgänger running around and where the stolen money is, it's you. But it's not safe. Not with the tools they have at their disposal and the bounty they've put on your head."

Her eyes searched his face. She was just inches away from him. The warmth of her breath tickled his cold skin. He wanted to wrap his arms around her waist and pull her to his chest. He wanted to tell her that she was brilliant and impressive, and he believed in her calling to do what she did with computers just as much, or even more, than he believed in his own to be a US marshal. And more than anything he wanted to admit just how very much he wished he could kiss her.

"Come on!" David called. "We've found the kittens!"

"We're coming!" Jonathan stepped back like a man waking up from a dream. He steeled his resolve. He didn't know how, but he was going to make things right for her. He needed to. "I'm going into town with Amos this afternoon. He says there are some disposable phones that have been donated to the store. I'll use one to check in with Chief Deputy Hunter. And I need you to stay here."

"But it's not safe!" she said. "What if Doppel-Dex is still stalking Hope's Creek? What if he recognizes you?"

He shrugged. "That's risk I need to take. But I don't think he will. He doesn't seem focused on finding me, just you."

He tried to pull away from her arm, but still she could feel her heels digging into the snow. "Wait! I want to stay with you. I don't want us to split up and either of us go off alone."

"I know," he said. "But I can't be by your side every hour of the day, and you were supposed to be assigned to a new agent soon. Miriam, Mark and Rosie will stay home today. If they see anyone coming, they'll hide you in the cold cellar. Trust me. I won't be gone long, and you will be safer staying here than coming into town."

How could she trust she was safe somewhere without electricity or even a telephone?

Lord, You brought me here. Help me trust in You.

It was hours before Jonathan and Amos left to go into town. She didn't know quite how long or even how to tell time without incessantly glancing at her phone. But it was long enough that she was able to play with the barn kittens, pat the horses and then get a long explanation on how cows and pigs had to be kept at opposite ends of the barn because, as Samuel put it, they "weren't friends." Then it was a trip to the henhouse to meet David's favorite chickens. When she returned to the farmhouse, Miriam taught her how to bake fresh bread for lunch, before taking her on a tour of the pantry and cold cellar to choose pickles and preserves for lunch.

It wasn't until the sun had already crested the sky and started its descent into the afternoon that Jonathan pulled her into his arms, gave her a long hug and the promise he'd be back soon, then climbed into the buggy with Amos and left. Celeste sat on a chair in the living room by the fire and watched the sky long after they'd gone.

For a while Miriam and Rosie sat with her in the living room. Rosie was knitting what seemed to be a long, thick scarf and Miriam was sewing a quilt for the new baby. Celeste sat, listening to the quiet rustle of fabric and clicking of needles as conversation flowed gently between them like a three-part harmony. They spoke about their farm, the foods they'd grown for the winter and their faith.

The two other women excused themselves to go upstairs, but when Celeste got up to follow they waved her down. She wasn't sure if they wanted her to rest or wanted to talk privately without her. Either way, she thanked them and stayed, enjoying the peaceful crackle of the fire, the rustle of the trees outside and the occasional clopping of a buggy going past. After a while a large cat, orange and impossibly soft, appeared at Celeste's feet and, after rubbing around her ankles, leaped up, curled onto her lap and nudged her hand. She ran her fingers through his long fur, feeling the deep rumble of his purr in her fingertips.

The front door creaked. She looked up to see a short man with a wide-brimmed hat and a long white beard stepping over the threshold.

"I'm Eli Mast," he said. He took off his hat. "I'm not sure if you remember, but we met last night?"

"Yes! Hello!" The memory was fuzzy and yet she knew there was something about the old man that both then and now made her feel safe. She'd started to rise when he waved her back down.

"No, sit," he said, "Zeb doesn't like most people and is very particular about who he chooses to sit with. If he's decided to sit on you, he must have decided you're something special."

He hung his hat on a peg by the door and settled into a chair. But it wasn't until his blue eyes, filled with a strength and wisdom that belied his age, fixed on her that she saw the resemblance between father and son.

They sat without speaking for a while, watching the flames dance against the wood.

"So, you are the woman who brought my son home to me," he said.

A sudden flush of heat rose to her cheeks and she raised her hands to cover it. No! It wasn't like that at all. Oh, how to explain it?

"I'm a witness in an important court case involving computers," she said slowly. "And your son Jonathan is a US marshal whose job it is to protect me."

"Yes, yes, I know," he said. "You used the internet to solve a bank robbery and now the robber is using the internet to get people to come after you."

She felt her lips part slightly in surprise and closed them quickly before it showed. "That's pretty much it, yes."

"I know the outward circumstances of what brought you here," he said. He ran his hand down his long beard. He spoke quietly, like someone who knew he was nearing the end of his life and was trying to make every word matter. "But the Lord isn't about outward circumstances now, is He?"

She shook her head. "No, I don't believe He is."

"I've been praying for a long time that *Gott* would return my son to me at the proper time. Now you're here."

Yes, that was what she wanted to believe to. That God had brought her here. That this house, this home and his family were part of God's plan. And that somehow, in some way, God's plan included Jonathan—the handsome, amazing and broken man her heart was being drawn to deeper and deeper the more time they spent together. Did she risk hoping for that? And what if she did give her heart over to hope, and that hope was dashed and her heart was broken?

How would Eli feel when his prodigal son retrieved his gun and left again? How would she feel when she left this place, and went with Stacy to settle into her life in the city and never saw Jonathan again?

"You don't believe God directs our lives?" Eli asked.

Oh, how could he be asking her that at the very moment when she was so close to having everything she'd ever wanted and yet knowing it could never be hers?

"I believe that God has a plan for my life," she said. "I believe God is calling me somewhere. But if it has anything to do with my being here, I don't see how."

The man nodded, and for a long moment he didn't say anything. Then, when he'd paused so long she thought he'd drifted off or given up the conversation, he said, "My grandsons told me they showed you my garden today."

"They did." It was one of many things they'd pointed out to her while running down the path.

"See any potatoes, did you?" he asked. "Or carrots? How about pumpkins?"

There was a twinkle in his eye that hinted at the younger man he'd once been.

Celeste found herself smiling. "No, all I saw was snow."

"But still you believe there was something planted under the icy ground that would grow there in the spring?"

Her smile grew wider. "Why, yes, I believe I do."

Where was he going with this? Before she could ask, the front door opened. Amos came in, shaking the snow off his boots, then David and Samuel rushed toward him, followed by Miriam just two steps behind them. The boys ran to greet Eli, and she smiled as he turned his smiling eyes toward his two young grandsons. The cat leaped from her lap. She stood up and stretched, excused herself from the happy babble of conversation and walked into the kitchen.

Yes, Lord, I can easily believe that there's a garden underneath that snow. That the trees will bud come springtime and that apples will grow in the fall. That corn, potatoes and wheat are going to burst out of the ground. What do You want me to take from that, Lord?

The kitchen door opened slowly. She spun. It was Jonathan, snow covering his hat and dusting his broad shoulders. There was a cardboard box in his hands, large and damp from the snow. They stood there for a long moment, looking at each other, her lips not even knowing what words to form.

"You're back," she said.

"I am," he said. He knocked the snow from his boots and crossed the kitchen floor. "I brought you something."

He set the box down on the table, then stopped, pulled off his hat and hung it up by the door. She pulled the lid back. It was printer paper from an old-model dot-matrix like she'd had back in early childhood, with little holes down each side of the page from where they'd attached to the printer, and the pages connected at the bottom, end over end in one long, endless stream. She lifted the first page out. Her fingers slid over the tiny letters and numbers, almost unable to believe what she was seeing. "It's Dexter Thomes's code."

"Yup." He pulled off his gloves and set them on the table. He was shifting his weight from one foot to another with the same nervous stance of a boy who'd brought a girl flowers. "Amos had an old printer in the shop that had been donated and was considered too old for anyone to use. The system was so old I didn't even know if it would work. I printed as many pages as I could before we ran out of paper and ink. But it's a start."

"It's amazing, thank you." Her fingers ran down the page, her mind coming alive like a computer booting to life. "I can definitely start on this. And who knows, maybe by the time Dexter Thomes's court date comes…"

"That's the other thing I have to tell you." He crossed the space between them and reached for her hands. She set the paper down and let him take them. They stood there with his hands holding hers for a long moment. She looked down at their linked fingers. There was something so natural and comfortable about it. Was Eli right? Had something been planted? Was this part of God's plan?"

"Dexter's lawyer has launched an appeal based on the fact somebody has Poindexter's website up and running. His lawyers are trying to claim that means you identified the wrong man."

"That's impossible." She shook her head. For a moment, her fingers started to pull away from his.

"I know." He tightened his grip on her hands. "But it means you have to be in court in a little under four weeks to testify against him."

Four weeks? The words hit her like a punch to the gut. But the trial hadn't been scheduled until March.

"There is no way I'll be able to analyze all of Dexter's data that fast. Not without access to the internet. And if I go into the court case blind, without having proved where the money went, there's too big a risk he'll be let go and set free." And something told her that if that happened he'd never stop looking for her and she'd be in hiding forever. "How will I even find time to work on all this data if I'm busy settling into a new life in witness protection? Stacy will barely have time to help me integrate into my new life before I'm yanked back out again to go to court."

Unexpected tears rushed to her eyes as frustration and sadness battled with the sheer exhaustion of the past few days. Would she even have the same cover life before and after the trial? Or would she have four weeks in one strange place before turning around and starting over again somewhere new?

And just how many hours will it be before Stacy arrives and I have to say goodbye to this place and to you forever?

His fingers brushed the tears away, tracing the lines of her face and tilting her head with her tear-filled eyes up to meet his.

"I can't help you with the data," he said, his voice deep with emotion in a way she'd never heard it before. "Hunter will not budge one iota about you going online or having access to electronic devices, even if I'd been open to it, which I'm not. But I do have what I hope is good news. I talked to Hunter, Stacy and Karl, and we've all agreed. The safest place for you is someplace where no electronic device, cell phone or security camera can find you. We're delaying settling you into your new life in Pittsburgh until after the trial. You're going to spend the next four weeks living here, like the Amish, with me and my family. What do you say?"

Chapter Thirteen

Happiness filled Celeste's heart like a cherry blossom tree bursting into bloom. Suddenly she found herself throwing her arms around Jonathan. She hugged him hard. For a second she felt him resist, like he wasn't sure what to do. Then she felt his arms, strong and warm around her, pulling her close and holding him to her. And for a long moment she just stood there, thankful for his embrace, thankful they weren't about to be separated and thankful for him.

"Sorry, I didn't mean…" she started, not quite able to believe she'd just thrown her arms around him like that, or that he'd responded and hugged her just as tightly. She let her arms fall to her side and stepped back. He loosened his grip on her body, but to her surprise, he didn't let her go completely. Instead, he stood there with his hands resting gently and protectively on her lower hips. "Ever since I found the code that traced back to Dexter Thomes and proved he'd stolen the money, everything in my life has been such chaos. It's like I've been tossed and thrown around in a hurricane never knowing what's going to happen from one second to the next. The idea I could actually spend the next few weeks somewhere peaceful, quiet and safe with people like these…"

And a man like you…

Her voice trailed off. It was the closest thing to joy she'd felt in a long time. Temporary happiness, she reminded herself. Still, she'd enjoy it every moment that God allowed it to her.

"Are you sure it's okay with your family?" she asked.

He nodded. "I asked them first. I will use a series of disposable cell phones to check in with Hunter and Karl. I'll only check and send texts outside the home, and they'll only call in case of an emergency. I'm going to move into the *grossdaadi* house with Pa. You will stay in Mark's room, and he will move in with his brothers. Pa invited him to stay with us, but he's conflicted about that. I understand. He's pretty protective. But between the new baby coming and Pa getting older, Amos and Miriam need a lot of help around the farm. They see us being here, even for a few weeks, as an unlikely answer to prayer."

"So, you know about the baby?" Celeste asked.

"Yup, I was so excited when Amos told me. I love babies."

She smiled. Her hands slipped up and rested on his arms, and they stood there for a long moment, holding each other lightly while the noise and bustle of the busy Amish farmhouse echoed from rooms in every direction. His dark eyes searched her face, and there was a depth to his gaze like a series of books he only just begun to open up to her, but which she'd now have countless long days and nights to read. Then he let go of her and she stepped back. He ran his hand over his jaw.

"Not sure I'm all that thrilled about having to shave, but only married Amish men have beards."

She laughed, happiness bubbling up inside her. *Thank You, God!* She and Jonathan would actually have a few short weeks together before they had to finally say goodbye.

Late-January sunshine streamed through her bedroom window, but the morning chorus of birds had barely begun to reach Celeste's ears when it was overtaken by the sound of a door slamming shut. She sat up. Her heart beat hard in her chest as fear poured like freezing cold water over the gentle warm glow she'd woken up in every morning for the past two weeks.

What's happening, Lord? Have Dexter's minions found us? Do we need to run?

Shoving back the quilt, she pulled herself to her knees and looked out the window, just in time to see Mark stride across the field. She sighed. Knowing him, he'd run out the door in a rush, slammed the door by accident and now felt embarrassed about it. But as she watched him stop by the fence, catch a breath and drop his head as if to pray, there was no mistaking the way his shoulders dropped and how emotion racked his frame.

She dropped back down onto the bed as her pulse raced and her heart ached. Mark seemed to love God and his family in a such a raw, genuine and protective way.

While the rest of the family had embraced their decision to hide her, Mark still wasn't at peace with it. It was like the young man couldn't bring himself to trust Jonathan or to shake the worry that his uncle was going to hurt Amos and Eli again. She couldn't even say he was wrong.

What am I doing here, Lord? I love being here so much and I'm really growing to care for this family. But they've all seen so much pain already and I don't want to ever cause them any more.

The last few days living with Jonathan's family on the farm had been like living inside a greater peace and happiness than she'd ever dreamed of. She'd awoken most mornings to Rosie at her door, asking if she needed help getting dressed. Then there were the daily trips to the barn with David and Samuel to collect eggs, milk the cows and feed the animals, and long multicourse meals with the family. She'd spent hours with Rosie and Miriam learning how to sew, cook and speak some words of Pennsylvania Dutch, while Jonathan was out with Amos and Eli, slowly repairing their relationship while they worked side by side.

At night she'd sit quietly by the fire, going over Dexter's code with a pencil and eraser, looking up to see Jonathan's keen eyes on her face as she slowly found and unraveled the patterns that she saw, in the hopes of finding something before the trial. Day by day, the tension that she'd gotten so used to living with faded from her limbs, along with that nagging headache no pill had been able to rid her of.

Yet, like a small jarring rock in the bottom of her shoe, she'd never been able to shake the knowledge that one day soon she and Jonathan would be leaving.

The knock on her door was lighter and more timid than usual.

"Come in." Celeste swung her legs over the edge of the bed. Rosie's face was pale. "What's wrong?"

"Papa found Mark with a cell phone," Rosie said. "He said he took it from the store because he wanted to find out if Jonathan was telling the truth about you."

Jonathan stood in the kitchen, watching through the window as his nephew disappeared into the fields. The memory of having been the one to explode in anger and take off running in that very direction burned a little too acutely in his memory.

"What did he find?" he asked. Anger burned like hot coals in the pit of his core. He wasn't even sure who or what it was he was upset at. He'd known things might be tense with his family when he'd decided to hide Celeste here. But he'd assumed that they'd protect her and keep her safe. The discovery that Mark had a secret contraband cell phone had shot a worrying hole through that. "Tell me he didn't let anyone know where she was."

"Of course not," Amos said. Jonathan didn't turn, but he could feel his older brother standing behind him. "He says he didn't even turn it on. And I believe him."

But he could have. If Amos hadn't found the phone while the family was getting ready to head out on a day trip to visit friends, who knew what Mark might've seen or done when he'd managed to get somewhere where with Wi-Fi access.

"He is a *gut* young man," Amos added. "He has a good heart. He's just struggling."

Struggling because he can't trust me. And I don't blame him after what I did.

Jonathan ran his hand over his jaw, missing the softness of his beard. Shaving it off every morning was an unexpectedly uncomfortable daily reminder that he'd reached his thirties without a wife or family of his own.

And now he was causing unexpected chaos and pain within his brother's.

As if sensing his thoughts, Amos's large hand brushed his shoulder. "This is not your fault, bruder."

"Of course it is." Jonathan turned back. His brother was dressed to go out for the day, with his hat already on his head. Miriam, Eli, David and Samuel were outside with the horses loading the buggy. Forgiveness felt like a choice his brother and father had decided to make, a gift they'd chosen to give him, and each of them in their own way had slowly been figuring out how to rebuild what had been broken. But Jonathan would never forget that he was the one who'd broken it.

Footsteps creaked on the stairs. He looked up, feeling his breath catch in his throat as he met the gaze of the woman standing one step behind Rosie.

"Celeste." He crossed the kitchen instinctively. His hands reached toward her. The morning sun illuminated her features. Did she have any idea how beautiful she was? Or what it did to his heart every time she even just walked into the room? Whatever strange attraction he'd felt that first moment he'd stepped through the smoke back at the safe house to reach for her hand to help her to safety had only grown each moment they spent together. The fact he'd be leaving her life in just two weeks tore at his insides in a way he couldn't begin to understand.

She paused a few steps away from him. Her hand reached for his, and as their fingers brushed it was like, in that moment, everyone else had faded from the room. Her eyes searched his face. "Is everything okay? Mark seemed pretty upset and Rosie said he had a cell phone."

He let his fingertips linger on hers for a moment, just

a few hesitant inches away from taking her hand. Then he let go and slid his hand over the back of his neck.

"Everything's fine," he said, willing it so as he spoke the words. "Mark was just worried for his family. He doesn't trust me and probably doesn't know whether to even believe the story we told him about who you are and why you're in witness protection. I don't blame him."

"Do you want us to delay our trip?" His brother's voice jolted Jonathan's attention back to the kitchen.

"No." Jonathan shook his head. Amos and Miriam had postponed this day trip to visit a nearby family twice already. He couldn't keep asking his family to put their entire lives on hold for him. Especially since he'd gotten the impression Miriam's pregnancy was taking a greater toll on her than she'd been letting on. Amos had already confided in him that she'd been on bed rest for the third trimester of her pregnancy with the twins. It was good for them to go and spend time with friends while they could.

Still Amos hesitated and Jonathan could read the thought in his eyes. "If Mark comes back…"

The words trailed off and Jonathan couldn't help wondering how many times he'd left his father and brother with that same worry.

"If Mark comes back before you're home," Jonathan said, "I'll speak to him if he wants to talk and give him space if he doesn't."

Amos nodded. They went outside. Goodbyes were said, hugs were exchanged and Miriam gave Celeste final instructions on setting the fire and heating the stew for dinner. Then Amos, Miriam, Eli, Rosie, David and Samuel loaded into the buggy and left.

Jonathan and Celeste stood on the front porch and waved them off until the family disappeared from sight. He turned and looked at her. Her long blond hair was tied back under a dark bonnet that framed her face perfectly. The beauty of the light of the winter morning was nothing compared to the simple lines of her face.

"I'm worried about Mark," she said.

He nodded. "I am, too, but Amos seemed pretty convinced that he didn't even turn the phone on. We've asked my family to take everything we've told them about you on faith, without any evidence at all. Maybe that was too much for Mark. Maybe he was hoping that if he looked you up online he'd discover that you really are one of the good guys."

"Good gals." Celeste's correction came so quickly he would've laughed if it wasn't for the very real worry in her eyes.

"Still, I don't know what to make of the fact that Mark had a secret cell phone," he admitted.

"Neither do I," Celeste said. "He seems like a such a great young man. He stepped into action to save my life back at the store. I don't even want to think about what would've happened if he, Rosie and your whole family hadn't protected me."

"Then don't. Focus on the fact that Amos has faith in Mark." *And let me worry about whether or not my brother is wrong.* He stretched out his arm. "Let's walk."

"Okay." The flicker of a smile returned to her lips. He felt her fingers on his sleeve as she looped her hand through his arm and wondered if she had any idea of the impact that even the simplest touch had on him. They stepped off the porch and walked out into the wintery morning together.

What was it about this woman that made his heart race like a teenager's? No one had ever affected him like this before. He'd taken the biggest risk of his life and let her into his estranged family. And she hadn't rejected him or judged him. Instead, it was like she'd stood by him as he'd started sweeping up all the broken pieces of his life and putting them back together. Snow glittered and sparkled as it crunched under their feet. Bright turquoise-blue sky spread above them. The curve of Celeste's arm fit so perfectly into his it was like it was always meant to be there.

He'd never risked opening his heart for anyone before, and here he'd been overwhelmed by a fierce, protective need to care for her that made him feel both stronger and weaker than he'd ever been. All he knew was he was dreading the day he'd have to say his final goodbye. His eyes rose to the sky.

I don't even know what to say, Gott. *It's still so hard getting used to talking to You. Just please, make something good of this mess. Bless my family when it's time to go. Be with Mark and guide his heart. Strengthen me to say goodbye to Celeste. Bring the right man into her life to give her the future I so wish I could...*

He sighed, feeling so much more inside him that he couldn't find the words to say.

"Were you just praying?" Celeste asked after a long moment.

"I was," he said. "I've been praying a lot more recently. It's hard not to here, especially around my father. He seems to pray constantly. He's been reminding me how. I never realized how patient a man my father was, or how what I saw as a refusal to talk to me when I was younger was just him feeling lost in his worries about my mother's declining health and then her death. He says God worked in his heart slowly over time after my mother died and I left, chipping away at his stubbornness and teaching him patience. Part of me thinks he's always been that way, underneath it all. He was always very patient with my mother."

He ran his hand slowly over his jaw.

"You do that a lot," she said. "It's like you're trying to stoke the beard that's no longer there."

He chuckled. "I didn't even realize I was doing it. Yeah, I do miss the beard. But Amish men don't grow beards until they're married."

"You could always grow one and say it was part of your cover. We could say your wife is back on your other farm taking care of your children." There was a lightness in her voice that made him realize she'd meant it as a joke. But he felt himself frown. No, he couldn't. Didn't she see that? He couldn't pretend to be with another woman, even an imaginary one, while he had feelings for her. Celeste laughed. "Too bad you didn't think to create a cover story where we were married. Then you could've grown yours out like your brother and father."

He stopped short, pulled his arm away and turned toward her.

"Don't," he said. "Don't joke about that."

"I'm sorry." The smile dropped from her lips as quickly as it had appeared. "I was just joking. But don't people create cover relationships when they're in WIT-SEC?"

Yes, they did. But the point was that he wasn't about

to pretend for one moment he had a relationship with her. He wouldn't—he couldn't—and he didn't even know how to explain why.

Her hand brushed his arm. Her eyes searched his. "Jonathan? Tell me what's wrong. You look upset. If I've insulted you somehow by implying you'd ever pretend to be in a relationship with me, I'm sorry."

That snapped his eyes back to her face. This again. Celeste's nagging doubts that despite all evidence on the contrary she wasn't worth much and was certainly nothing special.

"You think you insulted me?" he asked. "Are you kidding? Any man would be proud to stand beside you and call you his wife—even if it was just a cover story to fool the criminals on your tail."

He shook his head. How did she not get it? His mind flashed back to the conversation they'd had when they'd pulled up to the diner and he'd realized that she had no idea how truly special she was. And now that he'd had a glimpse of her curious and brilliant mind, and her deeply caring heart, it was impossible to the point of infuriating that she didn't realize that about herself. Well, he might not be able to be the man of her dreams, but at least he could let her know that she was worth so much more than she'd been led to believe by the creeps who had trolled her life.

"Celeste?" He turned and grabbed both of her hands in his. His cell phone buzzed in his pocket alerting him to a text message. No, he could afford one second to ignore it. "You're extraordinary. You hear me? You're a beautiful, brilliant and kindhearted woman who deserves more than a pretend relationship, especially with a man like me."

He watched as her lips parted in surprise, and he jumped in quickly before her beautiful lips could form words.

"I know this isn't the kind of thing someone in my position should ever say to a witness they're protecting," he said. "Not to mention it might seem doubly ridiculous considering we only met a couple of weeks ago. But I couldn't live with myself if I didn't tell you, just once, that you're amazing, Celeste. You're the most extraordinary person I've ever met, and with every moment I spend with you, I see more clearly that you're beautiful inside and out. And if you weren't in WITSEC and if we didn't both know we only have just two weeks left in each other's lives, then I would tell you that you've already touched my heart and I would very much like the opportunity to get to know you better and see where this could lead. Not that I don't think you deserve someone far better than me."

Celeste's mouth opened wider, but no words came out. Then she bit her lower lip. Everything inside him willed her to say something and break the awkward silence following his admission.

The phone in his pocket buzzed again with another text message. He had to check it.

"Jonathan, I…"

His phone started to ring. He dropped her hands and stepped back. "Hello!"

"Marshal Mast? It's Chief Deputy Hunter." The familiar voice was clear and strong. "I need you to bring Celeste in immediately."

Chapter Fourteen

Celeste watched Jonathan's face as he listened to whatever his boss was telling him. Her heart was still racing from the words he'd said just moments ago, and now, before she could even begin to wrap her mind around it, there'd been an emergency call.

She pressed her hand against her chest, feeling her heart beat against her palm. Never, in her whole life, had she imagined that a man like Jonathan would ever say those kinds of things about her. Did he have any idea how much she admired and respected him? How very attractive she found him? Or how much it had meant to her that a family as amazing as his had accepted her with open arms?

"Okay. Understood. We'll check in again once we've cleared Hope's Creek." He hung up the phone. Then he looked down at Celeste. "Dexter Thomes's lawyer filed an emergency appeal. Someone leaked that you thought you'd seen him out of jail, and they're trying to use that to say that you might not be a cognitively reliable witness. The judge has agreed they can call you in for questioning."

In other words, Dexter Thomes's lawyers were going to use the fact that a criminal who looked like him had come after her to prove she was nuts and didn't know what she was talking about. A shiver spread through her limbs that had nothing to do with the wintery cold. "When?"

"Tomorrow."

"But I'm not ready!" she said. "I've barely made a dent on the data. I mean, I've isolated some birth dates, but I don't know what to make of them. I was counting on having another two weeks. Plus, I promised Miriam I'd have dinner ready for them when they got home tonight. How soon do we have to leave?"

"Right now," he said. "I mean, we can talk quickly for a few more minutes if it helps get your head around things. Ten tops. Then we have to head back to the house, get changed back into *Englisch* clothes, pack up and go."

"We'll come right back, right?" She tried to convince her lips to smile. There was no way this was as bad as it sounded. There had to be a glimmer of hope, a silver lining, somewhere. "After all, Miriam and I are supposed to be having a quilting lesson tomorrow. And I promised the twins I'd help them name the barn kittens."

Her attempt to lighten the mood fell flat as she saw the sadness move across his face.

"We won't," he said. "I'm sorry, but this is it for this cover story."

He couldn't be saying what she thought he was saying. This was so much more than a cover story. This was a family. This was more happiness than she'd ever known and a glimpse of a life more wonderful than she'd ever dared hope for.

"But what about saying goodbye?"

"There is no time for goodbyes. I'm sorry. We'll leave a note, of course. We have no way of contacting Amos and Miriam, and we can't just hang around at the farmhouse waiting for them. We don't have the time. Karl and Stacy will meet us just outside Philadelphia. The four of us will stay in a hotel under assumed names. Tomorrow you'll testify at the emergency appeal. Then you'll continue on to your new cover life in Pittsburgh."

The fact he'd said "you" not "we" hit her even harder than the knowledge these were her final moments living as the Amish.

"Am I still going to be reassigned to another marshal?"

He shook his head. "I don't know."

"Am I going to be saying goodbye to you tomorrow?" she pressed. "Is this our last day in each other's lives?"

"I don't know." Jonathan's voice cracked, a pain moving through it that seemed to call to the ache inside her own chest. Then she felt the warmth of Jonathan's hands on her shoulders. He pulled her closer. "But here's what I do know. I know that I have faith in you. I know that you're going to be great. I know you're going to get up on that stand tomorrow and convince everyone that Dexter Thomes is Poindexter and you identified the right man. And then you're going to walk out of that courtroom, head held high, knowing you've done everything you could do. I know that, no matter what happens next, you're going to have an amazing life."

She turned her face toward him, feeling dozens of words she'd never say cascade through her mind like text rolling rapidly down her computer screen. What kind of life could she possibly have if it meant never seeing him again? He had no idea what his confidence in her meant to him or just how hard it had hit her heart moments ago, when he said that if circumstances were different he'd have wanted a future with her.

There's nothing my heart wants more than a future with a man like you.

No. Not a man like you. You, Jonathan.

You and only you.

"You're the bravest woman I've ever met," he said. "You're so smart, so strong and capable of so much. You just need to have the courage to see who you really are, step out in faith and be that person you were made to be."

Well, she didn't feel brave, she didn't feel strong and she had no idea who she was meant to be. But she knew that any second now his hands would leave her shoulders, they'd head back to the farmhouse to pack, this moment alone with Jonathan would be over and she might never get another one like it in her life. Her heart quickened, like she was standing on the edge of a diving board waiting to take the plunge, or like it had in the moment she'd decided to put everything on the line to pursue Poindexter online.

She took a deep breath, stood up on her tiptoes and slid her arms around his neck.

"I don't know how to say what I want to tell you right now," she said. "I know we've only got seconds, and I'm more than a little afraid of saying this all wrong. I really like you, Jonathan. I like you so very much. And I really wish this time we've had together here didn't have to end."

His eyes darkened. "Me, too."

She risked taking another step toward him and found herself standing on the tips of his boots. He smiled.

Then she felt his hands slide down her back. He pulled her into his chest. She stretched up onto the very tips of her toes. He bent his face down toward her. They kissed. Their lips brushed over each other and settled there as if they were made to be together.

Then she pulled back and laid her head against his chest.

"I really don't want to leave," she said. "I don't want to leave this place. I don't want to leave your family. I don't want to say goodbye to you."

He stroked her head. "Believe me. I want us stay here every bit as much as you do."

She felt tears building at the corners of her eyes. "But you can come back. I can't."

Slowly, gently, he wiped her tears away. "Don't you get it? It will never be the same here without you."

He took one last look around his family kitchen, feeling awkward in his civilian clothes. His gun sat heavy in its holster. He looked at the remnants of the quick meal of bread and cheese that he'd insisted Celeste try to choke down before running upstairs to get changed. He'd debated keeping them in Amish clothes until they'd made it outside Hope's Creek. But he wasn't about to take his family's wagon and horses without knowing how he'd return them, and it would take about an hour to hike to where Mark had parked the truck. It would be much harder for Celeste to hike over hills in her dress, and once they were outside Amish country the clothing might bring unwanted attention. He didn't know how long it would take until they reached somewhere she'd be able to change. If they slipped through the back door and through the forest, no one should spot two *Englischers* leaving an Amish farm. It wasn't the easiest option, but it would have to do.

He'd insisted they leave only the briefest note for his family—*Sorry, we had to go. Will write when we can.*—telling Celeste that his family would understand and that anything more could put all of them in danger if it ever fell into the wrong hands. She'd taken the pen from his hand and added in her own handwriting, *Thank you so much for everything. Ecclesiastes 3:11.*

"It's from a chapter of the Bible that both your father and I love," Celeste had said. Then she'd turned away and run upstairs, though not before he could see the tears glistening in her eyes.

A large family Bible sat on a table in the living room, its pages supple from the countless times his family's hands had brushed over it. Part of him wanted to flip it open and read what the verse was that she'd referenced. Instead, he sat down at the table and dropped his head into his hands. He never should've told her how much he cared, and he really shouldn't have let himself kiss her.

Celeste believed that *Gott* called people to things. She believed *Gott* put dreams and desires in their hearts. Well, first the desire to go into law enforcement had burned so deeply inside him that he'd lost his family over it. And now the urging in his chest to hold Celeste in his arms again ached more than he could bear.

The door swung open behind him. Jonathan leaped to his feet.

"So you change back into *Englisch* clothes as soon as my family leaves?" It was Mark. The young man shrugged. "And you brought a gun into my family's home."

Jonathan swallowed back his pride and chose to take

a leap of faith and trust the young man. "I'm sorry. We're dressed this way because we're leaving. My boss called. Celeste has to be in court in the morning."

Mark's eyes widened. "You're leaving?"

"Yes, and I'm not bringing Celeste back." Jonathan's broke Mark's gaze. He walked over to the sink, grabbed a cloth and wiped down the table. "I will write letters to both Amos and my *pa* as soon as I can."

"I want to believe you, but I can't." Mark's arms crossed. "What is so urgent that you can't wait even a few hours to say goodbye? Tell me you didn't come back only because you needed something and now that you don't need us anymore, you're leaving."

Jonathan opened his mouth, the desire to defend himself threatening to overpower the decision not to. The truth was far more complicated than that. He'd left because he had felt he had to. He'd longed to return for years. And, yes, Celeste had been the reason, but Mark would never know how hard it had been to walk up that front porch and knock on the door.

Before he could speak, footsteps creaked on the stairs, followed almost immediately by Celeste's voice. "Mark!"

Mark's arms unfolded. He nodded to her. "*Gude mariye*, I hear that you're leaving."

"We are." Celeste crossed the floor. She was dressed in her blue jeans and sweatshirt, but her hair was still tied back in a bun as it had been under her *kapp*. "Please tell everyone in your family goodbye from me and how very sorry we are to leave this way. Unfortunately, I have to be in court tomorrow and we couldn't wait."

"I will." The young man nodded slowly as if his brain

was processing. He turned to Jonathan. "How are you going to get back to your truck?"

"On foot."

"I will take you in the wagon," Mark said. His chin rose. It wasn't a question. "It will be much faster than walking."

Jonathan rocked back on his heels. On the one hand, the wagon would be much faster. But would it really be safer? Though it was clear his brother believed in Mark and trusted him, Jonathan had never found it easy to take anything on faith. Seemed he and his nephew had that in common.

Mark cut his eyes to Jonathan as if reading the doubt in his gaze. His arms crossed.

"I still don't trust you, and I don't think you trust me," Mark said. "But my faith teaches that I have a responsibility to take care of strangers and those in need, even when it's hard. And I know it would hurt my family if they found out I had an opportunity to help you and turned my back on you. Even if you turned your back on them."

Then Mark turned to Celeste. Something softened in his face, and for a moment the seventeen-year-old somehow looked both very grown-up and very young.

"My friends tell me that you are a very good person. They say you risked your life to help thousands of people who'd been robbed and stopped a very evil man. I was stubborn. I didn't know what to think when I realized you were here with my uncle. I took one of the phones from the store so I could look you up and decide for myself. But, after praying, I decided that I didn't need to go to the internet. I could trust my friends and my family and my faith."

"Thank you," Celeste said, stepping forward before Jonathan could say anything. "I believe you and I'm thankful for your help. I'm sorry for whatever happened this morning, but I'm glad that you stayed home and that God brought you home at the exact right moment to help us."

Jonathan gritted his teeth. It was fine for Celeste to decide she trusted Mark or even to view what had happened that morning as part of God's plan. But what evidence did she have really? What was it based on? The fact he'd helped her back at the store? The fact Mark's family believed in him? The sincerity in Mark's eyes? Despite the fact that Celeste and his father, Eli, were so very different on the surface, they both looked at the world through the same lens of faith. They both had this crystal clear belief that God talked to them and guided them. Well, he didn't have the luxury of believing the same thing.

His cell phone buzzed. He glanced down, and as he read the text from Karl he heard himself groan. He ran his hand over the back of his neck.

"What's wrong?" Celeste asked.

"Whoever's running Poindexter's site has put out a call for people to patrol the roads in certain parts of Pennsylvania, including Hope's Creek," he said. "They're offering double the reward for anyone who manages to spot you and stop you from making it to trial. Also, they've located my truck. We're trapped."

Chapter Fifteen

Celeste lay flat on her stomach in the back of the wagon, hidden under several layers of blankets, feeling the rock and jostle of the boards beneath her. It had taken only moments for Jonathan to decide that Mark's offer was the best way out of Hope's Creek undetected. He'd fired off a message to Karl and got a pickup location for a new, fresh vehicle, almost an hour out of town, while Mark got the wagon hitched and Celeste had hidden their belongings in the back. The whole thing from Karl's first text to pulling out in the wagon had taken under fifteen minutes.

Since then, though, the minutes had stretched, long and unending, with nothing but the sound of the wind whistling in the trees, the rattle of the wheels and the clop of the horses on the road beneath them, as Mark drove the wagon slowly and steadily out of Hope's Creek. This was probably the slowest getaway escape imaginable. The thought would've made her laugh if it wasn't for the doubt and fear gnawing in her core, which seemed to intensify every time the wagon slowed or she heard someone calling out to Mark in greeting.

Lord, I'm so scared. This is all starting to feel very real. Be with us. Calm my nerves. Help me to get to court safely. Help me to be strong on the stand.

She felt a warm hand brushing hers in the darkness as Jonathan stretched out for her from his hiding place on the other side of the wagon. His fingers wrapped around hers, enveloping them and holding them tightly. She squeezed him back with all her might. Then she let herself relax. For some time they just lay there, side by side, their hands linked in the darkness.

Finally, she felt the horses slow.

"Okay, I think this is the place," Mark said. "But it's just an abandoned junkyard."

Jonathan's hand pulled away from hers. She felt him shift his position in the back of the wagon beside her. A glimmer of sunlight slipped in through the blankets as Jonathan peered out. She moved onto her side and glanced through the gap, but saw nothing except the pale blue of sky ahead.

"Do you see anyone?" Jonathan asked.

"No one." Mark's voice filtered through the blankets from the front of the wagon. "This place is empty."

She heard Jonathan breathe what sounded like a prayer of relief under his breath.

"There should be a red pickup by the back fence, with California plates and a rack on the back," Jonathan said. "Pull up beside it."

"Got it," Mark said.

For a moment there was only the sound of the horse-drawn wagon moving over the snow. She reached out for Jonathan's hand again but couldn't find him. The wagon stopped. She felt the blankets move back and saw the mixture of lights and shadows shift as Jonathan crouched up. "Looks good."

She scooted onto her knees so she could see, then felt his firm hand on her shoulder gently pushing her back down.

"Stay down," he said. "Wait here. I need to check out the truck and the surroundings."

"Okay, be careful," she said, but wasn't sure he'd even heard her before he'd hopped over the side of the wagon. She lay back on the cold floor, closed her eyes and prayed. Something about Jonathan's warm and tender touch had filled her with so much hope. Feeling him pull away made her feel like part of her was missing. She needed to get a hold of her heart. Jonathan was not a permanent fixture in her life or someone who'd always be there to help her weather the storms. No, he was leaving her life, and soon. The quicker she stood on her own two feet the better.

"Okay, Celeste, you can come out now," Jonathan called.

He pulled the blankets back and grabbed their bags. She looked around. The carcasses of old and broken cars, half buried under the snow, spread out to her right. Tall fencing surrounded them on every side. She pushed the blankets off entirely and stood. Jonathan was carrying bags to the truck.

Mark stood beside the wagon and offered her a hand down. Standing in the snow, she paused, wanting to hug him but also knowing he'd probably feel more comfortable if she didn't.

"I wish I could find better words to say than thank you. *Danke.* Thank you for everything you and your family have done for me."

A slightly sad but entirely genuine smile crossed his face. "You're welcome. Safe travels."

"You, too," she said. "I hope God blesses you all so much for everything you've done for me."

She felt movement behind her and turned to see Jonathan at her shoulder. He nodded to Mark and they exchanged a quick and awkward goodbye. She followed Jonathan to the truck. He unlocked the doors and they got inside. He started the engine, but she remained still, her hand on the seat belt, watching through the windshield as Mark turned the horse and wagon around, and started toward the entrance.

"Everything okay?" Jonathan asked.

"No…" Celeste's voice trailed off.

Something was wrong. Something was gnawing at the pit of her stomach hurting her with each breath, but she wasn't sure what.

The screech of tires filled her ears. A car, brown and streamlined, flew into the parking lot, swerving to a stop in front of Mark. The horses reared. Mark's body jerked as he tried to steady them.

"Get down!" Jonathan slid a protective arm around her shoulder.

A large figure holding a gun jumped from the car and charged toward Mark. Even at a distance she couldn't mistake his form. It was Doppel-Dex. The imposter yanked Mark down from the wagon with one hand. With the other he pressed the gun into the side of Mark's head.

Chapter Sixteen

"You can drive this truck, right?" Jonathan grabbed her by the shoulder with one hand and turned her to face where Mark now knelt, shaking, on the ground. With the other he pressed a cell phone into her hand. "Celeste! Tell me you're able to drive this truck and get out of here."

Through a junkyard, in the snow, with someone she cared about down on his knees with a criminal's gun to his head?

"Absolutely." She gritted her teeth.

"Great." Jonathan reached for the door. "If anything happens to me, as soon as the entrance is clear, I expect you to gun it. Okay? Don't look back. Just get as far away from here as you can and call Stacy or Karl. They'll send someone to get you."

She felt the quickest brush of Jonathan's lips over hers. Then he jumped from the truck, slammed the door and started toward where Mark now knelt. Her limbs shook as she slid her body into the driver's seat, and she watched through the windshield, silent prayers forming on her lips, as Jonathan strode toward the gunman.

Doppel-Dex shouted, and while she couldn't make out the words at a distance, there was no mistaking the ugly menace of his tone. He cuffed Mark so hard across the face he nearly fell forward. The teenager's shoulders shook. Jonathan stopped walking. His hand twitched toward his gun. Her heart stopped. Jonathan was going to shoot a man in front of his Amish nephew. It was the only way to save his life.

But then the US marshal raised his hands high above his head. A gasp crossed her lips as she watched him toss the service weapon he'd only recently been reunited with into the snow. Could he be surrendering to the one man who'd been chasing her since the farmhouse? Was he offering up his own life to save his brother's son? Jonathan knelt and placed his hands on his head. There was a pause, then Doppel-Dex dropped his grip on Mark's shoulders and turned his gun on Jonathan.

"Where. Is. She?"

She heard that all right. Even at a distance, those three words snapped in the air like a bullet's crack.

But whatever Jonathan said in response was so quiet she wasn't able to catch the sound of his voice. Mark turned and pelted toward the wagon. Doppel-Dex spun back toward him. Jonathan launched himself at him like a linebacker. The criminal's gunfire echoed in the air above them. The horses whinnied as Mark grabbed the reins and spurred them on. The wagon clattered through the junkyard. Jonathan and Doppel-Dex wrestled for the gun. The wagon cleared the gate and disappeared down the road.

Thank You, Gott. Celeste buckled her seat belt and gunned the engine. The truck flew forward, toward the two men and the open gate beyond. Doppel-Dex tossed Jonathan to the ground. Jonathan reared up, blocking the larger man's blows. She breathed a prayer and yanked the steering wheel to the left, denting the corner of a wrecked hatchback as she forced the vehicle to a stop. She leaned over and shoved the door open. "Jonathan! Get in!"

He jabbed a quick blow to Doppel-Dex's face, knocking him back. Jonathan ran for the truck, scooping up something off the ground as he ran. It was his service weapon. She threw the vehicle into Drive the moment his body landed in the seat, even as he was still closing the door behind him. She aimed for the junkyard exit. Jonathan buckled his seat belt, then rolled down the window, released his weapon's safety but didn't let off a shot. Jonathan growled. "I don't have a clean shot."

She looked up. Doppel-Dex had dived behind a pile of debris. "You want me to stop?"

"Absolutely not," he said. "Keep driving. I'm not going to stick around and play cat and mouse for a criminal in a junkyard. How's Mark? Did he get away okay? I couldn't really see where he went."

"He's okay," Celeste said. "He got away."

"Thank *Gott*."

Funny, the Amish word for God had been the one that had slipped from her lips, too. She reached the gate and took another glimpse at the rearview mirror. Doppel-Dex was scrambling to his car. She hit the road and turned in the opposite direction of the way she'd seen Mark go.

"I told you to gun it and get out of here," Jonathan said.

"I wasn't leaving without you!" she said. The sound of an engine gunning roared behind then. She urged the truck faster. In the rearview mirror, Doppel-Dex swerved through the gates and started after them. She fixed her eyes on the road ahead. Behind her she could hear Doppel-Dex firing. Jonathan shouted for her to stay low. The back window exploded into shards of glass. *Help us, Lord!* She heard the sound of Jonathan returning fire. Then, as she watched in the rearview mirror, the pursuing vehicle suddenly jolted and swerved off the road and into a ditch.

"What just happened?" she asked.

"I shot out his tires," Jonathan said. He reached for his phone and it was only then she realized she still had it, wedged between her palm and the steering wheel, in a white-knuckle grip. She relaxed her fingers. He slid it from her hand. "I'll call it in, and I'll take over the driving as soon as I know we're clear and safe. That was a minor crash. He should be okay."

She focused on driving and waited while he called both Karl and Chief Deputy Hunter. He ended the call and sat back on the seat. He frowned and his brow knit.

"They'll send law enforcement to look for him," he said. "I don't know how big the operation will be."

Holding the steering wheel with one hand, she reached over with the other and brushed the back of his hand, but he didn't take her fingers. "I'm sorry he got away."

"It was the right move," Jonathan said without really looking at her. "I was not about to risk your life by trying to apprehend him when I'm with you. Catching him was not worth losing you. Nothing is more important to me that making sure you're safe and alive. You matter to me. You have no idea how much." His fingers parted, making space for hers. His thumb ran slowly over her hand. She glanced his way, and as their eyes met, something moved through them, so deeply in their core that it was like he was seeing her and she was seeing him for the first time. She shivered. "Celeste? There's something I need to tell you. Something important that I need to let you know. I..."

He choked on the words before he could say them.

She squeezed his fingers. "Jonathan? Is everything okay? Whatever it is, you can tell me anything."

She waited as silence filled the truck and the man beside her struggled to find the words to say. His eyes closed. She watched as he swallowed hard.

Then he pulled his hand away and crossed his arms.

"Never mind," he said. "Karl and Stacy are en route to meet us. They'll escort us to a hotel on the outskirts of Philadelphia where we'll check in under assumed names. Tomorrow, all four of us will escort you to the courthouse. If Doppel-Dex is not apprehended, there's a possibility he'll strike there." His mouth spread into a tight smile. It was an impersonal and professional grin, missing all the warmth and tenderness she'd gotten used to seeing on his face.

He lapsed into silence again. It was uncomfortable, like a walled fortress encasing him that she wasn't welcome to enter, and it made her stomach ache.

She kept waiting, minute after minute and hour after hour for the wall to fall, for them to go back to that natural, easy, comfortable way they usually were together. But even after they stopped to switch drivers, stopped yet again for food, and then finally met up with Karl and Stacy just as that sun was beginning to set, Jonathan's professionalism and silence remained, and that incredible mind and heart she'd begun to care so deeply about stayed out of her reach.

Artificial yellow light filtered through the curtains of Jonathan's rectangular hotel room, clashing with the shining red block numbers of the alarm clock on the other side of his bed. It was quarter to six in the morning. An hour before his alarm was set to go off and two before it was time to escort Celeste to Dexter's trial. Doppel-Dex had still not been apprehended, and law enforcement would be on alert for some kind of attempt on Celeste's life at the trial. Karl lay fast asleep and snoring lightly on the other hotel bed. If Jonathan had managed to get any sleep, his aching body wasn't aware of it.

Instead, his mind had returned, again and again, to that moment in the truck right after he'd made the call to let Doppel-Dex go in order to ensure Celeste's safety.

He'd just been about to foolishly blurt out to Celeste the words he'd never imagined saying to anyone, let alone a witness he was protecting.

I think I love you.

But how could he ever say those words to Celeste? Knowing what a short time they'd known each other? Knowing that it was highly unprofessional and that as a marshal and witness they could never be together? Knowing that she deserved so much better than a man like him? He rolled over onto his side, balled his pillow and tried to punch it into a shape that would fit comfortably under his head.

His family had forgiven him for leaving them the

way he had. He knew Celeste would accept him despite it, too, and that she'd tell him God had forgiven him.

Jonathan wasn't even sure if what he wanted was forgiveness. What he felt more than anything was anger. Not freshly angry over something new that had happened. No, this was like a deep-seated anger that had burrowed in him years ago and had never gone away. He'd been angry when bullies had attacked them. He'd been angry when Amos had told him he couldn't be a cop, when his mother had died and when he and his father couldn't communicate with each other. He'd been angry when he'd left home without looking back.

He'd been angry long before Celeste had come into his life. She'd gotten him praying again. She'd gotten him hoping again. She'd been the missing piece that had brought him back to his family and the life he'd left behind. And as much as he longed for a future with her, he knew there was no way it could happen.

I'm tired of pretending I'm not angry at You, Lord! Why did You take my mother from me? Why did You place a calling on my heart when the only way I knew how to pursue it was to rip me away from my family? Why did You let me meet Celeste, and start falling for her if You were going to take her away again?

Enough. He couldn't sleep, he couldn't pray, he couldn't think and he didn't much like what he was feeling. He opened the nightstand drawer and found a hotel Bible. He dropped to the floor on the other side of the bed, sat with his back to where Karl lay sleeping and looked out at the Philadelphia skyline outside. What was that Bible verse that Celeste had written on the note for his father? Ecclesiastes 3 something?

He found Ecclesiastes in the middle of the Bible and

started skimming. It wasn't until he hit the point about there being a time to plant and a time to harvest that he really started reading. He'd found it. The section both his father, the farmer, and Celeste, the computer programmer, loved so much, about how there was a time for everything.

And then he read, "He hath made every thing beautiful in his time: also he hath set the world in their heart, so that no man can find out the word that God maketh from the beginning to the end." And then a couple more lines down, "I know that whatsoever God doeth, it shall be for ever: nothing can be put to it, nor any thing taken from it."

He set the book down and laid his head in his hands and prayed.

Gott, I don't get what You're doing in my life or what You're making out of me. I know I want the peace that my pa has. I want the joy that Amos has found. I want the hope that Celeste has in You. So, I'm giving up trying to figure it out. Just show me what You want me to do.

He wasn't sure how long he sat with his palms pressed up against his eyes, or when exactly he'd fallen asleep. All he knew was that when he woke up, the light of the real living sun was streaming down onto his face and Karl was standing over him with a cell phone in his hand.

"That was Stacy," he said. There was a flicker of something in his eye when he said her name that Jonathan couldn't quite read. "She and Celeste will meet us in thirty in the lobby. We have to go. The hearing was pushed up by two hours because of the chaos at the courthouse."

He was on his feet within a heartbeat. "What kind of chaos?"

"When news leaked online that she was going to testify today, people showed up in droves. The courtroom is crowded. There are people gathered outside with signs."

Jonathan stopped short. "What?" People were coming crossing the country to see Celeste? "What people?"

"People who were robbed by Dexter Thomes," Karl said. "People she was trying to help. She may not have found the money they lost, but she stepped up and caught the man who robbed them. Your girl is a hero."

"She's not a girl—she's a woman," Jonathan said quickly. Maybe if Karl learned to be smarter with his mouth, Stacy might one day look at him the way he sometimes looked at her. And Celeste definitely wasn't *his*.

Their phones both beeped. Karl reached his first.

"It's Hunter," Karl said. "Poindexter has posted online that if Celeste shows up to testify, she won't leave the courtroom alive."

Chapter Seventeen

"Everything okay?" Celeste leaned toward Jonathan and whispered as they sat side by side in the back of Karl's vehicle as his colleague eased them through traffic and up to the courthouse.

It was a question Jonathan had felt her asking in a dozen different ways—words, looks and gestures—ever since he'd walked into the hotel lobby and his eyes had brushed over her form. It was a question he still didn't have an answer to. She'd looked exquisite, he thought, in a long blue *Englisch* dress with a high collar and a pale blue scarf, the color of the morning sky. Her blond hair was tied back in a loose bun at the nape of her neck.

"Of course," Jonathan replied, knowing that he wasn't really answering the question she was asking. "Everything is fine. Dexter Thomes will be under armed guard, you've been well prepared for your testimony and I'll be keeping you safe every step of the way."

But is everything okay between us? He could read her green eyes asking the question. He tightened his smile and broke their gaze.

No, it wasn't. Because there could never be an *us*.

Guide me, Gott. *I'm trying to trust You have a plan.*

He glanced through the window at the crowded courthouse steps. A sight filled his eyes that was both one of the most incredibly incongruous and yet surprisingly joyful things he'd ever seen—his *pa* and Mark stood on the sidewalk outside the courthouse.

"What are they doing here?" Laughter spilled from Celeste's lips as she squeezed his hand and he let himself feel her there for one long moment before pulling away.

"I honestly have no idea!" He waited for Karl to safely park the vehicle. Then he got out, keeping Celeste close to his side. Stacy and Karl took up protective positions on either side of him and Celeste.

"Pa! Mark!" Jonathan called. The older man and the young man made their way through the crowd, oblivious to the curious looks of some of the *Englisch* as they passed. "How are you even in the city?"

"Mark's friends from the *Englisch* church heard that Celeste was testifying today," Eli said. "When we got back to the farm, he told us what had happened and said he needed to come see you."

"You drove?" Jonathan blinked. While the Amish didn't drive or own cars, many weren't opposed to getting a ride in somebody else's car when the situation required it. Not that he could remember his own father taking a ride anywhere except to the hospital with his mother.

"The *Englisch* pastor drove us in his church van," Eli said. "He is a good man. We talked on the journey. He said he wants to send some of his young people to help volunteer in the shop, and has offered to give Mark a mentorship at the church, helping with the youth program while he decides whether he wants to be baptized. I like this idea very much, and I think Miriam and Amos will, too. It will keep him close to God and home, while he figures out what God wants him to do."

The glow in Mark's smile said that he did, too. Not only did the young man seem no worse for wear after being threatened by Doppel-Dex, there was something in his stance that would've made Jonathan think he'd grown a whole year or two in maturity overnight.

"I'm very proud of you," he said. He suspected that Mark would one day choose to be baptized in the Amish faith. "I am glad to see that you're not repeating the mistakes I made. I wish I had been as wise and faithful when I was your age, and not as stubborn and angry."

"You saved my life." Mark said the words slowly, like he was reading off a thoughtfully written list. "You risked your life for me. You sought peace with the enemy before resorting to violence and weapons. I'm sorry that I doubted you."

"I'm not," Jonathan said. "I'm glad you were looking out for your family, and in a way, you giving me a hard time helped me get my mind and heart straight."

"All that matters is that you're open to God's calling now." Eli clasped him on the shoulder.

"We'll meet you here after the trial," Mark added. "We'll talk more then, Onkel."

Uncle. The word swelled something unexpected inside Jonathan's heart.

They said quick goodbyes, then Jonathan walked up to the courtroom steps with Celeste by his side. It was one thing for his father to tell him to listen to God's calling. But what was God saying? They entered the building, went through security and down a hallway, where they were greeted by lawyers. Then it was time for him to escort her into the courtroom and into the witness-box. They stepped into the courtroom, and for the first time since the ordeal had begun he laid eyes on Dexter Thomes. The hacker sat tall and arrogant in the dock, seeming to somehow project a swagger that implied he'd be sauntering out a free man. His signature tinted glasses were gone, his beard was trimmed and his shaggy hair was pulled back in a ponytail. His eyes tracked Celeste's every motion like a hawk. Doppel-Dex was nowhere to be seen.

"I'm nervous." Celeste's voice was so low Jonathan barely caught it as they approached the witness stand.

"If you get scared look at me," he said quietly. "I have your back."

The trial resumed, and then all he could do was sit there and watch as the prosecutor walked Celeste slowly but thoroughly through every detail of how she'd tracked Dexter Thomes online and why she was convinced he was Poindexter.

A man slipped into the back of the courtroom and took a seat, and Jonathan found his well-tuned senses turning toward him. The man was tall, bald and clean shaven, with a face so hollow it bordered on skeletal. He was fiddling with his phone and something about him sent a shiver of warning down Jonathan's spine.

He nodded to Karl and glanced the man's way. Karl nodded back.

"It's like seeds planted underneath the soil…" Celeste's voice dragged his attention back to the witness-box. "There are always patterns in the data, even when they're hidden so deeply you can't see them."

She sat up straight, her head held high and her eyes focused as Dexter's defense attorney took over the questioning. Despite every assault the defense attorney could launch on her integrity, intellect and judgment, she remained utterly unshaken in her resolve that, yes, Dexter had stolen the money.

"But you told officials that you thought you saw Dexter Thomes in some rural town in Pennsylvania." The defense lawyer smirked. Jonathan bristled. He wasn't even trying to prove that Dexter Thomes was innocent, just discredit Celeste.

"I saw a man who looked like him," she said. "I did not see him."

"Like you saw a pattern in code that nobody else could see," the lawyer said. "And we're supposed to take this on faith?"

He said the word *faith* as if it was a dirty word. Jonathan winced. Was that how he'd sounded when she'd explained it? For a moment Celeste didn't answer. Instead, she looked at Jonathan. Their eyes met and a soft light dawned in her eyes. A smile crossed her lips and it lifted something in his own heart.

"I believe in the sun even when it's hidden behind a cloud," she said, her eyes on Jonathan's face. "That's not blind faith. That's knowing that something is real even when I can't see it."

Her eyes then turned to the judge.

"Before I went off-line, I downloaded a copy of Dexter Thomes's background data on his site. Over the past two weeks, I've been working on it the old-fashioned way, with a pencil and paper, line by line, trying to find the pattern. Now I know I've finally found one. And if you gave me a laptop right now and access to the internet, I would be able to tell you exactly where the money has gone."

Jonathan blinked. How was that possible? Confidence seemed to radiate through her, taking his breath away. It took everything in his power, all his strength and resolve not to tell the judge to listen. But there was nothing he could do other than listen as she argued her case, as she proved her mettle and her worth, as she shone like a light and explained, in words that were above his head, what she was able to see in the data and why she thought she could continue to follow it to the end. Finally, after a sidebar between the judge and lawyers, somebody brought Celeste a laptop. The courtroom fell silent as everyone held their collective breath and watched her fingers fly over the keyboard, typing, exploring, scrolling and dissecting. Then she gasped.

"And I've done it!" She spun the laptop around toward the judge. "I've found it. Well, I've found him. I've known for a while that Dexter was searching birth dates and social security numbers, but I didn't know why. He was looking for his half brother, a petty car thief called Casper Harrison."

Instantly the smirk fell from Dexter's face as cell phones began to ping around the courtroom. People rustled in their chairs. Something was happening. And by the smile on Celeste's face, he was certain she knew what it was.

Jonathan glanced back to the bald man in the back of the courtroom. He was gone.

"Casper and Dexter look different enough," she went on, "but apparently enough alike to be able to fool people. Dexter stole the money. He sent the money to Casper, who's been using it to pay people off for tracking me, or at least he has been." The chorus of phone chirps grew louder. Even those who'd apparently had the good sense to turn their phones to silent were checking them. "Because I just found the money and sent it back—a simple reverse payment algorithm. I'm guessing the sounds you're hearing are people getting notified by their banks that the money is back in their accounts."

Gasp and murmurs spread across the courtroom, which turned into babbles of conversation, laughter and even applause. Dexter's head had fallen into his hands.

Celeste's gaze met Jonathan's again and held it.

"I also deleted Poindexter's database on me," she said. "Every trace of the pictures and videos that he was using to track me is now gone. More importantly, now everyone in the world will know that he's lost his money and has no way to pay the bounty. So, there's no reason for anyone to come after me or the people I care about. And the money trail I uncovered will give investigators everything they need to keep Dexter in jail for a long time."

A high-pitched siren filled the air as a voice in the back of the room shouted, "Fire! The building's on fire!"

Instantly the voice was joined by a chorus of shouts and screams as people ran for the exits. Jonathan was on his feet and running for Celeste, his single-minded focus latched on her face even as he could hear pandemonium and chaos erupting around them. For one agonizing second he thought she was going to freeze again. Instead, he watched a silent prayer cross her lips. Then she leaped from the box and ran for him. In an instant, he caught her around the waist. His hand slid around her as he steered her toward the closest exit. Smoke poured down the hallway to their left.

"Come on," he said. "They're evacuating the building. We've got to go."

"Wait." She grabbed his arm, and her heels dug into the floor. "What if it's another smoke bomb like back at the safe house? What if it's not a real fire? What if Doppel-Dex is trying to create a diversion?"

He glanced at the docket. Dexter was being ushered out by bailiffs. His head was bowed.

"I don't know." Jonathan steered her into the crowd of people and toward an exit. "But we're not going to hang around here and find out."

A split second that felt like a decade passed.

"Okay," Celeste said. "I trust you."

Thank You, Gott. They joined the crowd and hurried for the exit. Within a heartbeat, Stacy and Karl had joined them, flanking them on either side. They jogged down the hallway, through the doors and out onto the court steps. Sunlight filled his gaze. He gasped a breath and glanced around, then realized who was behind them. Dexter Thomes had been evacuated through the same door they had. He guessed the usual exit they'd have taken him through been blocked somehow due to smoke.

Were Celeste's suspicions right? Was this nothing but a diversion?

"Karl, Stacy." He spun to his colleagues. "I think there's something wrong—"

Before he could finish the thought, something banged and flashed, filling his eyes with blinding light. Voices screamed. People shouted. Thick green smoke swamped the courthouse steps. His eyes flooded. Painful smoke seared his lungs. Someone had set off a smoke bomb. He felt something hit him hard and he pitched forward, almost falling down the steps as the sound of Celeste screaming filled his ears.

Chapter Eighteen

"Celeste!" Desperately his eyes scanned through the smoke. Amid the chaos of people and panic, he could hear Celeste's desperate cries still hanging in the air.

Help me, God. I'm blind! Guide me! Show me where to go!

"Jonathan, Karl, I've got eyes on the suspect!" Stacy shouted. "He took Celeste around the left side. This way!"

Jonathan turned and ran toward her, Karl one step ahead of him, as they pushed through the crowd and the chaos. His eyes locked on one form. Dexter Thomes was wrestling with a guard, fighting for his gun. The hacker yanked the officer's weapon from his holster.

"Dexter Thomes has got a gun!" Jonathan yelled.

Help me, Gott. I can't save Celeste and stop Dexter.

"We've got him!" Stacy yelled. "You go get Celeste." She stopped on a dime and spun toward the criminal. "Drop your weapon!"

Jonathan ran in the direction Stacy pointed. The scene played before him in an instant. Dexter fired. Stacy cried out in pain as her leg crumpled beneath her.

She dropped to the courtroom steps, but her weapon was held sure in her hands. She rolled onto her back and fired, Karl's steady and sure bullets joining hers as he ran toward her. Dexter fell, but not before another burst of gunfire escaped his weapon. Karl threw himself between Stacy and the bullets. He wrapped his body around his partner, and they tumbled down the steps together.

Gott, protect them!

He couldn't let himself stop. He ran through the smoke and he saw them, Celeste's blond hair tossed loose from her neat bun and her limbs thrashing as she fought for life against the grip of the hulking, bald man he'd seen in the courtroom.

He was already on his way. He burst through the door and found a long dark hallway in the bowels of the courthouse parking garage. He ran down toward the end of the hall just as a fresh smoke bomb erupted in his face blinding him.

Help me see the way!

The sound of a struggle echoed in the distance. Celeste was calling his name. He followed her voice, praying with every heartbeat that he found her and that she would be all right. He sprinted down a hallway and up a flight of stairs. He'd found her once before, back in the farmhouse when the air was thick with smoke and his fellow US marshals had been fighting for their lives. He would find her now. He rounded another corner and then he saw her.

Celeste was being dragged along the hallway by the tall, bald man. There was something in his stance that Jonathan knew in an instant, even stripped of the wig, fake beard and glasses. It was Doppel-Dex. It was Dexter's half brother.

"Casper!" He pulled his weapon and aimed it directly at the man. "Stop right there and let her go, or I'll shoot!"

Casper turned and dragged Celeste around until he was holding her up in front of him like a human shield. He pressed a gun into the side of her head. She'd taken back the money his brother had stolen. She'd robbed him of his privacy. She'd exposed his identity and his crimes for all the world to see. Now he had her.

"You're not going to shoot me!" Casper snapped. "Because if you so much as flinch, I'm going to shoot her first. You're going to turn around, go back and I'll let you know when I've decided where you can send the ransom money. I'm not leaving with nothing."

Jonathan whispered a prayer under his breath, raised his service weapon and centered the man in his sights. "Let her go and drop your weapon, or I will shoot."

"Do you really think you're fast enough and a good enough aim to make that shot without killing her?"

With Gott*'s help.*

Jonathan fired.

She heard the blast of the bullet, closed her eyes and felt a prayer move through her heart. Then she felt Casper's grasp weaken and release. He slumped to the ground.

"Thank You, God." She suddenly felt her knees wobble.

In an instant, Jonathan was by her side. "Celeste. Are you all right?"

"I'm okay." She pulled back a sob. "You rescued me."

He reached for her, pulled her toward him and brushed a kiss across her lips. Then he let her go. He turned toward the man lying bleeding on the ground and checked his pulse.

"He's still alive," he said. "His breathing is shallow, and he's going to lose consciousness. But if medical attention gets to him soon enough, he should live. Quick, find me something to help stop the bleeding."

She yanked off her scarf and passed it into his hand. He pressed it against the man's wound. She looked at him, this handsome, brave and incredible man trying to save the life of someone who would kill them both without a moment's hesitation.

Her fingers gently brushed against his shoulder. "You're incredible."

"I would've killed him, Celeste," he said. "Please don't doubt that. If I had to choose between your life and his…"

His voice trailed off as if too much emotion had suddenly choked the words from his throat.

"I know," she said. "You would have taken his life to spare mine. Still, you tried to find a way that nobody died. Not today."

He smiled. "Not today."

"Jonathan!" A voice rang out down the hallway. It was Karl.

"Down here! This way!" Jonathan called back. "We have one hostile down but alive. Requiring medical attention and to be taken into custody."

"And Celeste?"

"Safe and well!" Jonathan shouted back. Karl ran toward them, barking orders quick and sharp to whoever was on the other side of the walkie-talkie. Then he ended the call. "Is Stacy okay?" Jonathan asked.

"Minor injury." A smile of relief turned up the corners of Karl's lips. "Bullet just grazed her. She'll be fine. She's plenty tough. We're not sure if it was my bullet or hers that took Dexter Thomes down, but either way he's back in custody."

Thank You, Gott.

"Did you see my father and nephew?" Jonathan stepped back as Karl arrived, and let him take over.

"Last I saw they were helping evacuate people. Your dad said something about evacuating a barn."

"That sounds like him." He reached for Celeste's hand. They stepped away as what suddenly seemed like a crowd of officers, medical staff and others came running down the hall. Jonathan pulled her aside and moved along the hall until they reached a large window overlooking the snow outside.

"We only have a second," he said. His forehead wrinkled. "Not long. Karl is an incredible marshal and can take over for a few moments. But that's all we've got, seconds, and I don't know where to start."

"Then let me go first," Celeste said quickly. "I love you, Jonathan. I love how you think. I love how you question and how you search. I love how hard you wrestle with things. I love how deeply you care. And I don't know what happens next, but I feel like you're in my life for a reason, and I can't wait to find out what that reason is."

"I love you so much." He stared at her in amazement. "I never knew my heart was able to love anyone this way."

He brought his mouth down toward hers and she

tilted her face up to his, and for one brief moment they turned their backs on the chaos around them and their lips met.

Celeste awoke the next morning to the sun rising high in the sky and the sounds of birds chirping outside the window. She stretched, feeling the warmth and comfort of familiar quilts around her.

There was a gentle knock on the door and then it flew back as Rosie ran in.

"You're here! You're really here! I thought it was a dream!"

Celeste laughed. "Yes, I'm here. It kind of feels like a dream for me, too."

Everything had felt surreal since the moment she'd taken the stand, being grilled by lawyers and having her sanity questioned, and then she'd looked out and met Jonathan's eyes. In that moment, everything had clicked, from what she'd seen in the data while scouring through the pages late at night to how she'd managed to see Dexter where he wasn't.

The answer was relationship. The answer was family.

"Mamm said you arrived in the middle of the night with two *Englisch* cops," Rosie said, perching on the end of the bed.

Celeste nodded. That was close enough. After Casper was arrested and she'd given her statement to the police, Jonathan had somehow talked Chief Deputy Hunter into letting them return home to the Mast family farm, as long as Stacy and Karl came with them. The two US marshals had driven in one vehicle while she'd ridden in the small church bus beside Jonathan, his arm around her shoulder and his hand tightly holding hers.

It was only for one night, just until they sorted out what would happen next and what needed to be done. But one night back in the Amish farmhouse, knowing she was waking up to see Jonathan in the morning, was already more happiness than she'd ever expected to have.

"An important *Englisch* lady is in the kitchen waiting to talk to you," Rosie said. She fidgeted slightly, holding out the fabric in her hand. "I was wondering if you wanted to wear one of my Sunday dresses. Mamm said you might want to wear *Englisch* clothes."

Bright yellow and pale pink fabric lay in her hands. Celeste smiled. "I would love to borrow one of your dresses, thank you."

For as long as she was in this family's home she would dress as one of them. She felt pretty adept at pinning her dress and cap on by now, but she was still thankful for Rosie's company as she got dressed. Then she followed the young woman down to the kitchen.

The beautiful wooden table had been transformed into a conference table. Stacy and Karl sat side by side, with Stacy's leg still in a splint from the bullet that had grazed her the night before. Jonathan sat on the opposite side, dressed as a marshal. At the head of the table was a striking woman, with keen eyes and graying black hair swept up into a bun. Everyone rose as Celeste entered.

She turned to Jonathan. To her surprise and disappointment, he didn't meet her gaze.

The woman stretched out her hand. "Chief Deputy Louise Hunter," she said. "It's a pleasure to finally meet you."

"Thank you, it's great to meet you, too." Celeste crossed the room, took the other woman's hand and shook it. "What brings you here?"

"You." A smile crossed the chief deputy's lips. "I wanted you to know personally that Dexter Thomes and Casper Harrison have both been remanded into custody and prosecutors believe it's such a clear-cut case thanks to the evidence you've provided. We will continue to be vigilant about either Thomes or Harrison finding a new way to come after you and seek revenge. But I can't imagine law enforcement is going to allow either of them near a computer or unmonitored phone any time soon. And now that you've stripped them of the stolen money they have no way to pay for hit men. So, it's unlikely you will be considered an active target."

"I don't know what that means," she admitted. Again she tried to meet Jonathan's eyes, but he looked away, and the absence of his gaze dug at her as if someone was missing.

"It means that you're free to pursue other opportunities, another life," the chief deputy said. "And I'm here to offer you one. We have a secure facility in Colorado. It's both home and office to a number of federal officers and support staff. We'd like to hire you as an on-site data consultant. Your computer skills and expertise are second to none. You'd be safe inside our faculties in the unlikely event someone should ever come after you, as well as being able to use your skills to serve your country."

It made so much sense. She wasn't an Amish farm girl. She was a data analyst and a computer programmer. She was an excellent one. God had given her skills. She needed to use them. Yet, as her eyes scanned the simple kitchen, with its wood-burning stove and family table marked from hundreds of long meals and conversations, she couldn't help but think of all she'd be losing.

"Thank you," she said. "That's an amazing opportunity. I need to think about it."

She crossed over to the back door, feeling Jonathan's gaze on her. He stood. She tugged on her boots, grabbed her cape and bonnet, and stepped out into the snow.

She'd taken less than ten steps down the path to the barn when she heard the door swing open and shut behind her, heard Jonathan's voice calling her name. "Celeste! Wait!"

She turned. There he was, running up the path, with his straw hat and coat thrown over his *Englisch* clothes. She crossed her arms.

"You knew about this," she said. "That's why you wouldn't look at me."

"Of course I knew," he said. He reached for her hands. But for once she didn't reach back. Earnest eyes were locked on her face. "You're extraordinary, Celeste. You're so talented and incredible at what you do. You need to use those talents."

She stepped back and tossed her hands in the air. "Even if it means spending my life in a cement room, day after day, at a laptop…and without you?"

The last two words seemed to land and echo in the air.

Without you. Without you.

Something pained moved across his face. "But you're so good at what you do."

"I know." A smile crossed her face. "I am. But what if God is calling me to something more than that? Don't you want more for me?"

"What kind of more?" he asked.

He stepped in closer, but again she didn't let him take her hands.

"I don't know!" she admitted. "I just don't."

"Neither do I," he said. The side of his mouth curled into a smile. He stood there for a long moment, in the snow and early-morning sunshine, his face turned to her and his eyes on her face. "I'm still lost, Liebchen. But at least now I know I don't want to be lost without you."

He closed his eyes for a long moment. Then he nodded, as if hearing an answer or making a decision. He reached for her hand and she let him take it. "Come on, I need to ask my boss a question."

His hand tightened in hers. He led her back to the house and opened the back door.

"Chief Deputy Hunter?" he called. "I'd like to request heading up a trial project of US marshals who place needy and desperate people within Amish communities. It makes so much sense in light of the challenges posed by cyber warfare. We've learned from our experience with Dexter Thomes that few people look beyond the bonnet. The fact we'd be off the grid makes it harder to trace people. The friendliness of the Amish community is welcoming to outcasts and strangers."

Chief Deputy Hunter waited, looking from Jonathan to Celeste and then to their still-linked hands. Her gaze returned to Jonathan's face. "The idea has some merit. I can see it working well. Anything else?"

"There is," he said. She felt his hand tighten on hers. "I can't do this alone. I'm going to need a civilian partner, someone who knows how to look out for threats and can analyze data. I want to suggest that you create a position for Celeste here, as well, where she can help support people placed in this program and do other data analysis as required for WITSEC."

She pulled her hand away. What was he saying? That

he wanted her to stay with the Amish and join him in his work? Hope flashed in her heart. Did that mean he was opening the door to more?

"I think I'd be able to sell this idea to the higher-ups," Hunter said. "On the condition we create secure cover stories for you both, and also create a secure data facility perhaps disguised as a barn or other building, where you have access to cutting-edge technology. Are you interested in taking on that kind of job, Celeste?"

To live with the Amish but continue using her skills to help people? Yes, her heart knew its answer. Yes, this was what she wanted very much. She glanced at Jonathan. "Can I talk to you for a minute?"

"Sure." They stepped back outside.

"You told me some Amish use electricity and technology in their places of work, but not at home, right?" she asked. He raised an eyebrow, but nodded. "I'm only taking this job if I can still maintain that kind of balance in my life. I'm not going back to being online 24/7. I want all the cutting-edge technology WITSEC would supply me with to stay in the office. I want to live the *plain* Amish life outside of work hours."

"I understand and I think I can get Hunter to agree to that." A smile curled on his lips. "I want to go back to living like the Amish, too. But I'm not going to become baptized, so I can stay in law enforcement. Now I have one more important question."

He dropped to one knee in the snow at her feet. Her breath caught in her chest.

"I know where my heart is calling me, Celeste," he said. "It's calling me to you. It has been ever since the moment we first met and I know with every beat of my heart that it'll always keep calling me to you. I know it's sudden, but I don't want separate lives and cover stories for us. I want one life. One story. Together. So I'm asking you, please marry me, Celeste. Be my wife, share my home, share my family and build on it with children of our own."

The happiness that filled her heart was greater than she'd ever known, but when she opened her mouth she found just one word tumbling out. "Yes!"

"Yes?" He leaped to his feet. "Did you say 'yes'?"

"Yes!" she laughed. "Yes, I will marry you, Jonathan. Yes, I will join your family and raise our children near the Amish. Yes, I love you and my heart feels called to join with yours."

"Thank You, God!" A prayer crossed Jonathan's lips. Wrapping his arms around her waist, he pulled her tightly to his chest. She felt his heart beating against hers. Then he kissed her, deeply and lovingly, holding her securely in his arms until they heard David and Samuel banging on the window, calling them in for breakfast.

* * * * *

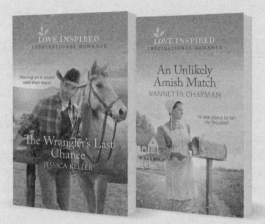

SPECIAL EXCERPT FROM

LOVE INSPIRED
INSPIRATIONAL ROMANCE

Can the new teacher in this Amish community help the family next door without losing her heart?

Read on for a sneak preview of
The Amish Teacher's Dilemma *by Patricia Davids, available in March 2020 from Love Inspired.*

Clang, clang, clang.

The hammering outside her new schoolhouse grew louder. Eva Coblentz moved to the window to locate the source of the clatter. Across the road she saw a man pounding on an ancient-looking piece of machinery with steel wheels and a scoop-like nose on the front end.

When he had the sheet of metal shaped to fit the front of the machine, he stood back to assess his work. He knelt and hammered on the shovel-like nose three more times. Satisfied, he gathered up his tools and started in her direction.

She stepped back from the window. Was he coming to the school? Why? Had he noticed her gawking? Perhaps he only wanted to welcome the new teacher, although his lack of a beard said he wasn't married.

She glanced around the room. Should she meet him by the door? That seemed too eager. Her eyes settled on the large desk at the front of the classroom. She should look as if she was ready for the school year to start. A professional attitude would put off any suggestion that she was interested in meeting single men.

Eva hurried to the desk, pulled out the chair and sat down as the outside door opened. The chair tipped over backward, sending her flailing. Her head hit the wall with a painful thud as she slid to the floor. Stunned, she slowly opened her eyes to see the man leaning over the desk.

He had the most beautiful gray eyes she'd ever beheld. They were rimmed with thick, dark lashes in stark contrast to the mop of curly, dark red hair springing out from beneath his straw hat. Tiny sparks of light whirled around him.

"I'm Willis Gingrich. Local blacksmith." He squatted beside her. "Can you tell me your name?"

The warmth and strength of his hand on her skin sent a sizzle of awareness along her nerve endings. "I'm Eva Coblentz. I am the new teacher and I'm fine now."

Don't miss
The Amish Teacher's Dilemma
by USA TODAY *bestselling author Patricia Davids,*
available March 2020 wherever
Love Inspired books and ebooks are sold.

LoveInspired.com

LIEXP0220